MOONSHINE MAFIA

by

JON MARPLE

A Crime Caper
Inspired by True Events

BookBaby.com

Table Of Contents

This book is a work of fiction, although certain characters, incidents, and dialogue are based on real-life events from the author's rich array of Scots-Irish West Virginia, Appalachian relatives. Having been given such a grand gift of characters to live with and write about, their stories gave wings to the author's imagination and flights of fancy to create a work of fiction.

Illustrations by Robert Santoré visit www.RobertSantore.com

Library of Congress Cataloging-in-publication Data has been applied for.

ISBN 979-8-9891742-1-8

CHAPTER I

FIRE IN THE HOLLER

Billy McCoy had two sons: Boo, seventeen, and Beau, fifteen, each of them slightly dimmer than the other. One summer evening, having grabbed a fruit jar of their daddy's corn squeezin's, they got properly juiced sitting on the front porch in old rocking chairs, watching the sun fade over the lush-green, rugged, wooded forest snuggled in the hills of West Virginia. Prohibition was the law of the land, and that made the illegal moonshine even sweeter to the boys.

They both were wearing dirty coveralls—they called them "britches"—denim that covered their front with a strap over each shoulder. Boo thought it was cool to let one strap hang down, unbuttoned. He thought it might impress Fanny Fitz, a girl who lived a mile down the hollow. No shirt. No shoes. They both had on torn, beat-up straw hats, pushed up and back on their heads.

Boo was bored. He turned to his brother and said, "Let's go over to McKenna's still and fire us off a few shots"— the still being the place where Pappy McKenna and his family made illegal booze, which was called "Mule Kick Moonshine."

Beau said, "Now why for we gonna do that?"

"Cause that Lamar McKenna is payin' too much mind to Fanny Fitz, that's what for. And I got a powerful curiosity in that gal. Fanny tells me he's a-comin' over all the time. Just droppin' by. Sniffin' round like some damn hound dog."

Boo's voice was picking up steam and irritation as he said, "He's onto the scent all right, and I'm a gonna put an end to it. Never liked that sumbitch. He's way too old for her, anyway. The all high and mighty McKenna's. Puttin' on airs cause they got that damn shine selling all over the place. Mule Kick. Mule Kick, my ass. Think they the kings of the holler. That sumthin', ain't it? The Kings of Devil's Run Holler, West By Gawd Virginia. Big deal."

"Damn, simmer down, Boo. It does occur to me that if we shoot up Pappy McKenna's still, he might just take offense. And that boy of his, Lamar. He is a bit touched in the head. Man's crazy. No tellin' what he gonna do if'en he found out it was us. Hey, maybe he's off in prison. Spends half his life in one jail house or another."

"No, he's here. That's what I said, he bother'en Franny." Boo paused and said, "What, you gonna tell the McKenna's we shot up their damn still? Whose gonna know if we don't say nothin'?"

"Well, that seems like a funny way to send a message to Lamar by shootin' up Pappy's still."

"Have a few more hits and it won't matter if it's funny or not."

Boo and Beau did just that. They each grabbed one of their Pa's hog guns and disappeared into the twilight, hooting and howling. This was not to be a sneak attack.

The boys fired a total of seven shots at the still. They were generally good shooters since they had been shooting at critters, large and small, from age seven. But not this night. The shine had taken hold.

The boys were wobbly as they fired the Big Hog Gun. Beau fired off the first round. It went straight at the Northern Star, a considerable distance from the still. As he fired, his front foot slid forward and down the damp, slick hillside. Beau pulled the trigger as he was halfway to the ground, falling backward. His butt hit first. Then his head. The buckshot headed skyward. Boo burst into uncontrolled laughter, coughing and spitting.

Getting control, Boo said, "Damn, Beau, the still is down there and here you are shootin' at the moon. Pa is right, you can't shoot for shit."

Eventually, two shots hit the still, before the boys ran back to safety.

The pellets put two holes through Pappy's prized copper pot. Not only would Pappy have to set about repairing the pot, but the shot also destroyed that day's batch of moonshine liquor.

And, as Pappy was to later observe, those copper pots cost real money.

Pappy and Lula McKenna's place sat near the back of Devil's Run Hollow—about five miles up the mountainside running out of McMechen, West Virginia, hard by the Oho River, just south of Wheeling.

To get to the hollow, you had to go up 21st Street. The street was paved for about half a mile and then turned into crushed gravel for another half mile, then a trail of dirt and mud. The ruts in the road were deep and well-formed. The brush, shrubs, and tree branches reaching across part of the trail could scratch up a car.

The trail was like the people who lived there; if they knew you, they welcomed you with a warm embrace and offered you food and drink. But if they suspected you might be there with bad intentions, like the mountains around them, they could be rugged, jagged, hard, and dangerous.

The trees in the hollow are rich and full with shades of green and brown luster. In the fall, those same trees are bright with a myriad of color—vivacious reds; sharp, distinct, burnt oranges; and deep, golden yellows, mixed with the dazzling white and pink of flowers and brush that may last through those first few frosty days. . . hillsides full of brilliant beauty. Thick and pushed together so close that not a single tree is visible, the hills and the mountains become a simple vast array of foliage. Once seen, it is unforgettable.

A creek ran by the road to Pappy's place, adding to the beauty as it moved quietly downstream over white stone and scattered rocks. About halfway up to Pappy's place, there was an old, abandoned mill with a large pond of water that always seemed cold—sweet too, if you took a taste.

Young boys from town and the hollow would come to the pond in the summer and skinny-dip. They would climb a cliff rising out of the water. At about sixteen feet, the cliff leveled and the boys could stand there as if it was a diving platform. The water looked, and was, a long way down. But once up, there was only one way down. "Geronimo!" they would shout as they jumped. The boys played in that mill pond with a joy that is gifted only to the young and innocent.

Pappy had three or four stills hidden in that hollow. No one really knew how many.

They were Scots-Irish from Ulster, that part of Ireland carved out for Scots, who then become indentured servants working the land for church, king, and the nobleman land owner.

They lived in small one or two-room thatched cottages with walls made of wattle and woven strips of wood covered with a mixture of straw and clay, called dung. They owned little. Everything—their animals, homes, clothes, and even their food—belonged to the Lord of the Manor.

They had little freedom. But they had their family and the clan . . . a community of like sufferers. They also had their home-brewed whiskey. They left Ulster and brought their whiskey-making pots and coils and knowledge of how to make what would be called moonshine, liquor made by the light of the moon.

The McKenna Clan made their way to Boston sometime before 1770. They fought with the Patriots against the despised King George. They sought freedom and land. They found both as they burrowed their families and kinsmen deep in the Virginia mountains of Appalachia.

They only asked to be left alone. And for a long while, they got their wish.

Moonshine was all Pappy ever knew. He played on the banks of the creek feeding the stills when he was three. By eight he was doing small jobs to help build, maintain, and make the shine. By twelve, he knew almost all that his father could teach him. By sixteen he was running the operation because his father, Henry, had gone off to the federal prison in Atlanta for making and distributing illegal liquor. Three years he was gone.

Pappy was smarter and more determined than his older brother, Robert. Before Henry left for prison, he placed Pappy in charge of the stills. Robert was to protect the house and put food on the table, hunting and fishing and helping his mother with the farming and the livestock.

When Henry returned, Pappy was the boss of the entire moonshine operation and it stayed that way the rest of Henry's life. Robert was gone, left home for the State of Washington and a new life. Pappy was nineteen, over six feet tall and mountain-man hard. He was set to marry Lula McCreary from Winchester, Virginia. Lula was sixteen. Pappy met her on a bootlegging trip, delivering Mule Kick to the local bars, politicians, and farmers.

He and Lula would have three children—twins, Lamar and Loretta, and a younger boy named Lloyd—who became known as "Hooch," a tribute to his driving skills getting liquor down the mountain, past the lawmen and to the bars and speakeasies of prohibition America.

Lula loved all the children with motherly devotion, even Lamar as he walked a criminal path from the beginning. Pappy didn't care much for Lamar and his ways, but he doted on Hooch. Hooch was his boy. He treated Loretta like a girl, tolerated her, but just barely. Of course, she adored her father. Pappy played favorites and didn't care if anyone objected.

Pappy's three children all went their own way. Loretta sought religion and found it with the Mormons and became a fiercely loyal Christian. She wanted her children to be far from the hollow and their illegal ways.

Lamar joined the Mormon church as well, but just to please his sister, who was constantly trying to push her brother to a Christian life, free of criminality. He was, in reality, a career criminal.

Hooch became a policeman by day and a bootleg driver on weekends. Everybody liked having an inside man with the police. Hooch's raid tips kept the moonshiner's out of jail on more than one occasion.

It wasn't hard to figure out who had shot up the still. Boo and Beau took care of that, bragging to the Fitzgerald girl the very next morning. Fanny Fitz, as she was called, spread the word, and it got back to Pappy by noon.

Pappy sent word for Lamar, who had a long rap sheet and living in McMechen, to come see him immediately. Said it was urgent. He got there about five to find Pappy on the porch sipping some Mule Kick with Lula by his side having a lemonade. Lamar often wondered if his mother spiked that lemonade, because she always seemed happier in the evenings than during her working day. Lamar had laid it off to thinking she was happier because her chores were done. Now, he wasn't so sure.

Pappy said, "Lamar, those idiot McCoy boys done shot up one of my copper pots. In fact, it was the one we just bought about six months ago. We can't let that stand. I gotta get Leroy now to fix the pots, and we lost a full day of liquor.

Lamar said, "You want me to knock some sense into 'em?"

"No, nothin' like that. I want you to get over there and set fire to Billy's shed. Not the house. This is not worth that kind of attention. I doubt Old Man McCoy knew those boys were gonna do something as stupid as to what they done. That should do it. Let 'em know we got an eye on 'em."

Lamar said, "Well, Pappy, I can surely do that. Yes, I surely can."

Lamar, always there to be Pappy's "avenging angel."

Lamar waited till midnight before approaching the McCoy place. The chicken coop was on the edge of the woods where Lamar stood. The tool shed was on the other side of the yard, past the house.

Getting over to the tool shed meant walking in front of the house and risk getting seen. Lamar thought it better and quicker to torch the hen house. That was right in front of him.

The hen house was three times larger than the tool shed, and in Lamar's mind, that made it a better target. It was quiet. There was a window on the side of the shed that Lamar looked into. The hens were quiet. Looked liked they were all sleeping. The birds were lined up, side by side on wooden platforms, sitting on their nests. Lamar thought this would be easy. He had brought along some rags and gasoline in a fruit jar. The hen house was enclosed in chicken wire. Lamar wanted to set the fire up close. He unlatched the door to the coop. He stepped in quietly, leaving the door open.

Two steps in and he was attacked by Marty.

Marty was a very large, Rhode Island Red, big and vicious. He jumped to attack. He got to Lamar's gut and peck, peck, peck. Hard and fast. . . wings moving with lightning speed . . . squawking and pecking . . . now pecking away viciously at any part of Lamar's body he could reach. Stomach. Legs. Ankles. When one peck hit Lamar's left testicle, Lamar let out a scream and gave Marty a kick that sent the rooster flying backward. Released from Marty, Lamar ran from the coop, Marty in hot and relentless pursuit. Lamar got the coop door closed in time to escape the beast. Lamar ran along the fence to the back of the hen house.

Lamar could see lights coming on in the house and men starting to move. Marty had come around to face Lamar through the chicken wire. He started pecking through the wire but couldn't touch Lamar.

Lamar grabbed his matches and with bloody, shaking hands, soaked and lit the rags, then threw them over the fence toward the hen house. One of the rags landed near Marty. The rooster, facing the challenge, attacked the fiery rag, which then caught him on fire. Now ablaze, Marty ran into the hen house. The straw in the house was quickly blazing. Marty stopped squawking. It was quiet now.

The quiet broken when the McCoy men busted through the door of their house with rifles. They had thrown on pants with suspenders. No shirts. Billy McCoy shouted, "Who's out there? I'm gonna shoot, you son-of-a-bitch." And shoot they did. Four shots. Two more followed. None hit Lamar since he had already run back into the thicket of brush and trees and disappeared.

He ran as fast as he could to get away from the gunfire. He didn't stop until he got back to the safety of Pappy's house. He quietly disappeared into his old bedroom, lit a candle, and took off his clothes. Naked, he looked at the bloody mess made from Marty's attack. Blood dripped to the floor.

Lamar murmured, "That little pecker-head needed to die a fiery death."

It was the talk of the hollow.

Everybody had an opinion. Ladd Moore, a neighbor of both families, said to his wife

Rowena, "Old man McCoy was damned fortunate that it wasn't his house Lamar set on fire. Might have killed off those idiot boys of his instead of the hens and that rooster. Might have done the holler a favor if those boys were given an early exit from this earthly existence. They are dumb sumbitches, and they started the whole thing. What's Pappy supposed to do, just let his still get all shot up? I think he used admirable restraint."

J. J. O'Sullivan, another neighbor and good friend of Pappy's said, "This ain't no business of the law. It's done over with right now. Any kind of law interference would be just chicken shit."

J. J. thought that kind of clever...the chicken shit thing, being as it was a hen house set on fire.

The general consensus was that there was no crime involved. The boys shot up Pappy's still. Lamar burned down the hen house. No need to go any further. We are all just mountain people here, and we take care of our own problems. We all are making shine, so let's just get back to business as usual.

As soon as it was reported by the police, the local press, taken by the grief shown by Billie McCoy over his prized rooster, picked up the story and started to have a little fun. The headline in the Moundsville Daily Echo read:

Marty, the Rooster, Murdered at Midnight.
Who Murdered Marty?

The Wheeling Register picked up the story the next day and ran a satirical obituary. Apparently, it was a slow day at the paper.

MARTY, THE ROOSTER
Dead at Three!

Marty, a beloved Rhode Island Red rooster, died on Thursday at the age of three. He was murdered in a cruel act of arson by an unknown party. He died a hero's death at Devil's Run Hollow, just outside McMechen. Twenty-four hens perished with him.

The night of the murder, Mr. McCoy said they were awakened by loud squawks from Marty, followed by screams from the unknown intruder. It was around midnight last Thursday evening. Apparently, the arsonist got into the McCoy's coop, where he was attacked by Marty defending the hens.

A memorial service will be held at the Free Baptist Church in McMechen this coming Sunday, followed by a BBQ. Mr. McCoy wanted it known that no chicken would be served, only pig or cow.

Marty is survived by Billie McCoy and his wife Beatrice and their two sons, Beau and Boo.

J. J. started calling it the "Marty Murder" and that's what stuck. Everybody had a good laugh, and after a few days it was mostly forgotten.

Billy McCoy didn't forget.
He wanted hot justice.
Now.

CHAPTER II

THE LAW STEPS IN

Billy McCoy got in his 1917 Ford Model T to confab with Sheriff Cletus McCoy, his second cousin, twice-removed, the sheriff of Marshall County, West Virginia.

Although everybody in the hollow was enjoying a good laugh over the 'Marty Murder' Billy McCoy found no such enjoyment. Billy wanted Lamar arrested and jailed. Right now. Today. He wanted Cletus to push the district attorney for a long jail sentence. He wanted Cletus to push for fifteen to twenty years. That seemed about right to Billy. Lamar had murdered Marty, the best rooster Billy had ever had, as well as twenty-four good laying hens. The very thought of Marty's heroism clouded Billy McCoy's eyes as he drove down the rutted road to town.

Sheriff McCoy was best known for his speed trap along the north-south road from Wheeling to Glen Dale and on to Moundsville. The speed along the road was twenty-five miles per hour. The sheriff had the county reduce the speed limit to twelve miles per hour between Glen Dale and Moundsville. A speed limit sign was posted behind a mulberry bush. It was almost visible to a driver, but not quite.

The traffic fines from the trap supported the entire sheriff's department for the year, every year, and the sheriff's re-election was assured for the next several election cycles. Locals were not stopped by the sheriff and his deputies, just visitors passing through.

Cletus McCoy had been raised up in the hollow. He graduated from Union High School, same as Loretta and Hooch, but his reading skills were limited. His natural aggression transferred nicely to playing tackle on the football team where he could, and did, attack people with a fierce vengeance.

Coach Iron Mike Hagler said to his assistant, Pop Holmsted, "Pop, we gotta watch that McCoy kid. I never said this before about one of our players, but that boy is. . . I don't know the right word for it, but I think it is psychotic. Kinda crazy. If we let him practice every day and go after our own boys, we might not have a team to put on the field Friday night. Kid just loves to go after people, and damn he hits hard. Let's hold him back from practice and turn him loose on game day."

The sheriff was also well-known for an infamous traffic stop he made in the speed trap. He and deputy sheriff, Freddie Bloom, stopped a new Model T with four young men inside that looked like college boys. The sheriff, who didn't like many people anyway, particularly wasn't fond of college kids. In general, he didn't really cater to any kind of kids or education.

The sheriff stopped the car, approached the driver side window, and said, "What's the rush boys? Why you goin' so fast?"

The driver said, "Sorry, Sir. I didn't know I was speeding. Isn't this a twenty-five zone?"

"No, it is surely not. This here stretch of highway is a twelve miles per hour zone," the sheriff said, raising his voice somewhat on 'twelve miles per hour zone'.

"Where you goin' so fast anyway?"

"Fort Lauderdale, down in Florida. It's our spring break."

"Where you from?"

The driver said, "Chicago. We go to college there. Northwestern."

The sheriff exploded, "Don't you go lyin' to me, Boy. I can see those Illinois plates, and by God, I can read 'em! I ought to run your asses in just for lyin' to me. Right now follow me down to the next intersection. See that building sittin' up on that hill?"

The boys glanced at each other and quickly looked away, not saying a word about their Illinois plates.

The driver said, "Yes, Sir."

"That where we are goin', so just stay right behind me. You got that?"

"Yes, Sir."

"Off we go then."

The boys followed the sheriff to a one-room makeshift building, built for just this purpose. They parked in a dusty parking area in front of a dirty-white building with a sign above the door that read:

Thaddeus C. Thomas

Justice of the Peace

Marshall County, WV

Once inside they stood before Justice Thomas, who was seated in a big, black chair with a desk in front and large gavel in his right hand. He was on a platform two feet above the floor, where the boys stood, looking somewhat bewildered.

The Justice was a small man, fifty-two years old, standing no more than five feet five. Thin body. Thinning hair. Narrow, small nose and pinched, scowling lips. The chair was bought for the previous J. P., who stood six four and weighed around three hundred pounds. No one, including the sheriff, wanted to tell Justice Thomas that his head didn't rise more than halfway to the top of the chair, and his feet didn't touch the floor. Deputy Bloom once said, "Damn, Thad looks like a kid taking his dinner at the big people's table and his daddy had to pick him up and place in the chair." The oversized gavel added to the comic effect, since it appear to be a sledgehammer in the Justice's small fist.

The four hapless teens stood before the Justice.

Justice Thomas said, "Which one of you boys was driving this here car."

"Me, Sir."

"What's your name, Boy?"

"Donald C. Purrington the Third."

"What's the 'C' for"?

"Courtland."

"So your name is Donald Courtland Purrington the Third."

"Yes, Sir."

"That's quite a handle. Well, Donald Courtland Purrington the Third, how fast were you going when the sheriff stopped you?"

"I'm not quite sure."

"Did you know the speed limit where you were driving?"

"I thought it was twenty-five."

"Thought did you? Well, Sheriff McCoy, how fast do you estimate Donald Courtland Purrington the Third was going before you stopped his speeding?"

"Well, Thad, oh. Excuse me your honor. I would estimate a considerable amount over twelve miles an hour, the posted speed limit."

"Mr. Purrington, do you have anything to add or refute the Sheriff's testimony?"

"I guess not. I must have just missed the posted speed limit, but I sure wasn't going very fast at all."

"Fast or not fast, you were going over twelve by the testimony of Sheriff McCoy here. The court finds you guilty of speeding. The fine is twenty-five dollars or the lot of you can spend the night in jail. Your choice."

The boys starting talking to one another.

Purrington turned to the Justice and said, "Mr. Justice, I don't think we can pay twenty-five dollars. If we did, we wouldn't have enough money to get back home, let alone go down to Fort Lauderdale."

The Justice said, "How much you got?"

The boys conferred again.

Purrington said, "Well, we have about ten dollars, and we then could then go on to Florida."

"Since you boys have been right respectful to the court and seem like well-behaved sorts, the court is gonna make a rare exception and reduce your fine to ten dollars."

Justice Thomas raised the big gavel high over his head and brought it crashing to the desk and said, "So be it. Sheriff, collect the cash and let 'em go. And, boys, slow down when you come back through here."

Purrington said, "We already got another route planned, your Honor."

Deputy Bloom gleefully told the story at the station house the next day. Everybody had a hoot. The Sheriff's legacy had been born.

Billy McCoy said to the sheriff, "It was Pappy that sicked his boy Lamar over to the hen house that done it."

The sheriff said, "That Lamar's been in and out of jail all his life. Best he be put away with serious time."

"Damn straight. I had enough of those McKenna's. Always have. Cletus, you see to it. Do us all a favor."

"I think maybe eight to ten. That ought to keep him outta trouble for a while."

Old Man McCoy said, "I was thinkin' more like fifteen to twenty—that would do it."

"That might be a wee bit stiff in some people's eyes. This is a hen house and some chickens after all, Billy."

"Now you just wait a minute here, Cletus. We are talking about Marty and that . . ."

The sheriff interrupted and said, "Billy, we already been over what a special rooster and all that. In fact, you have now gotten worked up over that bird for about the third or fourth time. I got it. Marty is your third son but Billy, he's a rooster. Try to keep that in mind, would you?"

"Yes, but Marty . . ."

The sheriff had stopped Billy again, this time with a raised hand that said . . . enough.

What Boo and Beau had done to occasion the arson was not discussed. Old Man McCoy didn't offer, and his second-cousin, twice-removed, didn't ask.

McCoy got in his old Model T and rode back up the mountain, satisfied that Cletus would pursue Lamar vigorously but somewhat disappointed that Lamar may not get fifteen to twenty for his dastardly crime.

Pappy knew the sheriff would come after Lamar. The McCoy's and McKenna's had never been overly friendly. Pappy thought, 'Damn Lamar. Just can't keep his mouth shut. If he had done the tool shed like I told him, nobody would of said anything 'bout it. But no, Lamar's gotta set the damn chickens on fire and now out there braggin' about it'.

With the sheriff's surly attitude about the hen house fire, which was what everybody was calling it, Pappy thought briefly about cutting off Sheriff McCoy from his free shine; however, budgetary concerns overrode his moral outrage, so he decided to kept the sheriff and deputies on the take.

Five or six times a year, the sheriff and a caboodle of newly appointed deputies entirely consisting of county politicians, bureaucrats, relatives, and friends of the sheriff would "raid" the McKenna's.

The raiders would drive up in their pick-up trucks and Model Ts and park in Pappy's front lawn. Pappy would open up a barrel or two, and the sheriff and his crew would then sit around and drink up all of the Mule Kick they could get down their gullets and then leave, each taking a few jars with them on the way out. The sheriff would get two quarts of the 140-proof brew.

The trip down the mountain was an adventure for the lawmen since they were all drunk on Mule Kick, and that was not regular shine. Lorenzo Tribbett, from further up the holler, said, "That Mule Kick hits you right upside your head and then let's you know it's gonna take shelter therein for a spell."

One particular trip down, down the mountain after a McKenna raid created a mountain legend that was oft repeated. Bubba McCoy, the sheriff's fifteen-year-old nephew, drove his car off a mountainside and damn near got killed. Bubba ended up in a full-body cast and missed his entire fifth grade of school. Never went back . . . to school, that is. But it did take Bubba a full three months to get out of the body cast and back just in time for the next McKenna raid.

Bubba didn't drive back this time since he had passed out after drinking what most figured was almost a quart of the 140 proof Mule Kick. They just threw him in the back of Billy Ray McCooty's Dodge pickup truck with the wood panels along the back and dumped him in his front yard. Bubba weighed 250 pounds and couldn't be lifted, so McCooty left him there in his front yard, passed out on the grass. They said Bubba didn't wake up for fifteen hours. Slept right there in the grass, morning dew and all.

The neighborhood kids gathered around him after school and stood there just looking at him and wondering if he was dead or alive.

When Bubba did become conscious, he sat upright for several minutes, legs splayed apart, his head bowed, just staring at the grass. No one said anything. The kids were keeping a respectful distance, but were ready to run if the creature came at them. Slowly he rose to stand, his big body unsteady. He waddled slowly into the house. The kids just stood there for several minutes looking at the door where Bubba had disappeared, then left without speaking a word, seemingly dumbfounded at what they had just witnessed.

Since Lamar had a long rap sheet from the age of fourteen, the law went after him hard. The arrest got some attention in the press, but the trial lasted one hour and forty-five minutes. The jury was out ten minutes.

Billy McCoy was the star—and only—witness for the prosecution.

The Assistant District Attorney prosecuting was a young peacock, Johnson J. Juice, 'J.J.'or 'Juice'.

Juice called Billy to the stand and said, "Mr. McCoy, what happened on the night of March 16 at your home up in Devil's Run Hollow?"

"Well, it weren't a pretty sight. Mostly cause I lost Marty."

"Marty? And who was Marty?"

"He was a rooster, but he was a lot more than that to me. A Rhode Island Red, he was."

Billy's voice cracked just a bit.

Juice said, "Take your time Mr. McCoy. We all know this is hard for you."

"Thank you, Sir, "Billy said. "It's all right, I'm ready to tell the story. Well, Marty was the best damn rooster God ever created."

The judge, Arthur B. Corbin, said, "Mr. McCoy, this court does not tolerate foul language. Please do not curse, or I will find you in contempt."

Billy said, "Excuse me, your Honor, but I ain't been cursing, and I am pretty sure of that."

"You said 'damn,' and there will be no more of that."

"But that ain't a real cuss word, is it? That's jist everyday talkin'. It's not like fu—"

The judge quickly jumped in and said, "Don't say it, Mr. McCoy, or you will be in contempt, and you will spend the night in jail. And, yes, 'damn' is a curse word, and you will forthwith refrain from the use of that word and any other of analogous content or context."

Billy sat confused and said, "Well, all right. No more 'damns' are you gonna hear outta me. I guess that goes for 'hell-damn' too, right? Cause I sometimes combine those two words to make a particular strong point."

The judge just stared at Billy, then turned his attention to Juice and said, "Counsel, would you proceed please, and get to the point quickly before I lose my patience."

Juice said, "Mr. McCoy, you were telling us about Marty, your rooster."

"Yes, well, Marty kept the whole hen house happy. He didn't let anything near that coop. One time Larry Clover, when he was about five or six years old—that's my wife's little sister's kid—got in that hen house, and I swear, Marty was about to peck his toes off. Mind you, you didn't want to get too close to that little fella cause he would come after you right away. Funny thing is, Larry is afraid of chickens to this very day. He won't even eat 'em. Stays entirely away from anything to do with chickens."

The judge said, "Counselor, kindly keep your witness out of coon hidey holes, and Juice, get to the point, will you please?"

"Yes, Your Honor. Mr. McCoy, just state the facts of what you know."

"Well, Lamar, here came over and burned down the hen house, and I lost Marty and twenty-four active laying hens, plus the hen house too."

"Thank you, Billy. That will be all."

"Juice, do you have any further witnesses?"

"No, your Honor, that's it."

Lamar got two years in the West Virginia State Penitentiary, just around the corner and three blocks over from the Marshall County Courthouse.

Lamar was released after sixteen months for good behavior. The warden was asked how a McKenna could do anything that could be mistaken for good behavior. Warden C. K. Koblentz thought about that and told the reporter, "That is a substantial question right there, but in this institution, he didn't make any liquor, and I know that is against his nature. That was pretty good behavior right there because you don't want a bunch of cons on that Mule Kick stuff the McKenna's offer up. Even the thought of that gave me some deep concerns. He also got additional time off for the job he did while enjoying our hospitality here."

The reporter then asked, "And what job was that?"

"Well, Lamar made sure the salt and pepper shakers were filled up before every meal. Six months of that got him one month off his sentence. I don't mind sayin' that Mr. McKenna was one of our best at the salt and pepper shaker detail we ever had. That, and of course the no booze makin', got Lamar out a little early, and that turned out to be for everybody's benefit."

Warden Koblentz was self-satisfied with his clever answer. He wasn't aware that Lamar was using his access to the food service area to steal all the things he needed to brew up some prison moonshine.

All the cons were grateful.

CHAPTER III

LAMAR WALKS THE STRAIGHT & NARROW

Pappy and Lula planned a big welcome-home Sunday dinner for Lamar on his return from the state penitentiary in Moundsville. All the family would be there, friends too. Everybody from the hollow was invited except, of course, the McCoy family.

Lamar wanted a particular friend there too, Larry Pritchitts.

In his various trips to Moundsville, Lamar had gotten to know most of the career criminals within a hundred miles of the tri-corner of West Virginia, Ohio, and Pennsylvania. He became attached to a criminal family across the river from Wheeling in Vinton County, Ohio, the Pritchitts. Whenever Lamar mentioned the Pritchitts family from across the Ohio river, he loved to crack, "One of the greatest feats of all time; Wheeling . . . West Virginia across the Ohio River."

The Pritchitts didn't think of criminal activities as . . . well, crime. To them it was life in the family. Lamar shared the same view. That's the way it had always been with them. If they weren't bootlegging moonshine, then it was robbing banks, stores, or other opportunities. If they were trapped or feared getting caught in one of their capers, they'd shoot their way out, if that's what it took.

Lamar had found a willing underling in Larry Pritchitts. They overlapped doing time in Moundsville. Larry was an easy target for the inmates—take his food and cigarettes, bully him around. Larry lived in fear he would be killed, until Lamar got him protection from the Ku Klux Klan, the largest and most violent gang in the prison. Larry was left alone after that, and Lamar had a loyal ally.

Lamar held a unique position in the prison with the inmate population. He knew the system better than anyone. He was smarter than most. He was personable, and above all, he could make moonshine. He was a talker that loved dispensing advice on how to beat the system living in the squalor of a prison. He knew what he was talking about because almost half his life had been spent in jails and prisons.

Larry thought Lamar a criminal mastermind. Larry didn't seem to wonder why, as a criminal mastermind, Lamar kept getting caught in his various escapades and would be sent to prison with alarming frequency.

Lamar found Larry smart enough to do as told and just barely smart enough not to screw it up too much. Larry was overweight, twenty-eight years old, and generally wore overalls with an undershirt. The shirts were cut off at the sleeves in the summer, long-sleeved in the winter.

He also suffered from a severe case of Tourette syndrome. When stressed, his right hand would start a skittish tic. If further stressed, his left eye might, oddly, do the same. Both tics, the eye and the hand, would be in perfect harmony, ticking at the same time.

Once, during a night robbery, Larry got more than overly stressed. His hand and eye tic became more pronounced, and then he starting hopping on his right leg, his left leg bent at the knee and off the ground, offering no assistance whatsoever. The family decided that was his last heist, which greatly distressed Larry. The bad news caused a torrent of curse words that appeared in almost every sentence he uttered for the next several days.

Four days before the big shindig, Lamar called Larry and said, "Larry, get your fat ass over here. I got some really good work for you."

"Lamar? Is that you? I'll be gawdamn, it is good to hear from you. You out? I thought you had two years comin."

"Yeah, I did but listen to this . . . I got it reduced to sixteen months for good behavior."

"Cut off my legs and call my shorty! The hell you did."

"The warden let me out early because he said I wasn't making any shine for the inmates."

"That don't sound like you, Lamar. What, you gone soft on me?"

"Larry, what do you think? Hell, no I ain't gone soft. I was makin' Mule Kick right in the kitchen. Dumshit warden didn't know anything about it. Course, Pappy slipped a couple of bulls on the outside a little squeezin's to make 'em look the other way. The cons had many a good night on my makin' Mule Kick. Made a little money too and eased my time a bit. I had 'em all treating me like a prince. The Coloreds. The Germans. The Irish. The Slavics. KKK. All of them."

"Nobody knows their way around a prison that is, being an inmate, more than you, Lamar."

"Anyway, I got some big things for you, Larry; you gonna like every one of them. So get yourself a bus ticket and get here Saturday night. Pappy's got a big welcome home Sunday dinner, and knowing the way you like to eat, I'll tell Ma to put three more chickens on the fire and bake four more apple pies."

"I don't like apple pies no more."

"I was just sayin', Larry."

"Well, I was over at Aunt Hester's not more'en two weeks ago Sunday, and she put some bad apples—"

Lamar cut him off. "You can tell me when you get here."

"Oh, Okay. See you Saturday night. I'm lookin' for some action. My family turned again' me and won't let me go on a single heist with them. My own family, Lamar, turning again' me like that. Sometime they don't have no compassion at all. It's sad, Lamar. Just plain sad."

They were all there, being it was a Sunday, and nobody was working the still or anything else, for that matter. The family, the friends, the neighbors, except for the McCoys.

Lamar's mother, Lula, had made the Sunday dinner: fried chicken with all the trimmings. Potato salad, corn, cornbread, peas, sweet creamed carrots, greens, apple pie, and she even did up some grits because they were Lamar's favorite. Many of the women brought dishes as well. It was a wonderful feast.

Hooch said, to no one in particular, "It's truly justified that they were eatin' chicken, given the circumstances of Lamar's unfortunate incarceration, and it was a shame it isn't the McCoy's chicken, but then their hen house is a little short of birds at the moment."

R. J. and Edith McNulty's son, Rosco, aged thirteen, sat on the porch and starting picking out a tune on his banjo called The Cuckoo—a sprightly quality to it, and that got some people starting to dance—clogging, flatfootin', and buck dancing.

Then Red Bascom sat down with his fiddle. The McNulty boy paused to let Red get situated, then picked out the melody to The Cuckoo in double-double tempo. Red answered with

the same timing and rhythm. Then Rosco played the next stanza, and Red again answered in perfect sequence. Gracie May Carter came up next with her dulcimer and followed Roscoe's lead as well; all the while Roscoe set the pace with the melody that was answered by the fiddle and now the dulcimer. Old Man Twitty sat in with a jug and tooted along with the band. Bobby McKinney started to hit the washboard with some enthusiasm. Two more fiddles and another banjo joined in. Roscoe's banjo kept the music going. They moved from song to song flawlessly.

The music kept playing, and the dancers kept clogging. Children had joined in. Old people, too. Johnny Lee Atkins, an old man of eighty-nine, was holding his cane above his head, dancing away. He needed the cane to walk, but not to clog.

Everybody took a turn. They danced and danced—with a partner or not, with two or three partners, none of it mattered. Move those feet fast and keep smiling and laughing. Stop and take a little touch of Mule Kick. It seemed to make the dancing better.

Pappy said to Edith, "That boy is a natural picker. I think he's the best we've had in the holler."

"Oh, Pappy," Edith said, "You just can't believe it. That boy started pickin' when he was about two. Nobody taught him a thing; he just started playing. Hum a tune and he will play it back with some rhythm, too. Just the darnedest thing you ever seen."

Everything was served family style on a long table. Chairs and smaller tables surrounded the rest of the front yard, where the family took their food and talked to each other. Everyone talked at once and repeated it when they thought that they weren't being heard. Children were running and yelling and playing. It was a happy, joyful sound, and altogether, a marvelous sound.

Everybody was happy, for as Pappy put it, "At this here particular time, not one McKenna was in prison."

Pappy speculated that hadn't happened for about seven or eight years since Will Junior, a cousin, just got released from the Ohio State Penitentiary over in Columbus. Will Junior got caught making a delivery to the south end of Columbus. Pappy said that barely counted, since Will Junior only did six months.

Pappy went on to say, "That prison over in O-hi-ah is living in high cotton compared to Moundsville. Those Moundsville bulls over there are meaner than a junkyard dog with fourteen suckin' pups."

For drinks, the kids and some of the woman had lemonade or tea, but for all the men it was Pappy's finest, Mule Kick. It was generally thought that quite a few of the woman may have spiked their lemonade or tea with a touch of the Mule. A few bold women just drank the Mule Kick, straight up, just like the men.

For the men, Ball fruit jars filled up with a rich, slightly caramel-colored liquid that looked downright innocent. Pappy was the only moonshiner in many a mile that aged his brew in charred oak barrels for three months. That give the liquor a rich flavor and caramel color. He'd pull those barrels on special occasions and charge double, even triple for that booze. You take a swig of Pappy's shine and that mule kicked you right in the head, and you felt it right down through your body and out your toes. That kick in the head was what made the McKenna's brew about the most popular moonshine within two hundred miles of his stills.

What Pappy was most proud of was selling in Kentucky. Kentucky moonshiners had a solid reputation that got Pappy's competitive juices flowing. He just didn't like the Kentucky people, either. He said on more than one occasion he never liked or found a man, woman, or child from Kentucky worth a good fart on a rainy day.

He had once bought a pig there, in Kentucky, and the bacon off that hog gave him looseness of the bowels for a week, so Pappy didn't much like Kentucky pigs, either.

Lamar was greatly enjoying the party in his honor as he saw Jack Walker, Loretta's son. He caught Jack's eye and with his left hand low by his side made a motion with four of his fingers, indicating that he wanted Jack to come over.

Larry stood next to Lamar. As Jack sidled up to Lamar, he said, "Jack, this here's my good friend Larry Pritchitts from over in Vinton County, Ohio. He's gonna stay with me awhile till I get settled in."

Jack nodded, and Larry said, "Hey, I saw that Ohio State, Denison game you played in. You were all over the place."

Jack said, "Denison was a pretty easy match-up."

"What you score, three-four touchdowns?"

"What I remember is that I didn't score any touchdowns against Michigan. They skunked us, thirteen to zip."

"You guys missed number 10."

"Chic was a great one. Came back from the military the next year and put me back on the bench."

Lamar looked furtively over his right shoulder, left, and then back to the right. Jack thought that was because Lamar had spent a good part of his life in jails and prisons and that caused him to have a suspicion nature. He didn't want others trying to listen into his ruminations and conversations. Lamar thinking that what he said was important and his gems of wisdom and discussions of future criminal activities should not be overheard. They were much too valuable.

When Lamar was sure there were no eavesdroppers, he said, "Jack, look at you. Big and strong and almost as good-looking as your Uncle Lamar. So you gonna be a lawyer? Larry, my nephew here, is gonna be a lawyer. Maybe he can keep us outta trouble; what do you think of that?"

Larry said, "If he could keep the likes of us outta trouble, I believe he would be the first to do so."

Lamar said, "Hey, I got a good one for you. This guy came up to this really stacked woman and—"

Hooch step through a crowd around the men and interrupted what was sure to be a nasty joke and said, "Dammit, Lamar, don't you go corruptin' Jack. Keep your damn jokes to yourself. Jack's out of the holler, and Loretta is gonna keep it that way."

Hooch said to Lamar, with Jack standing next to both of them, "Where you gonna stay?"

Lamar said, "Loretta has that rent house over on twenty-first street. She is gonna let me stay there. Got a job over at Willy Jack's barber shop so I can pay a little rent. Not much though. About half of what Loretta charges for that place."

"You gonna run a game out of the barbershop, maybe run some numbers?" Hooch said. Jack's interest picked up with the reference to his father. He listened with considerable more interest.

Lamar replied, "Oh, I wouldn't do that to Willy Jack. Or Loretta. She's got me on my best behavior, and I am walkin' on the path!"

Hooch just turned and walked away from Lamar as he said, "Lamar, your name and good behavior—that just don't seem right in the same sentence."

Lamar replied to Hooch as he walked away, "Hey, Hoochie, boy. The warden said I got released for good behavior; did you hear that? Good behavior. That is now my middle name. Lamar 'Good Behavior' McKenna." Lamar and Larry both laughed. Hooch, and Jack, did not.

Hooch thought, 'Now that is funny: Lamar on good behavior. That sure as hell ain't gonna happen'.

Jack just took all of this in as he looked at his two uncles . . . talking about him as if he wasn't there. He liked both his uncles. Lamar was interesting and always in some sort of jam that was generally so bizarre that you didn't know if you should laugh or cry. Besides, Lamar's capers were mostly kinda stupid, Jack thought, and he would be off to prison every couple of years.

Hooch was just fun to be with. He seemed like he was always doing some kind of crazy thing that wasn't wrong, just different from everybody else. Like the time he followed the speeding fire engines in town in his high-powered, fire-engine red Ford, racing through the streets following the fire trucks as if he was the fire chief. Jack was about ten, and to the young boy, fun just didn't get any better than that.

Hooch was also the bootlegging driver of the family. Pappy said once, "Man, that Hooch can drive the hooch better anyone you ever see. Last week he had the state regulators, the federal officers, and that other thing . . . what is that called, Hooch?"

Hooch said, "The Alcoholic Beverage Control Commission of West Virginia. ABC they're called."

"Yes sir, them's the one. Tell 'em how you did it, Hooch," said Pappy with a certain pride in his voice.

Hooch, like all of the other McKenna's, never passed up an opportunity to appear on center stage in a McKenna talk fest and so stood up to address the crowd.

He paused to get everyone's attention . . . hitched up his pants . . . tilted his hat back ever so slightly and then heard cousin Myrtle say in a loud and sassy voice, "Oh, for gawd's sake, get on with it, Hooch!"

Scattered laughter followed.

Hooch had the yard's attention and said, "Well, I'll tell you this. You gotta have the car, and Pappy's always said that. You gotta have that souped-up Moonshine Motorcar. Now we have that Model A, and fortunately I happen to be quite a driver, but I also happen to be a better mechanic than ol' Buster in town."

Buster sitting on the porch next to the now-quiet band said, "Hooch, that'll be the day. You couldn't get that T over thirty-five miles an hour without me telling you what to do."

Undeterred, Hooch said to the crowd, "Don't mind him. I need him to hand me the tools." Now Elwood Eps yelled from the back, "You are so full of bullshit, Hooch. Get on with it before we listen to how you won some shit-race over in Martinsburg."

That did get a big laugh since Hooch was well-known for his bragging about races he'd won and he told each race as a story to be heard and repeated.

Hooch continued, "We got this here Model T that Pappy bought a few years back, and that's the best you can get. Me and Buster souped that T up. You know we can get ninety gallons of Mule Kick in there and still get it up sixty-five to seventy miles an hour." Another voice from the crowd said, "Hooch, no T can go that fast."

Hooch said, "You are right about that, but we mixed the T up with our special sauce, and she runs like she's pitching a hissy fit with a tail on it. You got the car, and you can outrun anything the gov-mints got. Plus, those boys haven't raced cars with other bootleggers like I do. We get together over in Morgantown and trade secrets and try to kill each other in a big dirt field. Damn, that is good stuff and believe me, those boys will run you down and run you over. They know what they do'in' and so do I. And, Pappy, I read in this magazine about Ford's new V-8. We can get one for only four thousand dollars, so you better up the production!"

Elwood Eps than shouted, "Hooch, so what happened last weekend with the regulators? Get to it boy!"

"Oh, yeah, I forgot that was the point of me being in front of you, right?

"That was pretty easy. I'd like to tell you we just outraced the bunch of them lawmen, but boys and girls, we are a lot smarter than that. Pappy here got a tip from a certain lawman, whose name will go undisclosed, that the bastards would be at the foot of 21st Street with an ambush. The common misconception is that 21st is the only way down this holler. Those boys waitin' for us were loaded too and not with Mule Kick, but Thompson machine guns. Can you believe that? Machine guns against us good folk just makin' a little hooch. To avoid that trap we just went down a certain route north of 21st that our good brethren here have made and kept it secret, so I shall not disclose that either. To make it simple for Elwood and a couple others gathered here in hospitality and friendship, I will explain in a way they can understand. We took the other north route, got on the highway, and off we went to deliver our precious product. No one was injured. No one even shot at. Your humble bootlegger delivered again and about twenty speakeasy's up in Wheeling and Pittsburgh made their customers very happy all weekend long.

At that point Hooch had a big smile on his face, tipped his hat, and sat down. He even got a big hand of applause with some hooting and howling thrown in.

Jack had seen the brothers get in real fights. They didn't seem to like each other at times; other times they were laughing and joking. Once they got in a fight at a Sunday get-together over some silly thing.

They were really going at it, and Loretta said, "Willy Jack, get over there and stop that right now." Loretta had that strong constitution she got from Pappy, which was very demanding, bossy, and prone to smacking anyone that didn't strictly fall in line with her orders.

Willy Jack said, "Now, Loretta, they can work it out."

Loretta had a spoon in her hand that she had been using to dish up the potato salad, and she whacked Willy Jack on the arm, which left an immediate red bruise surrounded by the residue of potatoes, mustard, and mayonnaise as she said, "Git over there!"

Willy Jack did as told this time. He stepped between the fighting brothers, his arms out in front to push them apart and said, "All right boys, that's enough."

Hooch, however, had already loaded up his punch, and bam! He connected all right, with Willy Jack, smack on his left cheek. Willy Jack went down, dazed and almost out. That did stop the fight, just not the way Willy Jack had in mind. Willy Jack sat there on his butt with his pork-pie hat sitting high on his head and to the back right with a stunned look on his face. Jack thought that look on his daddy's face and that hat tilted back like that and he couldn't help but start to laugh.

Jack had been to Moundsville Prison with his mother to visit Lamar on many occasions. His mother went every Sunday. She brought food and cigarettes to Lamar. Loretta didn't approve of the cigarettes, but she was aware that the prisoners used them as barter, so she made sure that Lamar got them.

She never missed a week.

Loretta had always tried to take care of her twin brother. When he got out of prison, she would get him a job. A place to stay. Feed him and put him up if necessary. Willy Jack didn't like Lamar one little bit but tolerated his wife's caring and loving nature toward her twin brother.

Loretta was as religious as Lamar was a criminal. Both devoted to their cause. Loretta was determined to get to heaven and just as determined to keep Lamar out of the fiery furnace of Hades. The heaven part seemed to be working for Loretta—at least in her mind. The keeping Lamar out of Hades . . . not so much.

Willy Jack said of her frequent visits to Moundsville, "Loretta, you ain't gonna change the boy. He is what he is, and what he is a man that can't stand his-self unless he is up to criminal mischief."

Loretta kept trying anyway.

Willy Jack had a deep and devoted love for Loretta but often wondered how he got involved with this family, as his father was the Commission of Water and Waste in Marshall County—a respectable family with a high government position, now part of a family that by their own admission was a criminal enterprise. Lamar, of course, had taken criminality to another level.

Well beyond moonshine.

CHAPTER IV

THE LAW COMES A-CALLIN

Henry and Willa Mae McKenna, Pappy's parents, were both born in Devil's Run Hollow. Like the generations of McKenna's before them, they never left. Raised two boys, Pappy and Robert.

Henry was a hard man. Had a mean streak in him, too. He sometimes carried a hickory cane. He didn't need it to walk. He used it to occasionally whack a worker at one his stills or just to keep it by his side if he got some unannounced visitors. He wasn't above giving Pappy or Robert a hit across the backside either.

Willa Mae, ran the house with a loving discipline. She was a strong woman who had the reputation of having a photographic memory, what the mountain folk called a 'recollective' mind. She could read a magazine or newspaper or the bible and recall the image in her mind in great detail. Her woman friends from the hollow loved to sit with her and get caught up on the news from the outside world.

Both Henry and Willa Mae were closer in spirit and temperament to their ancestors rather than the forthcoming generations. They lived in what looked like a rundown shack. Inside, however, rooms had been added over the years. Beneath the house was a fruit cellar. It was comfortable for the family. Outside, they had a barn for the cows and mules, a chicken coop, a tool shed, and a pigpen.

Henry and Willa Mae, like all of the mountain people, wanted a piece of land that belonged to them, and they wanted freedom. The freedom to be with their own. Freedom from an intrusive government. Freedom to make a living as they saw fit and as their ancestors did.

When the McKenna's finally found their land, it was in the far reaches of colonial Virginia, about the time that Wheeling was settled. Fort Pitt was further up the Ohio River.

They were at last isolated from the dual demonic evils of discrimination and tyranny.

They provided for their families with land that wasn't suited for farming, but they could farm an acre or two of corn and a vegetable garden. They had some farm animals. A milk cow. Two, three steers. Chickens. Pigs. A pair of plow mules.

And they had their stills.

When the United States freed itself from their British overlords, it wasn't illegal to make your own liquor. Then the young government, desperate for money, started taxing whiskey. The tax, when not paid, made moonshine illegal. But in Appalachia, this was their way of life and they didn't stop. The government could call it legal or illegal—the boys in the hollow would keep turning it out the way it had always been.

At one point Henry said to his sons, "Hell, that George Washington hisself did the same thing we do, but it ain't at night, and he called his still a distillery. So maybe that's what we ought to do...don't operate stills by the light of the moon but in daylight and call it a dis-still-ler's. We don't got no more stills, boys, just dis-still-ler's."

As people settled along the river and in Wheeling, the McKenna's liquor got the reputation of being the best moonshine coming out of the hollow and for a hundred miles in any direction. It provided a living, more so than their neighbors, but they never showed anything uncommon. They looked, acted, and dressed like their neighbors.

Henry and Willa Mae didn't want to stand out, and they didn't. But they sensed a heavy disturbance moving their way. Willa Mae thought it like a thunderstorm that could be seen far off in the distance; you could smell it, taste it, feel it, see it moving slowly, directly at you— the growing intrusion of what was called civilization, creeping, crawling up the mountainside, into the hollow to destroy all the McKenna's had known for over a 150 years.

They didn't know that the storm was about to bear upon them with murderous vengeance.

It was early on a Tuesday. Henry and Willa Mae were taking coffee and cornbread in the kitchen when the dogs started barking. The sheriff of Marshall County, Weston Wallace, was pulling into the front yard.

The sheriff was easygoing as sheriffs go. He and Henry had an easy working relationship. Every month or so, Henry hosted a get-together for the sheriff, his deputies, and his friends. After much drinking and a lot of laughter, the sheriff and his deputies would leave with a good supply of Mule Kick. In return the sheriff would let Henry know if any lawmen were going to be sniffing around the hollow.

Almost every year, the local district attorney would get a warrant to hit one of Henry's stills. The DA never did get an arrest. In fact, they never found a still. Not one. Once they found too much Mule Kick in the kitchen, slightly over the limit for personal consumption, and Henry had to pay a $125 fine. That was it.

Henry came out and sat on his front porch and quieted his dogs as the sheriff moved slowly out of his car. The sheriff moved slow because of the potbelly that carried him around. That belly moved and directed him. It was if the sheriff had no control over his stomach. That belly controlled the whole man. The sheriff was helpless, the belly took him where it wanted to go. Right now it was pointed directly at Henry.

Henry couldn't help it; he stared at the belly. The sheriff's shirt always looked like the middle two buttons were ready to Pop off and give relief to the heavy burden that was Weston Wallace's stomach. Henry wondered, if the buttons were popped, if they would fly directly toward him. He had once noticed that the sheriff had a hard time reaching the pedals of his car because his stomach pushed him back from the steering wheel too far for his legs to reach.

Henry, a man of few words, said, "Sheriff," by way of greeting.

"Henry, I got some troubling news. Some state people came in yesterday, from that new commission they call the 'ABCC'—Alcohol Beverage Control Commission. Three of 'em. They look like hard cases. Checked into the hotel, and my gawd they had a mess of guns. The bellboy that packed everything to their rooms saw the guns. Heard 'em talkin' and heard your name mentioned. The sumbitches never even paid me a call to tell me what the hell was goin' on. They used to have done that. No more, they just show up with their guns, wearin' those suits and fancy hats."

"You want a pinch?" Henry said.

"Not right yet seein' as I have to drive down that damn road to get back to civilization. I jist might take a jar or two with me when I go." The sheriff thinking that was a fair trade for his information. Henry nodded. He turned his head slightly and said, "Willa Mae. Would you bring the sheriff some lemonade and a couple of quarts?"

Henry paused for a moment and then said, "When is this blessed event gonna take place, do you think?"

"I would suspect right away. Probably not tonight, but tomorrow be my guess. I guess you heard what happened to that farmer over in Winchester. Fella grew apples and made a little home brew. Just enough for his family and any friends that dropped in. Not a moonshiner, just a guy on his own fixin' a little. Damn revenue man shows up asking for directions. The friendly farmer asked him if wanted some tea. Guy says okay. Then the farmer says 'You want a little somethin' in it'? Tryin' to be neighborly and all. Guy says yes. They have a friendly chat and the guy leaves, then comes back with two others the next day. They got guns out, so the farmer gets his shotgun and tells them to get the hell off his property. His son, about seventeen, eighteen, starts cussin' at the regulators. Anyway, damn state man takes a shot at the boy hits the boy in the foot and the kid goes down. The farmer fires back. The regulators shoot him. Kill him dead. Then walk up to the boy and shot him in the head. Just killed the both of them. They found three and half gallons of liquor in the house and left. All this in front of the wife and children."

The sheriff looked down at the ground, ashamed at what they agents had done.

"I heard. Bastards are a bad bunch," Henry said.

Willa Mae served the lemonade and gave the sheriff two quarts of Mule Kick.

The sheriff's belly directed him back to the car and down the mountainside.

Mid-morning the day after the sheriff informed Henry of the coming raid by the regulators, Henry met with the men of the hollow. All were moonshiners.

Ladd Moore was there with his brother and a cousin. All of the Moore's were in their mid-thirties and had been in the hollow as long as Henry. The McCoy's were there: Isiah, Billy's father, Billy and his brother. And the O'Sullivan's, six of them with Sean being the spokesperson. All of them hotheads.

Willa Mae, Mrs. McCoy, and Mrs. O'Sullivan were there as well.

They were all dressed about the same, trousers that seemed slightly too large, except Isiah McCoy who didn't work much and had gotten heavy in his sixties and wore oversized coveralls, and Billy McCoy who wore the same. They all had shirts with no collar buttoned up to the top, still slack on skinny necks. Suspenders. Isiah and half the O'Sullivan's had old, worn jackets that looked like the remnants of a suit that was beyond its time.

They all wore beat-up fedoras with a soft brim and indented crown that was pinched near the front on both sides. Henry had no hat.

The older men sat at the table taking coffee. The younger men and boys sat in chairs or stood, each with a coffee cup in their hand.

Pappy and Robert were standing in the back. Pappy, twelve; Robert, fifteen.

Henry said, "Everybody comfortable? Need more coffee just give Willa Mae there a nod and she'll help you out. Help yourself to those corn biscuits, yonder." Henry nodded at an oak side table that was near the coffee pot. Next to the biscuits was a smaller bowl filled with butter, and next to that another bowl filled with strawberry preserves.

"We gonna have some visitors from that the new state commission that is tryin' to shut us down. The sheriff said there will be three of them, but they may have more comin. Said they looked like thugs in suits," Henry said.

Ladd Moore spoke up. "So what you got in mind, Henry?" Ladd was generally a voice of reason compared to the McCoy's and O'Sullivan's. Those two families were always looking for a fight—if it be with fists, knives, or guns, it didn't matter. They found an odd joy in conflict.

Sean O'Sullivan in particular was expressive and opinionated. Sean's nature was demonstrative. He laughed big, he loved big, he hated bigger. He had been with Teddy Roosevelt and the Rough Riders in Cuba and had sailed around the world as a merchant marine. He'd had eight professional boxing matches and untold fights in bars where he would walk in, take off his jacket, and say in a loud voice, 'Step up, men, I can lick any son-of-bitch in the place. Five dollars a fight. Winner keeps it all. Just step up and put up your money and your fist'. For his efforts he had multiple scars above his eyes. His face scarred. As he was feared by his enemies, he was loved by his friends, and in the hollow, everybody called him a friend.

Sean spoke up, loud, and said, "I'll tell you what you ought to do with these gawdamn fuckin' regulators, Henry, you want to ask me."

Isiah said, "Damn it, Sean, we all know what you would do, so just shut up for a minute and let's hear what Henry has in mind and watch your language we got women and young people here."

Henry said, "Well first, thanks for comin over here, but I look at this as a problem that is the same for each of us. Me today. You tomorrow. So we gotta put aside our little spats and do what we have always done and close the door when the outside world comes callin' with bad intent. Particular, the thugs like the state has on their payroll. Sends them to our front door and to our stills. We are not gonna let that happen here. We all got stills, so what I want to know, gentlemen, are you with me on this one or not? If you say nay, just leave now. You will still be my neighbor tomorrow. If you stay, you gotta know this could be a rough one. These men are not comin' to get our liquor. They are comin' here to get me and mine, and they will be back tomorrow to get you and yours, just like they did to that poor sumbitch down in Winchester and it appears these are the same bastards that shot and killed those poor soul's over there. So if you want out, now is the time."

Not one of the men moved. They sat waiting to hear what Henry was going to do.

Henry said, "I got more than one still. I think everybody here knows that. Two are deep in the holler. One is closer to the road where I think they will be goin', and we are gonna make it easy for them to find. That still will be our Judas goat. We put a little smoke into the air and them bastards will think they struck the mother lode. We gonna get ourselves fixed over there in the bush. Me and Sean will be at the still. The rest of you will be hidden in the scrub. We don't necessarily want gunfire, but if them boys open up, we teach them a lesson they won't forget. Any questions?"

There were none. Everybody sat silent for a minute, each man in their own thoughts. Then Henry said, "Pappy, you stay here with the women. Make sure they are safe. Robert, you go with me."

Pappy had never been cross with his father since he was seven. He disobeyed something silly and childlike, offered up a loud, "No I won't!" Henry smacked him hard against his backside with the hickory cane. Then he hit him again. And as Pappy started crying, Henry hit him a third time. Henry said, "Make that the last time you sass me, boy."

This was the second time. Pappy said, "I'm not stay'en here. I want to go with you and Robert."

Henry was more sympathetic this time, a little pride showing through, since Pappy wanted to join the fight. He said, "Son, you can be a hero some other time. This time we need you here."

"Pa, you got Miz O'Sullivan and Miz McCoy with Ma. They got guns, and it is my interpretation that nobody wants to mess with any of these women in an untoward way."

"But this could get pretty rough. There might be some firecrackers goin' off," Henry said.

"Pa, I can shoot better than you."

Henry said nothing. Pappy thought, 'I'm gonna be there even if Pa don't want me there'.

Devil's Run Creek was clear water, unspoiled, sweet and cool. This creek was why the early McKenna's settled deep in this hollow. A place that was isolated, which made it safe, and with this wonderfully perfect cold, clear water.

Henry thought the regulators would not go to the house, rather, they would go right to the still. Either, they had a tip to where the still would be, or had an idea that it would be in a certain area along the creek. What Henry didn't know was that a con from Moundsville had made a deal with the district attorney for less time in exchange for the location of the still. That con wasn't from the hollow. He learned about the still from a bootlegger inmate that had picked up some of the McKenna's liquor for a delivery to Pittsburgh.

The regulators thought this would be easy. They were experienced. They were arrogant and held the mountain men in low esteem, thought them stupid and uncivilized. And they had fire power. Each had a handgun and a Winchester rifle. The big man of the group carried a pickax to put to use on the stills, but these agents were inclined just to shoot the still and anybody that got in their way. It was more amusing that way.

The mountain men all had rifles. The O'Sullivan's carried Winchesters, as did Paddy and Robert. The others carried Kentucky Long Rifles. They all were deadly shots, and they had set the ambush site. They took cover surrounding the still in a semi-circle—a perfect killing zone, with their bodies hidden in the shrub and underbrush.

They settled in and waited for the regulators. They didn't have to wait long.

Henry heard the dogs bark in the distance. The barking stopped. They could see flashes of light off in the distance as the light bounced and disappeared through the trees and then reappeared. They could see a car approach the still and stop. They heard nothing but the natural sounds of the land at twilight. The lights disappeared. They heard the quiet close of car doors and a louder noise as the men checked their weapons and loaded up. Click, click. The woods seemed quiet now. The could hear the regulators approaching—not noisy, but not trying to hide their presence.

True to his word, Pappy was there, hiding behind an oak tree, Winchester in hand. He felt queasy, nervous, but refused to show it. The men seemed tense to Pappy, but they all had a grim look of resolution. The men were hidden in the brush about fifteen feet apart, each with their hat pulled down, each holding their rifles ready to fire. Slouched down.

Three regulators approached slowly, and the lead man, William W. Dobbins, said sharply, "McKenna. You two put down your guns. Put 'em down. Right now."

Henry didn't respond.

Dobbins said it again, "Put down your guns."

Henry said, "Who are you, and what are doing on my property carrying weapons and yellin' threats? We don't take kindly to bein' approached like that."

The regulator said, "You know who the fuck we are, McKenna. So put down the Goddamn weapons. Now!"

Henry said, "Show me your warrant or get off my property."

Dobbins said, "We don't need no fuckin' warrant. You got a still, and we are gonna bust it up and take you down this mountain and put you and your buddy there in Moundsville for a good long time. Now you can go with us standing or be dead on the ground. This is your last warning, McKenna."

"We know what you bastards did over in Winchester. That's not gonna happen here, so you best turn tail and get back in your car, or you will die on this spot."

Dobbins laughed. Laughed hard. "What, you gonna shoot us? We the government, McKenna. You shoot us, you gonna get up close and personal with Old Sparky over in Moundsville. We take you in; you do a couple of years. So just put down those pea shooters of yours, and we can do this peaceable."

Henry said nothing.

What Pappy most remembered about this moment was the stillness. The birds were gone. The wind was still. No animal or man said a word. Then a single shot startled Pappy. Made him flinch. Then the noise of ten, twelve shots from rifles seemingly fired as one. Pappy had not fired.

The first shot was fired by the agent closest to Sean O'Sullivan. The bullet hit O'Sullivan high in the upper left shoulder, spun him around so that he fell into the wall of the still, bounced backward toward the shooter and then to the ground.

The mountain men fired back before Sean hit the ground. The regulators got off the first shot and no others. They lay dead or dying not thirty feet from the still. Every shot fired hit their intended target. Two were killed instantly. One had been hit in the stomach, hand, and leg. He lay on the ground, breathing hard as Henry approached. Henry shot him in the head.

One of the others had been shot through the eye and in the chest. The third had a shattered arm and neck and three holes in his chest.

The battle was over within seconds of the first shot that was fired.

The mountain men walked slowly toward Henry and the dead men.

One of the O'Sullivan's ran to Sean and put a cloth over his wound to stop the bleeding. Sean said, "We get all the sumbitches?"

Henry said, "Yes, sir, Sean. We got 'em. Got 'em all. They won't be killin' nobody else anymore."

The others were silent as they looked at the bodies, not unlike they had just killed a dear or a bear.

Finally, Henry said, "Robert, get the car and take Mr. O'Sullivan to Dr. Moore. And hurry up about it. Don't tell anybody what happened. Nary a word. Wait for the doc to patch up Sully and get him home."

"Pappy, bring around the truck. You boys get the cash off these bastards, split it up. Take the guns if you want, but you will have to keep them hidden for a while."

Young Billy McCoy said, "Can I take this one's shoes? Those are pretty fancy."

Henry said, "Well, Billy, I can appreciate your love of fine leather, but I think we better leave them dressed as if for the funeral, don't you think? Those shoes may not fit your particular look with you generally wearing britches about 100 percent of the time. It might be a contrast and lead to some questions. We sure as hell gonna get some more of these bastards up here looking for these three, and those fancy shoes will look mighty strange with your usual apparel."

Isiah said, "Where you gonna put 'em, Henry? Gonna take 'em over to Ferguson's pig farm?"

"I got just the spot," Henry said, "where they will be gone and forgotten."

CHAPTER V

Land And Freedom

The raid by the regulators had been three years ago. The feds filled the hollow with agents looking for the bodies of the three agents. They offered a reward of five hundred dollars. No one laid claim to the money. They found some stills, which they destroyed. They did not find the agents, dead or alive. In time, big-city crime run by the Mafia drew their attention away from going deep in the hollows of Appalachia. It was safer going after the big city mobsters than the Appalachian mountain men.

Dalton X. Dicks was assistant director of the Bureau of Prohibition of the United States of America. He had been charged with finding the agents that had disappeared in Devil's Run Hollow. All of his efforts had failed, and he had run out of patience.

Dicks came to Moundsville in foul humor to meet with Sheriff Weston Wallace, District Attorney, David McClure, and West Virginia Director of the Alcohol Control Commission Calvin McPherson.

The four of them met at the Marshall County Courthouse, an imposing, large building on Court Street with four ninety-foot Romanesque columns placed boldly in front holding an arched roof rising magnificently heavenward. The building sat on a rise of twenty to thirty feet from the street. That rise, and the columns in front, gave the building an appearances of being above the fray, reaching skyward for divine guidance. Cannons and monuments on the grounds honoring past military glories added to a sense of celestial presence.

Dicks sought no such spiritual inspiration. He was in a rage and said, "Gentlemen, this is ending right now. Today. I be damned if I am going to let some worthless, good-for-nothing hillbilly like Henry McKenna kill off three of our agents and then just let him go back to making shine as if nothing happened. We cannot have that. Make's us a laughing stock, doesn't it? We don't have enough to get him on the murders, but by gawd, he is a moonshiner, is he not Wallace?"

"That he is, Director," said the sheriff.

"Has he done time for that, McClure.?"

"No, he has not."

"Well, he is about to do just that. Here's the deal. He can cooperate with us, take a plea and we ship him off to Atlanta to do three to five. If he refuses, we go to trial and he goes to that hell hole of a prison you got around the corner, and we will be sure to tell that murderous warden you got over there he has free rein with McKenna. What's that guy's name? The warden, the one that keeps beating inmates to death with the bullwhip? That guy, what's his name?"

"Jeremiah Smith," McPherson said.

"How many men he bull whipped to death now?"

"Eight."

"Eight inmates murdered under the hand of that bull-whipping son-of-a bitch warden."

"Sheriff, you get your ass up in that hollow and tell McKenna he is getting three to five in Atlanta or Moundsville. Lay it out for him real clear. He takes the plea and goes to Atlanta this Friday, or he goes to trial for moonshine and he gets Mr. Psychotic in Moundsville. MClure, get the papers ready for McKenna to sign."

McClure said, "Commissioner, McKenna is slippery. We don't exactly have any evidence to get a conviction on his moonshine."

"McClure, let me check my shit-a-meter about that. Okay, I just did. I don't give a shit. Get him pissing on one of your statues down there. Anything. It don't matter. Be sure to remind him that if he doesn't take the plea, the next McKenna arrested will take his place in Moundsville and get the treatment that is his. This threat of what could happen; that's why he's going to take a plea and leave with my marshals on Friday."

Turning to the sheriff, Dicks said, "Mount up and be the bearer of this grand news to Mr. McKenna. Let's get this show moving."

Dicks shoved some papers into a battered briefcase, stood up, and marched toward the door. He said to no one in particular, "We are going to put McKenna in Atlanta, close this case, and I hope I never have to come back to this fuckin' hillbilly haven."

The sheriff left the meeting and went to the station house to pick up Deputy Bloom.

He entered the station, found his deputy on the phone talking to his wife, and said, "Let's go."

Freddie Bloom said, "Gotta run, Hon. Looks like an emergency."

He turned to the sheriff and said, "What's up?"

"I'll tell you in the car."

They got in the car and Deputy Bloom said, "Where we headed?"

"To see Henry McKenna."

That was the only thing said during the trip up the mountain.

The dogs let Henry and Willa Mae know that a car was approaching.

Henry was sitting on his porch when the sheriff pulled into the front yard. Willa Mae was in the house, but alert when she saw it was the sheriff and his deputy.

The two law officers walked to the bottom of the three steps leading to the porch. The sheriff noticed that the middle step had dropped on one side a few inches before it had become lodged against a two-by-four block of wood, which now supported the step. The sheriff took off his hat. Henry couldn't help but notice the struggle the shirt buttons were having to stay put around the Sheriff's middle.

"Henry, the gawdam feds want a piece of your hide, and they aim to get it one way or another."

Henry remained stoic. He didn't flinch. He didn't smile. He didn't cringe. He continued to stare at the sheriff without a word.

"They want you to do three to five in Atlanta. Take a plea. If's you don't take the plea, I'm supposed to pick you up now for a moonshine trial, which will put you in Moundsville and turn you over to that crazy warden with the feds lookin' the other way. And one other thing, and you're not gonna like this, if you didn't take the deal now to go down to Atlanta, then next time a McKenna has a misstep with the law, they would be goin' to Moundsville and have to deal with that blood thirsty warden over there."

Willa Mae had stepped on to the porch. She said, "You mean by lookin' the other way from that murderous warden? Be a death sentence for my Henry, now wouldn't it, Weston?"

"Sadly, I do Willa Mae I'm sorry. It's not my doin'."

Henry said, "When you comin' back?"

"U.S. marshals be up here on Friday, early afternoon. There won't be no trouble. I'll be right there watchin'."

There was silence from everyone. Willa Mae felt dizzy. She said nothing more. She turned and went back inside. No damn lawman, not even Weston Wallace, would see the hurt in her face, see her body tremble, see her hands shake, witness her broken heart.

Henry turned his head slightly, looking at the woods. It was as if he was looking through the trees and down into town and all the way to Atlanta. He heard birds chirp. He heard one of his beagles bark.

"There's a gallon over yonder. Take it with you," Henry said, nodding to a jar toward the corner of the porch.

The sheriff said, "It don't seem quite appropriate to be takin' some Mule Kick under these circumstances, but I thank you, Henry. Tell Willa Mae I'm awful sorry about this. I did my best to stave 'em off."

He turned to leave and said, "I'll see you Friday. Early afternoon."

It was the first time the sheriff had ever left Henry's place without some Mule Kick Moonshine.

That night, the McKenna's place in Devil's Run Hollow looked peaceful, tranquil. Nearing twilight with the fading sun still shining, the trees around the property were showing their brightest colors of early fall in gold and green and brown. The farm animals were settled. Lightning bugs were starting to glow here and there. Everything suggested it was time for an easy moment of leisure, laying work aside for the day.

Inside the house, dinner was finished. Willa Mae was clearing dishes. Robert and Pappy washing and drying. Henry had a corncob pipe and sat in an easy chair. He was hitting the pipe bowl in the palm of his hand, clearing the old tobacco out, getting ready to light the new.

Firewood wood crackled and warmed the room.

Robert reached for his banjo when Henry said, "That won't be necessary tonight, Robert. I got something to discuss with you boys."

Henry got up and went to a hutch in the corner of the kitchen, pulled out some Mule Kick, and poured three fingers.

Robert said, "Pa, you mind if'n I had a little of that stuff?"

Henry said, "Well, that's why we make it, ain't it? Try not to go overboard. You too Pappy, if you are so inclined. This here is a serious discussion tonight, so take a short jar and no more."

Henry paused and said softly, almost to himself, "Yes, it's serious all right, the most serious we ever had."

The boys poured their drinks and sat down in front of Henry. Willa Mae was moving slowly around the kitchen, fussing with this and that, but fully tuned in to what Henry was saying.

"Sheriff came up to me today. Said those feds wanna send me to prison for moonshine. Can't get me for the incident. Want me to do three to five down in Atlanta."

Pappy said, "Don't they need to find a still and have a trial and all that? How can they just say 'we're sending you off'?"

"Because they can, Pappy. They the government and they can concoct anything they want and push us mountain folk around. They want me to take what they callin' a plea. I just give myself over to them and serve the time."

"Why would you do that?" Robert said.

"If I don't, they will pick me up and put me in a holding cell in Moundsville, and they got a crazy warden there that bullwhips his inmates till they are dead. That's what he would do to me. Whip me to death. Said if I don't take the plea then next McKenna picked up—that might be one of you, boys—they would see that they got the same treatment as I would've got. I don't have a choice, boys, I gotta go."

Pappy thought he heard his mother take a deep breath. Robert turned his head to the side. Didn't want anyone to see the tears in his eyes.

"I'm gonna be gone for a spell. That means you boys are now the responsible men of this household. You gotta run the stills, take care of the animals, keep food on the table. Take care of your mother. It's a lot to ask, but you can do it. I know you can. You been gettin' ready for this day since you were born."

Pappy said, "Pa, when you leaving for Atlanta?"

"Tomorrow afternoon. Pappy, you and I will go over to the stills and tell the boys. Get 'em started on the day. Keep an eye on that new boy, Leroy. I don't know if he has been properly introduced to a workday yet. You help 'em out. You work harder than they do, set the example. You know what to do, and after tomorrow you will know better. You always seemed to have the feel of makin' Mule Kick. Robert, you're good with that rifle, so you help your brother out with the still when he needs it, but you keep food on the table. Tend to the crops, the cattle and all, and you make things as easy as you can for your Ma. These three years will go by real fast, and all this nonsense will be behind us. The good thing is that none of the regulators want to come up in our holler for fear of not comin' back. Let's just keep it that way."

Pappy said, "When do you pay the boys?"

"We can get into the books and the business of the stills tomorrow."

Henry sat back and paused. Took a sip. The boys did as well. Henry felt good about having the boys sippin' with him. Gave him confidence they could face the enormous task in front of them.

Pappy said, "About this Mule Kick. What makes it so much better than the other shine here in the holler, Pa?"

"Couple of things, Pappy. The first are the copper pots that have been handed down forever and the new ones might even be a little better. The other thing is we slow heat, don't over boil anything. Then we distill our mash three times. Nobody does that. And finally, and don't let this out because this is what gives it the smooth taste and slight color, we then keep the liquor in oak barrels for three months. That is a long process, but it produces the best liquor made under the sun, or I should say, under the branches in these woods where nobody can see what we be doin'. And that, my boys, is why we can charge double or even triple of anything else a man can buy."

The boys took a sip with a little more respect as to what they were drinking.

"I need you to remember this, boys. This land we have and the freedom that we enjoy is special. McKenna's have been on this property, in this hollow, a long, long time. When men come up here to take what is ours, we deal with them. It's all we got. We fought long and hard to get here, and no sumbitch is gonna just walk up here and take away what is ours. Those thugs that came up here to kill us got what they deserved. We were justified. Why it was justified, is important for you to know. Our family history is important to know. We don't write a lot of things down, and for good reason, we don't want the outside world to know. You've had bits and pieces of our family history thrown at you over the years, but what I'm tellin' you tonight, I want you to remember, and you will pass it on to your family. You got that?"

Robert and Pappy nodded.

Henry said, "You boys know when the McKenna's came to the shores of America?"

Robert said, "I bet it's been about the time of the war between the states."

"No, it was before that. Before the revolution from the those damn Brits. About

1770-something. They were a family of Scots, like from Scotland, over in the old country. They had no property or way of making a living in Scotland. The bastard king of England said they could have land in part of Ireland if they moved there and worked the land, and after a period of time it would be theirs to own. He called it Ulster. So the family moved there and worked the land for some nobleman. They got nothing. They couldn't even kill a squirrel or bird for food. Couldn't shoot deer. Just worked the land—barely enough to feed the family. It was worse in Ulster than in Scotland. The king had lied. But that is what them bastards do. Look what they are doin' to me right now. They lie, they cheat, they steal from the people with no power. The king and the Church of England, line their pockets and keep the people under foot. Then there was a famine, and that did it for the family."

Henry paused, took a sip, took a puff on the corncob pipe, and said, "About that particular time, rumors got around that the American colony was lookin' for people to settle and they would get free land. Free land! The family Left Ulster and farmed in Llandrindod, Wales, for thirty years to save up enough to get on a boat for America. Can you imagine that, boys? Thirty years. Leaving everything behind to go to a wild frontier, nothing but unknowns, knowing that you might be killed by Indians, the weather, or just plain old evil. Knowing that you will never see your friends and relatives you leave behind. One legend has John T. McKenna, the leader of the family right then said, 'Hell, don't worry about what might happen—the boat ride over will probably kill us all anyway'.

Henry took a pull from his Mule Kick and said, "John T. and company landed in Virginia. Cleared land. Grew corn, apples. Stuff like that. And, of course, they brought copper pots and coils for their still. They made home brew. They all did. The Scots damned near invented makin' whiskey. As civilization closed in, the family pushed west until they found this holler. Here, in this holler, they finally got their wish. Land and freedom. As much land as they wanted and they had freedom from the law, the authorities, the gawdamn Brits, the King. Everything. So they moved to the very edge of the frontier, the boundary of the Ohio River. They made their brew and lived off the land. They traded their liquor for corn and vegetable seeds and animals and goods that could be used on the land."

All three took a swig. Henry said, "On a story night, this here stuff is good for sippin'. Don't rush it. Let it settle. Enjoy the goin' down burn. That's when Mule Kick Moonshine is the best." Henry paused, looked at the fire and said, "About this same time, the American Revolution came to Virginia and the McKenna's went to war for a cause. It was the first time they went into battle of their own free will. Before, it was a nobleman or the King telling them to grab their pitchfork and scythes cause you gonna go kill some poor sumbitch from a hundred miles away before that sumbitch kills you."

Pappy said, "So what happened?"

Henry said, "The Brits and the Loyalist, American traitors that remained loyal to the King, took to the mountains and started hangin' and shootin' the men folk that wanted freedom and independence from their masters. Destroyin' everything in sight. That was just the wrong thing to do to people of an independent spirit. John T. McKenna and about a thousand others got together and marched done further south to put a stop to the carnage. They met the Brits and traitors at a place called Kings Mountain."

"How many McKenna's were there, Pa?" Robert asked.

"We had five men in that army. One of 'em lost an arm. Our people taught 'em a lesson. Those frontier men had hunting rifles because they were so accurate, and they could hit a deer from two to three hundred yards away. The Loyalist had muskets, and that made a big difference in the fight. A musket was easy to load but piss poor with what'cha you were gonna hit. Shoot them damn things, and you didn't know where the pellets would fly. The frontier men had no battle plan, no sense of military battle. Really no leadership. They were told, do what you think is best. What they did best was shoot to kill. I'm telling you boys, that it was almost a massacre. Total defeat for the Brits. They surrendered. The Brit general, Ferguson, was killed. I was told this was the only battle of the war where Americans fought each other. Turns out this was one of the key battles of the war of revolution. Some said the turning point, because it wasn't long after that the Brits called it quits."

Robert smiled and said, "Sounds like the McKenna's won the whole damn war, Pa."

Willa Mae said, "Robert! You watch your language, boy"

"Yes, Ma. Sorry."

Henry said, "The McKenna's fought to free America. They fought for this Union in the war between the states. We claimed this land right here in this holler over a hundred years ago. This is our home. We have managed to be free. Free from the federals getting in our lives and free to make the best damn whiskey in this here great land of ours. The bastards have always wanted to take it from us, and if they try, well you know what we do to defend ours. This land is ours."

Henry paused as he thought about those words of freedom. He said, "Now what we always done, became known as moonshine liquor. They say it's illegal. Not to us it ain't. You boys have a big job in front of you over these next years. But you have been taught the business since you were five, six years old. You know it. Especially you, Pappy. Tomorrow morning, I'll show you know where I keep the cash, and we will go out together to talk to the boys we employ and tell 'em how it's gonna be for a spell. Robert, you see anybody near our cash stash in the fruit cellar, you shoot to kill and don't be hesitant about it."

"Yes, Sir."

Their jars were emptied. It was 2:30 in the morning.

CHAPTER VI

ON THE ROAD TO ATLANTA

Making moonshine often required Henry and the others to work at night, and they usually slept in late. Not on this day, the day Henry was to be picked up by the sheriff.

As the rooster crowed, Henry was beside the boys in their shared bedroom and rockin' their oak made beds. "Time to take over, boys—git your britches on, take care of your business, and get ready. You're gonna be the men of the house now."

Five minutes later, Willa Mae was serving them breakfast. Grits, gravy, and biscuits. Fried eggs and smoked bacon. Coffee. Henry was eating when they came in. The boys quickly caught up and finished.

Henry said, "Follow me, Lads."

Henry took the boys outside and around to the back of the house.

In back was the entry to the root cellar. Swinging the doors, back they walked down five steps, and there was another door made of solid oak, and it was locked. Henry unlocked the door and lit three candles scattered around the room.

The room was fairly large, all underground. It was all brick and oak. The walls had been bricked in. The floor was oak and well-covered with seeds and stems and dirt. Each wall was lined with four inches of oak shelves. Solid. Substantial. The shelves had baskets filled with dried fruit, potatoes, pumpkin, onions, apples, and covered jars with Honey and vegetables. There were fresh fruit and vegetables available as well.

Scattered on the floor were round storage barrels. They were filled with seeds, corn, and all manner of things. They reminded Pappy of the cracker barrels in several of the stores in McMechen, where there always seem to be farmers and mountain people sitting around and having cracker or peanuts and soda Pop as they shared talk and insights as to how the world could be a better place if the mayor or the sheriff or the president would just do this or that.

Henry went over to a seed barrel. He said, "Give me a hand here, boys." Henry told them to tilt this seed barrel over and empty the seeds into a half-filled barrel.

Henry said, "Now boys, this here barrel has a false bottom in it. See down here." The boys could see that about a third of the barrel had contained seeds. Now they could see a flat bottom that had two small latches to keep the lid in place. Henry detached the latches and pulled the false floor upward.

What they saw were two bags—two pig bladders tied at the top. Henry pulled out one of the bladders and said, "These pig bladders keep the cash preserved, just like with some of the food."

Henry then opened the bag.

Pappy looked into the bag and saw money—bills. Dollar bills. Five-dollar bills. Twenty-dollar bills. He even thought he saw a ten-dollar bill. He saw bills with pictures of men that he had never seen before. He saw bills that were larger than the others. Slightly different colors. He was amazed. Stunned. The bills were not in stacks. They had been thrown into the pigs bladder carelessly. All of the bills looked used. They were very wrinkled and even looked a little dirty.

As the three of them stared at the cash in the pig's bladder, Henry said, "Boys, this is what prohibition has brought us. And keep in mind this is a 'cash and carry' business. We make the Mule Kick and sell it for cash money. We pay the boys that work on the still, do the driving, and do the delivery in cash. I keep the record of the cash in my head. Nothing is writ down. You boys are gonna have to do the same. Somebody come snoopin' around the root cellar, they better have a good reason, or you just shoot 'em and take 'em to where the agents went and they will never be found. Yes, sir. That's what you do."

They brought two cars. The sheriff led the way. Deputy Bloom was with him. The second car was black. The black Model T had two men. The driver was about twenty-eight and the passenger about thirty-five, fit and broad-shouldered. They had on dark suits with bolo ties and western-style businessman's hats. U.S. marshals had come to drive Henry down to the Atlanta federal prison—a harsh, maximum-security, men-only facility. Some of the most dangerous men in American were found there. Still safer than Moundsville.

The family stood on the porch. Henry had a small satchel in his hand. His boys stood on either side of him. Willa Mae stood by the screen door.

The sheriff stood at the foot of the steps, with Deputy Bloom behind him slightly and to the side. The marshals stood five feet behind the sheriff. They both carried rifles cradled in their arms.

The Sheriff said, "Time to come along, Henry."

Henry turned to each of his boys in turn and shook hands with them. Nothing was said.

As Henry stepped down into the yard, the youngest marshal came forward carrying large and ugly-looking handcuffs and approached Henry.

At that point, Willa Mae left the doorway and moved away, not wanting to see her Henry being cuffed. The boys stood mute.

Sheriff Wallace said, "Can't you boys do that in the car."

The young marshal ignored the remark and cuffed Henry in front of his boys. He then grabbed Henry roughly by the arm and led him to the black car and guided him into the back seat.

The sheriff had been holding his hat. He turned to the boys and nodded, put on his hat, and returned to his car. They pulled away.

Pappy and Robert both had tears streaming down their faces, afraid for their Pa. Resolute to be manly, but both fearful of what lay ahead.

They went in the house to comfort a weeping Willa Mae. She had collapsed on the sofa, sobbing. That was the first time in their lives that Robert and Pappy saw their mother crying—a sight they never forgot.

CHAPTER VII

THE HOUSE ON 21ST STREET

Lamar and Larry moved into Willy Jack and Loretta's rent house the day after the big welcome home party. It was an easy move. Both men had a single suitcase. The house was fully furnished, on 21st Street in McMechen, just off the corner of Marshall. Go up 21st and you would hit Pappy and Lula's place in about three miles.

The house on 21st Street had been the family home of Wesley and Edith Walker. Five bedrooms. They bought the house because Edith wanted a large family. She got it. Five girls and the youngest, a boy they named Willy Jack.

Wesley became the Commissioner of Waste and Water for Marshall County, Edith was active in the Methodist Church and was the local chapter president of the Women's Temperance Union. They were solid, substantial citizens. Responsible and sober. Community and church leaders. Respectable and respected.

Wesley was a sober man, but on one occasion he came home late and drunk. The next morning coming down the stairs, he saw his wife and girls. Willy Jack had not been born yet. Each child and Edith were at the foot of the stairs. They were all in their Sunday best, each sitting on their suitcase.

Edith said, "Wesley, what do you see here?"

He said, "Looks like you are dressed up and ready to go on a trip."

"I want you to look at these girls. I want you to look at me. Because if you come to this house ever again in a drunken state, you will never see us again."

"Edith, I just got carried away a bit with the boys. That's all, nothing to get all worked up over."

"Does this look like I am serious about what I just said?"

"Yes, it surely does."

Nan, the five-year-old, started to tear up and cry. She said, "I don't want to leave Daddy. I don't want to go anyplace. Can't we stay here, Mommy? I want to go to my room."

"Wesley, what are you going to say to your daughters? This is your decision, and it will be made right now."

"Edith, it was just this one time. I never done anything like this before."

"Wesley! What are you going to tell your daughters?"

Wesley paused. The thought of losing his family overwhelmed him. It tore at him in a frightening instant.

"Girls, Daddy made a big mistake, and this won't happen again. Ever again."

With that, Helen stood and embraced her husband. The girls gathered around both of them.

Wesley said, "Edith, I'm so sorry. I love you, Honey. I love the girls. This is my whole life."

Edith said, "Wesley, I love you too, but I am serious about this, and after all I can't have my husband a drunk with me president of the Temperance Union, now can I?"

Just then, little Nan said, "Mommy, can I get out of this dress? It itches."

When Willy Jack was sixteen, his father went into McMechen General for a simple gall bladder operation. W.J. was a tenth grade student at Union High School, just down Marshall Street from the family home. It was early fall, and Willy Jack was in his history class, thinking more of the football game against Bellaire on Friday night than the lead-up to the war of 1812.

Mr. Gates, the vice-principal, walked into the class and spoke quietly to Miss Adams.

He then turned to the class, looked at Willy Jack and said, "Willy Jack, would you gather your books and anything else you have and come with me? Don't worry, you're not in trouble."

All the students looked at Willy Jack. He gathered his things and left with Mr. Gates.

Mr. Gates said, "Willy Jack, we are going to Mr. House's office. He has something to tell you."

No other words were exchanged.

As they entered the principal's office, Mr. House was seated at his desk along with a policeman in a side chair. Two of his sisters, Nan and Ellie also students at the school, where seated in the room as well. Jack looked at a big, round clock over the principal's desk. The time was eleven-eighteen. That clock. That time, would be forever carved into Willy Jack's memory. The time when his life changed forever.

Mr. House said, "Girls, Willy Jack . . . I'm afraid your father did not do well in his surgery today. We really don't know the details, but Officer Tidwell here is going to take you home so you can be with your mother and sisters."

Wesley had gone in for what everyone said was a simple operation. He was to be out of the hospital by Friday. He had even joked with Willy Jack that he would be back in time to go see Union take on Bellaire and see, as he put it, Willy Jack in action.

The officer brought them home and walked them to the door. Their sisters and mother were in the front living room. They all had handkerchiefs to their faces. As Edith saw her three children on the front porch, she jumped up and raced to the door. She sobbed as she embraced them. They stumbled into the parlor, the four of them in a clumsy half embrace.

Edith braced herself and said, "Children, I have terrible news for you . . . your father died on the operating table today. He's gone. Our Wesley, our Daddy, is gone. He's gone to heaven, children. Gone to heaven."

At that point she collapsed on the sofa. Willy Jack had never known such confusion, such muddiness, loss—a fog that washed over him. The fog clouded his vision. He couldn't see. He couldn't hear. The fog enveloped him so that he couldn't move. His entire body was too heavy for him to stand. He slumped in a chair. His hands rose to his face. The tears flowed from Willy Jack. All were absolutely devastated.

Their mother sobbed, "No, No, No. Why? Why? No. No."

Willy Jack, at sixteen, was now the man of the house. The town, the county, offered few jobs to women. Willy Jack tried to continue with school. Tried to stay on the football team. Tried to see Loretta McKenna when he could. Tried to continue life as he had known it.

But reality hit hard. The family needed an income beyond the meager pension they got from the county. Willy Jack was the only one that could provide.

Thirty-two days after the death of his father, Willy Jack was hired by Wheeling Steel. His title: General Labor-Utility Boy. He was subject to be told by any worker, at any time, what to do. The men were always quick to tell him they wanted it done yesterday. It was the bottom of the working men's ladder. He was the utility boy.

At work, he put his head down and kept his mouth shut. He had his mother and five sisters depending on him keeping this job and turning it into a better one.

Edith died two years after Wesley. As before with Wesley, on an operating table, this time with gout surgery, which caused a heart attack. She never made out of surgery.

Without parents, Willy Jack was the sole provider for his sisters.

The Walker girls were all beautiful. Nan the youngest, became Ms. McMechen... when she was eighteen, just out of high school. Each of the young women had, in turn, many eager suitors. They were cautious, but eager to start their own families. They all married before they were twenty.

Willy Jack and Loretta married too. Willy Jack was nineteen, and Loretta, eighteen.

Willy Jack's promotions came quickly at Wheeling Steel. Every year he would move up that ladder another step or two. By the time he married Loretta, he was a foreman. He was in charge of many men his senior. Some resented his advance. He didn't care. He was resolute and persevered. He now had a wife to support and their son Jack, born nine months after their marriage.

Edith, following the wishes of her husband, left the house to Willy Jack. Wesley felt that the girls would marry well and would not want. It was his wish that Willy Jack should inherit the house.

Edith knew the great sacrifice that Willy Jack had made for her and her daughters. He'd lost his childhood, his innocence, his life . . . all in a horrible instant. He did not graduate with his friends. He didn't celebrate the state football championship with his teammates in what would have been his senior year. No senior prom. No proper teenage courtship and flirtations with Loretta McKenna. All gone.

He gave his childhood to show up at Wheeling Steel at seven every morning and walk into a large, dark, dirty building with coal dust in the air and the stink of the hard, rough men that sweated and cursed through long days as they turned fiery molten masses into steel. Men that fought, hard drinkers, and some that beat their wife and children. Men that didn't like the handsome teenage boy that advanced faster than they and took their abuse without a word of complaint.

One evening at bedtime, Edith walked by Willy Jack's bedroom. She could hear her son crying himself to sleep. All she could do was close her bedroom door and weep. Her heart broke for the heavy burden placed on her son.

Edith, like Wesley, felt like Willy Jack should have the house and all that was in it.

So it was done.

When Willy Jack got the house; he and Loretta were comfortable in a home close to the steel mill. They decided to rent the house on 21st Street. Then Lamar was out of prison and the house was between renters.

Loretta made it clear to Lamar that they needed the income from the house, but Lamar could stay there until he got his feet on the ground. Loretta thought that would be a few months. Willy Jack knew what his wife didn't; getting Lamar out of the house would be the next time Lamar went to prison.

When Willy Jack and Loretta married, the sisters were aghast—their brother marrying into the infamous McKenna clan. Unacceptable. Unbelievable. They refused to attend any of the wedding functions.

They refused to even talk to Loretta. Loretta was not welcomed into their homes. She would be an outcast from the Walker sisters. She was of the McKenna clan. No good moonshiners and bootleggers.

And, of course, there was the suspicion that Henry, Loretta's grandfather, had murdered those federal men a few years ago; the regulators that went up to Pappy's still never came back. Pappy said he never saw 'em and must have been some other shiners. He announced that suspicions would be better directed toward the McCoys on the other side of the hollow.

Now the sisters had the worst of the McKenna's, Lamar, in their family home. When Helen heard the news, she fainted and dropped to the ground in the parlor of her house she shared with Elwood Eps, her husband. Fortunately, Elwood was there with her at the time and was able to administer vapors to her almost immediately. Elwood, being a pharmacist, had plenty of drugs handy to give Helen as she passed out and flopped to the floor. She hit her head on the edge of the sofa as she went down, and it took seven stitches to close the wound. Helen did have a history of fainting at unexpected bad news, and on occasion good news had the same effect, and this may have been the most fainting-inspired news she ever received. She spent three days in bed recovering—not so much from the head wound as knowing a McKenna had taken over the family home.

The house was perfect for what Lamar had in mind. Along with the five bathrooms, the washroom had a bath, sink, and cabinets for towels and some bedding. The toilet to the bath was a separate attached room. All with indoor plumbing.

Downstairs was a parlor, living and dining rooms, kitchen, a small laundry room, and a smaller separate room in the back of the kitchen, which was used as a catch-all for the family, sometimes a family room for games or just private time.

Willy Jack worried that Lamar would introduce a criminal element to the house and his old neighbors.

He underestimated Lamar's criminal nature.

CHAPTER VIII

Larry Gets A Gun

The two of them, Lamar and Larry, were sitting in the kitchen. It was early evening of the first day in the 21st Street house. They each had a jar of Mule Kick they were nursing along. The kitchen table was a red-and-white checkered plastic cloth. Tex Williams singing, "Smoke! Smoke! Smoke! That Cigarette," coming from the Pathephone Number 12. Played on a 78 rpm, Shellac disc. Five minutes a recording. Lamar loved that machine.

Larry said, "Damn, Lamar. This is the nicest place I have ever lived. This is grand. It's almost like we got too much room. What you gonna do with all this space?"

"I got plans for it, Larry. I got plans."

"Like what?"

"I'll let you know. Right now I got another matter to discuss with you. I've got a guy, was a boss over in Moundsville, that was a pretty good guy. He wasn't there when you were, so you don't know him, and he don't know you. Most of them bosses are just looking for something so that they can put their baton on you. But Conrad was almost tolerable. He left Moundsville and is now the head of security over at Wheeling Steel in the Benwood Plant. He needs a night watchman for the trucking area. The trucks are filled up with nails, so there is not much to steal. The trucks have to be guarded at night. Now, Larry, listen to this, they have never had an attempt on any of the goods or trucks there so you won't have to do anything. Just stay awake. Think you can do that? That's all they require. That's where you come in. I got you an interview for that watchman job."

Larry said, "Would I get to have a gun?"

"Yes, Larry, you would have a gun. That's why when you meet Conrad, I want you to keep that damn restless hand of yours in your coveralls."

Larry said, "Coveralls? Oh, you mean my breeches."

"Yes, Larry, your britches. Keep that hand of yours in your pants. Even Conrad might think twice about putting a pistol in your shaking hand. That just might give him a thought."

Larry said, "What kind of gun?"

"Damn it, Larry, forget about the gun. You will be strapped, but don't ever pull the thing out. Don't even think about firing it off. Here's what . . . don't touch it. Don't think about it. Don't ever pull it out. Never, never, ever."

"Will I get a uniform?"

"Yes, Larry. A uniform and a gun. Larry listen to me, don't touch that gun. You got that?"

"But what if some bad guys show up and I have to fight 'em off?"

"Just go hide someplace, but don't pull your gun. Don't touch it, Larry. You got that? And, yes, some bad guys are gonna show up and I will have sent them. Probably be a brother or cousin or two that you may remember meeting at some time. So don't shoot at 'em. Your mother may be a bit pissed if you kill one of her sons."

Larry said, "Do I get a badge?"

Lamar didn't answer.

Instead, he took an extra-long pull out of the smoky liquid in the fruit jar and turned his attention to the song in the background, as Tex sang, "Smoke, smoke that cigarette. Puff, puff, puff . . . and smoke yourself to death."

The next day in the early afternoon, Lamar took Larry to the security offices at Wheeling Steel. The steel mills were dotted along the Ohio River from Wheeling to Steubenville, Ohio. Lamar parked and looked into the sky. Wheeling Steel's big plant with a half-dozen smoke stacks, most rising hundreds of feet in the air. The stacks belched gases into the sky. Black toxic smoke. The stacks so high that the smoke would hopefully blow away before it settled on the ground somewhat dissipated.

It looked like twilight, as black coal dust settled over the Ohio valley from the plants. Under the stacks you could not see a blue sky. The sky appeared as gray, with black spots that served as clouds.

Lamar had been given a pass to park and access to see Conrad. Larry's right hand was becoming restless. Lamar said, "Put your damn hand in your breeches." Larry's irritation was coming out as he said "breeches." He hit the "breeches" hard . . . poking fun at Larry. Larry didn't pick up on the subtlety.

Conrad looked the part. Beefy. Scowling. Tan pants and shirt. Mustache. He said, "Hello, McKenna. This who you got for me?"

"Yeah, and it's good to see you too, Boss. This here's Larry Pritchitt from over in Vinton County. In Ohio. Larry, say hello to Boss Conrad."

"Hello, Sir."

Conrad said, "So, Larry, you want to be a security guard, and you do know it's the graveyard shift?"

"It has been a fond desire of mine to be a security guard for quite some time now. Yes, sir, quite a few years." Larry pushed his right hand deeper in his coveralls, feeling his hand tic beginning to accelerate.

"What about the night part of it? Think you can handle that?"

Larry replied, "Oh, yea. I'm up half the fuckin' night as it is. Shit yea."

Lamar thought, 'here he goes'.

Conrad seemed unfazed by Larry's peculiar reply.

Larry then blurted out, "Hey, do I get a gun?"

Conrad said, "Why, yes, Larry. You will get a gun. Do you know how to use one?"

"I have been shootin' things since I was five. When my hand calms down I can come pretty close, even today."

Conrad said, "What do you mean, when your hand calms?"

At that point Lamar jumped in and said, "That damn Larry. Always jokin'. So Boss, we set here?"

"Go see Felicia, the girl at the desk outside. She will set you up for payroll and give you some other things to fill out. And Lamar, take him over to Schottenstein's over in Moundsville, and Abe will set him up with a uniform. Larry, you will have to buy your own uniform, but we provide your badge and gun. Can you handle that, boy?"

A little of the boss came out as Conrad hit 'boy' with a little nasty.

Larry looked at Lamar.

Lamar said, "We can handle the uniform. Anything else?" Lamar was anxious to get out of there. Being around Conrad made him uneasy.

Larry got set up with Felicia and got his marching orders. She was abrupt and bossy. As soon as they got in the parking lot, Larry pulled his hand out of his pants. It was shaking quite violently.

They headed to Shotty's, the common name for the store, to get Larry outfitted for his uniform. Larry could barely contain his excitement. He said, "Lamar, they gave me my badge, but when do I get my gun?"

"The lady, Felecia, said you get it when you show up for work the first night."

Larry kept starring at his badge, running his finger over the raised numbers, 4273. He pinned the badge to his coveralls, directly in the middle, high on his chest. He said, "There, Lamar, that looks pretty darn good."

Lamar glanced over to look at the badge displayed prominently.

He didn't say word, just turned his attention back to his driving and what he had in mind for the house on 71st Street.

Abe, the store owner, said to Larry, "Try these pants on." Shotty's had a section that was called, "Little Used," and the salesman had pulled these out of a stack of pants piled high on a table. If you wanted to find your size, you started looking for the tags on each pant.

Larry said, "These don't look much like the jacket."

Lamar said, "They look close enough."

Abe said, "These are the only pants in the store that are going to fit. Or come close to fitting."

Lamar said, "What size are they?"

"Fifty-two by thirty. But no matter what size you are, you're going to have to have them hemmed. Your friend here has an unusually body shape."

"He does indeed. These will do," said Lamar.

Then Larry said, "I don't like pants. I think I will just wear the jacket over my breeches."

"No you won't, Larry. You will wear these pants," Lamar said.

"How am I supposed to keep 'em up? I take three steps and the damn pants will be around my ankles."

"Abe," Larry said, "You got some suspenders for my boy here?"

"I got 'em in red or red. Which color would you like?"

Lamar said, "He'll take 'em in red."

"Do I get a hat?"

Lamar said, "We gotta get that in Wheeling. Abe, let's wrap 'em up."

They headed back to the house, and Larry said, "I thought the uniform would look a little better on me." He still had his badge on display.

Lamar said, "Larry, I don't know how to say this without hurting your tender feelings, but when you put on fifty-two-inch waist pants, and they need took up three inches, you gonna look more like Fatty Arbuckle than Rudolph Valentino."

"Whose Rudolph, what's his name?"

Lamar ignored the question and stared straight.

He thought, 'I need some girls'.

CHAPTER IX

PEACHES IS A PIP

Lamar and Larry were seated in rocking chairs on the front porch of the house on 21st Street. They were having their evening portion of Mule Kick from their fruit jars and watching the patrons come and go at the bar across the street.

"Larry, we need some girls for the house," Lamar said.

"What kind of girls?"

"What kind do you think, Larry?"

"You mean for a cathouse. That what we gonna do?"

"Yes, Larry, a cathouse. A brothel. A house of ill-repute."

"Well, in that case they ought to be kinda pretty."

"Yes, you're on the right track there, Larry, but you have to stay mindful that all women have something pretty about them, so you gotta look beyond the obvious."

"Ought to be nice to be around. I been around some mean ones, and we don't want that."

"There you go."

"I got it! We should get some of them women from a couple of the houses down home. We got four or five pretty active houses, and them girls seem to come and go pretty fast."

"Yep, sounds like we are on the same page now. You know any? I mean personally."

"Well, I don't so much, but I got a cousin, Bobby T, that knows 'em all. That man likes his ladies. I bet he could get a couple to move up here to our place."

Lamar let the "our place" slide.

"I know Bobby T from a couple of bank jobs. Let's do that. Let's give ol' Bobby T a call and see what he can deliver."

Bobby T called Lamar two weeks later.

"Lamar, Bobby T here."

"B. T, you stayin' clean?"

"After that last bank job we did, I got scared straight for twenty minutes or so."

"Never fun to have the cops shootin' real bullets at you, is it?"

"Not a bit."

"What you got for me?"

"I'm sendin' up three of the best from over here. A sweet, young thing that is new to the trade and one that is sexy and experienced."

"That's two, B. T."

"The other would be Peaches Fantazzi. She is the boss of the crew. Your madam, so to speak."

"Peaches Fantazzi? What, does she strip in her off hours?"

"No, that actually is her name."

"Peaches Fantazzi. That's her real name."

"Now, Lamar, listen to me a second here. Peaches knows the business. Larry tells me this is your first foray into the whore house business."

"That it is."

"Peaches knows it backwards and forwards, so to speak. She can be a real help getting you trained, just don't let her scare you."

"B. T., some of the bulls over in Moundsville scared me. The KKK scared the shit out of me, and last I checked. I ain't even colored. I don't think a little lady runnin' a crew of girls in a cathouse is gonna be one bit intimidating."

"One other thing. The bus fare is $1.10, and the girls want a $5.00 bonus to start. Like a signing bonus. Up front."

"What the hell, who they think they are, Babe Ruth?"

B. T. was silent.

"Okay, tell 'em they'll get their six-fifty when they get up here."

Lamar and Larry picked the girls up at the Wheeling bus station two days later.

They were easy to pick out of the passengers getting off the bus. They were young, very attractive, and well-dressed compared to the other passengers.

Lamar went up to them with a little strut and a big smile, both arms extended. "Hello, hello. Welcome to this side of the river. I am Lamar." He did a pretend bow. "And this here is Larry. I'm gonna take good care of you girls, and we all will make a little money."

The girl that looked to be the older of the three said, "Cut the bullshit, Lamar. I've already met you; guys just like you every stop I've made. I been in this shitty business for seven years, and each stop I pray to God this is my last. Let's set some rules early on here. I will run the girls, all of them. You don't talk to them. You don't smile at them. You don't even know they are there. You talk to me. And that includes anyone else at the house you bring in. I'll take three percent off the top, and it comes out of your cut, not theirs. Right now you are going to buy us lunch, and we can all get cozy."

Lamar said, "Okay," but thought, '...She sounded like some of the boss's over in Moundsville rather than a lady but she ain't no lady, now is she, Lamar'?

The bus stop had a fairly small diner. Seated about twenty with bar stools around a counter and tables set up with hardback chairs.

They got settled at a table. The waitress brought menus and still no introductions. Lamar said, "Well, what are your names, pretty ladies?"

The one that spoke at the bus stop said, "We'll order first and then get to that."

Lamar shut up and looked at the menu. Larry hadn't said a word and seemed to be confused with the aggressive woman. The girls got the White Plate special: meatloaf, mashed potatoes, lima beans, a drink of their choice, and banana cream pie for dessert. The young girl ordered a milkshake and a hot fudge sundae for dessert. Both Lamar and Larry got the special.

After ordering, the talkative girl said, "My name is Peaches Fantazzi. I'll be your madam, and as I said, you got a beef with the girls, you come to me. You have any questions at all, you come to me. You think you want a freebie, you come to me. In short, you come to me."

That got Larry's attention. "You mean I can get a free one?"

Peaches gave Larry a hard stare and said, "Well, since we are all being so nice and friendly here and letting the language flow, who the hell are you?"

"I am Larry Pritchitt." Larry sat up a straight. Pushed his chest out as best he could, showing off his security guard badge.

"And who is Larry Britches?" said Peaches.

"It's Pritchitt. Pritchitt. With two t's. Chitt at the end. Chitt, Pritchitt."

"Oh, rhymes with shit, you mean. Pritshitt. With two 't's. And who are you, Larry Pritshitt?"

"I am Lamar's right-hand man and also a professional security guard, that carries a gun. And, I got this here badge too."

"You don't say, Larry Pritshitt, with two 't's. No, you don't get any freebies. In fact, you do your housekeeping or whatever you do, and you stay away from the girls. Don't go near them, and don't even talk to them. Just keep your pecker holstered. You got that?"

Larry didn't answer but thought she sounded like Lamar telling him to keep his gun holstered. Peaches was one he would stay away from. 'She scares me', he thought.

Lamar didn't like Peaches' attitude much, but as this was the first whore house he ever had, he was thinking and moving cautiously. He even thought that having Peaches run the girls might work out to his benefit, giving him time to work out something to get some quick spending money before the big score. Yes, he thought, this just might work out with Peaches in charge of the house.

Peaches said, "Now this young thing is Amy. She is fifteen and green as a willow branch. Just been in the life for about six months. Both you boys stay away from her. No freebies here, understand?"

The boys said nothing. Peaches said, "Do you understand?"

Lamar snapped out of it and said, "Oh, yea. Yea. No problem."

"I mean it. You let me bring her along slow. And this is Samantha Ruby. You can call her Sam."

Lamar had noticed Sam right away. She had an attitude. Right then, as if on cue, she lit a cigarette, bringing it slowly to her lips, bright with red, leaned back in her chair, amused by the conversation, but above the buzz. Blue eyes. He heard a con say once that he had known a woman that had bedroom eyes. Sam had bedroom eyes and a 'catch me if you can, and if you do, I'll make it worth the chase' look.

Lamar thought, damn, this woman is sexy. I could get into this one.

The two girls didn't say anything. Peaches did all the talking. About three bites into her steak, she said, "We were promised five dollars and bus fare. Where is it?"

Lamar said, "Oh, back at the house."

Peaches said, "It better be, Buster. You have anybody else ready to go?"

Lamar said, "We may have one or two possibilities coming in next week."

Peaches said, "Have them see me. You don't need to get involved. We need a couple of days to get ready. We'll start Friday night and work the weekend. Monday is an off day. Every week. No exceptions. I collect from the John's and we pay the girls on Monday. We clear about that?"

He nodded.

Lamar thought, this is going to be one hell of a ride.

Then his thoughts drifted to Sam.

CHAPTER X

IS THERE A DOCTOR IN THE HOUSE?

Lamar had been out a month now. He and Larry were sitting at the kitchen table at the house on 21st Street. Dinner had been served to Peaches, Sam, Amy, Lamar, and Larry. The girls were in the front living area prepping for the evening.

Lamar and Larry were seated at the kitchen table sipping Mule Kick Moonshine from their fruit jars. Larry was smoking a Woodbine cigarette, thinking he would rather stay here than go to the steel mill for his night shift. Larry had on his big pants, security jacket, badge, and holstered gun, ready to make sure that Wheeling Steel's truck yard was secure through the night.

Lamar said, "Peaches is driving me to the poor house. Wait, she's not driving me there. I'm already there. Every day it is a new expense. This whorehouse business is costly to kick off. It's not as simple as you might think, Larry."

"How so?"

"Larry, look around. Do you see some expenses here and there?"

"You mean like the cook and the housekeeper?"

"That's a start. We got three women out there and we gotta have a cook? We gotta have a housekeeper? Now the sheriff is nosin' around and he wants a piece, and I am talkin' about cash, not a piece of the trade." He let go of his thought as his voice trailed off.

Larry said, "What about your poker night at the barber shop?"

"Well, the trouble is this," Lamar paused, then said, "The trouble is each of our money making schemes just started, and more cash is goin' out than what's comin' in. All of these things take a little time for word to get around. You just can't take an ad out in the Moundsville Daily Echo and say, "Hey everybody, we got a nice little whorehouse down at 21st Street. Why don't ya'll pop over at lunchtime and join in the fun. We got a little moonshine for you too. First shot is on the house. Take the edge off. And by the way, we will even give you a dollar chip to get you started playing a little poker. Back door entrance at 9 pm. on Wednesday and Saturday at Willy Jack's Barber Emporium."

Lamar, pleased with his ad for the Echo, took a big drink of Mule Kick that went down too fast and he started coughing and snorting. Recovering, he said, "We are full service here at Lamar's Happy Palace of Illegal and Illicit Vices."

Larry said, "Well, I guess you can't do that. What about the thing at the mill? I thought I was only gonna be over there for a couple of weeks. You know, it's harder than you think staying awake all night. And another thing, they ain't got no beds over there. I was thinking about going to Conrad and asking him if he would get me a cot or something. Maybe a big chair. I would be okay with a sofa; that might even be best."

"Larry, do not ask Conrad for a bed. All you have to do is stay awake. Walk around more. Gawd knows you could lose some weight."

"I can't walk much. It hurts my back too much. Every step I get this pain that starts in my back and shoots awful down my left leg. Right down to my big toe."

47

"I have not met a Vinton County boy that didn't have a bad back that kept him from workin' and put him on disability. I'm thinkin' it's more the, 'keep him from workin' thing' rather than that bad back thing."

"So when are we gonna do what we are gonna down at the steel mill so I can turn in my badge? Think Conrad would let me keep the gun?"

"Larry, sometimes you just shock me with your overall brilliance. But the steel mill job is big. It takes a lot of plannin'. We need a big truck. Some specialized equipment. All of that cost money. Thanks to Peaches this damn house is eatin' up my cash. It's like I'm married to the woman and I keep all her relatives in food, housing, and clothes until they get hired over at Woolworth's."

Lamar paused and sipped the bourbon. He said, "I got a job for us this weekend. It could be big. Very big. This job can finance the house here and the business over at the steel mill. When I was in Moundsville, I had a cell mate that was a bootlegger. Hear him tell it, he provided moonshine to some of our medical authorities up in Wheeling. So he makes a delivery to the wife of a rich doctor. Right to the house. Big son-of-a bitch."

"You mean the house or the woman?"

"What do you think? The house. Big house and a good-looking wife all ready to take delivery. Guess what happens next?"

"I would guess he would bring the shine inside. That's the most logical thing."

"Well, yes, he did give the lady the shine, but more importantly, he and the wife get to talkin' and hit it off pretty good. The doctor, it seems, don't pay much attention to the lady, which was fine with her. They start gettin' together whenever the doc is gone. Jelly, that's my buddy's name, says she was one frisky biscuit. He said that every other sentence, '. . . that woman was one frisky biscuit'. After a couple of months of this, she tells Jelly that the doc brings a lot of cash to the house and has it stashed there, but she don't know where. Wants Jelly to rob the place, find the stash, then split it with her."

"Why would he bring cash home?"

"Seems like he don't like to pay this damn income tax thing any more than the rest of us. And it's not just this one doc; I guess all of them do the same thing. Take the cash home and hide it. Hell, we got a very lucrative stream of cash here, hittin' one doc's house after another. I got it all set for this weekend. Seems like the doc is getting some fancy award over in Charleston. His receptionist told me the whole family will be going. So it looks like Saturday night. The doc will get an award and we will get a reward."

"So what happened?"

"Happened to what?"

"Your buddy and the wife. I thought they were gonna get the money and split it."

"He got picked up doing another job before he could hit the doc's house, and that's when we hooked up in Moundsville."

"Tomorrow when you hit the place, you gonna let me go along?"

"I think we will need four guys to pull this off. Be in and out of the house in an hour. Think we can get Bobby T over here to join in the fun? I got Curly from the barber shop. You and me. That ought to do it. Think you can handle it?"

Larry's Tourette's kicked in ever so slightly as he said, "Gawdamn, fuckin' right. Okay, you sumbitch. I'm in."

"Now settle down, Larry. Let's not get too excited just yet. Don't make me change my mind. But this should be an easy caper. In and out. Boom, boom.

"I do have one final question."

"Go right ahead, Larry."

"What the hell is a frisky biscuit?"   48

The four of them meet Friday night at the 21st St. house. Curly from the barber shop. Booby T, Larry's uncle from Vinton County, Ohio, Lamar and Larry.

Lamar told Peaches they were not to be disturbed under any circumstances.

Bobby T was as experienced at crime as Lamar. A tough, hard man. A forty-five and at the peak of his criminal career. A man that left no witnesses. You name it, at some point in his life, Bobby T had stolen it. The minute he walked through the kitchen, he sharp-eyed a butcher knife. That knife was under his shirt when he left the meeting.

Curly, was a curly-haired Italian barber working at Willy Jack's. Dark hair. Always in need of money because he raced cars at dirt tracks over the weekend. Put most all of his money in fixing up his car, which he also used bootlegging. He would take chances and had crashed the car in both of his pursuits. Almost every Monday, he would show up at the shop with an injury. Broke his arm once, which kept him out of work for three weeks, but other than that, a lot of sprained ankles, bruised shoulders, band-aids on various parts of his head and arms.

He had been busted three times. Boosting cars sent him to juvie went he was fifteen and again when he was seventeen. Bootlegging when he was twenty eight. That landed him in Moundsville for a year. To Curly his car was his world, his ticket to a better life.

Lamar set the scene. He had a map of Wheeling spread out on the table. "This house is right here on Elmhurst Street. We hit the place at two in the morning. Curly here is bringing the car and will drive."

Curly jumped in and said, "This sumbitch can move too. Nobody can catch us. And we got room for four, a little tight cause it is stripped down for racing, but also has under seat and undercarriage storage for the booze, so we will have room for the haul. I'm not sure where Larry is gonna sit his fat ass. I added a switch right on the dashboard that can cut the brake lights. That has saved me on more than one occasion haulin' shine and havin' the law on my tail. Cut those lights in the dark and the cops can't see where your car is turning. I make a turn in the dark, the cops come up fast and they try the turn too late, and bam! They can roll their damn cars. Happened more than once. We got beefy shocks so the car don't drop when loaded with West Virginia prime. I almost wish we had to outrace the law. Gawdamn, that is fun!"

Bobby T said, "Careful what you wish for, Curly." He smiled when he said it, but Bobby T had a way that a smile was not inviting.

Lamar said, "Now, lookie here. We want to pull the car up on the driveway and go around to the back of the house and park the car right by the back door. We will have ingress and egress from that door."

Larry said, "Wait a minute. What do you mean by ingress and egress?"

"That means in and out."

"That's what egress means, in and out."

"No, Larry. Ingress means in. Egress out."

"Why didn't you say so?"

"Larry, that's where we load up the car with the swag."

Larry said, "What kind of swag?"

"Larry, just shut the fuck up, will you? Let Lamar lay this out," Bobby T said.

Lamar continued, "I have been told that any cash is probably somewhere in the master bedroom. We want to take, of course, everything of value. Particularly gold and silver, and they have plenty of that. But what is gonna make this special is the cash. Me and Bobby T will look for cash. Curly, you will stay with the car. Anything look funny out there, you let us know. Larry, you gonna be the runner. When we load up the sacks, you take them back to the car, and then you two will stash 'em."

Larry broke in and said, "Lamar, you know I don't run too fast. Maybe I ought to be doin' something else."

"Larry, I was just saying 'runner'. You can walk the swag the thirty feet or so to the car and hand it over to Curly."

"Well, I can do that."

"Yes, you can. Bobby T, you take the downstairs and I will take the upstairs. Be careful with your flashlights. Don't go flashing them for the outside world to see. We are in and out in less than an hour. No more. If cops show up, we leave with what we have and turn it over to God and Curly. Any questions?"

Larry says, "Do I get to take along my gun?"

Lamar says, "No. Oh, Gawd no."

Bobby T says, "We done here?"

"Anything else, fellas? We got a lot to do tomorrow, but me and Larry will have what we need. Curly, when can you get the car here?"

"It's here right now."

Bobby T said, "Are the girls a freebie tonight? Come with the job? A little bonus?"

Lamar said, "Oh, man no. Peaches handles that. She is out front. Talk to Peaches and she will demand you pay. Curly, you can sleep here on the sofa."

"Hell no! I want a girl too."

"See Peaches. She'll set you up."

"But I ain't got no money."

"I'll pay for it and take it out of your cut tomorrow night," Lamar said. "Believe me, fellows, I would rather get chased by the cops tomorrow night than deal with Peaches over a night set-up for you two. That Peaches is a pip and she can hurt you."

Bobby T said, "Oh, yeah. She got a rep back home. She can run a pretty tight ship. That woman knows what she is doing. I know one thing for sure. She won't give no discounts for old friends. Even after I got her this gig."

Lamar says, "Right now she just might charge you double for setting up this gig. And by the sweet by and by, both you two stay away from Sam. I got an interest in that one."

The next night, the boys headed for Wheeling at about one in the morning. It was a half-hour ride. Lamar wanted a drive-by and look around the neighborhood.

As they approached the house on Elmhurst, Larry said, "Look at the size of these fuckin' houses."

Lamar was hoping that Larry's Tourette's remained somewhat under control. It was not a good sign when Larry started cussing.

Bobby T said, "Place looks dark. Looks like we can drive around back, and with those big trees, nobody can see in the back yard at all."

Bobby T was right: The doctor's backyard looked like a botanical garden. Big sycamores, white flowering dogwood, red spruce. Some white oak and sugar maple. Cyprus. Rhododendrons.

Lamar thought it was perfect. Get the car back there, and it can't be seen.

After three passes, Curly cut the lights and slowly pulled around the side of the house and to the back. Lamar and Bobby T approached the back door with a tire iron. They looked inside and then at each other. Bobby T nodded, and Lamar put the tire iron between the door and the casing and gave a hard pull. The door cracked and broke a little. Bobby T give the door a push. The door opened, and the two stepped inside and waited in silence for any noise, any sign of life. There was none.

Lamar turned to Larry and said, "Bring over the bags and the flashlights."

Larry's eye was twitching, but not excessively. Lamar felt somewhat relieved.

The house was a large Victorian. Every room seemed perfectly kept.

The three walked into the dining room. They saw several large cabinets taking almost one side of the room. They saw silver placements for at least twelve. Some of the flatware had gold handles. There was a soup tureen and what looked like an antique coffee pot with a full complement of trays and accessories. A big punch bowl. They were all pure silver.

Lamar said to Larry, "Load 'em up. I'm going upstairs. Careful with the lights."

Lamar quietly climbed the steps leading to the second level. He got to the top and saw a light hit the house from the road. He whispered down the stairs, "Kill the lights now."

Lamar heard Bobby T say, "Larry, kill your fuckin' light. Turn it off. Now."

It got dark and quiet.

Lamar moved slowly toward a window. He looked out and his heartbeat quickened. It was a cop car shining a light on the house. He had stopped right in front. Lamar was ready to run, but stood and waited.

The cop car moved slowly forward. His light hit the next house.

As the cop moved to the next block, Lamar went to the top of the stairs and said, "It's okay, but hurry it up. The sumbitch may be back."

Lamar looked in each bedroom and found the master bedroom. He stepped in and turned his flashlight on the bed—perfectly made up. The entire room was pristine.

Now where would the doctor keep some spare cash? Lamar started tossing the bedroom. He spent fifteen minutes and didn't find anything. He looked for false bottom drawers, under the mattress, a false room leading from the closets, every box in every closet. Nothing. Shit. 'The con must have been lying to me', Lamar thought, 'False alarm. What till I get my hands on that bastard'.

He started back down the steps. He heard a car drive by. Lamar froze in place. The car passed. He was halfway down the stairs and took another step—funny hollow sound. He stepped back up—solid sound. Not hollow. He tapped on the steps with the flashlight. The upper half, solid. The lower half, hollow.

As he approached the bottom, he said, "Bobby T. Get your ass over here and bring that tire iron."

Bobby T said, "Whatcha got?"

"I think there is a room under the stairs. Let's see what is in it. Check on the other side and see if you can find a door or latch or anything. I'll do the same over here."

Lamar shined the light slowly over every hinge, high and low. Bobby T was doing the same. Nothing.

They both looked for a small latch—on the floor, on the wall beside staircase. Nothing.

Bobby T picked up the tire iron and said, "Enough of this shit."

Bobby T started pushing on the panels every two feet or soon. He started on the right, slowly moving down. About three-quarters of the way moving from left to right, then a panel gave way and moved slightly inward and then swung open.

Larry had come up from behind. The three shined their flashlights into the dark closet.

Cash was stacked up about three feet high and two feet deep. American dollar bills. To the left were gold bars. Not small. Large, gold bars.

Larry said, "Jumpin' Jehoshaphat."

Lamar said, "Get those bags over here. Let's move 'em, boys!"

They started filling up the bags. They got more bags. They stuffed them too.

Larry was moving the cash and gold out to the car.

They were about half through loading up the case from the money room when Curly came in and said, "We are out of room in the car."

"What?" Lamar said.

"Out of room. We can't put another thing in the car. It's all filled up."

Bobby T said, "Shit. We can't leave this here. We gotta take it with us."

Larry said, "Let's take this back to the house and come back."

"It will be light. We can't get in here in daylight, and the doc is coming back tomorrow," Lamar said.

The four stood there, mute. Finally Bobby T said, "Let's check out the car. Maybe we can tie it to the top or something."

Lamar said, "I think it better be the 'something' and not the top."

"So this is it?" Bobby T said.

Curly said, "So let me understand this. We have as much cash and gold in the car as we do in the house, right?"

Bobby T said, "You got it."

"So what we have here is a transport problem. We just need another car to haul the rest out."

"That would be helpful. Shall we hot wire a neighbor's car? That could add to the excitement of the evening," Bobby T said.

"Nah. We don't have to do that. They got a phone in there; I'll just call my cousin. He lives ten minutes from here and he has a car. Get me to the phone. I'll get him here."

Curly called his cousin. He was on his way.

The boys got the cash and gold in bags. They moved the stash to the backyard and waited for the cousin to show up.

The wait wasn't long. The boys heard the soft hum of a motor, and headlights bounced off the trees. Cousin Sabatino was here.

He pulled around the corner of the house. There was stunned silence as the car pulled out and stopped.

He was driving a bright yellow cab.

When Lamar saw the cab, he was gobsmacked. He was pulling the best heist of his life and the getaway car was a cab. A bright yellow cab.

Larry thought it funny. Bobby T just stared at the taxi cab as if it just might go away.

Curly embraced his cousin and said, "Gracie, Gracie."

Lamar said, "Load 'em up and let's get the hell outta here."

They were loading the cab when a light hit the house from the street.

The cop was back.

CHAPTER XI

THE RACE IS ON

The flashlight from the street froze the boys in place. Lamar whispered, "Larry, put your head around the corner and see if he is coming back here or moving on."

Larry moved to the corner of the house and took a peek and said, "He's getting out of the car."

It was Curly that took charge.

He said, "Larry, stay there and see what he is doing. Here's what we gonna do. Lamar and I are gonna take off in my car, and I'm gonna go left. The sumbitch won't know what to do. But I'm bettin' he will give chase, take off after us. As soon as he gets three, four blocks down the street, Sabby, move outta here with your lights off and go slowly out the drive and to the right. Larry and Bobby T will be with you. I'll lose the copper and we can meet back at the house."

"He's comin'. Oh, fuck me, he's comin'," Larry said.

Lamar said, "Larry, get over here. Get in the taxi."

As soon as Lamar said 'taxi' he thought, '...how in the hell did I get into this. It was a simple break and enter. Done it a hundred times and now escaping with who knows how much cash in a damn taxi'.

Larry moved his big body as fast as he could, shaking hand, twitching eye and all.

The silver bowls, tureens, and other debris were scattered around the yard, left there to make room for the cash. Larry, hellbent on getting out, didn't see the silver antique punch bowl that the doctor had bought at auction for $549. He stepped directly in the bowl, his foot lodged firmly. He fell forward face-first into the moist grass. It stunned him. Didn't knock him out, but it might as well have.

Lamar said, "Larry, get your ass in the taxi." Larry couldn't move.

Lamar, who was already in Curly's car, jumped out and ran to Larry, where he stumbled over the antique coffee pot and fell head-first into Larry. Larry let out a hummmmph. Now they were both trying to regain their footing. Lamar pushed to get upright, slipped, and fell on Larry with his extended knee, catching Larry directly in the groin. Larry let out a yelp—not a scream, a yelp. Lamar thought it sounded like a pissed-off squirrel.

Lamar tried to lift Larry. That didn't work.

"Bobby T, give me a hand here," Lamar said in soft whisper. Lamar was now upright. He and Bobby T were lifting Larry. They got him to both knees, then one knee, then one foot, then two feet, and Larry was mobile again. They moved to the taxi. Bobby T shoved Larry into the taxi, antique silver tureen and all.

Finally in the taxi, Larry said, "My hat. My hat." Larry had worn his nightwatchman hat with his uniform, including his badge. No gun. Lamar had said no to that.

Lamar, who was now moving to Curly's car, grabbed the hat from the ground and jumped in the car. Curly revived the engine, did a one-eighty, then sped around the corner of the house, blasting down the drive past the startled cop, and made a left to the street.

The cop was completely taken aback. Flashlight in hand, all he could do was stand there and watch the speeding car race down the drive. The lawman gathered his wits and ran to his car.

The race was on.

Sabatino did as instructed and two minutes later quietly moved from the back of the house to the drive, to the street, turning right. He moved down the street and cautiously turned his lights on. In his rear view mirror, he could see the faint bouncing lights of the patrol car racing after Curly and Lamar.

Larry's hand was in full twitch mode. Hey eye twitch kept up the beat. Bobby T had a slight smile. They were just two guys going home in a taxi from a bender.

Within a block, Lamar was moving faster than he had ever gone before. He looked around the passenger seat for something to grab and hold. Nothing. 'Damn', he thought,' Curly is really going fast'.

Curly said, "The sumbitch is coming this way." Curly let out a whoop and another and another. Kind of like a coyote howl after a kill.

He started yelling, "Hot damn, hot damn, hot damn! We are livin' now, Lamar! We are livin!' You feelin' it, Lamar? Are you feelin' it?"

Lamar was speechless. His eyes were fixated on the road ahead, just staring straight ahead. His hands, now wet with sweat, were gripping the sides of the car seat. He was paralyzed. Immobile. His mouth wouldn't move. He thought Curly was truly loco and this was it. He would die tonight in a bootleggin' race car on a side-street in Wheeling.

Curly shouted, "Lamar, you look a little peaked. Watch this." Curly reached to a switch on the dash. He pulled it down. The lights on the back of the car went dark. Curly could see in his rear view mirror, the cop car bouncing, headlights moving up and down as the car's suspension gave way to the rough road.

"Now, you watch this, boy." Two intersections later, Curly took a sharp left turn and then notched up the speed, like he was on a straightaway in a race. Lamar wanted to throw up.

Curly slowed some. He was checking the rear view mirror to see if the cop would turn or go straight. The cop turned, but too sharply for the car to handle. The car slid into the turn. Bounced off the curb. Bounced again, only this time the wheels didn't clear the curb, and the car started tipping over. It didn't flip, but it did hit a fire hydrant, which stopped the car. This caused a massive mushroom spray of water twenty feet high exploding from the hydrant.

The cop car now fully stopped. The car was blowing off steam and coughing. Then it died out. In his stupor, the cop wondered how a thunderstorm had developed so quickly and so heavy. It felt like he was sitting inside a waterfall and unable to move.

Through his rear view, Curly saw it all. He started up with his coyote howls again, only this time louder and longer.

Lamar said, "Can you slow it down a bit now?"

Twenty minutes later, both cars were parked out of sight at the 21st Street house.

CHAPTER XII

AIN'T THAT PURDY AS A PEACH

At the back of the house, there was an entry to a root cellar. The doors were at an angle off the ground, pitched upward slightly at a fory-five degree angle. Like a swing gate, the doors to the root cellar opened, one to the left, one to the right. It was dark in the yard and as Curly and Bobby T opened the cellar doors and light came on in the kitchen of the house. Lamar went into the house to see who was watching them. He had his big flashlight in hand and was ready to use it. There was Peaches sitting at the kitchen table, smoking a Lucky Strike.

She said, "Welcome back, Lamar. How'd it go?"

Lamar was surprised to see Peaches. He stammered and said, "Peachie, what are you doing up at this hour?"

"I work here. I live here and I heard this big commotion you were making. So how did your score go?"

"What score? What you talkin' about?"

"Oh, please Lamar, you and Larry been flittin' around like some teenage boys on a panty raid. Then Bobby T shows up. You guys had a job. How'd it go?"

"It went okay. Had a little excitement getting away, but Peach, me and the boys got some work in the cellar."

"Gonna divide it up, eh?" Peaches said with a smile.

"Go back to bed and forget we had this conversation."

"Oh, I'll go back to bed but Lamar, Honey, I ain't likely to forget our little conversation."

The gang emptied the cars of the swag and cash into the root cellar. Sabatino left.

Larry took off his shoe and removed the tureen attached.

The root cellar was dark, damp, and unlit. Lamar flashed his light on a single string hanging from the ceiling. He pulled the string, and a dull, dusty light turned on. The light revealed a dirt floor. Shelves along three walls. Old jars, bottles, and other containers were on the shelves. A couple of old barrels were in a corner. Another one was on the floor. All were empty. There was a wooden table in the middle of the room. Several chairs were scattered about.

The money was in four bags. Bobby T picked up one of the bags and dumped the cash in the middle of the table. The cash made a large, round mound. A number of bills fluttered to the floor. Most of the bills were one dollar. But twos, fives, tens, and the occasional twenty could also be seen.

No one said anything. The men looked at the large pile of cash.

Then the laughter came, loud and long. The laughter of relief. The laughter of success.

The boys were rich.

Larry said, "Ain't it as purdy as a peach."

Lamar said, "Okay, here's what we do. Larry, clear that bottom shelve. Count out a hundred dollars and put it right there. We get ten stacks, put 'em together, and we start with the hundreds again. Let's get to it."

It was about four when they started. It took them three hours and twenty-two minutes to stack the bills in thousands. Light and noise from the street were drifting into the cellar.

There were fifteen stacks and what looked like another several hundred left over. Larry counted the loose bills, then said, "We got $15,745"

That caused a stir with the group. Someone let out a whoop.

Another said, "Sumbitch."

Lamar said, "As agreed. Our expenses come out first. Those expenses were $734. So I will take that. We gotta pay Sabatino, so what you think Curly?"

"We give him, hmmmm, maybe two hundred. He will think he was been twice-blessed by Madonna. Because what he do? Just drive over. Nobody see. He drive here and then go home. Back to beddy-bye. That's more than Sabby make in a year. So, yeah, two hundred ought to do."

"Alright, here's two hundred to Curly for Sabatino. So what's that leave, Larry?" Lamar said.

Larry reached for the pencil on the table. He started putting numbers down on one of the bills. He said, "$14,802."

"As agreed," said Lamar, "I take half. Larry, gimme that number?"

They all waited in anticipation. Larry was mumbling slightly, "Hmmm, six stacks . . . that's . . . hmmmm . . . then half again . . . that's five. Carry the . . ."

Lamar interrupted, "For Gawd's sake, Larry it's a little over seven large."

Larry kept scratching with the pencil and mumbling. Shortly he said, "That would be $7,405."

"Okay, Larry. Now divide that by three and you get your cut. Your cut too, boys," Lamar said.

Larry went through the mumbling and scratching process again.

Bobby T said, "Larry, get on with it. I want get out of this stink hole and get upstairs."

"That would be $2,468 a man. Other than Lamar, of course," Larry said.

Curly said, "Hot damn. I'm gonna have the hottest bottleggin', sumbitch car that anybody ever did see. Tell Willy Jack to shove that barbershop job where the sun don't shine."

"Hey, hey, just a minute, Curly," Lamar said. "You can't go out and start showin' off like your great Aunt Matilda just left you a fortune with a big house in Florida. Put this in the mattress or wherever you want, but don't start flashin' money around. That is a sure thing to cause the law to look up our skirts. Curly, you keep your job and your mouth shut, and by the Curly, you owe me five dollars for last night's fun and frolic. As to everyone, including me, don't flash this money around."

Larry said, "But I am sick of that nightwatchman job. I just sleep anyway. And who is this Aunt Matilda? I don't think I know her."

"Listen up. Larry, you gonna hang in there with the nightwatchman thing. Guys, this is just the beginning. We are cookin' up a really big hit over at Wheeling Steel. That's why we got Larry there now. We got an inside man there too. The score at the steel mill will make this look as small as Larry's pecker. That heist will be the biggest anyone has ever seen. So don't go callin' a lot of attention to our little group of banditos. And besides, we might just find a couple of more docs to hit."

Bobby T said, "Wait a minute. What the hell is over at the steel mill? Nails? What are we gonna do with a truckload of nails?"

Lamar said, "It's not nails, Bobby T." He paused for effect. "It's nickel."

"Nickel? Whatever. I goin' upstairs, get me something to eat, and stay with Peaches for the week. That's not too splashy for you, is it Lamar?" He hit the 'Lamar' kinda hard, letting Lamar know that he would do with his money anything he wanted. Lamar gave him a hard look back but didn't say anything.

Bobby T said, "Any more jobs we gotta talk about your 50 percent too. That's a bit steep for my taste, Lamar."

"There's nothing to talk about. You did pretty good with last night's take, didn't you?"

"We can talk about it later. Right now, I'm outta here." Bobby T picked up his cash and left.

Curly said, "Okay, lemme know when we have the next gig." He followed Bobby T.

Larry looked at his money and said, "Where can I put this?"

"Don't worry about it. I'll put it with my stash."

"I'm just confused about one thing."

"Larry, you are often confused about a lot of things, but what is it this time?"

"Have I even met my Aunt Matilda? Cause I just don't rightly recall doin' so."

Peaches was looking out her bedroom window. She had seen it all. She was in her bedroom and watched them leave. She saw them return and haul the bags into the root cellar. After her confrontation with Lamar, she watched until they left. She didn't answer the knock on her door from Bobby T, who then was forced to sleep on a sofa in the parlor. She saw Lamar haul one of the bags in the house. She heard him drag the bag into his room. She listened at his door and heard the noises that came from within. She went to the root cellar and found seven bills on the floor undetected by the five. She put the bills in her bra. She went back to her room to think. And plan.

She knew it all. And better yet, she knew what she was going to do.

CHAPTER XIII

LAMAR, YOU'RE LOOKIN' FINE TODAY

Lamar put the cash bag in his closet and collapsed into a deep sleep. He didn't wake up until three that afternoon. He threw on some clothes picked up from the floor and went to the kitchen for coffee and one of Cassandra's, sweet rolls. Lamar thought, 'Getting Casandra was a blessing. That woman cooks and cleans as well I can steal' and that makes her world-class'!"

The women were moving about in the living room, talking and laughing. Cassandra was starting to prepare the evening dinner. She said, "Lamar, wha'tcha doin' sleepin' in so late? You gonna wake up now? I got some meatloaf left over I can fix for you. You want some, Honey? Cassie fix you anything you want."

"Thank you, Cassie. I just want to wake up. I had a busy night last night and gotta do some calculatin'."

"If'n there is nothin' you want, I have some things to do upstairs. You calls me when you needs me."

"Thank you, Cassie."

Lamar was sipping his coffee, grateful for the empty kitchen. He thought, 'That damn Curly is one crazy sumbitch'. The police chase brought a smile to his face. The cash made him giddy. It brought him the means to pull off the steel mill job. They needed a big truck for that one and a bunch of other things. He could buy them now.

For the second time that day, Peaches startled him when she appeared and said, "Good morning, Mr. Sunshine." She was still in her nightgown.

Lamar didn't respond.

Peaches sat down next to Lamar and patted his arm and said, "Now don't be pouty, Darling. So you had a big score. Maybe your big ol' Teddy Bear, Larry, is right, you are a criminal mastermind. Don't be shy, tell Peaches all about it."

Lamar smiled at the thought of what turned out to be an inspired caper. He couldn't help himself, and said, "Peach, it was truly a fantastic evening with an electrifyin' bump in the road. Best heist of my life."

He told Peaches the full story. He simply couldn't hold back. He didn't tell how Curly had scared him shitless because, in his telling, he was the hero of the evening, never showing fear or hesitation, only his larger-than-life heroic deeds. He didn't tell her how much cash they got. Peaches didn't need that information. She got that piece of the heist puzzle out of Bobby T hours before.

Throughout the story, Peaches smiled, nodded, and gave the appropriate exclamations at just the right time:

"You did?"

"You are so very clever, Lamar!"

"And that didn't scare you?"

"That was just brilliant!"

All the while leaning forward, showing a great interest as well as ample cleavage to keep Lamar's interest level elevated.

She worked him. Worked him good. Found out all she needed to know. And then some.

Bobby T spent the week keeping Peaches company and drinking up a goodly supply of Lamar's Mule Kick. A week after the heist, he packed it up and went back to Vinton County. All he said to Lamar was, "Let me know when the next hit is." All he said to Peaches was, "See you soon."

Curly went back to work at Willy Jack's barbershop. That was just for show, since he was totally engrossed in souping up his car and adding every conceivable piece of equipment to get faster. He took bootlegging jobs on the weekend. He was living his dream.

Larry didn't seem to want much. Lamar kept his money stored with his own. Larry wanted a few dollars. Lamar provided.

It was Sam that approached Lamar. Sexy and sultry Sam. Lamar was taking coffee in the kitchen on the second morning after the heist. Sam came down the stairs in a long, satin gown that was sheer and light. Over the see-through gown was a flimsy robe that flowed behind and around as she moved. She wore pink slippers and had a pink ribbon in her hair, which was full and mussed.

Lamar caught her scent as she walked by him to the coffee pot. He liked what he saw. He thought that he could see through her gown. But it was just a tease. Lamar thought, 'You can see through it all right, but you can't see what you want to see'.

Sam poured a cup, sat across from him, lit a Lucky Strike, took a long pull, tossed her hair ever so slightly, and said, "Why, Lamar, you are looking good today. Downright spunky. I heard about your little caper. Did you boys have some fun?"

Lamar felt his heartbeat quicken ever so slightly. He always got a little nervous around Sam. He said, "Sam, we hit it big. You gonna see bigger and better from Lamar. Yes, sir. Much bigger and much better."

"What do you have in mind, Sugar Baby?"

"What's in my mind right now? Our long-term plans?"

"Oh, I know what's on your mind right now."

"So you think you know what I am thinking, right this minute?"

"Yes, Honey, I do. Mama knows everything."

"So tell me."

"You want to take me upstairs and do unspeakable things."

"Well, I think I can speak about them"

Sam reached over for an ashtray, put out her Lucky Strike, took a sip of coffee, and said, "Why don't we just go upstairs and you can show me."

Lamar's heart was racing now, but he just sat there. His legs seemed weak. His thoughts were muddy.

She reached out and held his hand and guided him out of the chair.

Sam said, "Just come with me, Sugar Baby."

Lamar was stretched out in Sam's bed. Sam lay beside him with her arm casually over his chest. "Was that good for you, Honey?" she said.

Lamar said, "Oh yeah. I'm still in the glow. Kinda dizzy and my thinkin' is all fuzzy."

She playfully reached down to touch him and said, "How is our big boy doing now? A little spent?"

"Sam, how 'bout this? I think we ought to take up together. I'll pay you for every night after work, and you can come over to my room."

"Well, Sugar, that sounds like a big commitment for me. You, too."

"Yeah, well maybe. I need someone. Someone I can talk to and trust. Bounce some things off 'em. You're smart. You got a level head. I need something stable like that. Besides, you might be the sexiest woman I ever seen."

"You call sleeping with a gal like me stable?"

"Well, yeah. I've only been out of prison a month or so. And this is my first."

"Lamar, that's just pure bullshit. You try out every new girl that comes along. Don't you think I don't know that?"

"Hey, I gotta see if they are worth keepin' around. This is a business I run here, you know. Gotta see if the product is worth offering."

"And the latest?"

"She's still here, ain't she?"

Sam was quiet, thinking about Lamar's offer. With him giving her a more or less steady income, she could cut back on the traffic some.

Sam said, "Why Sugar, that sounds just grand. But a couple of conditions."

"Okay."

"You stay away from the other girls. You pay me direct on Fridays. Don't run it by Peaches. And I am serious about the other girls. You do that, and it will cause disagreeable consequences. I have seen that situation before, and every time it leads to hard feelings and somebody getting fired, and it's strange you know, but it is always the girl that goes a-packin'. I don't want that, and neither do you."

Lamar heard a little less softness with her tone. More direct and business-like.

Lamar said, "What about breaking in the new talent? See if they any good? Something like that?"

"Nope. None."

Lamar paused, thinking of what he was getting and giving. He looked over at Sam. He felt so good with her. She looked so good. He wanted this.

Lamar said, "Okay, we got a deal. Let's shake on it."

"We can do more than shake on it. You ready, Teddy?"

"I sure am. And don't call me Teddy."

CHAPTER XIV

LET'S ROLL A QUIRLY

Near evening the next day, Lamar and Larry sat at the kitchen table. Both had a Ball jar in front of them half-filled with Mule Kick. Larry had a small bag of tobacco on the table along with some paper cigarette wraps. Lamar said, "Lemme see that shag bag."

Lamar looked at the bag, holding it slightly above his head. The printing read, "Buck Wheat. Bright. Fine cut. 1 ¼ OZ. Scotten, Dillon Company, Detroit, Mich." It had a stamp on it from the government.

"What happened to your Woodbines?" Lamar said.

"I'm gonna roll my own," Larry said, as he reached across the table and grabbed the shag bag out of Lamar's hand.

"Why in the hell would you do that?"

Larry was pulling a small white sheet of paper out of box.

"Well, it's a lot cheaper, and I got real intrigued after I saw that cowboy movie the other afternoon at the matinee down at the Strand, that new moving-picture place."

"You mean the one you took Roxy to see?"

"Well, yeah." Larry didn't want to talk to Lamar about how he and Roxy, a new girl, were getting along and how Larry was paying her for nights by the week now.

"Larry, I believe you are more than vaguely aware that Roxy is the daughter of a good friend of mine and that my mother helped raise the girl."

"Yeah, sure."

"It's not of great concern to me, but Quinn, Roxy's daddy, does some work for Mr. G, up in Wheeling. You do know who Mr. G is and what kind of work he does?"

"Yeah. Mr. G is the Greek guy that is the Big Gio."

"Yes, he is. In the absence of the Mafia, Mr. G has taken their place. Let's just say, he is the Mafia in this part of the world."

"What kind of work does Roxy's daddy do?"

"Very nasty shit. The kind where a guy goes missing one night and they find him floatin' down river three days later."

"That don't sound good. But funny thing, Lamar, you should see me float. I can't sink. You can't push me under water, I just bop right back up."

"Point here, Larry, you better treat her good or her Daddy is gonna show up and have a discussion, and you'll be floatin' downstream."

Larry said, "Oh, sure. Sure. Don't worry about that."

Lamar gave him a jailhouse stare, and he said, "This is serious, Larry. You be careful."

Larry said, "Okay, okay, I'll be careful. Anyway, this movie we saw, it was a Bronco Billy movie—had this guy in a black hat, and he rolled his own cigs. He called it a 'Quirly.' You ever hear that, a Quirly? All the cowboys did the same. All the bad guys, that is. Bronco Billy don't smoke, of course, he being the good guy. But this one bad guy rolled his own and did it with one hand. Cool as shit. So I bought my last pack of Woodbines. I'm gonna do my own."

Lamar watched as Larry filled the paper with the loose tobacco. He stacked it high on the paper. Too high. There was a string on the opening of the bag. Larry put that string in his mouth, reached up with his right hand (the one that shook), and pulled it tight, closing the bag but leaving it extended from his teeth, concentrating on rolling the Quirly one-handed, as the bad guy had done.

There was three times the tobacco that was needed on the paper. Nonetheless, Larry tried to close the wrap together. Loose tobacco was falling on the table, now on Larry's clothes, on the floor. Larry still had the shag bag hanging from his mouth. He pulled the bulging cigarette to his mouth to give the paper a sealing lick, forgetting he had the shag bag in his mouth. He licked the paper. The shag bag fell to the table and hit the edge, fully opening the bag, which in turn caused all the tobacco to go flying to the floor and all over his clothes. The lick of the paper left enough loose tobacco on Larry's face he looked like he had a Fu Manchu mustache with two tapered tendrils running from the sides of his mouth to his chin.

Larry looked at the mess. He still had the paper from the Quirly in his hand, devoid of tobacco since it had sought refuge on the table and floor and Larry's face.

Larry said, "Maybe I need a little more practice at this thing. That cowboy in the movie made it look so easy."

"Maybe you just ought to just go back to your Woodbines, Larry. When we go out tomorrow, I'm gonna buy you some Woodbines."

"Oh, I'm gonna master this. We Pritchitts are known for our perseverance. This time next week I'll be just like that black-hat-wearing cowboy. One-handed and all that."

Lamar took a long swig, sat down the Ball jar, and said, "Do they have any forklifts over at the mill?"

Larry had made a small mound of tobacco, gathered from the table and floor. He put it in his swag bag and put the bag string back in his mouth and pulled out another white paper wrap.

Larry said, "What mill you talkin' about?" Through his clutched teeth it sounded like "Whaa mule you talkin ahh-bot."

"The place you go to work five nights a weeks. Wheeling Steel. The steel mill."

"Oh, yea. Whaa wasss ur question?"

"Take that damn bag out of your mouth."

"Thas your question?" Larry seemingly had forgotten about the tobacco bag hanging from his mouth, tight between is teeth. Lamar reached over and pulled the shag bag out of Larry's mouth and placed it on the table.

"No, Larry. My question was this: do they have forklifts in the warehouse you babysit every night?"

"You mean those little cars with the thing-a-ma-jig sticking out?"

"Yes, they lift big items and move them from one place to the other."

"Lemme think. Yes, they do. In fact there are three or four of them around the place. One of them is older though and doesn't lift much, but that yellow one has . . ."

Lamar interrupted and said, "Can you get the keys so we can use them?"

"Well, I think they just leave the keys in the car, er, the forklift."

"Could you check that tonight?"

"What for?"

"Cause we need it for the stuff we gonna steal out of the warehouse."

"There ain't nothing there to steal as far as I can tell."

"Yes, there is," Lamar paused for effect then said, "Nickel."

"Nickel?"

"Yep. We gonna steal twenty some ton of nickel.."

"That sounds heavy. I don't think the forklifts can lift twenty ton."

Lamar paused and said, "Larry, you are right. But the forklift don't have to do the whole twenty ton at once. We are gonna load it on a truck. Maybe the truck can pull a couple ton a night. So it might take ten, twelve separate runs to get the twenty ton. Got it?"

"Yeah, but nickels. Like change in our pocket?"

Larry was still struggling with his Quirly.

Lamar said, "Damn, Larry. Why don't you use two hands?"

"Well, this right hand shakes a little and I didn't want it shakin' the tobackey off the paper."

"Looks like the one-handed thing is working well for you. Anyway, it is not nickel like a coin. These are nickel briquettes on big pallets. We gonna load 'em in a truck and ship 'em up to Erie, PA to Willy Jack's brother-in-law. Guy married to Willy Jack's sister. I think her name is Edith or Ethel or something like that. Starts with an 'E.' Anyway, the guy's name is Lou and he has a scrap iron business. He has some buyers. So we deliver to him, and he sells to his buyer."

Larry started on his third or fourth roll, this time with both hands and the bag again hanging from his mouth.

"So, Larry, what we need is a truck. Tomorrow you and me are going into Wheeling and go to Charleston Motor Sales and get us a big-ass truck with a trailer that can pull a couple of tons. Curly tells me that's the place to go. Curly then will soup it up and put shit on it to carry the load and not look like it is gonna flop over from too much weight."

Larry was making an even bigger mess.

Lamar said, "Larry, gimme that shit. I'll roll you one, if you promise to go back to your Woodbines."

"I shall preserver. It's what we Pritchitts do."

CHAPTER XV

GREATEST TRUCK VALUES IN AMERICA!

Lamar was excited to get going. Larry was sleeping in Roxy's room. Lamar decided it would be prudent to have Peaches get Larry. Lamar knocked and Peaches came to the door and opened it slightly. She had only her nightgown on. She didn't look happy. Peaches didn't like to be disturbed before noon.

Lamar said, "Peaches, darling. Would you mind retrieving Larry from Roxy's room?"

"Why don't you get him yourself. Door's right there, not five feet away."

Lamar stirred rather nervously and said, "Well, you know. I, ah, I . . ."

"Gawd, Lamar. For a big-shot gangster you have a perplexin' sense of morality. I swear I don't know what the hell is the matter with you."

"Tell him to hurry it up. We gotta a meeting in Wheeling. I will be in the kitchen."

Before Lamar could move, Peaches, showing her annoyance, crossed the hallway and knocked on Roxy's door. Roxy opened the door before the surprised Lamar could get to the stairs.

Peaches said, "Tell fat-ass that Lamar wants him in the kitchen yesterday."

"Okay," Roxy said.

Turning to Lamar, she said, "There, you happy now?"

Lamar turned to get away from Peaches. Walking down the stairs, he thought, *I swear, that woman terrifies me. Just absolutely terrifying. Maybe she's a witch. That would explain a lot. Especially my fear of her. That's probably it. . . she's a witch. Do those wooden crosses work on witches like on vampires? Maybe Sam will know. I gotta find out about that*.

He hurried to the sanctity of the kitchen and the comfort of Cassandra, her coffee, and sweet rolls.

Peaches stormed back to her room. She was thinking about the money, as she did every day. She knew it was in Lamar's room, but now Sam was in Lamar's room as much as her own. She thought, *With Lamar in Wheeling, I need to get Sam out of the house for a couple of hours to give Lamar's room a going over. Where can I send her*?

Lamar and Larry headed to the Charleston Motor dealership in Wheeling. Lamar was giddy—buying a truck for the biggest heist in West Virginia history.

Lamar thought, *'Larry's right, I am a criminal mastermind. Look at what I've pulled off in, what . . . three, four months? The house was now producing good revenue. The poker nights are doing good, although Willy Jack found a poker chip in the laundry and was starting to ask questions. Maybe I should move poker nights to the house. Set up in the parlor off the kitchen. I might even double dip, make money off the poker game and the house with the same customers. Yes, I think I will do that. I could even get Bobby T up here and start making book. That pays good. That is real gold. Bobby T might be a pain in the ass though. I would have to think about that. But runnin' book with all the rest. Yes, sir, Lamar, you are one smart sumbitch'*.

With Lamar in his reverie, celebrating his own brilliance, he turned left to Broad Street heading to the dealership and didn't see an ice truck almost on top of him. The ice truck driver hit his horn, braked, and screamed a stream of very creative cuss words. Lamar swerved hard to the left to avoid the ice truck and barely missed a trolley car bearing down on them. Lamar yanked his car hard back to the right. The car rocked and settled down. The two near crashes brought Lamar back from his dream world to the present.

The dealership was on the street. There was a Ford sign hanging from the front about fifteen feet up sticking out over the sidewalk. It said "Ford," in script. The windows had three panels of glass with "Ford" again displayed on paintings made to like look like awnings. "Ford" was on the window midway down to the left as well. "Ford V8" painted on the window to the right.

The building was old, red brick. There was an entrance to the left and double garage doors to the far right. A truck was in front with a sign that said, "The New Ford Truck." A Ford car was in front of the truck. Brand new. The sign on the car said, "The Only V-8 under $2,395."

Larry said, "This looks like the Ford place, all right. I think they need one more sign with 'Ford' on it, so they don't confuse it with a Duesenberg dealership."

"What do you know about a Duesenberg?"

"Oh, I know."

"You are a surprising young man, Larry."

Lamar and Larry entered the building. A salesman approached and said, "You ready for that new sedan out front? Catches your eye, don't it. That is one little beauty. Get you to church on time, yes sir."

The salesman had on cream-colored slacks, a white shirt, white-and-brown wing-tipped shoes, and a scarlet-and-gray striped tie with a clasp that read, "3rd Field Artillery Regiment."

Lamar said, "We need a truck—the biggest and most powerful one ya got."

The salesman stuck out his hand and said, "Pleased to help you out. I'm George and trucks are my specialty. And your name?"

"I'm Lamar and this here is Larry."

Lamar looked to his left and saw a poster of a truck with an open-bed trailer. The truck had several huge logs on the trailer with six men standing on or by the logs.

Lamar starred at the poster. It read:

"THE LARGEST LOGS EVER HAULED ON A MOTOR TRUCK"

Diameter at butt, ten feet. Total log weight, approximately two tons.

The salesman started to talk, but Lamar held up his hand and said, "I wanna read this."

"WORK THAT TAKES TRUCK STAMINA"

This is no spectacular stunt for advertising purposes, but a photo of a Kelly-Springfield truck on one of the trips it has been making for months on this job, over a wood's road, and not once has it quit. Six months of this kind of work is equal to about three years of the worst kind of ordinary trucking . . . and this truck is still going. Kelly-Springfield trucks have stamina . . . a constitution that is above the average. They work while many others are being worked upon.

1 ½ to 6-ton models.

"THE KELLY-SPRINGFIELD MOTOR TRUCK CO., SPRINGFIELD, OHIO
HIGH-GRADE MOTOR TRUCKS
The Big Brother to the Railroads."

Lamar had been in the store some ninety seconds and said, "I want one of those," pointing at the poster. "Six ton. With a covered cab and a covered trailer. You have that here?"

George said, "Well, no. We would have to put in an order for a Kelly. That would take a while. Lemme show the Ford TT's we have out back. The bestseller on the road."

Lamar said, "I don't want a bestseller. I want a Kelly-Springfield, six-ton with a covered trailer and cab."

"Lamar, the T's are right out back."

"Do you have a Kelly out back?"

"Well, yes, but it is not a six-ton. Just a little smaller."

"Let's go look at that."

George said, "You know that Kelly is gonna cost a lot more than the TT?"

"I don't give care about that."

Lamar looked at the smaller Kelly, glanced at the TT, and said, "How do you place an order for the six-ton? Let's get to it."

George said, "The truck is gonna run you $3,005. Covering the cab and the trailer will be another $750, for a total of $3,755."

Lamar said, "We got a deal, but I want you to put the best tires on it that you can get for driving on the highway. We ain't gonna be on loggin' roads, so I want a smooth ride and I want that upgrade part of the $3,755."

Lamar was enjoying this, thinking he is being smart with the tire upgrade for free.

George said, "I'll have to check with the boss on that one, but I think we can do that."

"How much you need now?"

"Well, lemme think here just a bit." George played with some meaningless numbers on his writing pad. "Oh, I think half now and half on delivery would make everybody happy, yes sir . . . that ought to do it."

"How much is that? Half, that is?" Lamar getting anxious now.

"Hmm, lemme see. That would be just a little under $2,000. Why don't we just round that off to $2,000 for now."

Larry jumped in and said, "What if we got it in red or yellow? Maybe orange? Make it really hot."

"I don't think we want that, Larry," Lamar said.

"Yeah, but that would make it look so great. We'd have the hottest-looking truck on the highway. No one could touch that puppy. People see the Kelly decked out, and they'll be talkin' about it back home."

Lamar turned to George and said, "We don't want it red or yellow or anything else. Just your standard brown. We'll be right back. Got the money in the trunk. Larry, let's go."

"I don't know why you don't want the truck to look special. Red would make it really great. Red, or yellow on that big rig. Nobody never seen anything like that."

"Larry, this is a car carrying contraband. We don't want it to stand out. We want it to be forgotten. Like it was never there."

"I thought we were stealing nickel and that other stuff."

"We are."

"How's this contraband stuff fit in?"

"Sometimes, Larry, you just gotta trust me."

"Well, if you say so."

"I say."

Lamar and Larry walked to the car, retrieved the money, and took it back to George.

Lamar said, "I'm gettin' my tires thrown in?"

"Happy to say you are, Lamar."

"When can we pick it up?"

"About five to six weeks."

They signed and left.

In the car, Lamar turned to Larry and said, "Damn, I love that truck."

Larry said, "So it appears Lamar McKenna is at last in love. And it's with a truck."

Right after Lamar and Larry left the house, Peaches knocked on Sam's door. Sam answered, not dressed for the day.

Peaches said, "Sam, Honey, I would like you to run a couple of errands for me. I have some things here I have to get done. There's two dollars in it for your time."

Sam said, "Lemme get dressed. You have a list?"

"Here's a list, some cash, and the keys to my car. I hope the old jalopy I bought starts. Have fun and get something for yourself."

She went back to her room and waited for Sam to leave. It wasn't long, and Peaches was unlocking the door to Lamar's room.

Peaches had heard Lamar come in the night of the heist. She heard him drag bags into his bedroom, so she was confident that the cash was in the room. But where?

'Okay', she thought, 'Where would I want to hide money? It's a big stash, so I would need space. Can't be a small space. Something like a two foot by two foot. Maybe larger. If I had cash, I would want it next to me. Close by'.looked in the drawers and closet. She saw an old suitcase in the corner of the closet and thought she had it. Dry well. Under the bed. Under the mattress. In the bathroom. Behind the toilet.

Nothing.

She said to herself, *'In the floorboards or the wall. That's gotta be it'*.

She started on the walls, looking for any divergent signs of the wall being tampered with. It took her all of twenty minutes.

Nothing.

A new search—the floorboards. Crawling on her hands and knees, she searched the floor for anything that looked odd or out of place. Ten minutes in, she saw the slight scratches that looked like the boards had been pried open. Lamar had a small tool box in the closet. She retrieved a screwdriver and a flat putty knife and went to work.

The boards opened easily. There were two bags. She opened the top of one and was staring at beautiful, dirty, grimy cash. She grabbed a handful and just looked at it.

Then she heard the door handle moving.

The door opened.

Sam stepped into the room.

CHAPTER XVI

Peaches Fantazzi & Samantha Ruby A Pair You Can Count On

Peaches was sitting on the floor, looking at the cash. Sam was standing in the doorway, looking at Peaches.

Peaches said, "Well, look who just showed up. Don't just stand there. Shut the door."
Sam did as told.

"Get over here. Look at this," Peaches said.

Sam walked over and stared at the hole in the floor. She bent over and looked closer.

Her hand moved to her mouth as if to stifle a scream. All that came out of the cool Ms. Sam was a throaty 'ahhh'. She sat down besides Peaches. It was more of a collapse than a sit.

Sam said, "That's a lot of cash."

"No shit."

"What are we gonna do?"

"So, it's 'we' now, is it?" Peaches said it with a smile, not wanting to show any hostility. Peaches accepting Sam. Trusting her. Peach said, "So how did you figure it out?"

"Oh, please, Peach. Lamar leaves for a two days, and you suddenly want me in Moundsville running around on this and that. It wasn't hard."

Sam suddenly was not the sultry woman of the night, being eyed by a man as she lit up. No, this Sam was sitting there looking astonished.

Peaches said, "Grab a handful of cash. Let's close this up, get over to my room and talk." Peaches had lost her cool, bossy attitude and was dealing with Sam as an equal.

They each grabbed a fistful and carefully put the floorboards back, looked around to see if anything else was amiss, then opened the door to the hallway and peeked out. No one there. Peaches put her finger to her lips, "Be quiet." They moved across the hallway and into Peach's room and dumped their newfound cash on the bed and looked at each other. Smiles turned to laughter. The laughter turned to giggles. Sam reached for the cash and grabbed a stack of bills with both hands and threw it up in the air. As the bills fluttered back to the bed, more laughter.

After the initial shock of discovery and escape, Sam turned to Peaches and said, "Okay, Madam, what are we gonna do?"

Peaches had a small table off to the corner of her room. She moved toward the table and said, "Well, let's talk about it. You want some coffee?"

"You got any bourbon?"

"Oh, yes. Yes. That is more appropriate, isn't it? You want OFC bonded or Coon Holler from Lamar's dad?"

"At this moment, I think I could use a little kick of the Mule."

"Let's do it."

The women poured and sipped. Looking at each other with satisfied expressions.

They enjoyed the moment.

Peaches said, "Let's look at the facts. Lamar has stuck all his money under the floorboards. It's probably Larry's cut too, since he wouldn't know what to do with his money, never having any to handle before. They probably don't know how much is even in there. There is also plenty of cash. Lots and lots. Bless their little thieving hearts. So, darling Sam, how we going to steal from the stealer's?"

"We could take it all and run off."

"An option, right. An option."

"We could just take a handful every so often."

"You are aware," Peaches said, "that if we got found out, Lamar might just outright kill us."

"You think Lamar would do that?"

"Sure, Lamar's life is built around money. So, yes, he is capable of murder over money. But I don't think he would kill you—maybe me, but he does have a soft spot for you."

Sam said, "No, we gotta make this foolproof. Lamar loves money more than our moneymaker's. What if we just took the money and ran?"

"Well, 'ran' seems to be the operative word. We don't have a runaway car. You couldn't count on that beat-up piece of junk of mine. And where do we go? We'd have those cons coming after us and Lamar would not give up."

Sam said, "We don't need all the money, do we?"

"No, we don't. How about his? We take a little out every week. Not enough to be noticed at any one time. Just keep dippin' in. Just like Lamar is going to do. Every day or so you know he is dippin' in to buy this or that. Buyin' a truck today. That's gonna cost a few thousand."

"Why's he need a truck?"

"I don't know. I thought you might be able to tell me."

Sam said, "I'll find out. Probably something to do with what he calls the 'Big Job'. Talks about it all the time. 'Biggest heist in history' kind of talk. That boy likes to brag, and he really likes to brag after we have a little session. He likes to show off that little pecker of his too. The other night he gets naked and stands there offering an inspection. Looking down at his pecker and says, 'Ain't Thor and the Brothers beauties'? Calls him 'Thor.' Wanted me to inspect up close and personal. Acting like I had never seen one before. I swear, Peaches, the more I know about men the more I realize they are so very limited in their capacity to understand women or much of anything else."

"I think we are getting a little off track here, Sam, but yes, I know exactly what you mean. Bobby T is more of a 'here you got what I want; how much you want for it' kind of guy. But back to the money. So we grab the money in handfuls at opportune times and be careful about it, and we don't get overly greedy about what we take."

They both paused at that point. Thinking.

Sam said, "So where are we gonna put our stash?"

"That's easy. We will do what they should have done. Put it in the bank."

"The bank? Whoa there, sister. That's a little too exposed for me. Too many things could go wrong with a bank account."

"Not if you use a safe deposit box," Peaches said.

"A what?"

"Safe deposit box. The bank has a room where they have locked metal drawers. The room is like a safe. The whole room, that is. It's locked up like a safe you go in. You rent a box in the room and you can put anything you want in your box . . . the safe deposit box. Cash, jewels, documents. Anything. Only the box owner can get in the box. It's like having your own little safe right in the bank. So we get a safe deposit box, you and me, grab the cash, take it to the bank and put the cash in there."

"So we both can get in the box?"

"Yes. In fact, we can make it so that only both of us, together, can open the box. We can take out or put in any time we want."

"And if we had to make a quick escape?"

"We grab and go."

"Together?"

"Together."

"I guess that makes us partners."

"I guess you are right about that."

"Another shot?"

"You betcha. And make that a double, Partner."

CHAPTER XVII

Curly's Dream A Bootleggin' Souped Up Six-Ton Truck

Driving back from the Charleston Ford dealership Lamar said, "Larry, my old friend, I don't mind sayin' that this purchase makes me happier than about anything I have done in my life."

Larry said, "How 'bout your first kiss?"

"Better. This is better."

"How 'bout your first hooch?"

"Please. Not even close."

"How 'bout when you first got . . . you know."

"Better, although you are getting warmer."

Larry paused.

"How 'bout Sam? Better than being with Sam?"

"Well, you may have me there. That is pretty fine stuff, right there. That gal has a strong hold on Brother Lamar here."

"I knew I would find something."

Lamar said, "Damn, can you believe that truck? I didn't even know they had things like that. Did you see those logs it was haulin' on the poster?"

"I believe I was standing right there lookin' at the same picture, so yep, I saw it."

"This is gonna make the Big Job so much easier." Lamar was now referring to the Wheeling Steel heist as the "Big Job"—not the job or the heist. No. The 'Big Job.' It had taken on a life of its own.

Larry said, "I don't even understand what this Big Job is all about. I do know one thing. Nothing happens in that truck lot and the warehouse. All night I don't see a solitary soul. That place is neglected, deserted, and ignored."

"Good. That's what I want to hear. You're doing a fine job there, Larry. Keep it up."

Larry wondered how he could do a good job when there wasn't anything at all to do. He checked in. Checked out. Picked up a paycheck on Friday, and that was it. He mostly slept.

"Yes, Larry. Yes, this truck is gonna make the Big Job so much easier."

"It cost enough."

"From what we gonna make off this job, that truck is petty cash."

"Where you gonna keep it? Parking it at a cathouse might draw some attention."

"Larry, I like the way you are thinkin' now. As to where we park the beauty, that is a serious question. Right now, I don't know. Maybe Curly will have an idea."

Larry said, "Why don't you just park in the lot at the mill? They got ten, twelve trucks, and nobody seems to notice much. Want me to check with the boss?"

"No. No. Most emphatically no. Let me pass it by my inside man."

"You mean, Conrad, my boss."

"You don't know that."

"Know what?"

"That Conrad is my inside man."

Larry paused.

"Well, he's the only one I've met at the mill. They don't have a security camera on the trucks and stuff in the daytime. Just me, at night . . . I still don't know how you make a million off'a nickels."

"They ain't nickel coins, Larry. It's the metal that makes nickels and steel stuff. They use it in the mill to make steel. You and me gonna be makin' a trip up to Erie in a week or so, and it will all be clear."

"I can't wait," Larry said.

Lamar seldom went to Willy Jack's Barbershop. Willy Jack didn't mind. He didn't like having Lamar around anyway. He put Lamar in the fifth and last chair. When Lamar didn't show, it meant the other barbers got more heads and made more money. When he did show, which Willy Jack knew wouldn't be too often, he didn't stay long. Oddly, Willy Jack noticed that he mostly showed up on Wednesdays and Saturday, Lamar's poker days.

Willy Jack had given the chair to Lamar only because Loretta wanted her brother to 'have a chance to get his life together.' Willy Jack knew that was never going to happen. Loretta, always hopeful, prayed that it would.

The barbershop was in Moundsville, near the courthouse on sixth street. The customers were most all associated with the courthouse—cops, lawyers, judges, clerks—pretty much the county bureaucratic operational machine.

On one wall were framed photographs of former mayor's. Another wall featured sheriffs. The shop had waiting chairs and magazines. Collier's, Popular Mechanics, Saturday Evening Post, and other assorted magazines and newspapers. The chairs were scattered around the open areas so that customers could see and talk to each other. In the middle of the seating area was a tin container filled with ice and soda Pop. If you searched around in the tub, you could find a beer or two. Willy Jack didn't advertise that, being a good Mormon Elder. A coffee pot with mugs was in reach along with a barrel of shelled peanuts—the shells were simply thrown on the floor and swept up every hour or so, the five chairs, each with their own sinks and cabinets to hold tools and towels.

The shop was a comfortable, homey meeting place for all things political, social, and religious. The shop served as the place to get a shave, haircut, catch a coffee or soda, and discuss evens of the day, and in particular, courthouse politics. The men all had an opinion, ready and eager to express their ideas, sometimes with raised voice, sometimes with laughter. It was a good place to hang out.

In the first chair was Willy Jack. He was a handsome man with a dark complexion and a heavy shadow of a beard. He looked Italian, but was not. He was quiet most of the time. Whenever his name was mentioned at the courthouse, it generally started with, ' . . that Willy Jack, over at the barbershop, he's a pretty nice guy, now isn't he'?

In the second chair, by seniority, was Curly, the Italian and he looked it.

The third chair was occupied by Keister Pitts. The called him 'Pop'. Pop Pitts. He was going on sixty. Had been in the war. A former merchant marine. Bar fighter. Prize fighter. His face was a map to his success as a fighter. Lots of scars tissue and a broken nose. Pop was a talkative, friendly, happy, working alcoholic. If Willy Jack didn't watch him closely, Pop would drink the hair tonic, going after the 10 percent alcohol. Give Pop a little buzz.

The fourth chair was for that man that would be at the shop for a few weeks and move on. An endless supply.

Lamar had the fifth chair, when he was there.

It was a Wednesday and Lamar was at the shop. He said to Curly about lunchtime, "Hey, mop head. Let's go next door. They got roast beef on the blue plate today."

Curly said, "Willy Jack, can you spare us two for thirty minutes?"

Next door to the shop was a diner. Black-and-white checkered floor. Red-and-white checked plastic vinyl table covers.

The waitress, Mildred, said, "So what's it to be, gents?"

Lamar said, "Why, Mildred, haven't seen you in a while. I'll have the blue plate special."

"Drink?"

"Coffee would be nice."

"How 'bout you, Curly?"

"Same. Thank you, Millie."

Millie smiled and said, "Nice to see you, Curly," as she walked away.

Lamar looked at Curly and said, "Hey, where's my 'nice to see ya'?"

Curly said, "I just gotta fight 'em off, Lamar."

Lamar paused and said, "I got some great news."

"I'm listening."

Mildred brought the coffee, and Lamar stopped talking. She left.

"I got us a six-ton truck that can carry a forest in one haul. You won't believe this sumbitch."

"How much we gotta carry?"

"Two to four ton."

"Four ton! Damn, Lamar, that's a load. Where's it goin'?"

"Erie, PA."

"Some tough roads gettin' up there. I take it's for the Wheeling Steel job."

"Yep, the Big One. Biggest heist in West Virginia history."

"Goin for the record book, are we? Gimme a little about the truck."

"Curly, you can't believe it. Made over in Springfield, Ohio. Six-ton. Diesel. We got a pretty big cabin for a driver and passenger. Big damn covered trailer."

"I believe you're talkin' about a Springfield Kelly. The best. What kind of suspension? We gonna need one hell of a suspension on a trailer that's gonna haul four ton. Damn, I didn't think that could even be done."

Curly, now thinking up ways to soup up a six-ton truck. He said, "You gonna have to check on permits and such for here and PA. I'll soup it up. Lay out the route. Do we need any hidey-holes?"

Lamar said, "Not now. But I got long-range plans for that truck, bootleggin' hooch to the big cities. But right now, just get it ready for the Big Job. A straight haul on the trailer with one hell of a lot of weight."

Curly had turned into a mad scientist. His mind was churning with ideas for the truck. A living, breathing Frankenstein of a truck.

He thought, 'I gotta have a name for this monster. It will be that special. When I am through with it damn thing, I'll will be able to outrace the police in a truck. Nobody else has ever done that before. In a fuckin' truck! Hell, Yes'!

CHAPTER XVIII

SWEET AS PEACH PIE

After meeting with Curly, Lamar went back to the house in high spirits. He went directly to his room. He looked around as he always did to see if anything had been moved. Three years in juvie and years in Moundsville would do that to a man. You started to live with a lot of suspicion.

Everything looked undisturbed.

He checked the floorboards where he hid the cash. When Lamar left his room, he always pulled a head hair, licked it, and stuck it on the floorboard to the bottom right. He looked for the hair. It was gone.

Lamar knew in an instant. Somebody had been into the stash. He got his putty knife and jammed it in the slots between the boards, grabbed the boards, and threw them aside. The bags were there. He quickly tore open the top. The cash was there. Same with the second bag. Everything appeared to be there. He wondered.

Lamar could feel his heart beating. His hands were clammy. He replaced the floorboards.

He took off his shirt and shoes and fell backwards on the bed, hands behind his head. He started to think it through, 'Someone has been in here and checked it out. Maybe took a little of the cash. Everything seemed in place. Maybe the hair just got moved by Cassandra cleaning or just blew away. Or whatever. I didn't tell anyone about the hidin' place, did I? Not Sam. Not Larry. Did I get drunk and start talkin' too much? Who? Peaches? Oh, Peaches knows everything, now don't she? She knew the money would be hidden somewhere, and she would be relentless. Absolutely relentless. Gotta be Peaches'.

He laid on the bed, hands behind his head, thinking. Now drifting off to sleep. His last waking thought was to keep his eye on Peaches, thinking, 'Maybe Sam could help me trap her. Yes, Sam would do that for me. She loves me'.

While Lamar schemed and slept, Peaches and Sam went to the bank. They took Peach's clunker and headed to Wheeling and the Central Bank and Trust. Neither Sam nor Peaches had been to Wheeling. Sam had never been in a city. Peaches had been to Cincinnati, but that was it for her.

Being the nail capital of the world had its benefits for Wheeling. It was one of the richest cities in the country. To the girls, it was sophisticated and exciting. The streets were alive. Street cars on rails. People moving vigorously, walking fast with real purpose. Women dressed in the finest. And the cars! The girls had never seen such sights. Yellow. Green. Blue. Black. They all looked like they had just come from a showroom floor.

The Central Bank building looked like a skyscraper to the girls. Peaches had heard about those tall buildings in New York reaching to the sky. The stopped to stare at the top of the bank building.

Sam said, "How many floors is that?"

"I don't know. Maybe nine or ten, but we don't have time to be tourist. Let's get in, get the safety deposit box, and get out."

A half hour later, they were on their way back to the house on 21 Street.

Later that day, the girls, all of them, were in the parlor getting ready for their nighttime customers. Peaches and Sam were happy to have a drink and relax with the girls before the night activities began.

Roxy, the new girl said, "You know what I don't like about this job? My feet hurt. Those high heels just kill my feet. Wearing 'em all the time. Up and down those stairs, ten, fifteen times a day. That Milt guy the other night? He wanted me to wear them the entire time. Can you believe that? And my shoes hurt my feet. I think I need new shoes."

Peaches said, "Hey, go over to Shotty's. Ask for Abe. He'll fix you up and probably won't charge you, but might show up in a day or two looking for a freebie."

Roxy said, "Maybe I'll get two pair then. Might as well make it worthwhile. You know another thing? I brush my teeth probably four or five times a day. That is tedious. But look how bright there are." She smiled, and everybody looked. "I'm not much fond of changing clothes, or getting in and out of them so many times a day. Changing seven, eight times the day."

Sam said, "That's how you make the money, Honey."

Peaches said, "I've got some good news for you girls. The firemen are coming over tomorrow night."

That caused some smiles, laughter, and general good cheer.

"Yes, a state convention in Wheeling. The chief said to expect about twenty of the horny little devils," Peaches said.

Roxy said, "So, what's all the excitement about a bunch of firemen other than it looks like a busy night?"

Sam said, "Well, Honey. These fellas are young and good lookin'. I think it's in their regulations that a fireman has gotta be fit and handsome. Smart, too. They are very polite. Lots of 'yes ma'am, no ma'am.' They treat us with respect and better yet, gratitude. They are so grateful. Kinda just makes a girl want to give her all. Not all book a session, but if they don't book, they look, and the lookers are always back, alone, before the convention's over. Plus they tip good, even the lookers tip and buy you all the drinks you want, so that adds a little money for us. They are just sweet as can be, and believe me, ladies, you almost feel embarrassed to be paid for it."

Sam said, "My favorite John is an old fella. Just comes to talk. I sit and listen to him. Nice guy. Just lonely. Drives over the bridge from Bellaire. His wife gets suspicious as to where he goes and follows him. See's the traffic coming in and out of the house and figures it out. So the next day, she shows up here. Can you believe that? She's as old as he is. Very polite. Little old lady in round-rimmed glasses and carrying a small purse that she has clutched in both hands and kinda holding it to her chest. She wanted to speak to the woman that spent time with her husband. Peaches thinks she's harmless and gets me. I tell her he sees me once a month, but all we do is talk. Nothing more. No hanky-panky of any kind. So she says to me, 'Why doesn't he talk to me?' I say, 'Honey, I really don't know, but maybe you need to be a better listener.' That seemed to break the old lady's heart. I think she would have felt better if I told her we were screwing like teenagers. Little tears coming down as she left. He must be seventy or so. I don't think he is going to be around much longer."

"Kinda sad, isn't it?" Sam said.

CHAPTER XIX

PILLOW TALK

Lamar was sleeping when Sam crawled into bed. It was a little after midnight. She was tired and didn't want to wake Lamar. But Lamar had been sleeping since early evening, and he wanted to talk. Sam was grateful it was only talk.

Lamar rolled over and put his arm around her. Snuggled in nice and tight. In a soft, loving way, his hand cuddled her breast. Sam didn't move or give any encouragement.

Lamar said, "Damn, you feel good. I was dreaming about your boobies. Delectable and lovely, ain't they? Don't you think that odd?"

"What, my titties?"

"No, me dreaming about your titties. Isn't that kinda odd?"

"Lamar, Honey, I think that is just you dreamin'. Nothing odd about it. Now if you want, one of these days I'll tell you some odd things men do and want to do with women. Your little dream falls far short of some of that shit."

"Well, for right now, I think I'll pass on that."

Lamar paused, and Sam thought he might be going to sleep. Ever hopeful.

Lamar perked up and said, "Hey, did you see Peaches today?"

"Of course, Lamar. I see her about twenty times a day, every day."

"How was she acting?"

Sam started to wake up . . . fast. Her intuitive antenna just went active in a major way.

"How was she acting? What do you mean?"

"Well, acting any different. Little happy, maybe. Little . . . different."

"No, she was the same bossy bitch that she usually is. No different."

"Larry tells me you two went to Wheeling."

Sam was fully awake at this point.

"Yes, we went shopping."

"Really? What you get? Anything for me?"

"Yes, Lamar. I got you a new tux to wear the next time you go up to see Pappy and get some Mule Kick. Thought you ought to look good. No, we didn't get anything. Oh, Peaches got some new shoes for Roxy. I don't think the child is used to wearing shoes at all, let alone heels."

"I wanna ask a favor of you, okay?"

"Fire away. I'm guessing I can say no."

"Keep an eye on Peaches for me. Let me know if you see her snoopin' around the house or in my room."

"I can do that. What am I watching for?"

"I think she is looking for my money."

"The money from your visit to the doctor's house?"

"Yes."

"You have it here in the house and think that Peaches might try to grab it?"

"I have it stashed all right. Away. No one knows but me where it's at."

"Okay . . . I'll watch her like a cat chasin' a mouse."

"Good. I want to catch her in the act."

"The act of stealing your money?"

"Yes. Stealing my money."

"And where is the most likely place I would find her in the act of stealing your money?"

Lamar stopped talking. Thinking. He said, "Right here in my bedroom. I wanted it right close to me."

"So if she is snoopin' around in the fruit cellar or the parlor or any other place in the house, I need not be concerned, right?"

"Right."

"So if you caught her in the act, what then?"

"What do you think?"

"You wouldn't kill her, would you?"

"I would make her wish she was dead."

Lamar started to drift off. Sam didn't say anything, but her mind was churning. Fully awake now, she thought, 'Me and Peach gotta be really careful. Good thing is he suspects but doesn't know anything. I'll have to talk to Peaches first thing in the morning'.

The next morning, in a quiet whisper, Sam told Peaches everything while the two of them were taking coffee in the kitchen.

Lamar walked in and said, "Good morning, ladies. Sleep well, I hope?"

Peaches said, "Good morning, Lamar. Yep, slept like a baby."

"Good. Just wanted to let you both know that Larry and I will be gone today and back tomorrow late. Gotta see a guy up in Erie."

"What, you going to open another cathouse in Erie, Lamar?" Peaches said.

Lamar smiled and said, "Nothing that exotic, Peachy my dear. Nope, gonna go to a scrap yard."

"Maybe I should let you know, Lamar, that we have those kind of places right here in the neighborhood, and you don't have to drive a couple hundred miles," Peaches said.

"This is big. Biggest heist of my life. This will put me on the map."

Sam said, "Lamar, Honey. It if is a criminal thing, and we all know that it is, the idea is to stay off the map, isn't it?"

"I'm talkin' about my criminal notoriety. The people that count in my world will all know. Put me in the same league as Mr. G in Wheeling or some of those Mafia guys in Youngstown, Cleveland . . . like that."

"A worthy goal, Lamar. Put you right up at the top. Glad to know that we all here will be a small part of your criminal organization. Contribute in any small way we can," Peaches said.

Both woman were thinking the same thing,,'Gotta be careful. Lamar may have set a trap. A set-up to catch us. We better be careful. Awfully careful'.

CHAPTER XX

Road Trip!

Lamar and Larry left for Erie early the next morning, driving Lamar's black Ford Model T, north on the 644 to Pittsburgh, picking up the 620 to Erie.

Lamar said, "Larry, this damned Model T is gonna give you a sore butt before we get to Pittsburgh."

"I thought we were going to Erie!"

"Well, yeah, but we going through Pittsburgh to get to Erie."

"So, why we talkin' about Pittsburgh?"

"We are not . . . Larry, my point is this Tin Lizzie is not the most comfortable ride you ever had, and you're gonna have a sore butt before we get out of West Virginia."

"I feel pretty comfortable right now, thank you."

"Come to think of it, you got a lot of paddin' down there, and that may just smooth the ride for you. These Ts are just not made for comfort. This con in Moundsville told me a joke about a guy trying to sell his T and couldn't find a buyer. Guy was asked, 'How'd you ever manage to get rid of that danged ol' Ford T?' He said, 'Well, it weren't easy. First, we advertised it for sale and nobody would buy it. Then, we advertised it for free and nobody would take it. Finally, I parked it around behind the house and moved away.'"

Lamar laughed. Larry smiled.

"You get it? They left the house and the car?"

"Why would they do that?"

"This may be a long trip," Lamar said. "You know, I ought to get one of them Stutz cars. Damn, they are sharp. Pretty yellow one. Anybody ask I'd tell 'em that it was gold, not yellow. Faster'n blue blaze's. Wouldn't Curly love to race that thing? They call it the 'Speedway Special.'"

Larry said, "Good thing you reminded everybody of no big spending cause cruisin' around McMechen in a big, fancy Stutz and wearin' those fancy new suits of yours just might be noticed in McMechen. And there is the hat thing you got going. I can't forget about that."

Lamar had bought new clothes. Fashionable, he thought. Plaid suit with large lapels. A big hat that really didn't fit well. Bright red suspenders. Wingtip brown-and-white shoes. Peaches said the costume was from the early pimp period. She went on to say, "And then he would get in that beat-up Model T. Look ridiculous dressed like that and driving around McMechen. It's McMechen, for gawd's sake, not a big city of sophistication like Wheeling."

Lamar said, "Hey, Larry, I got this outfit in Wheeling at the best men's shop there. The guy told me it was all the latest in New York and Chicago. By the way, thanks for leaving your britches behind for the trip. Those pants look better."

Larry was wearing his security guard pants. A clean white shirt and dirty boots completed his dress.

Lamar said, "We might have to get you some nicer shoes when we get back. If you're gonna go to business meetings with me, you gotta look sharp."

"Didn't you say we were goin' to a junkyard?" Larry said.

"Yes, but not exactly a junkyard. We are gonna see Willy Jack's brother-in-law, Lou Carney. He is married to one of W. J.'s sisters. Lou is a big-time scrap dealer. Scrap being a big thing in that part of the world because they can transport over Lake Erie and then across the pond to Europe. It's big business."

"The pond?" That brought Larry to a pause. "Oh, you mean the ocean. So we are goin' to steal the nails from the warehouse at Wheeling Steel, truck it up to Erie, and Lou is gonna ship it to Europe or someplace, right?"

"You nailed it, my man! By the way, it's nickel, not nails. I think it's going to Germany, but I'm not sure who the buyers are. Larry, this is the perfect crime. Better than stealing from rich doctors, although that was quite the gig, weren't it?"

Larry said, "Perfect. Yep, the perfect crime. That's why you are who you are, Lamar."

With Lamar headed for Erie, Peaches and Sam had a planning session in Peach's room. This time it was coffee, not bourbon.

Peaches said, "Did you see the way that damn fool was dressed? Leaving for his big meeting with a big-deal businessman."

"He said he wanted to look his best," Sam said. "So what you think we should do . . . about the money?"

"Seems like an ideal time to hit the bags again, doesn't it? Tell me again what all your pillow talk was about."

"Mostly it was about me spying on you. 'Keepin' an eye on you', he said. " The poor man doesn't seem to suspect me a'tall. And he is just possessed about that cash. I wonder why he didn't just do what we did? Put it in that lock box at the bank. That was pretty easy."

"Lamar doesn't much run in banking circles, Honey. His people don't believe in banks. Don't trust them. Think them are part of a big government conspiracy against them. Come to think of it, he went off on the bad treatment his people got from the King of England, couple hundred years ago. What the hell would the King of England have against the McKenna's? Anyway, they still hold that grudge against any authority, especially the government."

"Damn, now that is serious grudge-holding."

"That they can do. I got this John, runs a bank up in Martins Ferry. Can't be seen dealing with righteous girls like us in in Martins Ferry. Might run into his pastor or the mayor, so he makes the trip down here. He talks about banking and I ask a lot questions. I learn a lot. That's how I learned about the new lock boxes. But back to the business at hand. I've been thinking on this. We are going to have access to Lamar's room about anytime we want, not just the next couple of days, right?"

"I suppose so."

"He's gone for the night and most of tomorrow. If he suspects me and wants you to watch me, what do you think he might do?"

"Lay a trap."

"Right. This would be a perfect time for him to do that, would it not? Let's check out the room, but just to see if we can find anything. Not take anything. Let Lamar get comfortable again. Get his guard down a touch. Then we can follow our plan, but next time we take two hands full. That would be a pretty good payday."

"Yep. Two hands full? That, my lady friend, would be a hell of a hand job, and worth a lot more, too."

"Let's go over there and check it out."

It didn't take long. This time the girls saw the hair. Lamar had put one on each corner.

Sam said, "What you think?"

Peach said, "Damn Lamar is going to drive me to drink. When we move the boards, we will have to move the hair carefully. Hit the bags and replace the hair. Ready for the raid?"

"Sounds Peachy," Sam said.

CHAPTER XXI

Scrap Iron Is My Life

Lamar and Larry pulled up to the scrap iron yard on East Street in Erie. The yard took up a full city block, surrounded by a brick wall fifteen feet high. From the street, it was impossible to see into the yard. Brown, dead shrub climbed the wall. The bricks looked old and chipped. Above the wall, a huge smoke stack could be seen. Looked like a good two hundred feet high. Dirty white smoke slowly rose from the stack. A billboard outside the compound said:

CARNEY SCRAP IRON

Cast Iron and Metals of all Kind

By the Pound or By the Ton

Best Prices in America

Larry said, "Damn, this is a huge place. Almost takes up as much space as the steel mill. How do we get in there?"

Lamar drove the T slowly along the side of the big brick wall. He reached a road at the end of the frontage and turned right. He could see an entrance a short distance away. He pulled into the entryway, next to a guard house in front of a large, iron gate. A security guard looked up from his newspaper. He folded the paper and put it on his desk. Took a sip of coffee from an old mug, got up, opened the door, stepped out, and said, "Good morning, gentlemen. How can I help you?"

Lamar said, "We got a meeting with Mr. Carney."

"And your name is?"

"Lamar McKenna."

The guard was writing down the name and said, "How'd you spell that last name?"

"M, c, capital K, e, double n, a."

"Double what?"

"N as in . . . nickel."

The guard was slowly writing all this down. Lamar glanced at Larry with a 'can you believe this' expression.

Finally, the guard said, "Wait here. I'll check."

Lamar wondered what the other option was to waiting there.

They watched the guard pick up a phone and speak. He nodded and came back to the car.

"Mr. Carney is expecting you. Lemme open the gate."

The big iron gate moved slowly from the middle to the edges.

Larry said, "Damn, Lamar, you ever see a gate open like that?"

"Yeah, they got a dozen of 'em over at Moundsville Prison. Larry, try not to look like you never been any place outside of some West Virginia holler."

"Oh, I been plenty of places. You seem to forget I'm from Vinton County, Ohio."

"That's hard to forget, Larry."

Inside the fence, the yard looked like a bomb had been dropped in the middle. Junk piles of metals in immense stacks. At a glance he could see ten or twelve of these stacks. One of the stacks had a man on top throwing metal strips down off the pile onto the ground. He was as dirty as a coal miner, with bib overalls and no shirt.

In front of them was a two-story brick building. A sign on the door said, 'Enter Here'.

They did.

A woman was typing on an unusually large Underwood and didn't look up. The boys stood there waiting instructions.

Larry said in a soft voice to Lamar, "Look, the size of that typewriter. That thing is gigantic. You ever seen such a thing?"

Lamar said, "Yeah, Moundsville."

Lamar kept looking at the secretary, who was ignoring them.

She finished typing, pulled the paper from the typewriter, and held it above her head with a window-lit background.

She says, "I gotta check for typing errors. Mr. Carney has a fit if there is one little letter out of place. So, you must be Mr. McKenbie?"

"McKenna, double n."

"That Mac, he just never can get a name right. Follow me, Mr. Carney is waiting for ya."

Lou Carney was forty-five and a self-made millionaire, married to Willy Jack Walker's youngest sister, Nancy, who was called Nan. Lou and Nan met when he was twenty-four and Nan was nineteen. She had just come off a year reign as Ms. West Virginia and was working at the Marshall County court house in Permits. Lou was an up-and-coming, fast-talking metal salesman. He needed a transport permit to move metals from mines in Kentucky and West Virginia to Wheeling Steel.

Lou waited in line to get his permit, thinking about his first big sale . . . thinking about his fat commission . . . feeling good. His turn came. He was glancing at the order he had from the mill as he said, "I need a permit for . . ." Mid-sentence he stopped looking at the paper, raised his head, and saw Nan Walker. He was speechless before this beautiful young woman in front of him.

Finally he said, ". . . a permit . . . ah, a permit for moving . . ." The smooth-talking salesman had trouble explaining what he needed.

Nan said, "Let me see your paper, Mr. . . ."

"Lou."

"Mr. Lou."

"No, Lou's my name. I mean my first name."

Nan smiled and said, "Well, Mr. Lou, let's see what we can do for you."

Lou got his permit a few minutes later and left. Outside he sat on a concrete bench near a statute of a Civil War soldier. He didn't know why he was sitting there, but he was thinking about the clerk, Nan. He thought, 'That woman took my breath away. Apparently my ability to think as well. What do I do now'?

Fifteen minutes later, he got his answer. Nan came out with two other women, both older. They passed Lou without a glance, crossed the street, and went into the diner next to Willy Jack's barbershop.

Lou followed and walked in as the women were being seated. Lou went up to Nan and stood there. He didn't know what to say. Nan helped him out; she said, "Well, hello Mr. Carney. Was everything okay with the permit?"

Lou said, "Yes, I think so."

Lou just stood there.

Nan said, "Was there anything else?"

Silence, but this time Lou shook his head slightly.

"You're from out of town, aren't you? Did you want some company for lunch?"

"That would really be nice," Lou said.

Nan said, "Ladies, do you think you can do without me this one time so that I might give a proper West Virginia welcome to our visitor?"

She then turned to Lou and said, "Let's grab that table by the window."

They were married six months later.

The boys were shown into Mr. Carney's office. Like everything else around the place, it was big. Big desk. Big chair. And Lou, a big man. Lamar thought Lou was a good lookin' guy, maybe goes six feet, six-one. Curly dark hair. Big smile.

Lou moved quickly, confidently, stuck out his hand to Lamar and said, "So you're Loretta's twin brother. Happy to meet you."

Lamar took his hand and said, "And this here is my associate. Name's Larry."

"Larry," Lou said.

"So how was the drive up, boys? No breakdowns? Saw you had a model T. How'd it ride?"

Lamar said, "Everything was fine, Mr. Carney. Made it up here unscathed by car or Mother Nature."

"Oh, please call me Lou. I'm a scrap iron guy. Not a lot a guys can be pretentious about operating in an office surrounded by that mess outside."

"Yeah, that is quite an operation you got out there."

"So how are Willy Jack and Loretta and the kids?"

Lamar said, "Oh, they're just fine. Loretta being the ultimate church lady and W. J. just workin' along."

"What about the kids? What are they up to?"

"Well, you know Jack went off to Ohio State, got his law degree and is working with Spencer Sprat over in Wheeling. Young Willy is in high school, and Rebecca is in the second grade, I believe."

"Sprat, the Hilly Billy Hot Shot?"

"The one and same."

"How'd it work for Jack playing for the Buckeyes?"

"He played, but not all that much until Chic Harley graduated. Had a pretty good last year, but all anyone wanted to do was remind him that he was not Chic. Not quite fair. Young Willy is better than Jack, I'm told. He won the state hundred last year and is the fastest thing you ever did see. Maybe he'll go over to Columbus too, but I think he favors Morgantown right now. Rebecca, the youngest, is just a sweet little girl. Pretty too. Up there in Nan's league, I'm told. Gonna be a heart breaker, that one."

"Thanks for the update. Nan and I just can't seem to find the time to get down there, but I think they are headed here this summer. So, boys, tell me what you got."

Lamar inched closer to the desk and said, "We got nickel briquettes."

"That's what I heard. How much?"

"Oh, that's what I thought you would tell us. How much can we get for them?"

Lou said, "I don't mean how much money can you get, I mean how much do you have to deliver?"

Lamar said, "Oh, yeah. Well, as I read it, we could probably deliver two, four ton a week for maybe eight to ten weeks."

Lou said, "That's a lot of nickel B's."

Larry said, "We gonna get them from...."

Lou put his hand up and said, "No, no, no. Stop right there. I don't need or want to know where you get them. You bring 'em here. We unload and I pay you."

"How much?"

Lou had a rather large calculating machine on his desk. He started punching in numbers rapidly. Silence. Only the click, click, click from Lou's machine.

Larry started to comment on the big machine on Lou's desk, but Lamar quickly put his hand up to say stop, and Larry looked at Lamar, shrugged his shoulders to say what?

Lou looked up and said, "I can give you nine hundred and fifty dollars a ton."

Lamar said, "So we deliver two ton a week, we walk away with, what is that . . . what . . . . nineteen hundred?"

"You got it."

"So ten trips, how much is that?

Lou answered quickly, "That, my friend, is nineteen thousand."

Lamar said, "That buys a lot of friendship. And if we get a four-ton truck load, you can handle that?"

"No problem."

"And the payout would be double?"

"Sure."

"Yes, it does. One thing. How you going to move four ton? You have a couple of trucks?"

Lamar beamed and said, "We got a six-ton, souped-up Kelly-Springfield. Damnedest thing you ever saw. And we got a bootlegging' sumbitch drivin' it. He got it all fixed to carry the load. Yes, sir! This is the most beautiful piece of machinery you ever did see."

"I thought those Kelly's were for hauling lumber and such?"

"Well, Mr. Lou, you gonna see the beauty in a few weeks. So hold tight!"

"It looks like you have a well thought-out plan."

Larry said, "Oh, yeah, Mr. Lou. Lamar here is a criminal mastermind. He is the best in the business. Why last month we hit a . . .."

Lamar quickly interrupted with, "Larry, now Mr. Carney don't want to hear about that little caper of ours. Do you, Mr. Carney?"

Lou said, "What caper?" Saying it with a little shrug and an all-knowing wink.

"What do you do with it after we deliver?" Lamar said.

"I sell it."

"Yeah, to who?"

Lou stood up and leaned over his desk. Lamar thought he had a twinkle in his eye. He smiled slightly and said, "Lamar, I have a perfect buyer. Rich as hell and don't ask any questions. And they can be a little sloppy with their book work, making them the perfect . . . the perfect buyer."

Lamar said, "Okay, I'll bite. Who ya got?"

"The U-nited States of America, that's who."

Larry said, "I think we found the perfect crime."

Lou said, "Crime. I see no crime here. I buy from you and sell it to the Department of Defense of the United States government. I'm not involved in any crime here. I have no idea where you are getting the nickel. I won't ask, and you won't tell. So let's keep it that way, okay? When you bringing the first load?"

Lamar said, "Within the month."

"Thank you boys for driving up. I appreciate it. Get me those metals."

"Yes, sir," Lamar said.

Lamar and Lou shook hands and the boys left.

They drove out of the scrapyard floating on a cloud.

The perfect damn crime. What could possibly go wrong?

CHAPTER XXII

THE BIG TRUCK ROLLS

Two weeks after the trip to Erie, Charleston Ford called Lamar. The truck was in. Lamar hot-tailed it to Willy Jack's barbershop. Not to work, of course, but to see Curly. Lamar did two heads in the late morning and got up close to Curly and said, "Let's get lunch. I've got some really great news."

They moved to the door when Lamar, not asking permission this time, said, "Hey, W. J. See you in a few, Curly and me goin' next door." Willy Jack, sitting with a group of men around the peanut barrel and soda Pop, never looked up. He was totally fixated on the conversation with county bureaucrats. The hot topic of the day was one Leon Kalograpalus. Commonly called Leon K. or Commissioner K. or simply K, was in charge of garbage pickup for the County.

Eight men were seated around the peanut barrel, drinking soda pop, calling it coke, no matter the brand or the drink. The soda was in a battered, old aluminum tub, filled with ice, much of which had melted into cold water. There was a logo on the side of the tub, eroded and almost colorless, that said, "Drink Fruit Bowl. Nectar For a Nickel." The men would crack five or six peanut shells then drop the peanuts in their drink and the shells on the floor.

The barber chairs were in the background. Today, no one was interested in a shave or a haircut. It was all about Commissioner K. All the men had strong opinions that when spoken were loud, firm, and delivered with the righteousness of a self-absorbed Pentecostal preacher. The notion that one should wait their turn in the conversation was not observed. Several men were always vocalizing at once. The noise was rip-roaring for the small space.

J. T. Tibbs, County Clerk, had stirred the commotion when he said, "I tell you, Leon K. is connected to Big Gio, that damn crime boss up in Wheeling. K just gave the county garbage contract to Big G's trash-haulin' company, Good Will Trash. Good will, my ass. Bill Smith, over in Benwood, even had a lower bid, and he is right here. Local boy. Just ignored him, that's what the hell K did."

Deputy Sheriff Osborn kicked in and said, "I really can't commence talkin' none, since we got a little investigation goin' on about this particular commissioner having to do with corruption and money dealin' here and there. But what we are findin' out is that K and Big Gio are right friendly. Yes sir. Right friendly. It's part of the Greek thing, both being Greeks. We got the goods on the commissioner too, and when it busts open, it's gonna be big. I'm sure as hell gettin' to the bottom of it." The deputy took a deep breath and said, "I just can't comment on it, being it is an ongoing investigation and all."

Willy Jack said, "So Big Gio is the crime boss for Wheeling and here?"

Osborn said, "Damn straight."

W. J. said, "But he's not Italian. Thought you had to be Italian to be part of the Mafia."

Osborn replied, "He is Greek, but he has control of the crime . . . prostitution, gambling, trash, meat, runnin' books . . . stuff like that. But he answers to Guise Tortuga, up in Pittsburgh and Tugy the Tongue, as he is called, is connected to the mob through the Columbo's in New

York. The mobsters think Marshall County is too light for them, so they let the Greek run it. The eye-talians got their people up and down the river in Newport across from Cincinnati and up the river in Steubenville and Youngstown, Cleveland, them Ohio towns. Pittsburgh too. Big Gio pays tribute to Tugy the Tongue, being as Pittsburgh is so close."

Assistant County Treasurer, Otis Armstrong, said, "Well, fellows, Big Gio has got his meaty paws in Marshall County now. No telling where that will go."

Willy Jack said, "I sure don't like the sound of that. You think they are interested in going after barbershops?"

Deputy Chief Osborn said, "Willy Jack, and I mean no disrespect here, but I think organized crime has bigger pickin's out there then barbershops."

Willy Jack said, "I sure hope so."

Next door, at the diner, Lamar and Curly had taken a vinyl red booth in the far corner. Lamar looked right, then slowly to his left. Looked over Curly's head to see the long line of the same tabletops, checking to see if he could possibly be overheard. Mildred, the waitress who had a fondness for Curly, approached and said, "Hi, Curly, you doin' okay today? What can I get you?"

This irritated Lamar, being ignored again by Mildred, and he spoke up and said, "We are both having the blue plate with coffee."

She said, "You want the green beans, the green peas, corn, or the succotash for your vegetables?"

Curly said "Let's try the succotash Millie, Honey. What you think?"

Mildred smiled at Curly and said, "Just perfect."

Curly said "Lamar?"

Lamar, now fully irritated at Mildred's interest in Curly and not him, said, "Fine."

Mildred left.

"Curly, I got good news for you."

"Oh, yeah? So spell it."

"The truck is here. The Kelly-Springfield. Waiting for us at the dealership in Wheeling."

"When can I pick it up?"

"Soon as you can. How 'bout tomorrow?"

Curly was beaming. Lamar had gotten over his irritation with the Curly-centric waitress and likewise had a big silly grin on his face.

In timely fashion, Mildred delivered the Blue Plates. She said, "Anything to drink, boys?" Lamar said, "Coffee."

Curly said, "Mildred, Honey, I think I am gonna have a little iced tea. Just put your little figure in it and it will be sweet enough."

"Oh, Curly, how you go on. I'll be right back."

Lamar leaned half-way over the table top. He said, "So where you gonna soup it up?"

Curly took a bite of the meatloaf and said, "Hey, this ain't bad. Try some, Lamar."

Lamar didn't respond.

Then Curly chipped in, "Oh, where? My place. I got everything I need right there. Plus I got a couple of my bootleggin' buddies to help out."

"What they gonna cost?"

"Not much, we are always helping each other out. Besides if we ever need a back-up driver, they could be it, and I will get one or the other to ride shotgun up to Erie if Sabby can't go.

These are good boys, and they can drive almost as good as me. Damn, that last ride was a trip, wasn't it? I laughed my ass off when that copper turned the car and almost flipped. I still see that fire hydrant shootin' water one hundred feet in the air. That was the damnedest night."

"Keep your voice down." Lamar reached out with both hands making a downward motion. "You have what equipment you need?"

"Mostly. I may need a couple of things. I'll let you know."

"Get the best. We don't want anything to go wrong, and don't forget you will be pulling two, four ton."

"Lamar, I am not likely to forget that."

"You okay driving this rig? It's a big sumbitch. Big. A monster."

"Lamar, I'm gonna forget you insulted me like that. Of course, I can drive the damn thing. I can drive anything on wheels and fast too."

"Speed is secondary, Curly."

"Relax, pardner. Relax. You are just a little uptight here, Buddy. This is my turf. When you want it ready?"

"Can you do two weeks?"

"Curly can do anything. Two weeks it is."

Mildred, who seemed to have very good timing, came to the table and said, "Curly, looks like you enjoyed the meal. Even ate your succotash too. And look at you, Lamar; you haven't hardly touched your plate. Are you finished?"

Feeling chastised, Lamar waved his hand and said, "Yeah, take it away." Lamar pulled out $2.50 and laid it on the table. He said, "Can you get out of the shop tomorrow?"

"Sure. I'll just tell Willy Jack that I'm a little off my feed."

"Right now, tell W. J. I'll see him when I see him," Lamar said, smiling again.

"Can do."

Lamar thought, 'A legend in the making. Yes, sir. Lamar, you a legend in the making, and you are just about there'.

CHAPTER XXIII

NOTHIN' TOO BIG, YA UNDERSTAND
JUST A SMALL PIECE OF DA PIE

Back at the house from his meeting with Curly, Lamar parked the car as he saw Peaches coming through the back door of the house, standing there waiting for him. Lamar thought, 'This will not be good. It's either more money or some calamity has hit one of the girls. Probably money'.

As he approached the door, he said, "Why, Peaches, you sweet little thing, I bet you have some good news for me. What, we double the income this week?"

Peaches didn't smile. She said, "You got a trio of real interesting characters here to see you. I put 'em in the back parlor off the kitchen. I didn't want them scaring off the customers. And, by the way, they are not cops. That's for damn sure."

"What'd they say?"

"I need to speak to Mr. Lamar McKenna. And it wasn't an ask. I told 'em you weren't here and I didn't know when you would be back. They said they would wait. That was about an hour ago."

"Okay. Let's see what they want."

Lamar went to the parlor, walked in, and knew instantly . . . it's Pittsburgh or Wheeling.

One of the men stood up. He was about fifty. Dark hair slicked back. Had a brown fedora in his left hand. Fancy suit too. Brown with slight, pasty-white lines up and down. High, white, starched collar with a brown-and-red striped tie. Had a tie pin. Bright gold. Brown-and-white wing-tipped shoes. The same kind Lamar had.

He stuck out his hand and said, "Mr. McKenna, good to finally meet you. My name is Stanislavsky—you can call me Stan. Everybody else does. These two gentlemen are my associates." He didn't give their names. One of the men was big. Had a droopy dog face. The other was small and thin and looked like a smaller version of Stan. Dressed the same. He was alert and twitchy.

Stan went on to say, "I hope you will forgive the unexpected intrusion."

Lamar said, "No, no. No that's okay. Stan, you don't look like you are from around here."

Sitting now, Stan was playing with his hat brim. Moving it in small circle with both hands. A leg crossed. Looking comfortable, like he belonged right there and treating Lamar like he was the visitor. He said, "No, I don't suppose I do, but not far away. Would Wheeling count as being from around here?"

"Close enough. Can I get you some refreshment? You know we have Mule Kick here."

"Well, thank you, Mr. McKenna, but not right now. Perhaps I can take a quart or two back to Big Gio."

Lamar thought, 'So, Big Gio finally came calling. I knew this day would come, and here it is'.

Lamar hoped it didn't show it, but at the mention of the crime boss, he could feel his body tense. He didn't want to start sweating, but he feared it. Feared his body odor would be scented by these predators, and they would devour him.

"Big Gio?"

"Why, yes, Big Gio. Surely you have been expecting him to reach out and make acquaintance of another McKenna, maker of the fabulous Mule Kick Moonshine. I'm sure, given your extensive background, you are aware of the fact that Big Gio controls the prostitution business in this entire area. Clear down to Weirton and beyond."

"Yeah, I'm familiar. Got to know one of your boys over in Moundsville, Marcos."

"Yes, he did mention that he knew you quite well. Said you knew your way around the system. Got along with about everybody."

"Well, tell Marcos hello for me."

"You can tell him yourself. He will be seeing you every Monday to pick up your small donation to Big Gio."

"So what will my ol' buddy be expecting?"

"Well, Lamar . . . may I call you Lamar?"

"Stan, we are now on a first-name basis, and I sense about to be partners. Is it partners or associates, like these two, or what?

"Lamar, you are not a partner of Big Gio. What we are . . . we're your friends. We are here to protect you."

"Really, from what?"

"I'm glad you asked. Would you like our brethren from Pittsburgh coming down for a visit? How 'bout the boys coming up the river from Newport or down from Youngstown? You don't want those people in your knickers, now do you? We're West Virginia boys, just like you. None of us want those outsiders making inroads on our turf, do we?"

Lamar didn't respond.

Stan said, "You also want to keep the place open and feel nice and comfortable with police, the sheriff, judges. We don't want anyone that is running a nice little business like you got here, getting into trouble with the law. We control that."

"I do have the county wrapped up. I got a judge or two that likes our shine."

"Lamar, we can have the sheriff, the marshals, the police chief over here tomorrow closing down your house and putting you under arrest. Is that what you want? I walk out of here feeling like you are not our friend, that's what you'll be getting. Nobody wants that, now do we?"

Lamar said, "Stan, you are very a very persuasive man. You make me feel like I should be thanking you."

"I can understand your feelings, Lamar. But we both know where this is going to end up. We make a deal. You're a reasonable man. Besides, we been buying hooch from Pappy for, damn, how long, Sergio?"

Sergio, the smaller of the two men, said, "My granddaddy did business with ol' Henry McKenna before Pappy come along. So must be thirty-forty years now. Hooch, your brother, right? He shows up every Thursday afternoon with a delivery to our warehouse. Hooch is a funny guy, by the way. Funny guy. Big Gio ain't no small customer either."

Stan said, "Because of our family relationship, we are quite willing to overlook your little poker games at that barber shop. That would be all yours. Now if you start running book over there, and I know you thought about it . . . wasn't that one of your first juvie time, getting caught running numbers for that guy, Sammy something? Anyway, running a book is a more serious matter than a penny-ante poker match a couple times a week."

Lamar felt trapped. He thought, 'I got plenty of money. So I make a little less on the cathouse . . . besides, after the Big Job, it won't matter much at all'.

Stan said, "Big Gio appreciates Pappy and the business they do. That's why he is willing to overlook your past profits and start on Monday with the payments."

"Tell you the truth, Stan. There ain't been much profit. There are a lot of expenses getting started in this business."

"I'll thank Big Gio for his largess on your behalf. That will play better for you than 'I'm not makin' it cause I don't have any profits.'.Lamar, that's what everybody says. You know better than that."

Lamar said, "How much?"

"Given our relationship with your family and how . . ."

Lamar interrupted and said, "How much, Stan?"

"Let's give you a break and say thirty percent."

"Thirty percent of my profits?"

"Lamar, don't be foolish. You know how this works."

"Thirty percent of my gross? I don't make a thirty-percent profit on the place. I gotta make some money here to make it worthwhile. Let's make it fifteen."

"Lamar, your embarrassing yourself. You know we are not a negotiating organization."

"Fifteen percent. And you and your boys get a freebie right now. Plus a quart a week for Big Gio with my compliments. Couple of pints for your boys right now and a jug for you. What'cha say?"

"Twenty, plus the little perks you just named."

"Eighteen."

"Don't press your luck, Lamar. You got your eighteen, but that's it and only because of Big Gio's long-standing relationship with Pappy and Hooch."

Lamar thought, 'Well the girls are gonna have to take a little pay cut. Peaches will not be happy. So what else is new'?

It was the next morning at the house. Peaches had come into the kitchen for her morning coffee and muffin.

Lamar said, "How are you today, Peaches?"

Peaches said, "I'm a ray of fucking sunshine, Lamar. That's how I am."

She was getting her coffee when Lamar said, "About those fellas from yesterday."

"Yeah, you mean the two goons and the gorilla?"

Lamar just jumped in, wanting to get the discussion behind him. He said, "Big Gio's guys. We gotta give 'em thirty percent of the girls' take starting Monday."

"What the hell do you mean that we have to take thirty percent of the girls' pay? I believe that would include me as well. The short and final answer to that would be no fucking way. Not now. Not ever. No. No. No. And don't ask me again."

As soon as she exploded, Lamar thought, 'Maybe I should have waited until she got some caffeine and sugar in her'.

Lamar was distracted by Peach's outfit. She had on pink, tight, high-cut shorts and a cutoff T-shirt. The shorts and the shirt were cut high. Lamar noticed that if she moved a certain way, he could glimpse a little of the bottom half of her breast. He thought, ' That is very sexy—somehow, sexier than seeing the entire production. Maybe it is the thought of what was above the little showing at the bottom that was so sexy'.

Peaches brought Lamar back to reality.

"Lamar! Did you hear what I just said? No pay cut. None."

"Yes, Peaches, since the drunks across the street at Mutts Bar heard you, I think I got the message. Let's talk about it."

"I don't need to talk."

Neither said a word. She glared at Lamar. Lamar stared back at her. A stand-off. Lamar had no chance of winning that battle and spoke first.

"You saw the gentlemen here yesterday?"

"You know, Lamar. It's a funny thing. I work here. I live here. I'm here every day almost every hour. I have a small world. So when three thugs show up trying to look like big-city mobsters, yes, I happen to notice them. In fact, you may recall that I ushered them into the back parlor so you could enjoy a private conversation. Yes, I saw them. And I assumed they are from Big Gio and want a little . . . what do they call it? 'Vig' or 'tribute' . . . something like that. Look, everybody in this part of the world knows that Big Gio controls the business that we are blessed to be such a lovely part of. In fact, we . . . me and my girls, are the reason there is any business at all. So yes, Mr. Lamar, I did see the gentlemen from yesterday. And apparently unlike you, expected them. Sooner actually. This takes you by surprise?"

"Well, here we are in little McMechen. Why mess with us?"

"Damn, Lamar. For the criminal mastermind that you're supposed to be, you can be a damned simpleton about so many things. Let me spell it out for you. If you had one girl, in a one bedroom house, Big Gio would want a piece. He's got to do it. One little pecker-head like you gets away with no pay, everybody else thinks they can too. Don't you think the other cathouse pimps, and other lowlifes might want to stretch their freedom from tribute just a wee bit if Big G let just anybody set up shop and operate without paying the juice?"

Lamar paused, then said, "I'm not a cathouse pimp."

"Well, la-de-dah. Pardon me. So you are a just Pussy Promoter and not a pimp, is that it? What's the cost?"

"Thirty per-cent."

"Of what? Thirty per-cent of what?"

"The gross."

"Every penny that walks in the door."

"Yes."

"That seems excessive. The Newport boys controlled Vinton County. I think Bobby T told me that they took fifteen. You wouldn't tell me a little fib, would you, Lamar?"

"Well, it can't come from the girls. Sam would leave. Maybe the others might stay. I don't know. Hell, I might start looking around."

"I'll take care of Sam."

"I would assume that. So that leaves Peaches. You going to take care of Peaches."

Lamar had not thought that one through. He said, "What about you take a fifteen per-cent cut. I'll take care of Sam, and the other girls take the thirty percent cut."

"I take no cut. You deal with Sam. The other girls . . . fifteen."

"Eighteen for the other girls."

"Done."

Lamar bowed his head slightly as if defeated and said, "I don't like it but I guess I have to live with it."

Peaches said, "Oh stop your whining and take this like a man. We'll raise the price of the product by twenty percent to cover the loss. I'm going to write this up for you to sign, and if you have any more trouble with the bastards from Wheeling, don't take it out on me and my girls. It's your problem, not ours."

"I can't put anything like that in writing."

"Yes, you can and you will. I'll keep a copy and you will keep a copy and it will be our little secret."

"I'm not gonna sign."

"You will sign or you will have an empty house tonight. I'll put the girls on strike."

"You can't do that. Peaches, you're not a labor union."

"You want to test me out, Lamar . . . test me out."

"Are you always this difficult in the morning?"

"Lamar, I can be difficult at any time of the damn day. And another thing. Those three galoots from yesterday—you pay the girls. I don't give away my girls for the boss to offer like lollipops. In fact, my girls don't work for free . . . ever. You send 'em upstairs with no charge. You pay."

Peaches, now finished with her daily dose of coffee and muffin, patted her lips with a cloth napkin, laid it softly on the tabletop, turned to look Lamar directly in the eyes, and said, "This ain't my first rodeo, Cowboy."

She got up and left.

Lamar noticed the lower half of her breast as she turned to get out of the chair, then watched her leave in her short shorts, thinking, 'she really looks good leaving a room too. Well that went pretty good'.

CHAPTER XXIV

LAMAR CASES THE JOINT

As Peaches left, Larry was coming in the kitchen for his morning dose of caffeine and his damnable rolled up cigarettes.

Larry said, "Hey, Boss. Top 'o the morning to you. What's got you in such a good mood?"

"You really don't want to know. I mean really."

"No need to get onery with me."

"Yeah, sorry."

"I'm just feeling good. Hey, who were those guys that came in yesterday? They looked like they meant business."

"As a matter of fact. They do. Mean business."

"Roxy told me they were from Big Gio. She's seen 'em around."

"Roxy knows about this? I'll be damned. I guess they all know."

"Boss, when you send guys to the girls to do what they do, they tend to get acquainted. Sometimes they actually talk. The girls were curious and maybe just a bit scared."

"I guess so. Yeah, they were Big Gio's boys come a-callin."

"I'm surprised they didn't come sooner."

"Not you too. Apparently everybody was expecting them sooner. So don't start on me, Larry. Just don't start."

"What? What'd I say?"

"Forget it. Look, I wanna come up with you to the mill tonight. Gonna look around. See the layout. Check out the warehouse. A few things like that."

"So we getting close to getting something done. I can't wait to quit that damn job."

"Don't get all excited about quittin' your job. The Big Job is not a one-night heist. May take eight, ten weeks."

"A robbery every night for eight to ten weeks might get us free room and board in Moundsville for eight to ten. Even if the place is a like a cemetery at night, someone would surely notice that."

"Well, Larry, I got good news for you. It's not gonna be every night. It will probably be once a week. I gotta see the place and do some calculatin'."

"So we rob the place once a week for a spell, then I can quit?"

"It might be a little curious if you happen to quit the day after our last visit. We will need you there a little longer just to see if anyone gets snoopin' around."

"Damn, I was hoping . . ."

"I know what you were hoping, but you may have to stay awake a couple of nights until we get what we want out of there. It won't be long after that. Gotta play it by ear just a bit, got it?"

"I guess so. I got a real nice place to sleep right now. Did I tell you about it? It's back in the northeast corner, near . . ."

Lamar cut him off and said, "No, Larry."

"No what?"

"No you did not tell me about it, and no I don't want to hear about."

Larry's voice went soft and he said, "It is a really nice place."

"I'm sure it is, Larry, I wouldn't expect anything less out of a Pritchitt."

Wheeling Steel Corporation was big. Seventeen thousand employees stretched up and down the mighty and magnificence Ohio River from Benwood, just south of Wheeling, to Steubenville, Ohio, to the north. Between those two points were several other plants. The third-largest steelmaker in the country.

Lamar said, "Okay, Larry, here's what I want to see. The gate where the trucks drive in. The forklifts and, of course the warehouse where they keep the metals."

Larry said, "The gate is what we just went through. The warehouse is back down this road. The big building at the end."

"Let's go to the warehouse."

"Okay, follow me."

They walked along a crushed gravel road to the back. The entire yard and facility was dark and dusty. It seemed like coal dust and other pollutants just hovered in the air. It felt as though the toxins invaded your skin and started to tear apart your lungs, your heart, your everything. Lamar thought of these poor suckers that spend a life here and dead at fifty-five. Just as bad as spending your life underground digging in a coal mine.

Larry took out a ring of keys and started fumbling around, trying to find the right key for the warehouse door. A sign on the door said:

The materials herein may be toxic

Caution is advised

Lamar said, "Larry, would you speed it up please?" Larry kept trying one key after another. Three minutes later the door was open.

"Larry," said Lamar, "mark that key so when the trucks come it doesn't take half a night to open the damn door."

"Good idea, Boss."

They stepped inside. The warehouse was divided into large sections of various metals and machinery. By far the largest were stacks of packed bags on pallets, each bag sealed with a security seal.

Lamar made a beeline to those stacks. The pallets were about four feet high and four feet wide. A notice was printed on each pallet:

Caution! Nickel Briquettes.

Un-Sintered

2,005 pounds per pallet

Store in cool, dry well-ventilated area.

Harmful if swallowed.

May cause sensitization by ingestion or skin contact.

Do not handle until all safety precautions have been met!

Lamar and Larry read the notice.

Larry said, "How would you eat a brick? Says here, harmful if swallowed. How could you swallow a brick?"

"Briquette," Lamar replied. "Briquette."

"What's that supposed to mean?"

"Well, Larry, I will research that word the next time I go out selling encyclopedias door-to-door. I don't know what the hell it is. I would guess it looks and probably is smaller that a brick."

"So how could you eat a small brick?"

"I don't think you could."

"What does that mean," Larry said, pointing to 'sensitization'.

"I don't know what the fuck that means. Would you please shut-up and lemme think a bit?" What Lamar was thinking was about the weight, 'Two-thousand pounds a pallet. Two pallets could fit on the truck. Over four thousand pounds a run. That is perfect'.

He turned to Larry and said, "Where are the forklifts?"

"Right this way, Boss."

"What's with this Boss thing you've started up?"

"I'm reading this pulp fiction thing about big-city crime bosses. All their crew call Mr. Big, 'Boss.'"

Lamar said, "I think I like Mr. Big better."

They turned a corner, and there was a forklift. To Lamar it looked like a small, regular truck, with a forklift attached to the front. It said on the back panel, 'Truclift'. Beneath that it said Clark Tractor Co, Battle Creek, Michigan, USA.

There was a vertical lifting cantilever in the front. Lamar judged the levers to be about seven feet in the air. A lifting platform sat at the bottom. Lamar could see that you slipped that steel platform under the pallet, then lift it up. He could see that the entire unit would then tilt back about six inches, so the load would be secure. The machine looked new.

Lamar said, "I think we got it all here. We just pull the truck to the loading dock, lift a pallet over to the truck. Do that twice and off we go. Slick and smooth. Should be in an out in an hour."

"I still don't know what half those words mean on the side there."

"Don't worry about it, Larry. Just remember you're our key man here. Key man in the entire operation."

Larry said, "If I am, we may be in trouble."

Lamar felt good. Satisfied that everything was in place, he left Larry to his sleeping quarters, packed up, and headed for the house on 21st Street.

He was thinking of his bed, enjoying the warmth and touch of Sam lying next to him.

As soon as Lamar and Larry left for the steel mill, Peaches said to Sam, "No more work for you tonight, we got our own work to do. Let's get up to my room right now for a little planning session."

Peaches turned to Roxy and said, "Roxy, Honey, we get any more customers tonight, you get 'em set up, would you please? Sam and me have some work we've got to get done."

"I got it covered, Peach."

Peaches pulled out a bottle of Mule Kick and said, "You're going to need this tonight, Sammy. Take a couple of good swigs."

They sat at Peaches' small table. Just enough room for two. The only light on was in the near corner. A stand-up. Peaches had casually thrown a gown over the top of the lamp. Sam liked the soft glow. Peaches liked it because the dim light covered a wrinkle or two. What you can't see is not there, right? She had other articles of clothing strategically placed around the room. A negligee casually over a chair arm. Stockings draped over a side table as if Peaches had just taken them off but forgot to put them up.

Peaches said, "You like the little hints I throw around the room? Gets the boys thinking properly doesn't?"

"Peach, I know you're experienced in this profession of ours, but I think the boys are already primed and pumped well before they get to the bedroom."

"Well, I have to use all the tricks now. Getting old at twenty-seven."

"Peaches, I know how old you are."

"Well, tack on a couple of years then and you got it."

"Oh, you mean like five?"

"Moving on now. You ever see me really pissed off?"

"Peach, darling, I see you pissed every day."

"Yeah, that's probably true, but I am talking about really pissed. Powerfully pissed."

Sam took a look swig. Her throat started burning, and she starting coughing and laughing at her plight at the same time. She sprayed Mule Kick as half went down and half went out.

They both started laughing. Getting a little buzzed.

Sam said, "Okay, we've had our little girl talk. What's going on? Was it the goombah's from Big Gio?"

"'Goombah's?'"

"Yeah, that means a guy in the company or the outfit as they call it, you know, a mobster."

"My, my are you the one that gets around."

"I went out with this mobster fella from Newport, across from Cincinnati in Kentucky. He was a big-time criminal. Told me I was a goo-mar. A mistress of a five-member or something like that. Guy had a lot of money, and he was generous too. After a year I wanted to break up with him, but I was afraid to. Fortunately for me, he got arrested, and I packed up and got out of there. But yeah, they would call each other goombah's."

Peaches said, "I bet you have some stories to tell, but yes, everybody knew those three were from Big Gio on sight. Everybody but your very own lover boy. He thought that little ol' Lamar didn't deserve any attention from the big boys up in Wheeling or Pittsburgh."

"Lamar can be so good about a lot of things, but damn he can just be plain ol' stupid at times. I am surprised they didn't come sooner."

"Everybody in the house is surprised about that. So he's got to pay, and he tells me the girls have to take a thirty percent pay cut. Thirty percent! Can you believe that?"

"At a thirty percent cut, I'm inclined to grab and go."

"And I would be prying those floorboards up with my hands and ripping my nails. Grab it all and go to California. But Sam, Lamar is no match for your madam, the unfailing Ms. Peaches. No you don't. So here is what I got for you and the others. You don't take a cut at all. In Lamar's words, 'I'll take care of Sam.' So I would start letting him take care of Sam. I take no cut, but the young ones take a cut of eighteen per-cent and don't worry we will raise the fare to twenty per-cent to cover. We are a little under market anyway, so it won't slow down the business. No freebies either. Lamar is going to pay for them as well."

"That doesn't sound too bad."

"I am, however, still pissed. Look, Lamar is going to be gone half the night. I think we should have our own little burglary tonight. Whatcha think?"

"I think I'm going to get this last shot down without spraying the walls and we are going to increase our personal wealth tonight by fifty per-cent."

"Down the hatch and open the boards," Peaches said.

Peaches opened her door and Roxy was walking by with a customer. Peaches quickly closed the door. Waited a minute. Now heard Amy's door open. Heard a man's voice say, "Hey, this is pretty sweet."

The two women stepped into the hallway and quickly crossed over to Lamar's room. Peaches turned the knob. Locked. She turned to Sam and said, "Quick, gimme your key."

Sam said, "Shit. In my room."

"Get your ass in gear. Get it before somebody else comes up here."

A few seconds later, Sam was back.

Peaches said, "What took you so long?"

Peaches reached for the key at the same time Sam was trying to unlock the door.

The key dropped to the floor. They both looked down and with dim lights in the hallway, couldn't see the key. They both dropped to their knees and starting to push their hands in a circular motion trying to find the key. Another thirty seconds passed.

Finally Sam said, "I got it."

"Well, use it!"

Sam fumbled with the key and found the lock, and they were inside Lamar's room.

Sam said, "Let's not turn the overhead lights on. Too much attention."

Sam crossed the room to a side table next to the bed, which had a small light. She turned it on, and the room was filled with a dim light.

They went quickly to floorboards. In the dim light, they did not see any hair. Lamar must have forgotten. They slowly and carefully pulled back the boards and saw a small, white patch of paper drop from the undercarriage of the boards to the floor of the opening.

Peach said, "There's the trap. We gotta put that back in place when we get the cash. Damn, we should have brought a bag to put this stuff in."

Sam jumped up and went to a drawer where she kept her personal things and grabbed a pair of nylon stockings. Handing one to Peaches she said, "One for you. One for me."

They both started filling up the nylons.

Peaches said, "Better than Christmas. We get our own little stockings on the mantle." Holding the stocking in one hand, they both reached into the money bag with the other...once, twice, three times, and stuffed the money in the nylons.

Peaches said, "Shit. Let's do one more."

Sam giggled. Peaches laughed. They did one more hand full.

They attached the white paper to the bottom of the boards. They put the boards back in place, turned out the light, and made their escape back to the safety of Peach's room.

There, they drank, laughed, and got silly.

They weren't aware they had been just a little careless.

It was late when Lamar got back to the house on 21st Street. Sam was in her own room, passed out. Lamar went to her room, undressed, and fell into bed, immediately falling asleep.

The sun burst through the next morning. Both the wayward lovers had slept late. Sam woke first and stumbled her way to the bathroom. Coming out of the bathroom, she sat on the edge of the bed and rubbed her eyes. Lamar started to stir.

Then she noticed it. The stocking filled with money. The "Sock Pot," as she and Peaches were calling it last night, laughing like hell over that one. She wasn't laughing now. It was tossed carelessly on the floor off to one side of the bed, clearly visible. Sam froze. She got up as Lamar said, "Hey, you comin' back in here?"

"One second, Sugar Baby."

As she reached for the stocking, Lamar started to turn to her. She quickly grabbed the stocking and threw it under the bed. With the same motion, she stumbled onto Lamar and fell on top of him as she offered a girlish squeal.

Lamar said, "Well, well. Just what I had in mind. Sam, I can't believe how well things are going for me. I just think it, and it gets done. Just like right now. I think it, and here you are. It's just amazin', ain't it?"

Sam thought she knew all the tricks of faking an interest with men. Not this time. She was a frozen cod. She was in a state of near paralysis. Sam didn't know what to do.

Lamar, ever so grateful, was a selfish lover and was back to sleep within minutes.

As soon as Lamar closed his eyes, Sam made her move to get the Sock Pot from under the bed.

She went to the other side of the bed . . . where Lamar could not see here. She crawled under the bed to get the stocking. She reached out and got a hand on the stocking. Just then there was a knock on the door. Sam started furiously backing out from under the bed with the Sock Pot in hand when Lamar said, "Who in the hell is that at this hour?"

Sam was now on her stomach but out from under the bed. She said from the floor, "I'll get it, Honey."

Lamar said, "What? Man, I can't hear anything today. You sounded like you were in a well."

"I'm right here. Go back to sleep," Sam said, praying that he would.

There was a hook on the door with a flimsy robe over it. Sam grabbed the robe and quickly wrapped it around the money. She opened the door slightly.

It was Peaches.

Sam immediately put a finger to her lips and handed Peaches the Sock Pot.

Peaches mouthed, "What the hell I am supposed to do?"

Sam said, "Get it out of here. He's here."

Sam closed the door.

Lamar said, "Who's that?"

"The maid. I told her not right now."

Lamar said, "Come on over here, Sugar. I got time for a quickie."

Sam said to herself, 'I can do this. I think I can. I'm almost sure I can'.

CHAPTER XXV

IS IT LOVE? OR MONEY, HONEY?

Lamar felt good. He thought, *'The Big Job is comin' along good. Much to my satisfaction. The Kelly will be ready soon. Maybe I should go to Curly's place and take a look. The poker games are bringing in some good cash now. Moving the games from Willy Jack's shop to the cathouse was a stroke of genius. I got a bunch of cash in my bedroom. I ought to check that this morning. Peaches has the house hummin' along. The girls are happy. Damn Peaches is a pain in the butt, but the girl knows how to run a whorehouse and with Big Cie's dud, the house is running about the same as it was before. And Sam. Well, Sam was incredible. That woman knew how to make a man feel, well, like a man. Maybe I'm in love. Maybe I should marry the woman. Maybe I should stop thinking crazy thoughts. Yes, Lamar, you got it goin'!*

Just then, Sam opened the door carrying a tray of coffee, orange juice, and cornbread muffins.

She said, "Here you are, Sweet Baby." She put the tray on the bed.

Lamar noticed the sweep of her morning gown. You couldn't see through it, but there was a suggestion that any moment you would get a glimpse of something. Little peek of this or that. Lamar said, "Damn, woman, you do have great legs."

"None of that right now, Honey. Just eat your muffin and drink your coffee. I have some things to do this morning."

"Hey, we still have a little time."

"Lamar, aren't you the one! No, I have to scoot. It's my time to use the bath, and I am taking a nice long soak." She leaned over and kissed him on the forehead and walked out.

Sam headed directly to Peaches' room and softly knocked. Peaches opened the door, saw it was Sam, grabbed her by the arm, and said, "Get in here. Let me get us some coffee. We need to be awake for this discussion."

She poured coffee for them and said, "Okay, give me an update and spare me everything but the facts."

"Well, lover boy is in glow-land in my bed. He came in late and he has been all lovey-dovey. Even this morning he wanted . . ."

Peaches interrupted and said, "Stick to the facts. No rabbit holes to run down. Just tell me what happened."

"Well, nothing really. He came in late. I think he came right to my room last night, didn't go to his room. Oh my gawd, Peaches. I passed out when I left here last night. The stocking with the money was right on the floor . . . what did we call it last night?"

"The Sock Pot."

"Right. Anyway, he was being amorous and I thought I was going to have a stroke right there. I got him back to sleep, hopped out of bed, grabbed the stocking to hide it, and damn if he didn't wake up. I threw the sock thing under the bed and climbed back in for another go.

Got him drowsy again and then had to crawl under the bed to get the sock. That's when you knocked. When I was under the bed. Lamar says, 'who's that?' and I said something, and he said it sounded like I was underwater or in a water well, or something like that."

"Rabbit hole."

"Well, I opened the door and gave it to you. Really, Peaches, I was ready to pass out!"

"Okay. I took the money and hid it in the garage. Over in a corner beneath a wood pile. We gotta get it to the bank as soon as we can, so that is item one today. Get the cash to the safe deposit box in the bank."

The girls sipped their coffee and thought.

Peaches said, "How about this? Tell Lamar that we are going to Wheeling to get you a nice dress and shoes. You want to go out on the town with him looking your best. And if he wants to drive us tell him no, he can't because you are had in mind something really sexy and you want it to be a surprise. You know the routine. Promise him a big night and all that. We'll drive the jalopy and hope it makes it."

"I have to take a bath. That's a must."

"Well, get going then, gal."

Sam took off. Peaches started searching for her largest handbag.

Lamar and Larry were both still sleeping.

When Lamar woke after his trip to the warehouse with Larry and his morning tryst with Sam, he started thinking . . . about Sam, 'This woman gets the blue ribbon as best in show. Woman's got it all—smart, funny, great legs, nicely rounded mounds. How does she get that flat stomach? I don't have a flat stomach; she does. I think I'm in love. No, it can't be that—it's just months outta Moundsville. That'll turn any man love struck at the first female that comes along. Yes, that's what it is. But what if I didn't have her, how would I feel? Rotten. One rotten son-of-a-bitch, that's how. So maybe I ought to tie her down and put a ring on her finger. Can I handle that? I can always get a little on the side, can't I? Hell, I own a cathouse. She might not like that. Where could I get a ring? Maybe hit a couple of doctors' houses and check out the jewelry. Nah, the wife would have it on a finger. Maybe I could buy one cheap. Lemme think. Who steals rings? Four-fingers, that's who. That safe cracker who blows up safes and shit. He got out a couple months before me. Maybe I ought to see him. See what he's got. Yeah, I think I'll marry Sam. She might want to keep workin'. That's all right. Bring a little extra money into the family. Maybe I will tell her tonight. You don't need a ring to start makin' the plans, right?'

Lamar dressed and went to his room. His room was not cluttered. He was neat. His years in juvie and prison taught him to keep his personal items limited and in their place. Then if it was gone from its place, meaning stolen, he would know. Some guys you just can't trust.

Lamar didn't have many clothes, but he did have a large closet. He kept extra Mule Kick there. Put it elsewhere in the house, and it would quickly disappear. He tried it in the kitchen at first. Five gallons gone in an instant. Of course, the disappearance made a happy household of girls and whomever else wondered by. So he moved it to his room. He had more under his bed, plus a pint or two for personal use in and on his bed side table.

In the evening, he and Sam would have fun getting tipsy together. Once, after a particularly great romp, Sam jumped out of bed, grabbed a glass half-filled with Mule Kick, jumped back into bed and said, "That was so great, let's celebrate."

Lamar thought, 'Maybe that's when I fell for her. No, it wasn't just that, she is just so much damn fun, all the time. Yes, this woman is gonna be Mrs. Lamar'.

He had a full-length mirror in one corner. A small table and two chairs. The bed was wood. Solid and traditional. Like Willy Jack's family would want. Beautiful quilted bedspread.

Patterns in blue and green and white. It was a comfortable room, and Lamar felt right at home. In fact, without this house that Loretta provided, maybe none of his success would have happened.

He thought about his sister. *'She tries so hard to do good. All that religion. Trying to make everything and everybody better. Willy Jack was okay, but damn he don't like me'.* Lamar well aware of Willy Jack's feeling about him. He didn't care. Didn't matter a wit. He didn't like Willy Jack's condescending attitude either. He did like Jack, Loretta's oldest, and the other two kids, Willy and Rebecca. Jack, a lawyer with Sprat.. Lamar smiled and thought, *'Maybe that's why I like young Jack; I'm gonna need him someday. Loretta is leaving me alone. That's good. I sure as hell don't want her down here snooping around, just buggin' me to go to church. Maybe I'll show up this Sunday. Give the sis some hope that I am straight as a deacon. Maybe I'll take Sam with me. That would be something. Sam and me in a church run by those Mormons. I think I'll do that. Show some respectability'.*

As he approached the floorboards, he was quietly humming a tune, feeling good. His mood went from shine to shitty in an instant.

All four hairs had been moved. The paper was still in place, but the hairs moved. This was no accident. Someone had been into the stash. He quickly removed the bags and was relieved to see the bags still in place. He looked inside the bag. All cash, nothing strange. He pushed the bags away to see them better. One bag looked slightly less full than the other. He fluffed them up, thinking that would even them out. Still the bag that had been on top looked a little smaller than the other bag.

'Someone, was getting into the top bag and taking cash out. They had to be thinking that he just wouldn't notice because they weren't taking a lot. Just enough so he wouldn't notice. Sneaky. Sneaky. Sneaky and so very Peachy. It's gotta be Peaches. Anyone from outside the house would take both bags and be gone. Larry doesn't care. Sam doesn't know. None of the other girls could come in this room. Oh. Roxy might, but it doesn't fit. And besides, if Roxy wanted something, she would just ask her daddy, or Larry. No, it's got to be that conniving little thief, Peaches. No more cash out. It was starting to go fast with the truck and all the other stuff. Well, the Big Job is right around the corner. Then I got some cash flowin' again'.

He was anxious to catch Peaches now that he had convinced himself that Peaches, and only Peaches, she is the one and only, or as a lawman would put it, 'No known confederates'.

Still early in the day, Lamar knocked on Peaches's door. She answered, and Lamar said, "Peaches, my darling, may I have a word?"

Peaches opened the door and walked to her coffee station.

"Lamar, would you like some coffee?"

"Thank you, Peach. That would be welcomed. I need a little boost."

Both spoke with a little strain in their voices. Not overly noticeable, but just a little tense.

"Why thank you. You know I like it black."

"As I recall. What's on your mind, Sport?"

Lamar was taking a seat at the small table where Peaches and Sam had done all their conniving.

Lamar said, "I want Sam to have the night off. I'll pay for it so don't get your dander up. I have a little surprise for her."

Peaches was at full alert, looking for any clues as to Lamar's thoughts.

She said, "May I ask what is the occasion?"

Lamar, said, "Well, Peaches, are you sitting down?"

"I believe so Lamar, but what I am wondering is if you are going to tell me you need glasses since I am sitting here directly in front of you."

"Figure of speech, Peach," Lamar said with a little smile. "Nope, the big news is that I am gonna get married. Yes, sir, I think I'm gonna do it."

Peaches was flummoxed. She coughed up a little coffee, settled back in, and said, "So whose the lucky girl, Lamar?"

"Oh, come on. Don't do that. You know who."

Peach went a little pale. She wasn't going to pass out, but she thought she just might be close.

"You mean Sam?"

"Of course, who you think it was gonna be, you?"

"Lamar, I am eternally grateful that it is not me. But I'm a little confused here. You said married. So you and Sam have talked about this and she said . . . what?"

"No, we have not talked about this but we will tonight."

"So you haven't actually got her to agree to this as of right now?"

"Well, no, but I don't see no problem with that."

"Did it ever occur to you that she might not want to be Mrs. Lamar McKenna?"

"Well, no. It didn't occur to me. But I think she is just as much for me as I am for her."

"You mean, crazy in love, with the emphasis on 'crazy'?"

"Well, yes."

With the breaking news, the two paused to sip. Lamar had a goofy look on his face looking right at Peaches. Peaches was looking toward the window to her right thinking, *How does this affect me and the money Sam and I have in a joint account? I gotta get to Sam before this idiot does'.*

She turned back to Lamar and said, "This is great news. Maybe we can have the wedding here with a big celebration in the yard."

"Peachy, that's nice of you to offer my house, but I got a big family up that holler just behind us. I'm thinkin' I'll make it a back-country affair up at my parents place."

"That's sounds awfully romantic, Lamar. Make a girl real proud to be surrounded by the McKenna clan. Seems like you got it all worked out, Lamar. You being the mastermind and all. Maybe you can mastermind a weddin' too."

Lamar had quite a bit of work to do before his night with Sam. He made a list:

1. Get flowers.

2. Get candles. Maybe four or five, for tonight.

3. Talk to Four Fingers, if you can find him. Probably not.

4. Tell Larry.

5. Tell Ma and Pappy, Loretta. Hooch.

6. Get that new thing for Sam that she was talking about. The silk thing. 'Chemess.' Get her one of those. Maybe in peach.

7. Find out where I could buy the chemises thing. Peaches would know.

He went back to Peaches room. She was seated again at the coffee table with fresh coffee. Lamar said, "Let's punch this coffee up a bit. I got a busy day and not much time."

Peaches did just that. She said, "Okay, Lamar, what now?"

"I need some things and I thought you could help me out."

"Okay."

"First of all, I need to set the mood. I need some flowers and candles."

"Candles are easy. We got plenty right here. I'll give you as many as you want when you leave."

Peaches thinking, *'I hope, really praying that is very soon'*.

She continued and said, "The flowers, go down by the courthouse. You know that little market across the street from the back of the court house? Go there. The Italian that runs the place will have a nice little section in the back of the store. Anything else?"

"Lemme look my list."

Peaches could see a list he laid on the table. Looked like a third-grader had written it. Lamar placed his finger on the paper and ran it down, line by line.

"Here it is. I want to get her a couple of sexy things. You know like maybe some see-through stockings or one of those chemess things."

"Stockings are easy, but what's the other thing . . . a 'chemess'?"

"Yeah, a silk thing. You know, silky and sexy."

Peaches was stumped. She paused and said, "You mean a *chemise*. I think that is French and so you say *shuh-meez. Shuh-meez.*"

Lamar brightened up and said, "Yeah, that it's . . . a chemess, and a couple of other sexy things."

"That is a little trickier . . . but here's what you do. You might want to write some of this down. Do you have a pencil?"

"Oh, yeah, right here. Go ahead. I'm ready."

"There is a department store in downtown Wheeling. Right on Market Street. Right around Twelve or Fourteenth Street . . . right in that area. Takes up a big piece of the block. Big sign on the corner says, "The Hub." Go there and go up a flight to the women's shoes. It's back and to the right. There is a girl in there by the name of Daphne. Tell her Peaches sent you. She'll take care of you."

Lamar was scribbling it all down and said, "Peaches sent me. Daphne. The Hug on Fourteenth and Market."

"*The Hub*. Not *the hug*."

"Got it."

Lamar paused. He looked at Peaches with a hard stare.

'Not now', he thought. *'Not now, I'll talk to her about the money later'''*

CHAPTER XXVI

LAMAR ON BENDED KNEE...QUITE A SIGHT

In a state of high excitement, Lamar found Larry in his second-favorite spot in the house, the kitchen. As Lamar walked in, Larry was saying to Cassandra, "Miz C, you can make a ham-and-cheese sandwich taste better than a Thanksgivin' dinner. This here sandwich is so good it'll make your liver quiver and bladder splatter."

"Oh, thank you, Larry. I do believe you enjoy my cookin' better 'an anyone around here."

"I surely do, Lamar! Sit down and have the best damn ham-and-cheese sandwich you ever gonna have. Make you want to slap your grandma."

Lamar said, "Don't have time. We gotta a lot to do and we gotta get movin', so slap your granny and grab your sandwich. We goin' shoppin'."

"Shoppin'? You got another big truck in mind?"

"Come on. We can talk in the car, and no it's a far thing from a truck today."

Larry picked up his sandwich and soda Pop, and they headed to the car.

Lamar said, "By the way, you been up in the holler and pickin' up a new pattern of speech."

"You mean my new hillbilly talk?"

"I do indeed."

"It's like this—Roxy and me went over to Mutt's Bar the last couple of weekends, and they had some folks playin' and pickin' in there. Called themselves the Skillet Lickers. That's cute, ain't it? Skillet Lickers. Anyway, they have this peculiar way of singin' and talkin' and I'm pickin' up on it. Bein' from O-hi-ah, we don't talk like that over in Vinton County."

"I know how Vinton County folks talk, Larry. I spent quite a bit of time over hittin' those banks with your cousin, Bobby T, and his crew. So how do people talk over in Vinton County?"

"Well, it ain't like they talk around here. Over there I would say . . . lemme think here. I would call it High Kentucky talk. No, no that's not quite it . . . it's Sophisticated Kentucky speech. That's it. Sophisticated Kentuckian."

Lamar said, "There ain't nothing sophisticated about Kentucky, 'cept maybe the derby."

They hopped in the car and took off, leaving a trail of dust in their wake.

Peaches watched the car leave and quickly went to Sam's room. Sam opened the door, sleepy-eyed.

Peaches said, "Sam, get over here right now."

"Over where?"

"My room. Where else? We got some major planning to do. I'll get some coffee in you and wake you up. Hurry up! Just get over here. Don't get dressed; just throw on a robe."

A minute later, Sam dragged herself into Peaches's room.

"So what's up? I think I was dreaming when you knocked."

Peaches already had their coffee poured. They sat at the small table. Sam lifted her coffee as Peaches said, "Lamar is gonna ask you to get married tonight." Sam coughed with her mouth filled with coffee. A muffled humphaaaa, then coffee all over her pink gown.

Sam looked down at the coffee spill and said, "Damn. This is my favorite kick around. Lamar is . . . what did you say? Marriage? Tonight?"

"Not marriage tonight, but a proposal tonight. He is running around town right now getting you flowers and a teddy, what he calls a Che-mess, by the way. He paid me for your night, so you're not on call. He is gonna make it a big night."

"That is so sweet. You know Lamar does have some nice qualities about him."

"You mean you would consider it?"

"Why not? He is a good-looking man, and we know he's got some money. I could cut down my workload, maybe even quit altogether. There are some positives here, Peachy."

"Sam . . . Sammy. Are you vaguely aware of what Lamar does for a living? He is a criminal. He is a career criminal. He goes to some place where he gets free room and board every other year or so compliments of this state or that."

"Well, yes. He does have an unconventional lifestyle. That's for sure. But, Peaches, so do we, now don't we? Besides, he is not boring. Every day there is something a little crazy, something a little different. You know, I never had a guy ask me to get married. It's got me thinkin'."

"Well, think of this. You have also been stealing from him."

"So what? How's he gonna find out about that? We are not telling him and nobody else knows. Besides, as Mrs. McKenna, I could live off his cash. Might not be a bad way to go."

Both the women were now in deep thought as they sipped their coffee.

Peaches said, "Want a heat-up? By the way, soak that gown in cold water, wring it out, and then just dab it. Don't scrub. Just a gentle dab. That'll get rid of those stains."

Pouring the fresh coffee, Peaches said, "So you're gonna go along with this?"

"Let's just say, I'm contemplating real hard."

Lamar and Larry had picked up the flowers and were headed to the department store in Wheeling call the Hub. As they approached the building, Larry said, "I been here with Peaches. She gets things for the girls. Mostly upstairs with Daphne."

"Oh, you met Daphne?"

"Certainly have, and when you met her, you won't forget her."

"Really, why's that?"

"You'll find out."

"Well, lead the way."

Larry said, "What's this all about anyway?"

"I'll give you the whole story in the car goin' back. Right now, I want to get somethin' nice for Sam."

"If you are getting from Daphne what Peaches usually gets for the girls, the 'somethin' nice for Sam' just might be somethin' really nice for Lamar. Might that be the case?"

"You may have something there. You know, Larry, every so often you display superior insight to the strangest concerns of the human condition."

"We Pritchitts do have a way."

Larry headed to the shoe department on the second floor, near the back. He said, "There she is, over there," pointing toward the back.

Lamar's first thought when he saw Daphne was, *That may be the most beautiful woman I have ever seen. Blonde with a tint of auburn. About twenty-eight or so. Tall as I am. And in heels, taller. She looks like one of those Greek statues with over-exaggerated perfection'.*

Lamar approached her and said, "Excuse me, are you Daphne?"

"Why, yes, how can I help you?"

"Peaches sent me. Said you could help me with a purchase or two."

"You know Peaches, do you? Well, you're the first."

"First what?"

"She never sent any of her . . ." Daphne stopped herself. Then said, "Any of her friends here."

"I just wanted to pick up a couple of items, and she said this was the place and you are the one to talk to. I am kinda her boss."

"Oh, I see. That must be challenging . . . being the boss of Peaches."

She smiled, and said, "And who is the gentleman looking so good in his police uniform?"

Lamar said, "This here's Larry. He is my associate. He's a security guard."

Daphne said, "Well, good for you, Larry. I feel more secure now than I did a few minutes ago."

Larry, also taken with the beauty before him, just nodded, holding his security hat in hand.

"Well, follow me fellas."

Lamar and Larry appreciated the view as they followed Daphne and entered a room where women's lingerie was displayed on life-like mannequins.

Daphne turned to Lamar and said, "What did you have in mind?"

Lamar's first thought was he would like to see Daphne in that short little red thing that you could see through. He said, "I'm not sure. Maybe I can just look around." He was buying some time to gather his thoughts.

He said, "What do you think, Larry?"

Larry got up close to Lamar and said in a whisper, "I think I'm getting one."

"One what?" Lamar whispered back.

"You know," he said, pointing downward. "One of those."

"Get behind that mannequin over on the other side of the room and calm down. Look at the wall or somethin' and think about your job."

Daphne said, "Lamar, maybe if you could tell me the occasion I could help you pick out an item or two."

He said, "Oh, nothing special. Just a happy evening with a lady friend. She said she liked those che-messes. Things like that."

Daphne said, "A che-mess? I bet you mean a chemise."

"Yeah, that's what I said."

Daphne smiled and said, "Lot of people have trouble pronouncing that, Lamar. What color do you favor?"

"Peach. Yeah, peach. Maybe red or pink."

Daphne would pick an item and Lamar would buy it. He found he had trouble telling Daphne no and ending up buying three pairs of nylons, a garter, a pink and a peach chemise, a flimsy house gown and what Daphne called a "hostess gown," pink satin slippers, a boudoir cap (nicely decorated with lace and six, tiny, silk ribbon roses), and finally a semi-laced step-in corset of elastic with sections of pink at both the front and back.

Lamar didn't understand a word Daphne was saying and didn't want to expose his lack of knowledge, so he just kept quiet and would said, "Okay, I will take that too." His bill ended up being $189.42—one of Daphne's biggest sales from the lingerie room.

Lamar was in a state of part bewilderment, part embarrassment, and part seeing images of Daphne in any one of the items he had just bought.

Lamar gathered up his packages and gathered up a cooled-down Larry, who had been wandering aimlessly throughout the room. Reluctantly he said good-bye to Daphne, told her he would be back, and headed back to the house on 21st Street.

Lamar was feeling good. Headed back to the house, he wasn't even thinking about his lost money. Well, he did think about it, but it had become a secondary matter to the big event tonight and his shopping spree. Dealing with Peaches could wait, and besides, it didn't look like too much was gone.

Larry was playing with the lock on the glove compartment of the car. Opening it. Closing it. Click. Click. After the third click, Lamar said, "Larry, dammit, would you stop doing that?"

"Doin' what?"

"Playing with the glove compartment lock."

"Oh, yeah. I was just thinkin' and it helps me think if I can get some movement goin' in my hands. When I am contemplatin', I actually like to walk around and think. Seems like the walkin' helps me think. So the hand movement is my replacement since I can't walk right now, being as we are in a car. I discovered this about two years ago when me and Bobby T were gonna . .. ."

"Slow down, Henrietta. I got something big to tell you and I don't need a dissertation outta you about how you turn on your thinkin' apparatus."

"Okay, but Lamar, did you forget my name? You just called me Henrietta. I'm Larry, ain't I? That Daphne woman rattle your brain that much that you forgot my name?"

"I just said 'Henrietta' because you were goin' on like a little ol' lady and I wanted you to stop talkin' for a minute cause I got something big to tell you." Lamar broke into a little laugh and said, "That damn Daphne gets a man's attention real fast, don't she? Never seen anything quite like it."

"Well, I'm not a little old lady, Lamar." Larry was looking like his momma just got after him for wettin' the bed. Showing a little hurt.

"Hey, look, Buddy. I know you're not a little ol' lady. You're are my right hand man and all that, so please find it in your heart to forgive me, okay? So now can we get to the business of the day?"

"Well, I'm not stoppin' ya. And yeah, Daphne is plum pretty and tall as a drink of ice tea."

Lamar laughed and said, "Here we go. You go to Mutt's Bar this weekend and listen to the hillbilly singers?"

"I did indeed, and my vocabulary is increasin' every day and I'm gettin' smart as all get out."

"Glad to know it. Lemme me get right to it. I'm gonna get married to Sam."

"Married? What do you mean, married? You mean like a Ma and Pa kinda married?"

"Yep. Like a Ma and Pa. With a preacher and all that stuff. Gonna hitch up, proper."

"Where do you know a preacher from?"

"Not important, Larry. We got preachers on every corner in McMechen and up in the holler too. The thing here is Sam and I are gonna get hitched."

"Where's this blessed event gonna take place and when?"

"I don't know. I just got the idea in my head this morning. You are sure full of questions. I guess it would be up at Pappy and Ma's. More room there, and Ma throws a mean outdoor picnic and barbeque. I suppose the bride might like a say as well."

"I do like your Ma's pecan pie and cornbread muffins. Think she would have some of that?"

"Well, tradition dictates that you have what they call a wedding cake, so we would probably have a big weddin' cake?"

"I'm fond of cake. How's a wedding cake different from a real cake?"

"Well, it's a real cake, just a little fancier, I guess."

"I do like cake. So I guess congratulations are in order . . . congratulations to you and Miss Sam."

Lamar said, "Thank you, Larry," but he was thinking, 'Damn, that Daphne is something . . . yes she is. That girl is something else, indeed.

Peaches was in the kitchen taking a late afternoon tea and dipping with Fig Newton cookies. Her favorite. She was thinking about Sam and Lamar. Lamar and Sam: 'Married? Seems impossible. Why would Sam even want to marry a guy like Lamar who is always a scam away from five to ten in some prison? If Sam married Lamar, she certainly would have some control over Lamar's riches. Would she tell Lamar about our little Sock Pot? What would Lamar do? Demand it back for sure . . . but I don't think Lamar is the killing kind. But, would he? He's not Big Gio. I don't think. I gotta have another sit down with Sam'.

Sam was not with the other girls in the reception room, listening to "Oh Gee Oh Gosh Oh Golly I'm in Love." Up to her room. Not there. Down the hall to the bathroom. Peaches knocked and Sam said, "Who is it?"

"Peaches."

"Oh, come on in, Doll."

Sam was in the tub with bubbles up to her chin, a sponge in one hand rubbing gently on a her left leg, which was pointed to the ceiling. The bathroom was large enough to have a wooden chair in a corner next to a closet for towels and other bathroom essentials. Peaches pulled the chair close to the tub, took and seat, and said, "So you getting spiffy for the big night?"

"Well, it's good to have the night off for a change. I'm thinking I could get used to that."

Sam lowered her leg, put the sponge up, and said, "Peach, Honey, light up one of those cig's for me, would'ya? There, right on the counter next to the towels."

Peaches lit up a Lucky Strike. Took a puff. Inhaled. Let it out and handed the cigarette to Sam. Sam stretched and rested her head on the back of the tub.

Peaches lit her own Lucky, took a puff, and said," How you gonna play this tonight?"

"Well, I'm going to get out of here and look over all the nice things that Lamar got for me, select something really sexy, and head over to Lamar's little love shack, where I will apply all the wonderful tricks you taught me so many years ago and have Lamar laying on his back as flat as Samson after Delilah got through with him. I've always like that name . . . Delilah, don't you?"

"So sounds like you are gonna say yes to being Mrs. Lamar. Gettin' ready to visit him down in Moundsville, are you?"

"Lamar going off to jail every so often might be a bonus. Ever think of that? Give me a chance to reorganize myself without taking care of his needs and delights. Might even give me access to most all of his ill-gotten gains. There are some upsides, don't you think, Peachy?"

"I never quiet heard it expressed like that. 'Whoopee-do—my man's off to do three to five. I can start livin' now'!

"Peaches, I've never been married. Why'd you get married?"

"Because I thought I was pregnant, and I was sixteen."

"How long'd it last?"

"Until I realized I wasn't pregnant and the boy was a worthless idiot."

"Well, I kinda like Lamar."

"Sounds like true love."

They paused to take a long puff.

Peaches broke the silence and said, "So you say yes and start the wedding plans. What are we going to do about our little hidey-hole?"

"I've thought about that some," she said and took another long pull. "Maybe we do nothing. Maybe we just keep reaching in ever so often. Both of us. I don't think Lamar is going to open up his little piggy bank and say, 'Have it, Sam, my love.' What do you think?"

"Given those options, I think I would opt for just a little something ever so often. Build up a little security. So you think we could do that?"

"Probably a lot easier than what we are doing now."

"And why, dear Sam, would you do that?"

"Girls gotta have a little protection, don't she? A little getaway cash, just in case. As I said, I doubt that Lamar would be handing over much cash to me just for being Mrs. Lamar. You see him doin' that?"

"Handing over cash? To you? To anyone? I don't think so. I am assuming that he will profess his undying love to you tonight. It sounded that way when he came all dewy-eyed, asking about the fun store to get you some 'chemess' as he called it."

"Wait till I show you all the stuff he got me. Really nice things. I assume Daphne at Big Hub?"

"You got it."

"I'm surprised he didn't propose to her. Every man gets around her starts panting like a hound dog."

"Kinda of like you, sexy Sam."

"I don't think quite like Daphne."

Peaches said, "Okay, we stay on track.

"Absolutely."

"Wear your new 'che-mess.' Lover boy will like that."

Sam put on the chemise. The hosting gown over that. High heels. Red lipstick. Hair just so. Pretty, powdered, shaved, and bathed. At eight she knocked on Lamar's door.

Lamar opened the door with a bottle of champagne and a corkscrew. He had a robe on, opened in front. Underneath the robe he had on a Topkis Union men's underwear in soft, white cotton with shoulder straps and a body shirt that reached to his knees. There was a drop seat flap. Bottom, back. He also had on long, black socks with garters holding them up. No shoes, but white leather slippers. A very romantic look by Lamar's standards.

Sam took a look and almost broke into laughter. Instead she put one hand on a hip and one hand in the air and said, "So, sailor, how do you like the look?"

Lamar stood there, just staring at her. Up and down.

"Oh my gawd, woman. Get your sweet ass in here. Right now before I take you in the hallway."

Sam stepped inside. Lamar pushed the door closed with a foot as he pulled Sam close and kissed her with passion.

Lamar held out a bottle champagne and said, "Look at this, Baby. Dom Perignon Brut. The best that's made."

As he started to open the champagne bottle, he said, "Lemme look at you. You do fill out a chemess, now don't you? Some women are sexy. Some are downright beautiful. You, Miss Sam are sexy, sexy, sexy, and throw in the beauty stuff too. You do fill it all out, right nice."

She said, "Well, thank you, Lamar. You look right interesting as well."

He poured. He sipped. She drank half a glass with the first taste.

"Ain't you the speedy one. I guess I will have to catch up." They both emptied their glasses and Sam held out her glass and said, "Again."

Lamar complied. Within ten minutes, Sam was up to the evening's challenge, and Lamar was ready to grab Sam and be off with her to wonderland.

He did. They did.

Midway through their lovemaking, Lamar was intense. Sam was surviving. She was thinking, should she or shouldn't she? Playing the possibilities around in her head. She was startled when Lamar started making loud noises. Grunting, swearing, almost yelling and as a wrap-up finale, "Yes! Yes! Yes!" The noisy Lamar had made his first appearance.

Sam feared that Peaches would be running through the door at any minute thinking she would be just in time to save Sam.

Lamar, with a sweaty sheen over his body, rolled over and said . . . nothing. Until he said, "Baby. That was the best ever. I don't know how you do it, but damn you do."

She started laughing. Lamar thought it was because Sam had been so happily, well-satisfied with his performance.

The thought that crossed her mind was far from Lamar's five-star performance. She was thinking about that young doctor that came to see the girls last month. His name was, fittingly, Dr. Fox. The girls started calling him Dr. Foxy. They all decided that they greatly preferred Dr. Foxy to the elderly doc that was their regular. Young Dr. Fox was earnest and rather shy with the girls. He had a list of things to read off as part of his examination. Things like, "Do you have trouble with your stool?" Or "Do you feel like you are turning yellow or some other color?" Silly things like that. Then, reading the next item from the list, he said to Sam, "Are you sexually active?" Sam said, "No, I just lay there."

Dr. Fox looked up from his list and smiled and said, "Have you ever served in the armed forces?"

Sam reached over and patted Lamar on his tummy as if to say, "Good puppy."

Lamar got out of bed. He was naked. Beside the bed, he knelt on one knee. He looked serious. All that Sam could see . . . he was naked. Nothing was contained. He was flopping loose. The mighty Thor of Lamar had been reduced to a recessed nub as if searching for a home after a mighty battle.

Sam was mortified. She said, "Lamar, you can't do this in your current condition. This is not a pretty sight. Get your damn underwear on at least. Maybe your robe too. Cover up as much as you can."

Confused, Lamar hesitated.

Sam said, "Now, Lamar. *Now*. Get something covering every inch of your body."

Lamar jumped up and did as told.

Back to his proposal position, Lamar said, "Sam. You're the best sex I ever had. Will you marry me?"

Sam said, "Lamar, that is the worst proposal a woman ever received. An all-time worst. Why don't you try again?"

"What? What'd I say?"

"Don't, Lamar. Just give it another go."

He composed his thoughts, then thought some more.

"Sam, I am pretty sure I love you. Will you marry me?"

"That's good enough, Lamar. Yes, Lamar, I will take that chance with you."

Lamar started throwing off clothes and hopped in bed.

"Let's celebrate!" he said gleefully.

THE BRIDE WORE WHITE

The wedding was to be at Pappy and Ida Mai's place. The home where they raised Lamar, Loretta and Hooch and where Pappy kept two or three stills in operation.

Five miles up the dirt road from town. The McKenna's had been in this place for almost a hundred years. It was now their birthright. The house was old and from the front looked rustic. Humble. Small. But over the years, rooms had been added and the cabin greatly expanded, now too big for the elderly couple. The red spruce wood used to build the cabin had turned to a beautiful patina of dark gray and brown. The porch out front was filled with sitting chairs, a rocking chair and two small tables. All wood and all hand made.

A path from the front of the house, lead to a barn and tool shed. Beyond that, fenced in yards that kept a few animals; chickens, pigs, cows and goats. A corn field could be seen behind the barn. A vegetable garden part of the pasture as well.

Not far from the living area was a creek with rolling clear, cold water over white and brown rocks and stones. At the quiet times you could hear the sounds of the water moving southward to feed the Ohio River.

The area around the house was filled with trees. Trees in brilliant efflorescence with early fall foliage. The bright burnt orange and crisp scarlet of Sugar and Red Maple. Sycamore and Oak trees cast various shades of yellow, orange and red. Crimson Dogwood and the bright yellow of Walnut trees. Radiant greens of Oak, Ash and Basswood. A spectacular kaleidoscope of color and incredible beauty. Fallen leaves provided a soft and colorful path.

The McKenna's had fought for this land. Died for it. Crossed a violet ocean. Fought through thickets bush by bush. Tree by tree. They had cut and built and sweated, gave birth and buried their dead. This was their land now. They believed it to be the most beautiful, satisfying, giving place on Earth.

Pappy and Ida Mai had a favorite tree. An Elm, fifty-feet high. Broad, sweeping branches formed a canopy of shade. Under it's branches, this creation of a bounteous nature, provided cool shade from the summer sun. They called it God's tree. Over their life together they would sit under that tree and discuss all of life's blessing and problems. The would sip their coffee in the morning dew, drink their lemonade on hot summer's days, taste their shine in early evening's special moments. Pappy and Ida Mai loved this tree.

It was under the God Tree that Ida Mai told Pappy that she was going to have their first child; that turned out to be the twins, Lamar and Loretta. Here was where Pappy told Ida Mai her that he would gone for awhile---off to prison in Atlanta for Moonshining Under this tree Loretta was married to Willie Jack. And now under this tree, Lamar would be wedded to a woman that Pappy and Ida Lou had never met.

Lamar, of course, wanted the biggest shindig the hollow had ever seen. Every family in the hollow had been invited. Even the McCoy's. Lamar's crew was there. Larry and Curly. Bobby T was there..

Peaches was the Maid of Honor. Amy and Roxy, the bridesmaids. At one of the planning meetins with all the girls Peaces said, "Ladies, I think's it's been awhile since any of us have been maids, in the strictest sense of the word."

Hooch, was the best man. Ida Mai had cornered her son's and said, "Boys, I know this will be painful for the both of you, but there were be no fightin between you two today. We are gonna get Lamar married properly. God knows he needs it."

Larry was asked to be a groomsman. He said, "What's that?"

When told that he was to be part of the wedding and standing with Lamar during the ceremony, his eyes watered as he said, 'This is one of the greatest moments of my life'.

The McKenna's would only be missing Hooch's son, Nick, who was enjoying free room and board in Lexington, Kentucky, for robbing a floating casino in Newport.

It was a beautiful fall day for the wedding. Bright and sunny. The foliage was spectacular. Most everybody in the hollow and many from town were headed to the big event. Rumor had it that Lamar had hit it big and was determined to have the biggest, best party the hollow had ever seen. Lamar had hired a carpenter from the hollow to build a dance stage and add four more large picnic tables, which were now scattered about the yard along with chairs.

The wedding was to be at noon. The party would carry through the night. Lamar had hired a carpenter from the hollow to build a dance stage and add four more large picnic tables, which were now scattered about the yard along with chairs.

Peaches was Maid of Honor. Roxy and Amy were the bridesmaids. Curly and Bobby T joined Larry as groomsmen. Reverend David D. Dronsfield presiding. The Reverend was the minister of record at the Moundsville Prison. Every Sunday Lamar would help him set up a room for his preaching. Help with the chairs, put the song books out, round up some of the men.

The Reverend was a large, imposing man with a full beard. He had been an all-state linebacker at Union High School, all-conference for Marshall University. He looked like a preacher in a black suit, high starched white shirt, collared, carrying a large bible by his side.

The planning by the girls of 21st Street had been exquisite. All of the woman had been excited and eager to get things ready, and perfect for the big day. Peaches, of course, co-ordinated the effort. She become the wedding planner and did so with her usual magisterial efficiency.

The gown was the subject of intense conversation between all the women. They had almost universal agreement on a white, form fitting, gown with a modest trailing crown that flowed down the back. The bridesmaids were a purple, loose fitting dress that had puffy shoulders and long sleeves. The girls were almost happy with the selection. They bought the clothes at the Big Hub under the supervision of Daphne.

Lamar had a new brown suit of tweed with wide lapels, vest, white shirt and a red bow tie. He worn a large brown fedora that looked too big for his head. Larry, and the rest of the groomsmen worn their best pants, suspenders and a white shirt.

Larry drove the girls to Pappy's place, including Sam, about the same time that Curly drove Lamar.

About eleven in the morning, most all of the hundred and fifty or so people at the wedding were mulling about, drinking lemonade, sassafras tea, coffee, and a few if the men were spiking their drinkings with a touch of Mule Kick. All of the girls were in a back bedroom, getting Sam ready. Lamar was already in his suit and hat.

Seeing her twin brother, Loretta rushed up wrapped her arms around him with great enthusiasm, dancing with delight. Willie Jack stood stoically by her side.

Loretta said, "Oh, Lamar, I am so, so very happy for you. I knew this time, you would walk that straight and narrow. And look at you! All handsome and that woman of yours, she is just beautiful, Lamar, how did you ever meet her?"

"She just stepped off the bus and into my life, Loretta."

"You are doing so well. I am proud of you how well you are doing. Now, don't get nervous, but as soon as you two get settled in, I'm sending the missionaries over to the house so you can get Sam introduced to the church. Lamar, that would be a big step to you and Sam's eternal salvation. You could even get married again for all time and eternity. Can you think of anything better than that?"

Lamar was not thinking about his eternal salvation or his forever bliss with Sam, but of a couple of missionary's showing up at the cat-house.

"Loretta, that is so wonderfully thoughtful of you but why don't you let me and Sam get really settled in before you go and send some of the missionaries over. I don't want to spook the poor girl. You know she's from Vinton County and those people don't take kindly to strangers showing up at their door step unannounced. You do remember that incident two-three years ago when that fella shot the bible salesman and darned near killed the poor man. Told him to leave his property and the bible salesman said he just wanted to leave his personal testimony and bless the house before he left. Well, he left alright full of buckshot In an ambulance. Remember reading about that?"

"I do recall, Lamar. It was the talk of the church for a week or two."

"Well, that fella was Sam's cousin, twice removed. The shooter, not the bible thumper."

"Lamar, these missionary's are just the finest young men you could ever meet. One is from Salt Lake City, Utah, and the other, the quiet one is from Arizona, right next to an Indian reservation. He sure ain't fond of Indian's. Said they made fun of her on the school bus about his round, pink face. He does always kinda looked flushed. Anyway, he likes to take his shoes off during a sit down meeting. He does wear socks and that is certainly a good thing, but don't take offense if he goes and takes his shoes off when you meet him."

"Loretta, I am not gonna take offense cause you can't send these missionaries over to the house. This is all pretty new to me."

"Oh, I know it, Love. Just enjoy this day and don't worry. I'll get you out to church and you can meet them there."

Lamar said, "Not too change the subject, but how's our boy Jack doing? He about out of school? Damn, he has been at it a long time, hasn't he? And they told me he was the smart one." Lamar smiled, showing his sister that he was joking.

"He is getting out of law school in just a jiffy. Can you imagine that? We will have a lawyer in the family! The first one."

"Loretta, other than you, I don't know of any McKenna that got much beyond the sixth grade."

"Now, Lamar, don't forget about your brother."

"How can I forget him. He"s gonna be standing by my side in about an hour. And yes I know he graduated from Union too. Much to everybody surprise, I mingy remind your."

"Oh, don't be a stinker, Lamar. Hooch is doing very well, but so our you. Look it this turnout."

"So what is Jack gonna do with this fancy law degree of his?"

"Last summer he worked for a law firm in Wheeling. Doing mostly odds and ends. As soon as he passes the bar exam, he will start there."

"A law firm, you say? What kind of work to they do?"

"Criminal defense."

Lamar said, "I was hoping you would say that."

The Reverend Dronsfield was under the God tree. He said in a loud voice, it is time to commence the weddin. Where pray tell is Zachariah?"

He referred to Zachariah Tingle, the man who made the dulcimer sing like an angel. Zachariah had been drinking lemonade with, as he told his Sarah, just a little touch of Mule Kick.

Zachariah Tingle could play just about any instrument, instantly. Hum a tune, he could play it. And play it as no one else could. Some thought him some kind of musical genius. His favorite instrument to play was the dulcimer, a stringed devise that sits on the player's lap and is strummed. Ida Mai once said, "Hearing Zachariah Tingle play that dulcimer was as sweet and clear as a running brook on a hot summer day."

Zachariah settled in. Plucked the strings a few times to get the right sound. Looked over at the Reverend and nodded. The Reverend nodded back and Zachariah begin to play Here Comes the Bride with hard, tough hands that just seem to barely touch the strings and produce a melodic sound with a fitting cadence.

Lamar and the boys were standing to the left of the preacher. Only Peaches was to the right.

Sam stepped out of the house with her bridesmaid in back. Amy and Roxy each holding opposite ends of the trailing. Two little girls from the Hollow, Sally Ann Donovan and Leslie MacBoyle, walked in front, each carrying a basket of floral petals. The reached into the basket and threw the petals right and left supposedly in front of the bride, but more often than not, they landed well out of Sam's path.

As Sam moved gracefully toward them, Larry turned to Lamar and said, "Now that is a picture. I didn't know Sam could clean-up that good."

"That girl is full of surprises," Lamar said.

The Reverend gave a cough, cough as if to say, quiet boys.

Reverend Dronsfield said, "We come together on this day, in this place of great beauty and peach to wed the two before me in the eyes of God and all that are here today...."

Ten minutes later, on that lovely fall afternoon, Samantha Ruby became Mrs. Lamar R. McKenna.

As the couple kissed to conclude the ceremony, Peaches thought, "This is gong to be very interesting to watch the dynamics of these two. I wonder which one will kill off the other?"

CHAPTER XXVIII

THE DEVIL'S IN THE DETAILS

"Lamar, you just can't believe what me and Nikko done with this truck," Curly said. "Ain't that right, Nikko?"

Nikko said, "Damn, straight. Nobody ever done anything like this."

They were at Curly's property, three miles out of Moundsville, on a hillside. From where Lamar was standing he could see Moundsville down below and the Ohio River beyond that. He said, "Curly, you done right good of himself with this property. How much land you got here?"

"Ten acres and most all of it cleared. The farmhouse is livable but not very big. I got this great barn here and that's what I really like about the place. Look at all the space we got. This is sweet. Something I always dreamed about and I owe it all to you and the good doctor. Thank you, Doc."

Lamar tended away from garages and things of that sort, but he was astounded at the size of the garage-barn and all the tools and equipment. Two cars and a truck were being worked on apart from where the truck was. Just the cab to the Kelly was in the garage. The trailer was outside.

There were several chains hanging from rafters. Lamar could see that they were used to lift engines out the vehicles. The floor was solid concrete—grease spots here and there, but very clean and organized. Tools lined shelves. Workbenches by each working station.

"Curly, this looks like you could build airplanes in here. Damn, this is huge. I'm guessing all this stuff is the latest and greatest."

"Lemme put it this way. I don't object no more for paying five dollars to go to see a doctor. No sirree. And I am grateful the docs have a little larceny in 'em to steal a little from Uncle Sam. I was thinkin' about it the other day, and I realized they are just like the moonshiners. They don't like payin' those gawdamn income taxes neither. The doc's are actually one of us, don't you think?"

Nikko said, "Well, wherever you got the money to do this, Curly, there ain't a garage in all West Virginny that can top this one, right, Curly?"

"Yes, sir, and I been in every garage within a hundred miles. You know what, Lamar? We are startin' to get a very good piece of all the bootleggin' around here. Not just Pappy. I think we got—what, Nikko—half the hooch trade now? Takin' it all over the place. Not a cop car around that can stay up with what me and Nikko souped up."

Curly paused and leaned into closer to Lamar and said, "I got a little proposition with you about usin' this particularly little vehicle for runnin' hooch up to the big cities, Chicago and New York."

"You mean the Kelly? Slow down there. We gotta get the Big Job done first. Let's stay with that, before we start talkin' about big cities. Besides, it's one thing dealing with Big Gio and the Pittsburgh guys—you go foolin' around in the big cities and you start messin' with guys like Capone and his like. You make a mistake with those fellas . . .well, you know. So back to the job in front of us. You ready for the big boy to make its voyage? Kinda like the Wright

Brothers?"

"Oh, we gotta much better machine than those bike mechanics, right, Nikko?"

"Much better and much bigger," Nikko chimed in.

Lamar thought, 'What is this guy, Curly's monkey? Curly speaks and the guy repeats'.

As if reading Lamar's thoughts, Curly said, "Nikko here is a mechanical genius. He can make anything better, faster with more speed, torque, suspension. You name it, he can make it better. Not a bad driver either."

Nikko said, "Mr. McKenna, what we did here was pretty simple. We turbocharged and then supercharged, while increasing the engine displacement by over-boring the cylinders. We got creative with the suspension. Added new leaf springs to stiffen it up and help with load distribution. Plus we added a carburetor and installed more manifolds to bring more air up . . ."

"Nikko, Nikko," Lamar said, "Slow down just a bit here. You lost me on the carborundum. What I want to know, is she ready to pack a four-ton load from Wheeling to Erie and make eight to ten trips."

"Well, yeah, but lemme tell you about the suspension additions we put in."

"That's all right, Nikko. Curly, when you ready?"

"I was ready yesterday."

"Nikko your backup?"

"Yep, best we got."

"Be at the house on 21st Saturday night at seven. I'll get the crew and we can go over the plan. Can you saddle up Monday? May take most of the week, so you better clear things with Willy Jack. How 'bout you, Nikko? You ready to make a little money?"

"Happy as a pig in slop."

They met in the fruit cellar of the house on 21st Street. The barrels and boxes of seeds and preserves had been pushed to the side. The room was chilly and damp. A single dirty light bulb hung over a round table. Dust hovered above the table.

The floor was grimy from the years of spilled seeds and dirt.

The boys were all here: Lamar, Larry, Curly, Nikko, and Bobby T.

"Damn Lamar," Bobby T said, "really swingin' for comfort and luxury here."

"I don't want anyone overhearing this one," Lamar said, "Besides, I have fond memories of our money count in this very space a few short months ago. Nobody complained then. Anyway, this here meetin' is for the review of the nickel metal heist at Wheeling Steel, so let's get to it."

"That was one sweet night," said Bobby T. "We oughtn't do a couple more of those, Lamar."

Curly said, "Man that night was a hoot. And the money was sweet, sweet, sweet. Hey, Lamar, before we start, we gotta name the truck. That truck is one serious mover. Nikko and me got it down . . . the names that is, to a few here. We got Thunder and we got Goliath and . . . Nikko, help me out here."

Nikko said, "Thunder, Thor, Brutus, Goliath and Lumber Jack . . . you know, not a lumberjack like a, ah . . . lumberjack guy, but Lumber Jack, cause it was made to move timber and lumber and heavy shit like that."

"Well," Larry said. "I don't like that Lumber Jack. That just don't hit me as even close to what we doin'."

"Hey, Hey," said Lamar, "We got heavy planning here to do. We can get to the truck later and another thing, you can take Thor right off the table, right now."

Nikko said, "Why's that, we kinda liked it."

"It's personal to me, actually very personal, so just go with me, OK? Lamar said.

"Thor's been scratched. What else you boys have to offer?"

Bobby T said, "What about Nickel for the name? Since that's what we haulin'. No, maybe dime . . . or dollar. Yeah, the Silver Dollar."

Curly said, "Silver Dollar don't mean nothing. This truck ain't no Silver Dollar; it's big! Gigantic. The name has gotta demonstrate that power. No, I like Thunder or Goliath."

Larry said, "Didn't Goliath get killed by the slingshot guy? Don't we want the name of somebody that won, like maybe the slingshot guy?"

Lamar now getting into it, showing off a little, and said, "David."

Larry said, "You want to name the truck David?"

"No, that's the name of the slingshot guy, King David."

"Well, now I like that better for the truck, King David," Larry said.

Bobby T said, "How about Brutus? That names got spunk and strength."

Lamar had now turned pink, bordering on bright red. He said, "Dammit. I want to get to the business at hand. Let's just name the truck."

Larry said, "Lets vote. We can write the name we want, and nobody will know how we voted."

Lamar, pinker by the minute, measured out the words with a pause between each word and said, "We. Don't. Need. A secret ballot. Nobody cares how you voted. Let's just vote. We can take three names, so what are the top three, Curly?"

"Well, Thunder, Goliath. And what's the third?"

Bobby T said, "Brutus."

Larry said, "Hey, how 'bout Big Fella? Saw that in a movie a couple of nights ago. This guy went around and called everybody Big Fella. I thought that was pretty . . ."

Lamar said, "Larry, pipe down. Okay, we got three names here: Thunder, Goliath, and Brutus."

They voted. Thunder and Brutus were the finalists.

On the third ballot, Brutus carried the day, three to two. Larry couldn't abide Thunder because his Aunt Katie, from his mother's side, got struck by lightning twenty-two years ago next month in a thunderstorm. Lamar cut him off before he could get into the painful details of her passing. Lamar, Larry and Bobby T voted for Brutus. Curly voted for Thunder. Nikko abstained, too upset over losing the Goliath name.

Brutus it is.

"Finally," Lamar said. "Now let's get to the Biggest Heist any of us will ever be involved. It's the perfect crime. Lemme give you all a little rundown on the overall scheme of things. First of all, we got an inside man—in fact, we got two. Larry here, of course, is the night watchman, and our other man is high up with their security detail. We gonna haul steal nickel metal out of the Wheeling Steel warehouse that our friend Larry here, guards every night with his life at stake. This nickel is heavy. Comes on pallets two thousand pounds each. We takin' two pallets a trip for as long as it's safe."

Lamar had a sketch of the truck yard and warehouse. It was crude, but everybody could at least get the idea of the general layout.

Lamar continued and said, "This is where the truck will enter. Right here. Larry will be there to unlock the gate. Curly, you will move the truck to these loading docks at the side of the warehouse. Nikko is gonna bust a car to us for the rest of us ride in. We will follow the truck in and proceed to this gate here." Lamar pointed to where a doorway was to be.

"Okay, back in this area is where they keep the nickel. They are on big pallets. Two thousand pounds each. They have several different forklifts back there, Curly, so we will have to see which one is best to lift that much. Then Curly will drive the forklift over to the loading dock and load two pallets in there. Four thousand pounds. Two ton. We then close it down and get outta there. Curly and Nikko are off to Erie to deliver the goods."

Bobby T said, "So how many trips you think it's gonna take?"

"Maybe eight to ten," Lamar said. "They have a lot of nickel, but we can't make it obvious that so many pallets are missing. My inside guy will put invoices about this being shipped to various places, so it will look like some were used at other plants and places. It will confuse them for years."

"Any questions?"

Nikko said, "I got an idea. You say that the pallets are all stacked up, side by side, in this warehouse. We want to take a lot, but if we take too many, somebody will notice that stack go down. All this correct, Lamar?"

"Correct."

"So," Nikko said, "why don't we get my cousin just in from Italy to help us out with that problem?"

"Okay, I'll bite. What does your cousin . .. .what's his name?"

"Dante."

"So, how can Dante help?"

"He's a master craftsman. He can build anything."

Bobby T said, "Nikko, get to the damn point, will you?"

Nikko said, "Oh, sure. We take two pallets each trip, right?"

"Right."

"Then next trip we bring two pallets back. Filled with brick and replace the missing pallets."

The boys were startled, then started laughing. Bobby T said, "Curly, I thought your boy Nikko was full of shit. I gotta apologize. He's a damn genius!"

Lamar said, "Nikko, you've earned your spot. Monday night we go. This is just a simple pickup and delivery. Nothing more than that. We meet here at five to go over everything. And then we hit Wheeling Steel. They won't even know it!"

Lamar thought, 'This may just be the perfect crime. Larry is right. I'm a criminal mastermind. Yes, by gawd, I surely am. A fuckin' criminal mastermind'.

CHAPTER XXIX

BRUTUS IS A ROLLIN'

Lamar, Larry, and Bobby T were in a stolen car that Nikko provided headed for Wheeling Steel. Lamar's car was stashed to be picked up after they left the mill.

Curly and Nikko followed in Brutus.

Conrad, Lamar's co-conspirator, gave Larry permission to come in late. Lamar was thinking he had to keep giving Larry instructions up the last minute.

Bobby T said, "Man, that truck looks great!"

"I thought it looked pretty swell," Larry said. 'Brutus' in black with that that harvest gold background. Outstanding! I like the way they kinda tilted the name a little, like it was moving, and the swish lines coming out and over the name."

Bobby T said, "What the hell has happened to you, Larry? Harvest gold? Moving swish lines? I think you've gone a little squishy on us. You're starting to sound like some fuckin' queer. What you reading? Harper's Bazaar? Have it sent to you, monthly, is that it, Larry darling? Where you get this stuff anyway?"

"Where I get my new found fancy words is my business and mine alone," Larry said. "But for your information, I get educated at the moving picture show. Roxy and me go every time there's a new picture. This last one was about some poor farmers and their crop of harvest gold not coming in. I'll tell you, boys, those pictures shows are really increasing my vocabulary."

Lamar said, "Would you two shut up? We are on our way to the greatest heist in West Virginia history, and you guys are blabbing about the name on the truck and harvest gold. Brutus is fine. The painting on the side is fine, although I may remind you two that I told Curly don't make it memorable. We want it forgettable. But damned if he listened to me. Case closed. Can we start thinking about tonight? This is historical."

"Well, I like the color and the other stuff on the truck. I think it's sublime," Larry said.

Bobby T said, "Sublime? There he goes again. It is not 'sublime' at all, whatever the hell you mean by that anyway. There is nothing sublime about that truck. Larry you don't even know what sublime is, do you?"

Lamar said, "Boys, enough, okay?"

They approached the entry gate to the trucking and warehouse area.

Lamar said, "Larry, right here?"

"Yep. This'll do."

Lamar said, "But what do you do first?"

"I check around the lot and make sure nobody is in there."

"Very good, Larry," Lamar said, "Very good. And when you come out of the warehouse?"

"One light from my torch, meaning come on in."

"And if it is not okay?"

"I hit the torch twice, meaning get the hell outta here."

Bobby T said, "You need any help gettin' outta the car, Larry?"

Larry said, "Aha. Very funny. You know it is not right to make fun of a person that has physical issues."

Larry got out of the car and with both hands on his belt, which held his holster, gun, and other paraphernalia, bent slightly at the knees, and quickly rose while hitching up his pants and belt.

Larry said, "See you in five," and began the trek around the grounds to see if it was safe to enter.

Bobby T said to Lamar, "Where the hell is he getting all this stuff from?"

Lamar said, "I don't know but I suspect it's Roxy. Sounds just like her, and I think maybe Larry is greatly influenced by what she says. He was on a hillbilly jag last week. It passes."

They waited in silence for Larry's signal.

They didn't wait long. They could see Larry coming out of the warehouse heading to the entry gate. He flashed once. It was clear.

As they watched Larry approach, Bobby T said, "He's a beaut, ain't he? I never noticed before, but do you see how he doesn't walk in a straight line like a normal human? He kinda sways side to side. Step forward, move to side. Step forward, move to other side. Kinda like a penguin, ain't it?"

Lamar was silent, getting a stir in his stomach. Getting into the heist. A little nervous, but anxious with anticipation. Scared, but he was thinking, 'look at the reward'.

Larry unlocked and opened the gate. Lamar pulled into the lot, followed by Brutus.

Once in, Larry closed and locked the gates and got back into Lamar's car. He said, "All clear, Boss. Follow this road, and when it turns to go slightly to the left, go there. The warehouse will be just straight ahead."

"I know the way, Larry. We were there a couple of days ago, remember?"

"Oh, yeah. Well, then let's go," Larry said, a little edge now to his voice.

In front of the warehouse, Larry unlocked a door, went inside, and opened the roll-up door for the car. Lamar drove inside. Larry pointed to Curly to go around the warehouse where the loading docks were. Curly left and Larry closed the door.

Lamar breathed with relief. They were in place. Just load and go. Simple as pie.

Curly backed Brutus up to the loading dock. It wasn't a perfect fit. The truck was higher than the floor. Curly thought, no problem. They could work it out with a couple of eight-by-ten boards.

The nickel was back in the far side of the cavernous warehouse.

Scrap metal stacked high in one corner. It looked like a crazed steel worker had just thrown it in that direction without regard to structure. Pallets and billets, large and small, were stacked in meticulous order, like so many soldiers standing in line waiting for their mission assignments. There were used pipes and old ovens in a corner. Lots of them. Long metal bars that looked like small tubes that were twenty or twenty-five feet long were stacked on one another. Hundreds of them. Curly called them 'rebars'.

Larry said, "Lemme show you where they store the nickel." He then led them into the midst of the metal jungle.

"Here you go," he said, pointing at pallets that were full of nickel briquettes. Two thousand pounds each. One ton. One pallet.

Curly said, "Well, let's go. Get me saddled up to one of these new fancy forklifts."

The newest looking lift said "CLARK" across the side of on the cantilever. The system was designed to wrap the load with chains, then attach to the pulley, which then lifted the load upward to engage and move.

Lamar said, "You guys ever drive one of these things before?"

Curly said, "Hell, no. We ain't even seen one of these before. The drivin' looks like the easy part. Attaching the load is doable, but can this thing pick up two thousand pounds? It don't look like it could. What ya think, Nikko?"

"We can get it loaded, and the driving is no problem. Curly's right, can it pick up the load?"

"Let's stop jawin' and get it loaded," said Bobby T.

The boys strapped up the nickel load with chains across the middle and sides and attached them to a large iron hook hanging from the top of the mast. Curly took the seat and scooted around to get his butt situated just right.

Curly said, "Man, Nikko, this feels funny. The wheel turn on this must be really slow." Curly played with the steering wheel, started the motor and said, "Here we go."

Everybody stood aside.

Curly started the lift cycle. The engine turned and made a high-pitched whine, then struggled. The load didn't budge. Curly cranked it to an even higher pitch. The load moved. Slightly. Little more. Then an inch off the ground. Little more. Then backed off as the back end of the forklift begin its rise off the ground. The load only dropped an inch or two, but it came down fast, and the end of the lift bounced two or three times as it settled back down.

Nikko said, "Give her another try, Curly."

Curly did. Same result.

Curly turned his head from the driver's seat and said to Lamar, "This unit ain't gonna work. What about those others, Nikko?"

"They are older and don't look like they could take half of what this baby can do. Look, let's lighten the load, and this Clark will do just fine," Nikko said.

The sign on the side of the nickel said:

DANGER: NICKEL
TETRACARBONYL

Wear Protective Gloves, Mask and Goggles. May cause death or disfigurement without protective gear

DO NOT INGEST INTERNALLY!!

Lamar said, "Larry, we need some bags or containers to put the stuff in and lighten the load here just a mite. What'cha got?"

"I got a bunch of lunch sacks in the office, but I'm thinkin' you need something a little larger," Larry said.

"Well, yes," Lamar said, "something a little larger would be dandy. We are movin' a quarter ton or so here, Larry, so yes, something a little larger would be needed."

Larry said, "I think I know what we want," and waddled off.

He came back minutes later with about ten large burlap coal sacks that said:

BENWOOD MINE #9
WHEELING STEEL

Larry cut open the top of the nickel pallet, opened the top, and the boys got their first look at nickel briquettes.

Bobby T said, "They look smaller than I thought they would be."

"Ain't they a beauty in their own right," said Lamar, "Just kinda shiny and almost looks like silver." They all paused to admire the grandeur of it all.

Finally, Bobby T said, "Let's get with it, boys. This has already been the longest damn heist I have ever had the pleasure of being involved in. And we just standin' here lookin' like a bunch of tourists. Let's load 'em up."

They each grabbed the coal bags and started to load up the precious nickel.

It was hard work. They did four bags, tied them together, put them on the lift hook, and Curly started moving slowly toward Brutus.

Nikko said, "So that's it? That's top speed?"

The bootlegging wild man said, "'Fraid so. Damn, this is slow. Really slow." It took them two hours to load half the nickel. One thousand pounds.

But load it they did, then came the moment of truth: the remaining one thousand pounds.

They hooked it up. The forklift quivered briefly but lifted the entire load two feet off the ground. Curly drove and Nikko slow-walked to the truck along side the load. They had put runners leading into the truck with inches of wood on either side, which Curly navigated easily.

Brutus was loaded.

Standing in the warehouse, ready to leave, Curly turned to Nikko and said, "Damn, look at that."

Nikko said, "Shit. It's the morning shift."

They ran back to the rest of the crew. They were getting in Lamar's car.

Curly, said, "Lamar, wait a good gawdamn minute. We got company."

"What?"

"Yep, the morning shift is coming on right now."

Bobby T said, "What the hell time is it?"

No one answered, but Lamar said, "Are they coming this way?"

"No, but people can sure as shit can see over this way."

The problem was solved by an implausible source, Larry.

He said, "Highly unlikely anybody comes this way except Karl, my replacement, and he is late more often than not. I swear that man don't know whether to wind his butt or scratch his watch."

"Dammit Larry, get on with it," Lamar said.

"So here's what we do. I go out to the gate and open it. Lamar you lay back, and as soon as I get the gate open, you get outta here, fast. Curly, you just take your own sweet time. You be just another driver moving a load out of the warehouse."

And that's what happened.

The crew was exhausted but elated. Thunder took off for Erie. Lamar and Bobby dropped the hot car and picked up Lamar's T and headed back to 21st Street.

In the car Lamar turned to Bobby T and said, "Perfect, eh? Just perfect. Really no hitches. Well, couple of little bumps, but they turned out pretty easy to overcome. We gonna do nine more just like this, Bobby T. Ain't nobody gonna stop us." Lamar paused, then said, "Who'd a figured that Larry would save the day?"

Bobby T said, "Get me back to Peaches. I paid for the entire night and I get kicked outta her room at eight, and it's getting there quick."

Lamar wasn't even thinking about his stash of money in the floorboards, but Peaches and Sam had been up to their old tricks.

CHAPTER XXX

Trouble In Paradise

Curly and Nikko made the run to Erie with no problems. Lou Carney was there to greet them and inspect the merchandise, along with a chemist who verified the quality of the nickel as 99.9 percent pure. He paid the boys in cash. The next three weeks, three more runs without incident.

Lamar was walking with a swagger, feeling full of himself. He thought, The poker game, the house on ent firms t, and now the Big Job heist, all working and bringing in cash. Maybe I ought to expand. Start taking on Big Gio. Control all of the Northern Panhandle of West Virginia. Hell, maybe all of West Virginia. Big Gio wasn't the Mafia. He was just a guy like me. Maybe not as smart. All I need is a little more money. Have Bobby T bring in a few more Vinton County boys. Big Gio won't know what hit him. He's just a big fat-ass ready to be hit hard. Take him down. Be the crime king'.

Lamar's fantasy with Sam was waning. His thoughts were more on Daphne. He thought, 'I need a mistress. Sam was still as sexy as ever . . . but Daphne was in another league. Every big-time mobster had a mistress, didn't they'?

The house, poker, and numbers running provided almost daily instant cash. Lamar used that money as needed. Kept it handy in a small safe in his room. His floorboard money, he kept stashed away for bigger expenses, not the day-to-day matters.

It had been two weeks since he had needed the floorboard money. When he got the first payment from Lou for the nickel delivery, he paid the boys and decided to put the rest in his bank . . . the floorboards. Checking the bags, they looked light.

That night, Sam got to their room early. About ten. She looked drawn. Lamar was sitting in bed, in long underwear and black socks, sipping shine. He had candles on the bed stand, burning brightly.

Lamar said, "So, how was your night?"

"Just a delight. Did you hear what happened this morning?"

"Do tell."

"Oh, this was something. You know that guy, Chuck, from Steubenville? Comes over a couple times a month."

"I don't believe I made his acquaintance. So what'd he do?"

"Well, about nine this morning, the girls have come down for coffee and corn muffins. Cassandra makes the best corn muffins. You tried those?"

"Yes, Sam. And Mr. Chuck . . ."

"Just be patient, Cowboy. Well, Amy was the lucky girl that pulled the Chuck card and spent the night with him. So we're are all in the living room having our coffee and having girl talk time. Now Chuck goes about two-fifty, ugly hair coming out of everywhere on this big, round body. A beard that looks like it has never been cut, trimmed, or shampooed. So we are just sitting there, and here comes Chuck down the stairs naked as can be, yelling about how he paid for all night and by gawd the night wasn't over, and he wanted Amy back upstairs. So here he comes and all any of could see was this tiny little nub of a pecker sticking out. You could barely see the damn thing. All shriveled up and covered up with a couple layers of drooping stomach fat. That pecker was recessed. I swear, Lamar, recessed right into his body."

Lamar was smiling at the thought. He said, "So what happens next?"

"Oh, Peaches went right after him." She said, 'Chuck, get your fat ass back upstairs and get dressed. The night ended at eight and it's close to nine. What the hell is the matter with you'?

He just stopped and said, 'It's nine? In the morning'?"

Peaches said, 'No, numb nuts, it's the middle of the night. Of course it is in the morning.'

Chuck said, 'Oh, shit. My wife is gonna kill me'.

"He turned tail and believe me the sight of him going up the stairs was worse than seeing him come down the stairs. A few minutes later he is dressed and just flying out the door."

Lamar said, "You do get some strange ones passing through our little house. Sounds like Peaches handled it well."

"Peach handles everything well."

"Doesn't she, though. It's such a shame, I'm gonna have to kill her."

"What are you talking about, killing Peaches? Why in the world would you say something crazy like that?"

"I think you know why."

"Lamar, you are scaring me. Just tell me."

"She is takin' my money."

"What money?"

"I think you know."

"Know what? Stop with the games, Lamar. Just tell me."

"About my hidden stash from the doctor's house."

"Lamar, I don't know anything."

Lamar noticed a hesitation in her voice.

He said, "Tell me, Sam. Give me the whole story. You're my wife. I'm not going to hurt you."

Sam said nothing.

Lamar's face took on a menacing, wild look. His eyes focused on Sam with horrible intent.

Sam's heart was pounding. She was trapped. She didn't know what to do.

She said, "I don't know what you're talking about."

On his side now, his left hand grabbed her throat. He started to squeeze.

"Tell me, Sam. Tell me everything."

Sam pulled away. Jumped from the bed. Reached into the bed stand and pulled out Lamar's twenty-two pistol. She pointed it at Lamar.

Lamar laughed and said, "You ain't gonna shoot me, Sam. Put that damn thing down." Sam's hands were trembling. She didn't know if the gun was loaded. Lamar laughing at her. The humiliation of it.

"I'll shoot you, you son-of-a-bitch. I should do it anyway for you fucking around with Daphne."

"What? Daphne, I haven't done anything with her yet."

Sam looked for the safety. She didn't know if it was off or on.

She pulled the trigger just as Lamar turned his body. Instead if hitting him where she aimed, the bullet went into the fleshy part of his right butt cheek. Lamar's momentum carried him into the nightstand, which knocked over the candles and the fruit jar of Mule Kick, which then spilled from the glass—which started the fire before the candles hit the floor.

The moonshine quickly ignited the room. Lamar was on the floor, unable to move. Sam dropped the gun and ran out of the room. The gunfire had the house awake. Peaches was coming out of her room as Sam was running from the flames and Lamar. She was screaming, "He knows, he knows. I shot him. I shot him!"

Peaches said, "Get in here."

She pushed Sam into her room and moved quickly to Lamar's room. The room had exploded in a fury of flames. Lamar was struggling to move. Peaches ran into the room and got Lamar standing. He said, "Get the money."

Peaches got him to the hallway room and said to Larry, who was standing there with the girls and two customers, "Larry, get him downstairs and call the fire department. All of you girls get out of here. You guys too. Get. Go outside. The house is on fire! Roxy, get Sam out of my room and downstairs and out of the house. Hurry!"

Everybody was running now, Larry was half carrying Lamar downstairs, blocking the stairwell with his slow movement. Everybody was screaming behind Larry.

Lamar kept repeating, "Get the money. Larry, get the money."

Peaches opened the door to Lamar's room to get the money. The alcohol had the room ablaze. The heat from the room was overwhelming. Peaches quickly slammed the door shut raced outside to join the others.

The money was aflame.

And gone.

The moonshine in Lamar's room caused the fire to spread rapidly. Within minutes the room was destroyed as the fire moved to the other bedrooms. The flames reached upward to the ceiling and roof. Burning timbers crashed into the floor below.

Everybody had gathered in the front yard. The girls had thrown robes and blankets over their shoulders. There were two customers at the time. The left in a great hurry. One man, someone recalled his name as Chester, ran to his car naked. He tried to start his old jalopy with a crank that was in the front of the car. Young Amy said later that the vision haunted her in a nightmare for several week...Chester cranking up that car naked. In her dream, Chester had a really long arm working the crank, and his facial features had taken on a grotesque smile, looking right at her.

Chester's car wouldn't turn over. He cranked and cranked, and when he heard the approaching clang, clang of bells from the approaching fire, ambulances, and police, Chester took off. He ran across the gravel road to Mutt's Bar and rushed in. That was the last that was seen of Chester. Not just that night but forever. Never came back for his car. Rumor had it, he had moved to Alaska.

The Moundsville Fire Department from Central Fire Station Number One pulled up eight minutes after the fire started. They were led by Chief Bryson, who took charge.

Larry liked the fire chief's uniform—dark blue coat with gold buttons top to bottom. The top of the coat opened near the neck, and you could see the starched white shirt and matching dark blue tie. Larry really liked his hat. Big hat with a leather visor attached to a flared top that was adorned with a snappy insignia in the middle front. Printed on the medallion was "MFD." Larry thought for a minute that he might like to be a fireman. Then he saw the men carrying a hose up a steep ladder and had second thoughts. Maybe the nightwatchman job and stealing suited him better than climbing ladders and carrying stuff.

Most of the damage had been contained to the two bedrooms and the poker parlor downstairs.

Lamar was hauled off to the Reynolds Memorial Hospital in Moundsville.

Peaches thought it funny that maybe she and Sam had more of the money by stealing it from the robbers than the robbers did stealing it from the doctor.

Lamar liked being the center of attention at the hospital. Larry was in a chair by his bed most of the day, mostly reading pulp fiction novels from the old west, has latest addiction.

Everybody from the house, the gang, the barbershop, the poker game, his number runners, Pappy and Lula, Hooch, and even the bag man from Big Gio, Marcos, had visited. Big Gio sent a bouquet of flowers.

Everybody seemed greatly amused that Sam had "missed her mark."

Loretta came with flowers.

Lamar said, "Don't worry about the house, Sis. Pappy's got a crew down from the holler and they will have the house restored in a couple of weeks. It'll be better than ever."

"I'm just glad your OK, Lamar. You had me worried when I heard you'd been shot. I feared the worst."

"Oh, Loretta, just a little domestic disturbance that got out of hand, that's all. Just a little misunderstanding with Sam. We have since kissed and made up, so no more worries, OK?"

To each and every one, Lamar would sweep open his hospital gown, turn on his side, pull back the bandages, and say "Look at that," showing off his wound. It was a gruesome sight— black ridges around a red hole with a multicolored puss. When Sam saw it, she rushed to the bathroom and threw up. All of the women took a glance and immediately looked away. Some of the men did too, but Larry said, "That is one nasty-looking thing. How'd she come to shoot you in the butt, anyway?"

Lamar said, "I don't think that was where she was aiming."

"Where was that?"

"Ask Roxy, she can tell you."

With that Larry was quiet. Deep in thought.

The doctors had said that Lamar was lucky. The bullet did not hit any vitals. 'Lucky my ass, that damn thing was hot. Hot as fire. It was painful and could have taken my privates right off if I hadn't turned my butt over to take the hit'.

The second day, Peaches and Sam showed up. Uncharacteristically, both looked a little uncomfortable.

Lamar said, "Ladies, why don't you pull up a chair, and let's have a cozy conversation. Larry, would you close the door, and you can pull your chair over here too."

Peaches said, "Lamar, I . . ."

Lamar held up his hand for silence.

He said, "Ladies. You want to tell me all about it or are you both gonna play it cute?"

Peaches said, "About what?"

"See Peaches, that is exactly what I don't want to hear. I know what you did, and how you did it. So let's not be coquettish and play that little game. Let's get right to it. How much you did you and your sidekick here take? How you gonna get it back to me? Today. Right now. Immediately. Then we can all kiss and make up."

"'Coquettish'? That's a word I never thought I would hear from the crime lord," Peaches said.

"See Peach. Again, that's just what I am talkin' about. You think this is funny. You think I am just gonna let you joke about it. Let everybody know, 'Hey, anybody can steal from Lamar and just go have a good laugh. Hell, let's have a party. See how clever that gal is.' That what you think, Peaches?"

Peaches did not respond.

Lamar said, "Peaches, you know I could have you up in the holler by noon and no one, I mean no one, would ever find you or most likely not even know you were gone. Forget about you inside a week. Is that what you want? You want to go to the pig farm? Because I can arrange it right fast. So what's it gonna be, Peaches?"

Peaches and Sam looked at each other. Sexy Sam was not looking sexy just right then. Peaches was paler than when she had first walked in the room.

Peaches said, "Yeah, we found the stash. I found the stash. Sam just happened to walk in as I found it. We didn't take much, just a little shoe money."

"You took half a bag, and that is pretty damn significant. So stop the bullshit, Peaches, and tell me where is my money and when it will be back in my hands."

Sam said, "No really, honestly, Lamar, it wasn't that much."

"Sam," said Lamar, "Don't do that. I figure I owe you, Peaches, since you pulled me out of that blazing hell hole. The room in which you, Sam, tried to shoot me in the balls and then left me to be my own barbecue. So don't tempt me. These things happen in a marriage, so I am willing to forgive and forget. Well, maybe forgive. It's kinda hard to forget a bullet in a one's ass. And speakin' of asses, why don't you two get yours movin' so I can get my money."

There was silence. Lamar waited.

Peaches said, "We can't."

That startled Sam, but she kept her mouth shut.

"And why is that Peach, Honey?" Lamar's voice took on that edge again.

"Gone."

"You spent it all? On what?"

"We didn't spend it. It was in my room. Went up in smoke along with your stash."

"Up in smoke!"

The room got quiet again. Lamar was fuming.

Lamar said, "You two are gawdamn'd lucky women."

"How's that?" Peaches said.

"Couple of reasons. First one is the house will be repaired in a couple of weeks and you two can get back to work. Make up for your waywardness. Secondly, the Big Job is paying off good, so we still have money coming in. Without those two little things goin' on, you Peaches, would be pig slop. And Sam, you would get a good spanking. I might do that anyway."

Peaches said, "So we good?"

"Let's not get carried away." Lamar paused and said, "Sam, what the hell you doin' shootin' me like that?"

"Lamar, you were choking me. I thought I was going to die. What? You just want me to lay there while you strangle the life out of me?" Sam was now moving from terrified to righteous indignation and said, "And while we are at it, here we are not more than a few months after our wedding and you are sniffing around Daphne like a frenzied bloodhound."

"I told you I haven't done anything yet."

"See, Lamar . . . you haven't done anything yet. Well, that's a comfort."

Larry said, "You goin' out with Daphne, Lamar?"

Larry was impressed.

The women got up to leave.

Sam said, "I'm sorry I shot you, Lamar. Really I am. I just got so scared and I really didn't pull the trigger. The gun just went off."

"Well, I did get a little rough with you, so I guess we're even. And you, Peaches, no more stealing my money...and Larry's too."

"I won't make that mistake again."

Walking back to Peaches's jalopy, she said to Sam, " I really have to get another line of work."

Sam said, "I was thinking the same thing, but what would we do, Peach. It's what we got. By the way, did you note the comment, 'These things happen in a marriage? What marriages? Not any normal marriages that I know about."

"Sam, they are McKenna's. You never know what those people are gonna do or say."

While the girls were talking, Larry said to Lamar, "Daphne? Damn, Lamar, that's something. I'm impressed. Just like a big-time gangster. Yep, that's you now. A big-time gangster."

Lamar was wrapped in his own thoughts, 'A spanking. Never did that before. I bet Sam could get into that, might even like it. As soon as I get outta here....".

Sheriff Boyer, paid a visit as well. He was dressed in khaki. Khaki shirt with a big silver star badge that declared him the sheriff of Marshall County, WV. Had on a thin, black tie. Big belt. Holster with a Smith & Wesson, .38 Special revolver with a four-inch barrel and a swing-out cylinder, double action. Topped off with a cowboy hat that he didn't take off in the hospital room.

The sheriff said, "Lamar, so tell me what happened. I heard it was the happy bride that shot you. Little family disagreement?"

"Nothing like that, Sheriff. It was an accident. Hell, we were just playin' around in bed and the thing just got fired off and happened to hit me right here."

He started to turn over and show off his wound, but the sheriff said, "Lamar, you pull that tape back and I sure as hell will arrest you on the spot."

"No need to be so testy, but it is a sight to behold."

"I'm sure it is. So this is nothing but a little family incident. An accident. Is that your story?"

Lamar smiled. A little too smug. Had a little falsetto in his voice as he said, "Yes, sir. Mr. Police Officer, that's what happened."

The sheriff turned to Larry, nodding off in his chair, and said, "Larry, wake up. Would you give us a little privacy please?"

"Sure, I'll just go back to sleep here."

Lamar said, "Larry, I think the sheriff wants you to leave the room."

"Oh, okay. What for?"

"Just scoot. Go get a bite in the cafeteria. The sheriff wants a little private time."

Larry left and the sheriff said, "So what about the house? More specifically, what about my cut from the house and your other bullshit stuff?"

"Why don't you just get right to the point?"

"Knock off the bullshit. I want to get outta here."Lamar answered, "Well, Pappy is sending down some of the boys from up in the holler, and he tells me that the house will be restored within a week, ten days max. So it will be back to business as usual."

"I don't like missin' a week's cut."

"Cletus, I had my stash in my room and it's gone. Up in smoke. I gotta rebuild and re-cash.

I'm a poor boy all of a sudden."

"That don't matter to me. You still got the numbers, poker, and gawd knows what else. So Lamar, don't miss a payment."

The sheriff paused, and Lamar give him a little wink.

The sheriff said, "So this was just a little accident from some bedroom playtime, and you are not gonna charge your bride, is that it?"

"Why should I have her put in jail? She's a good little moneymaker."

"You got her still workin'?"

"Sure I do. Why not?"

The sheriff paused. Stood up. Pointed a forefinger at Lamar like it was a pistol and mock fired it off. He left the room saying, "You are one piece of work, Lamar. Don't miss a payment to this ol' boy."

CHAPTER XXXI

WELCOME BACK LAMAR, WE'VE MISSED YOU.

Mack Lyons made a discovery in the warehouse. There were seventy-seven coal bags missing.

After a twenty-year stint in the Marine Corp, Mack retired as a master gunnery sergeant with the military police. The troops called him 'Top,' as in the top man. As in, 'Top, Sir! And snap off that Sir like you mean it, Marine!' For an enlisted Marine, he could be your best friend and advocate, or he could be your worst enemy. A legendary investigator of crimes for the military police of misdeeds and mischief by marines of any rank. He would go after an officer or enlisted man with equal zeal. He was fair and tough, and he was the poster boy for dogged determination. No fancy degrees, but smart as hell.

After his retirement from the Marine Corps, he became director of security for all of Wheeling Steel's vast operations. Mack had been with Wheeling Steel eighteen years.

Lyons was pissed. He stormed past Felicia into Conrad's office and said, "What the hell is going on down here?"

Conrad said, "Why don't you tell me what the problem is and I'll tell you what the hell is going on here."

"You got seventy-seven coal bags missing from the warehouse."

"So? I think this company can afford to lose or misplace some burlap coal bags without you having a cow."

"This is how we track the coal being used. Without the bags, will don't know how much coal we are burning and how much to order. It has a big effect on cost."

"Mack, these are burlap bags. So the count is off a little, I can't see how it makes much difference."

"So you know nothing about these missing bags?"

"No, and I don't much care, but for you, Mack...Chief, I'll look into it and get back to you."

Mack stood and bent over the desk, getting up close and personal with Conrad, and said, "Yes, you will get off your ass and find out what's is going on in your warehouse, and you will get back to me in my office tomorrow at this time. And you sure as shit better have an explanation as to what's going on. You will also lose that fucking attitude, or you will find yourself back with all the lunatics and psychopaths at that thing over in Moundsville you call a penitentiary. You don't want to have a problem with this Jarhead, Conrad. Have I made myself clear?"

"Yes."

"Yes, what?"

Conrad paused, eyes burning with emotion, and then said, "Yes, Sir."

With that, Master Gunnery Sargent, Mack Lyons, turned and left.

He went directly to the warehouse. He was thinking about what was so valuable to steal in here. It didn't take him long to realize the most important metal in the warehouse was the nickel. In the nickel area, he walked the parameter. He paid close attention to the area closest to the loading docks. One area looked different. The floor wasn't as dirty. It certainly wasn't clear, Mack thought, but it certainly was a lighter shade of gray. Some of the pallets looked newer than the others. They looked better made as well. He found a crow bar and opened one of the newer looking boxes. He found bricks. No nickels briquettes. Just bricks.

His thought, "These pallets weight two thousand pounds. How in the hell did they move them? The forklifts were not designed to handle that much load. Or could they?"

Mack left the warehouse in deep thought. Back in his office, he got coffee, sat at his desk and thought, ' How do the burlap bags come into play? He thought of the metals. Think like a thief. The metals. The nickel has good value, but those pallets would be near impossible to move. What could you do with nickel? You would have to steal tons of it to make it pay. And is what they did. Say you stole it. What then? Sell it. Yes, but to who? That just doesn't make sense. How would you do it? You would need a big truck. A really big truck. How would you even get it in a truck? Could the fork lifts pick up that much? Maybe I ought to try it. See if it could lift that much'. If the forklifts couldn't do it, what then? Empty part of the load in bags, have the forklift do what it could. But load what the forklift couldn't handle, into...into the coal bags. Let the lift do the rest. The robbers would have to have an inside man. They would have to get in at night, and they could use the dark as cover. They would have to have keys or an insider. We have a night watchman there. Most likely be the night watchman then, right? Who else? I need to look a little closer at the night man'.

Mack went to personnel and found out that Larry was a recent hire by Conrad, found out Larry had done time in juvie and had a ninety-day jail sentence three years ago when caught robbing a house with relatives in Ohio. He thought, 'Why would Conrad hire an ex-con on to his security team'? Cause we have two insiders. Conrad and the con. My insiders'.

Mack met with Sheriff Cletus Boyer and said, "Cletus, we got a little situation over at the mill. Some sons of bitches are stealing nickel."

Cletus said, "Nickels? What you got nickels in there for anyway? That's a lot of risk and trouble to go through for nickels."

"Not nickel as in coins, Cletus, nickel as in the raw metal. It's used to make the steel. Part of the process. But here's the thing, the nickel comes to the plant in two-thousand pound pallets. That means they gotta have a big truck to move that much. A big truck couldn't get in the plant during the daytime. Gotta be at night."

"So what you need?"

Mack said, "Here's what we gonna do. I'm gonna post a guy to watch the warehouse. Might take a few nights, but he'll spot the gang going in and let me know. You have your troops ready. You gotta be there and in place within the hour. It'll take them at least that long to pack the load. When they come out. Bam! You got your arrest. In the meantime, get your detectives snoppin' around and see if you find any movement in big trucks. Buying, selling. Anything at all. Talk to some of their informants, call any of the dealerships and see if they've sold any big trucks recently. Anything like that."

Lamar and his merry band of bandits were now confident that the Wheeling Steel job was faultless. They had already made eight trips. Lamar was happy.

Uncle Lou, as the boys starting calling the scrap-iron king, paid cash upon delivery. It was all a big, happy family that had a party every week that you got paid for.

It was a relaxed, confident crew that pulled up at the gate at Wheeling Steel. Larry was there to unlock the gate. They pulled in and got about their business. Another milk run. Curly driving with Sabatino riding shotgun this trip. Nikko was on a bootleg run. The pay was better with less time.

What they didn't know was Mack Lyons' spy was in an office forty yards away with binoculars up to eyes as he saw the big truck approach the gate and Larry pull out his keys.

The spy phoned Mack.

Mack called the Sheriff and said, "Cletus, the bastards are here. Mount up and get your ass over here. They're in the warehouse right now. We got 'em. Full implementation of operation Nickle and Dime. Got it?"

"What time is it?"

"It don't matter what time it is, Cletus, get the troops and get over here pronto."

"Right. Okay, we are on our way."

Everything went as planned for Lamar's crew. They loaded up. Cleaned up the place. Locked up the warehouse. Lamar was feeling smug. Larry getting tired and was looking forward to getting some sleep. Curly and Sabby, rested and ready to roll. Bobby T bitching about something and nobody paying attention to him.

Lamar and Bobby T were in the borrowed car, this time compliments of Curly. The truck followed the car to the gate. Larry unlocked the gate and pushed a button to roll the gate open. Lamar pulled through, now anxious to get to bed and Sam. The car was halfway through the gate when bright lights went on in front of them—so bright that both Lamar and Bobby T held their arms up to shield their eyes.

They heard a man on a bullhorn say, "Stop! Stop right there! This is the Sheriff Cletus Boyer. Get out of your vehicles with your arms in the air. Do it now!"

Both Lamar and Bobby T hesitated. Curly and Sabby got out of the truck right away with their arms raised. Larry was stunned in place, unable to move.

The sheriff said, "You. The security guard. Pull your gun from your holster and throw it out away from you. You! In the car. Get out now with your hands raised. If you have weapons, pull them out and throw them away from you. Do it now! You in the truck. Get down and put your hands in the air."

Lamar and Bobby T did as told. Bobby T made a motion that he was going into the side of his jacket and said, "Don't shoot. I got a gun here and just pulling out of my pocket to put on the ground."

He reached to his side and pulled out a pistol with two fingers and raised his hand to show it. He then gave it a toss. He said, "Got another one. Don't shoot."

He bent over and pulled a gun out of an ankle holster. Repeated showing the gun and then tossing it aside and said, "One more thing." Over his right hip toward the back, he pulled out a big knife. It looked like a big knife the mountain men would carry. He tossed that aside.

Lamar carried a Smith & Wesson .38-Caliber Model 10 revolver. He pulled it slowly from his shoulder holster and tossed it away.

The voice on the bullhorn said, "On the ground now. Face down. Our officers are approaching. Do not move or you will be shot with intent to kill. I repeat, do not move!"

The sheriff, Mack, and the officers from the state, county, and local police approached the men now face down on the ground.

Now standing over them, the sheriff said, "Well, hello, Lamar. I wondered when you would show up. Welcome back."

CHAPTER XXXII

WILLY JACK AND LORETTA

Willy Jack Walker had loved Loretta McKenna since he was fifteen years old. Both were attending Union High School in McMechen. Ninth-grade home room. Every school morning, Willy Jack would see the cute, spunky blonde with the radiant blue eyes and sparkling personality come into home room and is heart would beat faster. She was smart too. Better at school than he was, too, Willy Jack thought.

She was a McKenna from up in the hollow, and everybody knew about the McKenna's. The stills. Jail time. Mule Kick. The one boy off to the West Virginia Industrial Home for Boys every other year or so, over in Pruntytown. "Juvie," it was called. Lamar was his name, Lamar McKenna, off to Juvie. Loretta's twin brother.

Willy Jack had heard it all. He didn't care. This was his girl, his love, his sweetheart. He knew it from the beginning. W. J., as he was often called, however, had the shyness of most boys at fifteen, and getting the courage to approach her terrified him.

Loretta thought Willy Jack was too quiet for her. Good-looking, he was that, for sure. But quiet and he always looked so serious. She didn't know if he was moody or just bashful. She did know his father had died and he quit school to work at the steel mill to support his family, which included his mother and five sisters. He had been in the tenth grade. He quit high school a to work at Wheeling Steel. The man of the house at sixteen.

Loretta was determined to live a clean, religious life. She wanted out of the hollows. Have a family in town. A man with a respectable job. Pappy and Lula knew she was smart. Smarter than her parents. Smarter than her brothers. Lula thought her daughter could do great things. Lula and Pappy always encouraged and supported her.

During the school year, Loretta stayed with her cousin, Cookie Tribett, going home only on weekends and not all of those. The girls were like sisters.

As they left school one fall afternoon, Cookie turned to Loretta and said, "I met these cute Mormon boys. They are missionaries."

"Missionaries? I thought that missionaries went to Africa or China or something like that," Loretta said.

"Nope. Well, I guess they do, but these missionaries came right from Utah."

"What for? Are they Christians or something else? Everybody here that I know are already Christians, so what are they going to do with us?"

"That remains to be seen." Cookie paused and said, "I know what I'd like to do with them."

"So you got anything going yet?"

"I'm workin' on it," Cookie said, smiling.

"So are they normal fellas?"

"Normal enough. They sure don't look like the boys from around here. They dress nice and sound smart. They do say strange things every now and again."

"Like what?"

"Like Jesus talked to their prophet."

"You mean in old times . . . like the Bible times?"

"No. In our time. Well, years ago, but now."

That brought laughter from Loretta. She said, "Well, at least we know they are not nutso! Having some personal talks with Jesus and all that. Oh, wait. He died, what two thousand years ago. So these guys have horns and tails, too?"

"Not that I noticed, but they are really cute."

Cookie said, "They're coming over tonight for dinner at the house, so you, my sister, will meet them in a couple of hours."

"Oh, I really can't wait. I'll look for the tails. You look for the horns."

The Tribett family and Loretta starting taking lessons with the Mormon boys. The Elders used the American Legion Hall for Sunday services, directly down the street from Cookie's house.

The missionaries were about twenty. They were called Elder. Loretta thought that funny. Young men called 'Elder Whiting' and 'Elder Lake'

After dinner that evening, the girls and the Elders were clearing the table. Elder Whiting said to Loretta, "What grade are you in?"

He was tall. Handsome. Not shy like Willy Jack. He was confident and liked to talk. Especially to Loretta. Loretta thought she would like to go dancing with him.

She said, "Senior. Graduating in the spring. Where are you from anyway?"

"Oh, a place in Utah south of Salt Lake City, called Provo."

"Whatcha do there?"

"My Dad teaches at the university and I was going to school there."

"So you are a college boy."

"Why yes I am, Loretta."

"How'd you get so tall?"

"How'd you get so pretty?"

Loretta couldn't help it. She could feel her face getting hot, turning just a little pink. She felt her body tingle ever so slightly. She said, "Why, how you go on and you an Elder in the church and all."

Loretta was washing the dishes, rinsing them and handing them to the tall, young man. Their hands would brush against one another. Their bodies moved in metered time together. Tik Tok. Tik Tok.

The Elder said, "Utah is a beautiful place. There, we have real mountains. Not these little ol' hills you call mountains."

"I like it just fine right here."

"You would love it there."

Tik Tok. Tik Tok.

Willy Jack and Loretta had gone to school dances, been to the movies together. They kissed once. A bungled affair. They were saying goodbye after a movie date night. Standing in the doorway of Cookie's house, Loretta was holding the screen door open with one hand. Thinking Willy Jack was leaving, she let the screen door close. But Willy Jack was turning to her for their first kiss. Their lips barely touched . . . as the screen door closed on Willy Jack. Hit him right in the head, hard enough that he saw stars.

Loretta then took charge and said, "Well, bless you Willy Jack. You are an awkward one ain't you. Come here, let me show you how it's done."

She then gave Willy Jack a kiss he would not forget.

Willy Jack said, "Ohhh."

"That's it? That's all you can say?"

He repeated, "Ohhh."

"Oh, boy. I gotta lot of work to do here," Loretta said as she closed the door.

Cookie broke the news to Willy Jack that one of the missionary boys was sweet on Loretta. Willy Jack was furious.

Cookie said, "W.J., don't worry none. He's gonna have to go back to Utah in a couple of months. He'll be gone."

Willy Jack said, "Well, does Loretta like him?"

"Well, of course, Willy Jack. We all do. They are nice fellas. But there is nothing to worry about. Look at it this way. They are missionaries, W.J. Missionaries! They got rules that they can't be livid about courting girls. They can't go on a date. They can't even be alone with a girl. I know that for a fact since I asked Tommy, that's the other one, Elder Lake, to step outside with me and he declined. Said no, he can't do that. And I was gonna plant one right on him too. No can do. Hurts a girl's feelin's, doesn't it? Anyway, they can't even get within spittin' distance of a female."

Willy Jack was not comforted. He said to Cookie, "When they comin' over?"

"Tonight for dinner. Don't you do nothin' stupid. First of all, this guy is a big boy. Way over six feet. Maybe six two or three. Yeah, and he is a couple years older than you."

Willy Jack waited till dinner time and then walked over to the Tribett house.

He knocked on the door, and Loretta answered.

Jack said, "I need to talk to the tall one."

Elder Whiting was in the background and Willy Jack said, "Would you step out here? We need to have a word."

The Elder said, "Me?"

"Yes, you."

Willy Jack stepped off the porch and into the yard. The Elder followed.

Loretta, Cookie, and Elder Lake stepped out on the porch. Cookie's parents looked out the front window.

Willy Jack sized the missionary up to be a couple of years older, six-two, maybe thirty pounds heavier. The missionary looked puzzled. Willy Jack was rolling up his shirt sleeves. Although young, Willy Jack had been working at the steel mill now for about a year. He had grown two inches and put on twenty pounds of muscle. Loretta noticed his forearms were rippled muscle.

"You makin' eyes at Loretta?"

"What do you mean? 'Making eyes,' what does that mean?"

"You damn well know what it means."

Loretta turned to Cookie and whispered, "Who is this guy? I've never seen Willy Jack like this." He was so quiet and shy with her. Not now. She had always thought of him as a shy boy. For the first time, she saw a man. A strong man. A fighting man that was ready to fight for her.

Willy Jack said, "Since you seem so confused, let me get a thing or two straight. Loretta is my girl. Your stay away from her. No more lookin' at her with suggestions. You got that? Is that clear enough? Because if it ain't clear enough for you, Elder, then I'm gonna make it real clear. Right here. Right now. So is it clear or not?"

The missionary was startled. He didn't know what to say. He stood there.

Elder Lake said, "Now look here. This is uncalled for. Elder Whiting hasn't done anything with Loretta."

Willy Jack glared at Elder Whiting and said, "He speakin' for you now? Cat got your tongue? What's it gonna be? You stayin' away from Loretta, or you wanna to take a beatin'?"

Elder Lake turned to Cookie's parents and said, "Brother Tribbit, maybe it best we come back another time."

The missionaries gathered their things in haste and left.

Willy Jack said, "Sorry to disrupt your dinner. Loretta, may I have a word?"

Loretta, now the shy one, said, "Let me get my sweater, and I'll be right there."

She thought as she stepped inside the house, 'This is my first date with a real man. Not a boy. This ought to be interesting'.

Their love story was just beginning.

CHAPTER XXXIII

You Don't Mess With
Loretta McKenna

Willy Jack Walker and Loretta Ruth McKenna wanted, needed, to get married. Fast.

The Walker family was a respected name in Marshall County. Wesley Walker, Willy Jack's father, was director of the Waste & Water Department. Solid citizens. Solid Methodist. Edith was president of the local chapter of the Woman's Temperance Union. Wesley and Edith had five girls and Willy Jack. The girls were all beauties.

His youngest sister, Nan, become a Miss West Virginia. They said she looked like Marion Davies, the movie star. Their eldest child, Helen, was student body president of Union High School. Mr. House, the principal, couldn't remember that ever happening before . . . a girl president. He said during her introduction at a student rally that "Ms. Walker is exemplary young lady in every way. You girls out there ought to be more like her."

This, of course, immediately caused most of the girls in the class to want to really smack her a good one in the next slumber party pillow-fight.

Helen was later heard to say with just a bit of sarcastic wisdom, "Thank you, Mr. House. I may, just maybe, get a date for the prom now."

But she did. Get a date for the prom, that is.

The McKenna's were quite the opposite of the Walkers, up in Devil's Run Hollow, brewing their Mule Kick. Town talk was that there was always going to be a McKenna in jail or going to jail. When Pappy heard that remark he said, "That there is a gross miscarriage of justice. Right now there is nary a McKenna any way near a jail house."

Lula reminded him that his cousin Bodie was just got pinched for bootlegging and is in the county lock up. Pappy said, "Oh, but that fella does does possess a proclivity for trouble"

Lula in her quiet way said, "Why, yes, Pappy. I think that's what folks are talkin' about."

Willy Jack and Loretta met with the preacher at the Walkers' church, Pastor Lloyd. The church building was a beautiful red brick affair with stained-glass windows. Loretta had never seen stained glass with religious scenes before, and she thought them about the most beautiful thing she had ever seen. One of the windows had names identified as "major donors." She noticed the Walker name prominently in a bright red against a tempered gray.

She thought this would be just the perfect place to be married.

The pastor was seated at his desk. The teenagers sat on hard wooden chairs on the other side. Loretta thought the pastor looked uneasy. A little nervous. Even looked a little pasty.

Pastor Lloyd said, "Well, it's good to see you, Willy Jack, and thank you for helping out with the potluck dinner last week. That is appreciated. And, you . . ." He looked down at a notepad before he said, "Loretta. Loretta McKenna. From up in Devil's Run Hollow, right?"

Loretta said, "That's right, Pastor Lloyd. But I will be living in town now."

"How can I help you folks?"

Willy Jack said, "Pastor Lloyd, me and Loretta are getting married, and we would like to get married right here in the church."

"That is wonderful news you want to bind your marriage in Holy Matrimony. That is the proper thing to do." The pastor seemed to run out of words and stopped talking.

Willy Jack said, "Can we do this right away? Like this Saturday?"

The pastor squirmed and cleared his throat. He looked down then gave a distant stare out the window to his right. Loretta knew what was coming. She'd had this kind of treatment all of her life. She thought, 'Here comes the McKenna thing'.

The Pastor said, "Willy Jack, you've come to this church all of your life. Your family has probably been in this congregation longer than anybody. When God has a need here, your family, all of them, are always ready to pitch in. Rally the troops too, so to speak. The best examples of Christians that I know of But . .. ." His voice trailed off at that point, lost for words.

Loretta said, "Getting to the point, Pastor, is that you won't marry us?"

"Loretta, you seem like a nice young lady. This is nothing personal about you. But there are certain members of our congregation that are uncomfortable having the marriage here, in the House of the Lord."

"So if not in the House of the Lord," Loretta said, "Where would these certain members have us get married?" Loretta's bright blue eyes burned with intensity as the anger arose in her.

"It's not what you think, Loretta," said the pastor.

"Really, so what is it, Pastor? You and I know exactly what it is. It is a bunch of privilege shitheads that are so locked as to what people might think that a moonshiner's daughter might step foot in their precious church. 'Oh, my God, a Walker is marrying a McKenna! We can't have that now can we? Makin' all that shine up there in the hills. Gettin' arrested for it. Bunch of ne'er-do-wells.' Pastor, I thought Jesus went to people like the McKenna's to bring them the gospel."

Loretta stood up and said, "Come on, Willy Jack, I don't want to have anything to do with this place or these people. And you, Pastor, you ought to get acquainted with the Bible. Because right now you look about as un-Christian as a little pissant. Let's get out of the place, Willy Jack, because it makes me feel dirty."

Willy Jack was beginning to a get a little better glimpse of the McKenna fighting spirit. He got up to leave with Loretta.

The pastor said, "Loretta, now listen here. I can marry you elsewhere, just not here, in the church."

Walking out the door with Willy Jack in tow she said, "Oh, really, not in God's house. Elsewhere? If you believe that is in any way acceptable, you are a bigger horses-ass than I thought, right Willy Jack?" Willy Jack declined to comment.

They left the beautiful Methodist Chapel and were married by Elder Lake at the American Legion Hall on Grant Street the following Saturday. Elder Whiting was not in attendance. His mission ended and he had gone back to Provo, Utah.

None of the Walkers attended. All of Loretta's family joined in joyous celebration, although no Mule Kick was seen—the Mormons disapproving of such things. Some of the men, however, were seen going out to Pappy's truck and were seen coming back with the back of their hands wiping their mouth and dribbles of liquid on the front of their breeches.

Jack Walker was born a robust nine pounds and nine ounces, nine months later.

CHAPTER XXXIV

JACK IS HAMBURGER'D

Willy Jack had a good job as a foreman at Wheeling Steel. By the time he was twenty-one he was married, had a child on the way, and was a foreman at the mill. His early advancement to foreman caused resentment by the older men, but Willy Jack worked hard, kept his mouth shut, and was respectful to all, especially those men that he outranked in seniority but now worked under his supervision. It was tough work with tough men, but he had a quiet way and a strong core.

He worked at the steel mill for ten years, until a friend, Fat Freddie Franklin, who was simply call "Fats," offered him better pay as a barber, and soon after that he owned and operated "Willy Jack's Barbershop" right near the county courthouse.

Loretta led the family. She set the dinner table and the goals for Willy Jack and the children. She desired most that her family have strong, Christian values as taught by her church. She was proud to be a housewife and mother. That is what she wanted, and that is what she got it.

They had three children. The eldest son, Jack; then seven years younger, Young Willy, then five years later, Rebecca. With Rebecca, Loretta finally got her real, live baby girl.

Loretta had drilled it into Jack from birth that he would go to college. Be the first of all of the McKenna's to actually graduate. She also instilled in him the importance of values. Especially the church's Christian values. She raised him to be a good Mormon boy. Hard work, family values, good intentions, and virtue. Jack knew no other way. He was aware, but not intimate with the McKenna's ways that sent his relatives to prison occasionally. Especially Uncle Lamar, because he treated jail cells like a revolving door.

But Jack didn't know his Walker family well, and he was raised a McKenna, not a Walker. The McKenna's were fun and always interesting. A Sunday at Pappy's was a festival of fried chicken, corn on the cob, mashed potatoes with all the fixings, and the best apple pie that could be found in Marshall County, followed by raucous discussions where everybody seemingly voiced their strong opinions on politics, religion, and the bad behavior of neighbors and relatives. A little kick of the mule fueled the discussion and lightened the day.

Pappy especially, was full of Irish blarney, exaggerated tales of daring and adventure and he was funny and entertaining without trying. Everybody laughed and loved and had a lust for life. Jack loved them all, even Uncle Lamar. His Uncle Hooch was his favorite. Hooch the bootlegger, had perfected the art of storytelling with just enough exaggeration to make it fun and interesting.

Jack found his place on the playing grounds of Union High School in the ninth grade. He tried out for football with just about every other boy in the school. There were at least a hundred boys trying out for the thirty-three spots on the team.

The head coach was Mike Hagler. "Iron" Mike, coaching football since the game became popular. Looking forward to his retirement now, Iron Mike had earned his nickname. Tough and relentless. He wanted tough kids from the poorest parts of town and the hollow. He looked the other way for a boy that smoked or generally raised hell. He didn't like pretty boys or boys that would wear a necktie to school or run for student body president. He was a hard-ass and he wanted hard-ass football players that played angry and liked to hit and only got madder and more violent when they were hit.

His assistant, Pop Holmstead, was in his late sixties. Been everywhere. Done everything. Canadian army dough boy. Pro football. Pro wrestling. Bar fighter. Great teller of stories. His swearing was a thing of poetry, and he was the only person ever that Iron Mike would allow to swear on his football field. No college degree, but was everybody's favorite substitute teacher no matter the subject.

He was also the one person the players could always go to, for whatever the problem. Parents giving them a bad time. Girlfriend pregnant. Girlfriend breakup. Not playing enough. Iron Mike hates us. Flunking a class. Pop would would always tell them the truth and he always seemed right even if the boy had to be told to stop whining and grow a pair.

The boys all loved Pop and he never let them down.

At the second day of try-outs for the football team, Iron Mike called to Pop and said, "Hey, Pop get over here."

Pop was on the field with groups of ten boys running a forty-yard dash. The boys that were too slow or too small were cut right there on the spot. Pop would say to the small, slow boys, "You can go get dressed now. Thanks for tryin' out."

Pop jogged over to Iron Mike.

Iron Mike said, "You see that tall, skinny kid over there? Watch him for just a minute."

Jack was with a group of boys trying out for quarterback. A younger coach was supervising. Kids that wanted to be receivers were running routes, so the wannabe quarterbacks could throw it their way.

Iron Mike said, "Watch that kid coming up." There were six boys trying out for the spot. Jack was to throw next.

There was a center that snapped the ball back to Jack. He caught it raised his right arm to throw and started to signal the receiving with his left hand...go deep, go deeper...deeper. When the kid was forty-five yards downfield, Jack let it loose and hit the receiver in stride fifty yards down the field.

Pop said, "Oh, my gawd. Did I see what I just saw? Who is that kid? It's too bad we don't pass the ball more than once every third game."

Iron Mike said, "Don't give up hope, Pop. We might be getting that down to every other game. Let's see if the boy can run. Get your five, six fastest guys over here and see if our passer can put one foot in front of the other."

Iron Mike called for Jack to come over to him. Jack did and the coach said, "What's your name, Son?"

"Jack Walker."

"Walker... Walker. You related to Willy Jack Walker?"

"That's my father, sir."

That set Iron Mike to thinking. He said, "I know your dad. Played a little and showed a lot of promise. Had to leave school to go to work. I get my haircut from him every so often. I knew he had some kids but. .. ." He paused. "Seems like yesterday and here you are. You know, now that I think about it, you look a lot like your dad."

"I've been told, sir."

"I don't believe he could throw a ball like you."

"Nobody can, Coach."

Iron Mike smiled. He liked it. Cocky at fifteen. Seems smart. Got an edge to him his daddy didn't seem to have. Iron Mike then remembered: 'Willy Jack married a McKenna . Those McKenna's are tough sumbitches. I wonder if this kid is tough, too? Let's see him run'.

Pop had his fastest boys line up. Some were three or four years older than Jack. Jack didn't like to lose at any competition and that included a foot race.

Pop said, "Okay, boys. You're gonna go from here to the forty. Coach Anderson is down there with his stopwatch, so go all out. Ready. Set."

Pop blew a whistle and the boys took off. Forty yards and under five seconds later, Jack finished ahead of all the boys by three yards.

Pop turned to Mike and said, "Hamburger. Let's see what the boy's got some sand."

The hamburger drill was this: About thirty players line up with a path between them. Fifteen on either side.

Iron Mike said to Jack, "Listen, son. These guys are not gonna tackle you. What they are gonna do is try to knock you on your ass. They are gonna hit you as hard as they can. Your job is to get through them without being knocked down. So run hard and stay on your feet. They get on the grass, they win. You finish standing, you win. Any questions?"

"Can I hit back?"

"Yeah, I guess so, but your goal is the end of the line standing, not knocking them on their ass."

"Thank you, sir."

Jack took the ball and looked down the line. He saw the players smirking at him. They were older. Bigger. Probably a lot stronger. Tough kids. Their fathers worked in coal mines and the steel mill. Most all of them were border line poverty. Many of them had been beaten by a drunk father. To all of them, they knew football was their only way out of crushing poverty and going to college.

But Jack didn't see the players; what he saw was the insults and humiliation of being that hillbilly kid from the hollow. A hillbilly. None too smart and always poor. Lazy, worthless hicks up there away from everybody with their funny way of talking and everybody marrying a cousin. Making their whiskey, drunk all night and sleeping all day.

Jack steeled himself. He would not go down. He. Would. Not. Go. Down.

The first three players on either side didn't touch him because his speed took him by them before their could react. Then the hits came. Right. Left. To the head, to the gut. To the knees. Boys launching themselves headfirst toward Jack. They came from all angles. Jack was snorting, snot pouring out of nose, tears down his face. All from his pent-up hatred of the insults and the taunts he and his family had thrown in their faces. A primal yell came from his very core. He screamed as he ran. The last four players were all seniors. Big boys. Linemen. Each over two hundred pounds. They got ready for the kill. Jack lowered his shoulders. Threw his left forearm out violently at the player on that side, hitting him hard in the face and putting him down. He lowered his shoulder on the right to bull his way through the two on the right. The closest player got the force of Jack's speed and shoulder. He fell back and took out the remaining boy on that side. Jack was standing leaving a wake of speed and violence in his path. He won. They lost.

He crossed the line now, screaming in a loud primal, animalistic roar. Now bending over, trying to get control of his body and emotions.

The coaches, players, and few spectators were all silent. No one spoke or made any noise. The players were stunned. Iron Mike turned to Pop and said, "My gawd, Pop. What have we got here?"

Pop said, "Never seen something like this before, have we, Mike? Maybe got the next Jim Thorpe here. Either that or the next Jack Dempsey."

Mike said, "I don't know about you, but I just found out when I'll retire."

"When's that, Mike?"

"The day this kid graduates."

Thirty-three boys made the Union High School Varsity. The boys met with their coach in the middle of the playing field. They formed a circle around the coach, the boys in front kneeling.

Iron Mike said, "All right boys, listen up. Hey 20 and 32 back there, when I say listen up, you shut your mouth right then and there. That means no talking. And you two guys, 20 and 32, you will give me four and twenty as soon as we are done here. You two have got to set the standards for these younger players. And the first standard is you don't disrespect your coach. Now for those you that don't know what four and twenty mean, it means you will give me four laps around the track and twenty push-ups. And that, gentlemen, is about the lowest we go. Next time it will be eight and forty, so when I say 'listen up,' that means you will shut up and shut up right then. Mid-sentence—hell no—mid-word, you shut up. And you two, All-State and all that, but that means you gotta lead and show the young kids how we play Union High ball. We don't screw around. Twenty?"

"Yes, sir."

"I don't believe I heard you, Stevie."

"Yes, Sir!"

"Thirty-two, Mark?"

"Yes, Sir!"

"For the rest of you, our first rule is no swearing. I might use a little swear word now and again—sixty-two year-old hard-ass and I can't stop swearing. I got it being Navy, and when you are in the Navy, you can swear all you want, but not here. Never. You swear on the field, and you will be pulled. Why do you think that? Lemme tell you. You don't play for yourself, you don't play for Iron Mike, you represent the people of this entire community. You play for them and we go across that river and play Bellaire, you represent all the people of West Virginia. So we dress right, we don't act up, and we don't swear. The major exception is Pop. He was in the Canadian army and we just can't break him. So let's get down to fundamentals. This here is a football. We wanna take this ball and get it over and into the end zone. This ball is precious. You backs, if you are runnin' with this ball and give it the other team, you will be benched. And Stevie, that goes for you too. All-state don't mean nothin' now. That was last year."

Stevie said, "That go for Mark as well?" Referring to the Most Valuable Player in the State from the previous year, Mark Grimm, "the Grimm Reaper."

"Stevie, you might have found a loophole. MVP in state, you may get a pass. Let's get back to our rules. You quarterbacks. You pass it away to the other team, you will be benched. If this ball is on the ground, you dive, you scratch, you kick, you crawl, and you get that ball before the other little bastard in the other color uniform grabs it. This ball is valuable. As valuable as your nuts, which brings me to the next topic of discussion."

Reaching in his pocket, he pulled out a strange-looking piece of cloth. To the young boys it looked like something that might be some kind of a slingshot.

Iron Mike continued. "This, boys, is called a jockstrap. You wear this when we practice and play the games. It protects your little peckers and nuts. My boys a few years ago didn't have these, but times were tougher then, and those boys could take a hit in the nuts like nobody you ever seen. They got whacked there so many times, those balls of theirs would get as hard as walnuts. Walnuts, I'm tellin' ya. Those boys were state champs, and they could take a hit. So get your mothers to take you down to Shotty's and tell them you're on the football team and they will get you fitted out and ready to play. You got that? Any questions? You, 82, whatcha got?"

Eighty-two said, "My Ma said I shouldn't wear one of those 'cause it will restrict my ability to make her a grandma."

Mike said, "Where did you Maw go to medical school?"

"I don't think she ever told me."

"What's your name, boy?"

"Merkle, Sir. Marty Merkle."

"Merkle, do people call your mom a doctor? Do they say 'Dr. Merkle'?"

"I don't reeal ever heard anyone say that."

"That's because, 82, your mom is not a doctor. So get down to Shotty's and get fitted out. The school board has decided that all of you boys will wear jockstraps, and that's it. No jock. No play. And don't ask me what the school board was doing wasting time on jockstraps for football players. I have no idea, although I would like to have heard the open discussion about that. Any questions? Yeah, what is it, 82."

"Do I have to take my mother with me to Shotty's to get the jockstrap?"

Iron Mike looked at the ground and thought, 'You get one of these every year and you just found this year's kid. Boy will probably grow up and be some smart ass lawyer'.

He said, "Take whoever you want, Mertly."

"Merkle, Sir. Merkle.

Coach said, "Okay, boys, on three. One, two, three."

The team answered back in a loud yell, "Union! Beat Bellaire!"

In Jack's first game against Bellaire, Stevie ran for two touchdowns. The Reaper ran for two more and tackled the Bellaire star running back from his middle linebacker spot so violently, that the kid had is fill of thirty-two and didn't play the rest of the game. Jack passed seven times for two touchdowns. Two passes in the end zone were dropped by his receivers. Union won forty to three.

CHAPTER XXXV

JACK'S EPIPHANY

Jack played every game at Union High from that first one through his senior year.

His final year was magic. Every game a blowout leading up to the final against their rivals, Wheeling. Jack was averaging three touchdown passes and two running a game. He scored eight times against Moundsville. Was the state's Most Valuable Player.

After the last season, Iron Mike did as he had promised. He retired as the State Champ and was soon inducted in the West Virginia High School Hall of Fame. Pop was right on his heels—he resigned too.

Jack was in Trig class, the Monday after the his last game. The vice-principal, Mr. Gates, walked into the classroom and whispered something to the teacher.

Mr. Blount, the teacher said, "Jack, Mr. House would like to see you."

With that the kids started whoopin' and yellin'. Thinking Jack, the Mormon jock who did no wrong, was in some sort of trouble.

Walking down the wide hallway with Mr. Gates, Jack was trying his best to think of what this could be about. He relaxed a bit when he saw Iron Mike sitting with Mr. House and another man.

Mr. House said, "Jack, sit down over here. I want you to meet Coach Wilce. He is the Ohio State football coach, and he wanted to meet you."

The coach stood and offered his hand. They shook.

The coach said, "Jack, we've been watching you for the last couple of years, and we think you would be a great addition to the Ohio State football program. We would like to get you playin' for us over in Columbus."

Jack said, "Thank you, Coach. I, ah, I. I really don't know what to say. I've kinda always thought I would go to WVU."

"WVU is a fine school, but we can offer so much more in Columbus. We have a program that could put you through school without any cost. And our team is a national power, not like WV, a nice little regional program."

Jack was starting to think a little clearer. He said, "Well, Chic Harley has kinda put you guys on the map. Whacked Michigan a good one too. Wouldn't I be playing the same position as Chic and he has a couple more years, doesn't he?"

"Chic is the best in college football, that's for sure. You're a better passer than Chic, right now. We'd take advantage of your talents, you can be sure of that. And you may have heard we are building a 65,000-seat stadium right on campus. It might be finished before you graduate. Sixty-five thousand, Jack, cheering you on."

Jack smiled and said, "You didn't mention anything about my running compared to Chic."

Coach Wilce said, "Nobody runs like Chic, Son."

"I know. I've seen him play."

When Jack walked into the Ohio State locker room, he quickly realized that his high school days as the big star were over. His first thought, "These guys are really big. No more, Jackie boy, are you going to be biggest and fastest on the field. Where's Chic? Oh, I see him. He's sure looks small. How's he do all the stuff he does on the field'?

Jack was standing, star-stuck, in a walkway, when he heard a deep voice behind him say, "Rookie. You. Get your ass out of the way. Move over there." He nodded toward an equipment manager on the other side of the room. The man with the deep voice, had a towel around his waist, coming from the shower. He was big, about two-thirty, Jack guessed. He had a dark stubble and a large head. He looked angry about something. It was the first time Jack had doubts about his football ability. He thought, 'Can I play with these guys'?

He did play, but he wasn't the "do everything" player like in high school. Every player around him now had the same story, the same background as Jack. His first year he was on the practice squad. Freshmen were banned from varsity sports their first year. The next two years, he backed up Chic and came in for passing on occasion or when the game was about over. His final year, Chic was gone and Jack started. He played well and made third-team all-conference. They lost to Michigan Jack's last game. George Halas of the Chicago Bears called and made a weak offer, but he was through with football and happy about it.

He stayed on for law school at Ohio State and was now ready to graduate. Jack was in the library at Page Hall. He was bored. What was said about law school was right: The first year they scare you to death. The second year they work you to death. The third year they bore you to death. As a law student, he was Order of The Coif, meaning a top 10 percent student.

Offers came in—Cadwalader, Wickersham & Taft in New York City. Tolles, Hogsett, Ginn & Morley in Cleveland. Worthington & Strong in Cincinnati. Three Chicago firms had sent invitations for interviews. A classmate and friend, John Bricker, wanted to start a firm with Jack in Columbus. A nationally known criminal defense lawyer in Wheeling, Spencer Sprat, wanted an interview.

Out of his boredom, he remembered the letter that he received from his sister several days ago. He pulled the letter from his briefcase.

Rebecca wrote, "Hello, Brother. Everything is pretty good here. Mother is as feisty as ever. She's been painting rooms in the house at her usual breakneck speed. She would do one room, then the other. Funny thing, she did every room in the house and then realized that they were all green! Different shades, but every room. . . green. She really got a kick out of that. You know, she is the Relief Society president at the Church now. Doing a real nice job, I'm told.

I am doing fine working at Woolworth's. It's okay, but I really am ready to settle down, but no candidates right now. Mother gave me this letter from her journal. I didn't know Pappy had gone to prison, did you? Anyway, I'll let you read it. Let me know what you think, okay? With love, Sis."

Sitting at a long table with other students scattered about, he began to read the letter from his mother's journal, written by her hand:

"To my children, who I love more than life itself, Jack, Young Willy, and Rebecca.

The first Christmas that I can remember was in Pittsburgh . . . was I five? Probably. My Dad here, rather than at home in McMechen, because he was hiding out from from the law. There was a warrant out for his arrest. He'd been bootleggin' Pappy's liquor.

We were living in an apartment on Liberty Avenue. Christmas morning found the little McKenna family waking from a sound sleep with 'Ho, Ho, Ho' and the scratching of reindeer on our roof (or so we thought). We hopped out of bed and the first thing I saw was a blackboard with the words, 'Merry Christmas from Santa Claus.'

A doll for me, boxing gloves and roller skates for the boys.

We had the best Christmas I thought any child could have. I'm sure my mother cooked a fantastic meal because Dad saw that we never were without food.

We had so much fun that day. Everyone was happy and just joyful.

Late in the day, Dad set up a ring in the kitchen, roped off with kitchen chairs. Our little brother, Hooch, was too small to box with Lamar, so Dad put the gloves on me and Lamar, my twin. Lamar got a little carried away, socked me a good one, and knocked me out. His first KO. It scared everyone to death, and Mom made us put the boxing gloves up.

Right before Christmas, she had taken us to Caldabaugh's, 'The store that has EVERYTHING'! We were allowed to choose one gift each. That's when I saw the doll!!!!! It looked exactly like a new baby and was the same size. It was the only thing that my eyes spied. The cost? Twelve dollars! Do you have any idea what twelve dollars amounted to then? But I knew Santa would bring it to me; I was such a very good little girl.

The boys got the boxing gloves and roller skates with rubber tires so they could skate in the house. Yes, my Mother allowed roller skates in the house!

And sure enough, that Christmas morning, Santa delivered my baby girl. I called her Mollie. I loved the doll and still do. Do you know I still have it? From that moment on I knew what I wanted: a family with babies that I could love and cherish. A good husband. I wanted out of the hollow. I wanted away from bootlegging and moonshine and all that went with it. I wanted my boys to go to college. The first McKenna's to do so. I wanted a church and a religion to guide us on a new path. I wanted to be close to the Lord, Jesus the Christ. And now I have all that. Now I want Lamar to mend his ways and become converted to the gospel.

A few days later, our Uncle Lee wanted to borrow the skates, and because the boys wouldn't give them up, he cut chunks out of the skates' tires. I think it was Uncle Lee and his mean-spirited ways and criminal activity that got Lamar so involved in going down that path to evildoings. But I will not give up. I will keep helping Lamar find the path to the Kingdom of God.

The next Christmas found us back in Devil's Run Hollow. Dad was gone off to prison now, and Mother was trying to make a roof over our heads and put food on the table. It was a great struggle for her, but she was one in a million and the best of mothers.

As I have grown older and thought many times of my dad being away from us, I used to put it in the back of my mind and try not to think of it. But our dad loved us, he wanted us to have a roof over our head and food in our bellies. It is the only time my dad was ever in trouble with the law, and when you think of how he was practically an orphan, how he went to work so very young and on his own from the time he was in the fourth grade. . . the struggles he had to overcome.

I'm proud of my Dad—even the hard lessons he had to learn, he learned, he overcame. He became a great man in my eyes, especially since he did most of his overcoming on his own, and he did it for me and my brothers and for you children, too.

Love,

Loretta Ruth McKenna Walker, your loving Mother, forever."

Tears formed as Jack finished his Mother's letter. He bowed his head so he wouldn't be seen—the football star crying in the law library. He notice teardrops on the sheet of paper. He put both hands to his face and wiped away the tears.

He felt such an ache, such pain, such an overwhelming sense of love to his mother and the family for Pappy, too, what they had all done to survive. He now understood what Appalachia was all about—the values they held, why their land was so terribly important to them.

He thought, 'All these people, my people, were doing was trying to survive. They only did what the family had done for centuries. They just wanted to live and let live'.

Jack Walker knew at that moment what he was going to do. He would go back to West Virginia, and he would defend his family. Much of the sacrifice, much of the suffering, had been to bring him to this moment in time, ready now to lead this family. Lead them to prosperity, teach them a better way. Defend them in the courts. He thought, 'I may not be Clarence Darrow, but this family will get my best. I owe that to them. It was their sacrifices that got me here'.

He closed his law books. His mission was now clear. He would go back home.

Back home to West Virginia.

CHAPTER XXXVI

JACK I NEED YOUR HELP

Spencer Sprat said, "C'mon in Jack. Sit down."

"Thank you, Mr. Sprat."

"Spence, is my name around here."

"Okay, Spence it is."

"Let's get the difficult stuff out of the way first," Sprat said.

His head was covered with unruly white hair. Looked like he didn't do much to comb it. He was a big man, shorter than Jack, but full-bodied, wearing suspenders holding on to rich-colored brown pants and a starched, white shirt. No tie. He was playing with a stogie, cutting off an end and lighting it up.

He took a puff and said, "You smoke, Jack?"

"No, I don't, but I do like the smell of a cigar."

"Oh, yes. One of the pleasures. Jack, we may have trouble, you and me, working in my office."

"Why would that be, Spence?" Jack said.

"I think you know why."

Jack smiled and said, "Is it because you went to that overrated, never-produced-much-good law school up in Ann Arbor, or because you were an all-American tackle at that same shitty, arrogant school playing club teams and building a big record? Michigan Man, my ass."

Sprat started laughing, hard. Smoke got caught up in the laugh and started a string of coughs. Jack was laughing, too.

Finally, Sprat said, "Damn, Jack. Maybe you got the balls to be something in this profession, even coming out of that cow college in Columbus."

"I do what it takes to win."

"I know that, Jack. I saw your play your last game high school game against Wheeling. Extraordinary play. Really magnificent, and I saw your last game against the Maize and Blue. No points for the Buckeyes, eh? That had to be tough."

Sprat sat up straight, took another puff, and said, "Well, let's get to it. Why in hell's unholy world do you want go into criminal defense work? You could go to New York or Cleveland and get on with one of the big firms. Go up to Cleveland with that firm that's got Rockefeller's business. Let that ol' man make you a millionaire."

"Yeah, I did get an offer from them—Tolles, Hogsett, Ginn & Morley."

"So why are you here?"

"Spence, you came down from that hollow over in, where was it... Mud Creek?"

"Mud Run."

"You went from Mud Run, to Michigan Law, to become the top criminal defense lawyer in the country."

"I have to concur there, Counselor."

Jack said, "So why did you start defending the undefendable?"

"This may shock you, Jack, but my pa and grandpa and. . . etc. etc. etc. . . . were all Scots-Irish moonshiners. Somebody's got to defend their sorry asses."

"Spence, I'm pretty certain you know my family name, since you're such a fan and all. It's Walker, but my mother's maiden is McKenna. Capital M-c-capital K-e-double n-a. McKenna. I think you are somewhat familiar with my family."

"Pappy's been here a couple of times. Really like Pappy. Straight shooter. Just like my grandfather. Lamar, of course. We ought to just get him an office with a bed. I met Henry once. Tough old nut."

"So we are both suckers for lost causes, Spence?"

Spence said, "Lost causes are the only ones worth fighting for, Jack. Come on, let's go. I want to show you the office I got for you."

"Does this mean I'm hired?"

"Jack, I hired you the moment you ran over that big-mouthed fat kraut in The Game. Guy goes two-fifty and you put him on his backside and just kept right on going. What was name?"

"Gaskamp. How'd you know I would want to come here?"

"Because, Jack my boy, you want to learn from the best, now don't you? And Darrow notwithstanding, Laddie, I am the best. The Hillbilly Hotshot. Hot damn!"

"By the way, what is the offer?"

"Work your ass off six days a week, shit wages, and forget about an outside social life. Oh, the bonus . . .you get to work with a bunch a criminals that will lie to you and not want to pay you and may have you shot and killed if you piss 'em off."

"Who could resist that sales pitch? What's the upside?"

"The Hotshot, Jack. You get to work your ass off for me. In five years I got a feeling that I'll be in second chair."

"Why do you think it'll take five years?"

"Because it took me three, and you're a Buckeye. Those farmers are slow learners."

"When do I start?"

"You started when you showed up for work today. There are three cases on your desk. Read 'em. You'll be in court with me today, right after lunch on the Murdoch file. Murder One. One of Big Gio's boys."

Jack threw himself into the work. He loved it. It fueled his competitive nature. He loved the courtroom battles. Loved working with a wild menagerie of characters that filled his day.

He loved it all.

Two years later, it was well past midnight when Jack got the call. The voice was urgent but not in panic mode. It was his Uncle Lamar.

"Jack, I need your help. They got me in County over in Moundsville."

"What's the charge?"

"Well, I guess burglary. They caught me and my boys taking a truckload of nickel out of a warehouse at Wheeling Steel over in Benwood."

"Nickel, did you say? You mean the metal?"

"Yeah, it was the perfect crime. We were . . ." Jack cut him off.

"Stop. Don't say anything else. Don't admit anything. Just say, My lawyer is on the way. How many in your crew."

"Well, me and our cousin, Larry . . ."

"You mean from Vinton County? That Larry, the one with palsy?"

"Yeah."

"Who else? Well, Curly that works in your dad's shop. His cousin, Sabatino, a backup driver, and Bobby T, Larry's cousin."

"You mean they caught you in the warehouse?"

"No, at the gate when we was leavin'."

"All right, I'll be there within an hour. Don't say or admit anything. You got that, Uncle Lamar?"

"Yeah."

"Lamar, I mean it. Don't say anything. I know how you like to talk. You know the system, you been there enough times."

Jack's first thought after hanging up with Lamar was, 'Mother is going to be devastated over this. She had such hope for Lamar. Thought she had got him to turn the corner. Put him in the Walker family house and he turns it into a whorehouse. Then damn near burns it down. Yesterday, there's Lamar in church. All smiles and hello's to everybody, Hi, Brother Jones, how you doin,' Sister Jones. The next day he's in County for stealing metal nickel. Nickel! And from Wheeling Steel. Spencer is going to want this one, but this is mine. This is why I came to this firm, to defend my family. And here it is. My time. But, caught in the act! At the mill. Wheeling Steel will put all their weight behind serious time. They can't let this go unpunished'.

Jack was throwing on clothes. Suit. Tie. Grab the briefcase. Business cards. Keys to the car. Out the door, thinking, 'What's the defense to men caught at the scene? How am I going to tell Mother he's done it big this time? Well, Jack, you wanted challenges. You got one now'.

Jack didn't know that reporters from the newspapers in Moundsville, McMechen, and Wheeling were already writing their story, which one would call the boldest, brashest heist ever in West Virginia.

The very oddity of the crime will attract a lot of attention.

Within two days, the reporters would be from the Pittsburgh Dispatch, the Cleveland Plain Dealer, the Cincinnati Enquirer, the Columbus Dispatch, the Frankfort State Journal, the Youngstown Bulletin, and not far behind, The New York Times and the Boston Herald.

The Erie Evening Herald and the Erie Dispatch did not send reporters.

They had no idea what they were missing.

CHAPTER XXXVII

LOCK-UP

The county sheriff's office was a square, two-story building made of limestone that had turned a dirty gray and black. Sheriff Boyer's office, along with staff and two deputies, were in the front on the first floor. Midway to the back were steel bars and a secure entryway to the jails. There were four jail cells in the back.

One of the cells was occupied by two inmates—young men about twenty-two, twenty-three. They had been sentenced to ninety days for selling moonshine liquor to four underage boys. The boys got drunk, stole a tractor, and went joyriding. They broke through J. T. Colter's fence down in South County and found themselves staring at the rancher's prize bull. The bull, a black Angus named Lucifer, took exception to the invasion of his pasture and started ramming the tractor. The terrified boys sobered up fast. Trapped on the top of the tractor, Lucifer took one run after another at the tractor, rocking it back and forth. With each hit the boys feared the tractor would tip over and the angry beast would be at them.

About seven in the next morning, J. T. Coulter came out to feed the cows. He was stunned when he saw that Lucifer had destroyed his tractor, and four teenage boys were trapped on top of what was left.

Sheriff Boyer tracked the booze, which started the whole affair, to the young men who now were now incarcerated in the cell next to Lamar's five. The two had jeans and dirty T-shirts on with long hair and stubble on their face. They played cards all night and slept during the day. They had a radio that they played all night. They got out once a week, on Saturday morning, to take a five-minute shower.

The cell at the far end was the drunk tank. Four filthy mattresses were on the floor, stinking of piss, alcohol, and vomit. The cells were cleaned every Monday morning. The mattresses were thrown out every year on January first—starting the new year clean.

The county jail was usually locked up at six at night and opened again at eight in the morning. Not this night. It was noisy—the lawmen giving orders and the reporters asking questions, all done at once.

The boys were escorted to the cells by eight lawmen. Lamar and Curly went into the cell next to the two inmates. Larry and Bobby T were next to them and Sabatino in the drunk tank.

Lamar made his call to Jack, and they waited.

At three in the morning, Jack arrived. He was taken to a room on the second floor, painted a pea green and with a square, plain, worn table and straight-back wooden chairs. Like everything in and around the jail, the room had a peculiar scent . . . a combination of jailhouse stench that seemed to drift and stick everywhere, mixed with a strong disinfectant.

The boys were led into the room, cuffed, and roughly pushed down onto the hard chairs. The lawmen left the room.

Lamar said, "Boys, this is my nephew . . . my sister's boy, Jack Walker."

Larry said, "Jack, you can't believe that cell. It smells awful, and those creeps next to us wouldn't turn down the radio. That thing was giving me a splitting headache."

"Larry, that is so like you," Bobby T said. "You concerned about your personal comfort when we are looking at two to five in Moundsville."

Sabatino said, "You guys are lucky, I got stuck in that . . . that, sudicio . . . Curly, how you say 'sudicio'?"

"Filthy."

"Si, filthio. Filthio. Really filthio."

"Filthy," said Curly, "filthy."

"Yeah, that what I say."

Jack said, "Okay, gentlemen. Shut up. No talking. It's time to listen."

Bobby T sat down glared at Jack and said, "Where's Spence?"

Jack said, "My name is Jack Walker, Lamar's nephew. I'll be representing you."

Bobby T turned to Lamar and in a loud voice said, "Lamar, you said we were gettin' the Hillbilly Hotshot and we got your nephew? That is one big fuckin' drop off."

He then turned to Jack and said, "So, hotshot junior, you even been to a law school or do you just carry Spencer Sprat's briefcase?"

Jack reached across the table and grabbed a handful of Bobby T's loose-fitting prison outfit around the neck and said, "What did I just say? I said shut up, no talking. It's time to listen."

He pulled Bobby T out of his chair. "Listen, you stupid son of a bitch. When I tell you to do something, you gonna do it double-time, you understand? I want you to get something straight . . . real straight. Lamar is my uncle. He is my mother's twin brother. You get that? My mother's twin. This is family, Bobby T. Nobody messes with my family. Nobody. Because you are not very bright, you have been in and out of jails, prisons, and various lock-ups since you were fourteen. You think you know the system? You don't know shit. You are looking at fifteen to twenty years here, and you will sit there and do what I tell you to do, or I will call the guard and have your ass hauled back to your grimy, crummy little cell, and I will not represent you, and neither will Spence. Are we clear now? I can get real cranky at three in the morning sitting in a jailhouse. So I say again, Are we clear now?"

Bobby T nodded.

Jack said, "I want to hear it. Are we clear?"

"Yes, I think so."

Jack didn't let go. Pulled tighter on his shirt. Tighter around his neck.

Bobby T said, "Alright, alright. I got it.

Jack pushed Bobby T back into the chair.

"I'm glad we got that cleared up. Lamar, where did the cops stop you?"

"Well, Larry here had just opened the gate, and all these lights came on. Damn near blinded me. Anyway, the sheriff was on the bullhorn telling us to get out of the car. See, I was driving my car in front of the Kelly Springfield. Jack, did you see that truck? It's a real beauty."

"Stay on point, Uncle Lamar."

"Well that was pretty much it. We got out of the car and they arrested us."

"Which side of the fence were you arrested, inside or outside?

"Side?"

"Yes, were you through the gate or not?"

"Oh, on the mill side."

"Were your carrying guns, weapons?"

"Yeah, we all had something on us."

Jack paused and thought briefly.

Jack said, "There is an arraignment and bail hearing on Wednesday in the mornings. As you probably know they will be charging you with various crimes of which you each will plead not guilty. The judge will ask if you understand the charges and how do you plead. You will answer, yes, I understand, and not guilty. That's it. Not another peep out of any of you. You got that Bobby T?"

Bobby T nodded.

Jack then turned to Sabatino and said, "What's wrong with you?"

Sabatino started weeping, his shoulders moving up and down, and he said, "Mia moglie e mia madre me uccideranno."

"Curly?" Jack said.

"He says his wife and mother are gonna kill him. Jack, he's not a criminal. He drives a taxi and has three kids. He was just my backup driver. He didn't do anything. Plus, he is a little emotional. He's being crying down in the cell block too."

"Tell him those women are least of his worries," Jack said.

"Okay, gentlemen. This meeting is over. I will see you on Wednesday. Don't talk to anyone about your caper or anything else. That includes guards, cellmates, each other, lawmen, prosecuting attorneys, and strangers in the showers. No one. Just don't open your mouth. At all. Any questions?"

Larry said, "Are you gonna get us out of here on Wednesday? It really is smelly in there."

Jack stared at Larry, picked up his briefcase, and turned to the door and said, "I'll see you on Wednesday."

CHAPTER XXXVIII

So Happy To See You Back
In Court, Lamar

The five were moved to the Marshall County Courthouse Wednesday morning and placed in a holding cell. All were in prison clothes . . . baggy pants and shirts with dirty, light gray-and-white horizontal stripes. The sleeves puffed out, which made their arms appear thin. Larry's pants were too short and exposed pale skin above the slipper-shoes issued by the jailers.

Lamar and Bobby T had a relaxed look. Curly looked puzzled. Sabatino appeared on the edge of tears. Larry looked happy to get out of the stink of the jailhouse. They were cuffed. Their hair has disheveled, hand-combed after their showers. Stubble growth was on their faces. With the exception of Sabatino, they looked like men who had done prior prison time.

The courthouse itself was an imposing structure made of brick, elevated about thirty feet above 7th Street on a gentle mound. Four seventy-foot columns rose to support a peaked roof with a spire on top, reminisce of a Gothic cathedral. A tall, ornamental tower rose above the majestic structure. In front, wide, fanned-out steps led to the front entrance. Above the entry, in black letters against a snow-white background, it read, MARSHALL COUNTY COURTHOUSE. The courthouse made a statement, as if to say, 'I'm an all-powerful clenched fist over all that enter here'.

The courtroom was beautifully crafted in wood. Old European craftsmanship. The room was dominated by a twenty-foot-long judge's bench, three feet above the floor. Tables for the lawyers and the accused faced the bench. Scattered about were tables and chairs for bailiffs and others. Behind the lawyer's table was a three-foot-tall railing. Behind that were seats for spectators and the press. A jury box, with seating for fifteen, framed the courtroom directly to the side of the judge's bench.

Peaches, Sam, and Roxy were seated near the back. Loretta and Hooch were in the front row.

The judge was Elwood W. Pickett, sixty-three—a beefy, bald man who walked with a limp, gifted from a mining accident when he was seventeen. That accident put him on the path to law school at West Virginia University. He had been a prosecuting attorney who then advanced to the bench. His reputation was tough but fair, with a lean to the prosecution's point of view.

The boys were brought in by sheriff deputies. Their cuffs were removed, and they were seated at the defense table. Jack was absorbed in his notes and said nothing but nodded to the group.

The prosecutor Lamar's nemesis from the Hen House case, District Attorney Johnson J. Juice, best known for his courtroom dramas against Spencer Sprat in two separate murder trials. Sprat got an acquittal in the first trial and a reduction in the second from Murder One to manslaughter, time served, in the second. Clear victories for Spencer. The last acquittal was well known since the defendant upon hear 'not guilty', jumped up and said, 'Thank y'all. I appreciate the not guilty, and I promise you I will never do it again'.

Juice entered the courtroom with his usual fanfare—slapping a back, smiling and pointing at another, having a brief joke with the bailiff, the fake laugh, winking at a reporter. With his ceremonial entry complete and at the prosecutor's table, he turned to Jack and said, "So Spence sent the second team, did he? Didn't want any part of the Juice on this one, did he?"

Juice was smirking at Jack and thinking, 'I'm gonna mow this rookie's grass. Chew him up and spit him out'.

Jack didn't take the bait. He stuck out his hand and said, "Jack Walker. Spence's in Cleveland on a murder case, but he told me to give you his regards and tell you he wishes he could beat you again."

"Spence is a funny guy. Walker? The football guy, right?"

"That's right? That your linebacker son I ran over in the Moundsville game? Seemed like a fine player till they carried him off the field. I hear he missed a couple of games after that . . . broken...what was it, collar bone right...yeah, I think so, a broken collar bone..right? So, how is the boy?"

Juice just glared at Jack.

The bailiff shouted, "Here yea. Here yea. All rise. The Honorable Judge Elwood Pickett convening in the Third Circuit Court, County of Marshall, State of West Virginia."

Judge Pickett entered from a door behind the bench with his bald head shinning and a black robe from neck to black shoes. Rumor had it that he worn only his underwear under the robe. The rumor originated with Candy, his personal secretary, so many believed the rumor to be true. Truth be known—it was, up to a point. He kept a shirt on. No pants.

The judge looked at the lawyers and nodded at the prosecutor.

"Johnson J. Juice for the State, Your Honor. We have five defendants caught in the act of burglary and . . ."

Jack stood and said, "Objection. Speculation. No evidence of any crime at this point."

"Sustained. Young man, we will get to you shortly, but let's try not to get too technical in the prosecutor's first sentence."

"Yes, sir. But the prosecutor should be more careful with his words."

Juice glared at Jack, thinking, 'This young prick. So this is the way? Okay'.

Juice then read a list of crimes that the men had allegedly committed: burglary, criminal trespass, concealing stolen property, larceny, illegal transportation, and several other lessor violations. He finished and sat down.

The judge nodded to Jack.

"Jack Walker for the defense."

Judge Pickett said, "You representing all of 'em, Counselor?"

"For the moment, your Honor."

The judge turned his attention to the defendants and said, "Would you gentlemen please stand? I am going to speak to you as a group, then ask a direct question or two to you individually. This question is for all of you: I want you to know that you have a right to be represented by your own personal lawyer. Do any of you choose to do that? Please raise your hand if you do."

No hands were raised.

"All right. I am now going to address you individually . . . starting with the man standing next to Mr. Walker. Your name please?

"You mean me?" Lamar said.

"Yes, Lamar, I mean you."

"Oh, well good to see you again too, Judge."

"Let's not get overly chummy here, Lamar, just state your name."

"Oh, okay. Lamar McKenna."

"Lamar, I heard you were released early from our lovely state facility down the street. Where are you living now?"

"Over on 21st Street in McMechen."

"Does the street have an address?"

"Oh, yeah. Six-one-nine."

"Thank you. How do you plead?"

Lamar looked tentatively at Jack. Jack nodded to Lamar and he said, "Not guilty, Your Honor."

The process was repeated with the others.

The judge then said, "Moving on, Mr. Juice. Let's address the question of bail."

Juice said, "Your Honor, there should be no bail. Several of the defendants are well-known by this court. I believe you have even presided over a McKenna trial or two over the years, so you are well aware of the history of this defendant. Larry Wells and Bobby T Wells are from Vinton County, Ohio, and could walk over the bridge and then we would have to go through the time and expense of getting them back in this courtroom. Curly Morizzo and Sabatino Santore are from Italy and could easily return. The state respectfully petitions the court to deny bail for all of the defendants."

"Mr. Walker?" said the Judge.

"Thank you, Your Honor. Lamar McKenna, and his family, are well-known in this community. Lamar, who is my uncle, could be released under my recognizance. Larry and Bobby T Wells could be released and confined to the house on 21st Street. Curly Morizzo has only a minor record from his juvenile years, and Sabatino Santore has no criminal record at all. Further, Sabatino has a wife and three children depending on his ability to provide for them. He has neither the means or ability to flee and is tied to his family. Additionally, your Honor, the allegations here involve no threat to anyone. Mr. Juice refers only to crimes against property, not people. No violence has even been part of the allegations. If it weren't for the unusual nature of the alleged crimes, the defendants would, in all likelihood, be given a release with no bail. We request a similar consideration."

The Judge nodded to Juice.

"There is a lot of speculation as to what these men might do, as they face long prison . . ."

"Objection. Speculation, bordering on outright blarney."

"Sustained, but again, Mr. Walker, this is an arraignment. You can strut your stuff when we get to trial. Mr. Juice, you may continue."

"As I was saying, there is much spec . . . thought, as to what these men might do or whatnot. But the Vinton County boys could walk across the bridge, then we would have to go drag 'em back. Who knows what the Wops . . . er, excuse me, the Eye-tal-ians would do. Lots of Eye-tal-ians are up in Youngstown and Cleveland who might give these boys a helping hand. Mr. McKenna could get up in the holler and no one could find him, not even our fine sheriff and his deputies."

"Thank you, gentlemen. You both made compelling arguments."

The judge had his fingers together, pyramid style. He bowed his head slightly, then looked at the ceiling and then down again.

He then said, "The Vinton County boys, Larry and Bobby T, have a $1,250 bond set for each because if we have to go trackin' 'em down over in Ohio, it will cost us that much to do so. The Italians, Curly and Sabatino, are set at $650. Now, Lamar is a special case, but I don't think he is gonna go a-runnin' because this here is his home, and he doesn't have another. So I am gonna put his bond at $1,000. And counselor, he is in your charge and so are the Vinton County boys, so you damn well better keep an eye on 'em or I will hold you in contempt. Trial will be two weeks from this date. Either of you have any trouble with that? Good. So be it."

With that he lifted his gavel over his head and brought it down hard on a round, thick piece of oak wood. He got up, as did all those present, and he disappeared through his door to his office . . . presumably to take off his robe and put on his pants.

Seated in the back row was Sheriff Cletus Boyer. As the gavel came down, he got up and left the courthouse.

He was headed up to Devil's Run Hollow to see Pappy McKenna.

CHAPTER XXXIX

MEET THE NICKELODEON FIVE

Later that day, Jack met with Lamar in the lawyer's conference room.

Jack said, "Let's clean up a couple of things, Uncle Lamar. Where were you taking the nickel?"

"To your Uncle Lou, up in Erie."

"This just gets better and better. Expanding from the McKenna's over to the Walker side, are we? So up to Lou's scrap yard. I thought that might be the case. I never imagined Uncle Lou doing stupid things."

"Oh, he's a smart one, all right. Didn't even wanna know where the nickel metal came from. And listen to this." Lamar paused for dramatic effect then said, "He had the perfect buyer!"

Lamar, gave a furtive look over his shoulder.

Jack said, "Go on."

Lamar broke into a big smile then said, "Only the United States of America, that's who. Specifically, the Department of Defense."

"Let's be clear here, Uncle Lamar. You delivered nickel metal to Uncle Lou, who then in turn sold it to the Defense Department."

"That is correct, Jack. The perfect crime."

"Perfect, but yet here you sit."

"That shouldn't have happened. That damn Conrad, the security chief, must have blabbed. Fuckin' snitch. There is just no other way they could have known."

"Watch your language, Lamar."

"Oh, sorry. It's just being incarcerated like this, around these criminals, makes me revert back to a former self that is much more crass than I have become. It's a protective measure I have learned."

"Step back just a bit. The security chief was your inside man?"

"That's right, he was a boss over in Moundsville, and we got acquainted."

Jack paused to think about the implications of both the security chief being the inside man and Uncle Lou selling the contraband to the Defense Department. 'Not all bad', he thought.

Jack said, "I have to have bail money for you and the boys, plus legal fees for the firm."

"Okay, we can do that. How much we talkin' about?"

"Well, you heard the judge. $1,000 for you. $650 for Curly and Sabatino. $1,250 each for the Vinton County boys. The firm will charge $1,000 each for the defense, and it may go up from there, depending on the length of the trial and where this all takes us. So that's $9,800."

"Damn, Jack. That's a lotta scratch. Bout all I got."

Jack didn't respond.

"Okay. You can pick up the money for all of us from Peaches over at the house on 21st

Street."

"Peaches?"

"Yes, Peaches Fantazzi."

"What is she, a stripper or something? What's her real name?"

"That's it. Peaches Fantazzi."

"So what I hear about the house is true. So mother helped you to start a new life and you turned the place into a brothel and about burned it down. And what? Is this Peaches your Madam?"

"Yeah, that's about it."

"Damn, Uncle Lamar, the older you get the more amazing standards you set."

Lamar said, "Watch your language." He was smiling,

Jack wasn't smiling. He was thinking about the conversation he was about to have with his mother.

Jack picked up his briefcase to leave and said, "I'll have you out of here by tomorrow morning."

Later that day, Bobby T and Lamar were in the exercise yard. The inmates were given sixty minutes to exercise, smoke, and converse. The yard had an eight-foot wire fence around it with razor ribbon on top. Two guards with shotguns stood outside the door entrance to the fence. Under a roof were several old weights for the prisoners to lift. Grandstand-type seating, six rows deep, near the weight lifting area.

Bobby T and Lamar were seated on the third row middle. The had the area to themselves.

Bobby T said, "Well, what are we gonna do about the Eye-talians?"

Lamar looked over his shoulder, turned his attention to Bobby T, and said, "What do you see as the problem?"

"Don't get cute with me, Lamar. You know damn well what I am talking about."

Lamar looked down this time. He said, "Curly's okay. Sabatino will fold the first time lawman says boo."

"I don't know if I share your enthusiasm about Curly, but yes, he does have a lot to lose. Just like us. You think he can control Sabatino?"

"I don't think Sabatino is controllable."

"How much do you think he knows?"

Lamar thought briefly and said, "Oh, not much Bobby T. But let's count it up. He knows everything about Wheeling Steel. Let's start there. And something that would be consequential to you . . . he knows about the doctor heist. As you know, he was there. Plus, he's been to the cathouse, so he could get Juice all over that. On the positive side, he doesn't know about the poker or the numbers."

"So what are you gonna do about it?"

"You mean, what are we gonna do about it?"

"Lamar, this is your fuckin' problem, not mine."

"Really, Bobby T. You think so? You better think again. This is our little problem."

Bobby T didn't argue. After a thoughtful pause, he said, "So what do we do about the Sabatino problem?"

"You got anybody from Vinton County?"

"Maybe."

Lamar said, "I've got an idea that we might use Big Gio up in Wheeling."

"The head mobster in the Panhandle? Why would he help us?"

"Because he gets a piece of everything I do. The cathouse, numbers, poker. Everything. I believe what I pay for is protection. It's his turn to step up."

"Did he squeeze you on the doc's house?"

"That too. I gave him a thou to keep it legit with him. He didn't know what we grabbed, so hell with him."

"Okay. Big Gio it is. How you gonna contact him?"

"Don't worry about it. I got a way."

"What, Peaches?"

"We see her tomorrow, because my nephew worked some magic. I'll get the ball rollin'."

Peaches was waiting and opened the door right away for Jack. Jack was surprised to see a very attractive woman in her early thirties who was dressed like she had been outfitted in New York City. She certainly didn't look like his idea of a Madam from Vinton County.

She said, "Hi, Jack. Come on in. Let's go to the kitchen. I have some coffee, and Cassandra made some apple fritters that are really amazingly good."

Jack checked everything as he walked through the living room into the kitchen. It was clean. Well-organized. Not what he would expect Lamar's cathouse to look like.

In the kitchen, Jack sat while Peaches handed him a coffee and fritters. She did the same for herself and then sat down.

"So the boys got caught, did they?"

"It appears so."

"How they holding up?"

"Pretty good. Lamar and Bobby T are fine. The veterans. They have been there, done that. Larry seems puzzled by it all, but okay. Curly's fine and Sabatino is a mess."

"There's your weak link."

"You mean Sabatino?"

"Yep. That boy is in danger."

"From?"

"I think you know."

"I'm not sure about Lamar doing anything like that, but Bobby T . . .?" He let his voice drift off.

"Bobby T has done worse, believe me. Your uncle . . . your uncle is more than capable. He damn near killed me and Sam a couple of times."

"Where is Sam?"

"Gone. She had a nice offer to work in Newport, Kentucky. Roxy's still here though. And another girl, Amy. I want to take care of them. Get them situated."

"Roxy, she's working here?"

"I thought you knew."

Jack's mother loved that girl. This will be devastating. Roxy was the daughter of a church friend who left her family to escape to Roosevelt, Utah, land of the dinosaurs. Her husband worked for Big Gio and threatened to kill her if she took their daughter. Loretta took the child in and raised her for years until one day her father showed up, picked the girl up coming home from school, and took her to Wheeling to live with him and an endless string of women."

When the father got tired of raising a child, Loretta was there to take the child in and mother her for three years, when the child left for Utah and her biological mother.

Peaches broke Jack's reminiscing and said, "Oh, let me get the money." She left the kitchen and returned with a small duffle bag. She said, "I think you will find it all there."

"You mean for all five?"

"No, just Lamar, Larry, and Bobby T. They wanted you to pick up the money for Curly and Sabatino at Curly's repair shop. Here's the address. It's not from there."

"Thank you, Peaches. So where will you be going—what will you do?"

"I saved up enough to lay back for a while, so I'm going to stay right here and maintain the house. See if I can help keep things together for the boys. Lamar will need some help. I wouldn't miss this circus for anything. And I have a front-row seat."

Jack picked up the bag to leave and said, "Indeed you do, Peaches. Indeed you do."

Jack's next stop was the one he dreaded most, meeting with his mother. He turned down Grant Street in McMechen and drove slowly toward the end of the street. It was the last house on the left directly across from a large, vacant lot that had been turned into a baseball diamond by the boys and men in the neighborhood. The backyard sloped gently down to the Ohio River. There was a small cottage behind the house where Uncle Pat lived—Cookie's uncle. He was a quiet, bald man who always wore a fedora. He would sit on his stoop and watch the boys play ball and the men pitch horseshoes.

The river was not to be approached by the children. Several years before, another relative, Walter Tribett, drowned in a boating accident with two others when they got caught in a whirlpool.

His mother, Loretta, made sweet tea and said, "Let's sit on the porch. It's a shame to waste such a nice day."

Jack saw the headline from the Wheeling Intelligencer on the kitchen table:

NICKELODEON FIVE HITS WHEELING STEEL

Loretta was raised with a grandfather, Henry, that had gone to prison for moonshine. She knew about the federal agents that were after Henry and disappeared. Her father, Pappy, had gone to prison for bootlegging. Her twin was in in prison as much as he was out. She was used to bad news. She had lived it.

But Jack was her shining light. The good son. The bishop of their little congregation of Mormons. Now a lawyer with the best legal defense firm in the state. He was everything to her. And now Jack had to delivery news that would hurt his mother to her very core. They sipped their lemonade, each knowing this was a conversation they didn't want to have.

Jack said, "Dad at the shop?"

"Where else?"

"Looks like this trial will be the hot topic at the shop for the next few months."

"There will be no doubt about that. So what's Lamar got his-self into this time?"

"It's bad, Mother. Pretty bad. Almost no defense to speak of. They were caught at the scene with the contraband in tow. The newspapers have it right."

"So this is why you came back, isn't it? To defend and elevate the family."

"It is."

Jack paused and looked to the empty playing field off to the north of the house. His mind filled with flash memories of playing endless hours of football and baseball, which the boys called "mush ball" because they never really had a new hardball, only mush balls.

"Well, the short of it is this; Lamar and four others were robbing Wheeling Steel of nickel pallets. Taking them up to Erie and selling them to Uncle Lou at his junkyard. Lou in turn was selling it the Defense Department."

Loretta's eyes clouded over. Her heart was broken. Broken again by her twin brother.

She said, "How long will he go away this time?"

"Mother, we don't have to get ahead of what may or may not happen."

"Is that fancy lawyer of yours going to defend them? What's his name . . . the Hillbilly Hotshot?"

"Spenser Sprat. No, Mother, I will be lead chair. Spence will not be on the case."

"I know you will do your best, Son. You always have."

"Yes, I will. Spencer will offer counsel too, and he is one of the best defense lawyers this country has ever produced."

"Yes, Sister Malan . . . she gets those fancy newspapers, showed me the article about him in the Cleveland newspaper."

"There's more, and I hate to tell you this. Lamar converted the 21st Street house into a brothel, and he has Roxy working there as one of the prostitutes."

Loretta screamed, "No, no, no. Not Roxy. Not my precious baby. No, God please no. Jack, she was like my own. Like my own."

"I know, I know."

She collapsed to her knees and startled to fall from the chair. Jack reached out to break her fall and collapsed to the floor with her. He held her in his arms as she sobbed. He felt her body convulsing and shaking uncontrollably. As he held her, tears formed in his eyes and moved slowly down his face.

He held her like this, his mother in his arms, now touching her hair, now holding her tight, now calming her as best he could. After what seemed like an eternity before her weeping stopped, she kissed Jack on his cheek. Jack helped her back into her chair. She took a long drink from her lemonade. Her face was a colorless mask, steely eyes bright with fight.

She said, "What are his chances for beatin' the rap?"

CHAPTER XL

PAPPY GET'S SERVED

Sheriff Cletus Boyer of Marshall County, West Virginia, drove a familiar road to get to Pappy's house. He knew the way since four times a year he and his deputies, friends, and relatives would conduct a 'raid' on Pappy's moonshine stills. The raids were conducted on the first Friday of every quarter.

The sheriff and deputies would pull up in Pappy's front yard with guns drawn. Pappy would come out of his house grinning and would always say, "Welcome, Sheriff. Let's have some Mule Kick. That started a party till about midnight when the drunk raiders each got a quart of Mule Kick to take home, except the sheriff. He got four quarts. This practice had been going on since the sheriff had been elected. Pappy didn't care much since the last sheriff had received the same courtesy, and the next Sheriff would too. Henry did the same for the Sheriff in his time. "

Pappy told Lula, "That is one hell of a lot of kick to give them boys, but I look at it as my tax, and the sheriff has done me a favor or two over time."

This trip the Sheriff was alone. He pulled up to the same spot of his Tuesday night social events, got out of the car and said, "Howdy, Pappy."

Pappy said, "I hear tell that Lamar was got his little tit in a big ringer."

"He sure does, Pappy. But Lamar is a resilient little pecker-head. No disrespect intended, Pappy. I feel bad about it since I had to be the arresting officer, but I had no choice. I got the call in the middle of the night from the chief of security over at the mill. Had to move on Lamar. Course, I didn't know it would be Lamar."

"I figured as such. Cletus, Lamar surely does keep comin' back for more. You know, I didn't raise him to be no criminal. He don't come from that stock."

"I know, Pappy. And look at Loretta. Angel on Earth, that one. She surely is."

"Lula got some lemonade in there, or we can sit here for a spell with a little something in it."

"Thank you kindly, Pappy, but I am makin' this trip on my own and I am gonna be missed shortly, so I gotta get back to servin' and protectin'."

"Well, it is no doubt troublesome news, so go ahead and spill it."

"Pappy, Lamar is goin' to a jury trial in two weeks. We gonna send notices for jury duty up to about everybody in the holler, since every single jury notice sent up here or given to the postmaster for them to pick up has been dutifully and faithfully ignored by the good citizens of this here holler. Same way in every other holler around here, too. This time I'm gonna give you a stack of jury notices, and you get some people down to the jury room that can read and write, and it wouldn't hurt if they were likable too—which would leave out every one of them McCoy's and probably the O'Sullivan's too. You can tell them if selected for jury duty they would be down there about a week and we will put 'em up. Room, board, the whole thing. So, Pappy, I am gonna bring the notices up here to you and you pass 'em around and make sure they show up when and where."

Pappy thought about what the sheriff said.

"So you want 'em on the jury?"

"Don't matter what I want. It's what you want for your boy. If he is to be judged by his peers, convicted by his peers, then by gawd we gotta have some peers on that jury. We can't have a bunch of city people that don't understand Lamar and his kind."

Pappy said, "Seems only fair."

"Damn straight, it is only fair. Pappy, with this gesticulation on my part, we square for the last seven years and the next seven as well."

Pappy stuck out his hand. The sheriff did too and gave Pappy his politician hand shake—hands clasped, with the sheriff bringing his left hand over the top to grip both the right hands.

Pappy said, "Much obliged, Cletus. I ain't gonna forget this."

"Pappy, it may be meaningless, but I want a fair trial. That's all I ask. Fairness . . . and acquittal."

"That's all any man can ask," Pappy said.

At the time Pappy was visited by the Sheriff, Jack was in conference with Spencer Sprat in the law firm's conference room.

"Jack, you got a nice retainer up front. You have to do that with every client, even those that are relatives or don't have much. Don't ever, and I mean ever, give away your legal service, or the services of this firm, for free. You do that and your clients, especially your family and so-called friends, will not respect you or the valuable services you give. Always charge, and don't be bashful about it."

Jack smiled. Spencer said, "That tickle your fancy, Jack?"

"Every Sunday at church I have at least one person come up to me and say, 'I didn't wanna bother you during your work day, but I have this one little question . . .' and I stop them right there and say 'Brother Freeloader, here is my card, call and schedule an appointment.'"

"I get the same thing over at the country club and those guys are rich. Damn freeloaders. Anyway, looks like you have this billing business figured out. So tell me about the case."

"Well, you read the newspaper reports. They're spot on. Caught them in the act. Stopped them right at the gate as they were packed up and ready to leave. The whole bunch of them."

"You thought about criminal trespass rather than burglary, didn't you?"

Jack laughed and said, "Yes, I did. Thought there might be a case that provided some relief, but nothing there that Dick Kennedy could find. If there is intent to steal, there is burglary."

"Yep, I've gone through the same process a time or two myself. But good work on the bail. How'd you pull that off?"

"Judge Pickett was reasonable, which surprised me. I don't think he likes Juice all that much, and I've got to keep my eyes on Lamar and the Vinton County boys, who are under my supervision and staying at my parents house in McMechen, that Lamar turned into a whorehouse."

"I was aware of the cathouse. You know Big Gio has a piece of Lamar's action, and it included the cathouse, of course. Watch Juice—he'll lie, withhold evidence, say anything, and the worse thing is, he's a first-class prima donna prick who thinks he is going to be governor next election."

"He thinks I will be easy pickings."

"You got that choirboy look about you, Jack. They just don't know that under that sheepskin is a fox. A clever fox that will eat your heart for breakfast and your liver for lunch. You know that they have started to call you Gentleman Jack over at the courthouse—like calling a big man 'Tiny,' something like that. What's your main line of defense?"

"Damned if I know. You have an idea?"

"Take a plea, young man. Take a plea."

"Would you?"

Hell, no. I would play that jury like Caruso singing Rigoletto. Poor misunderstood backwoods boys. No violence here. Wheeling Steel is a big, fat, lazy company that doesn't care about their workers. Get them implicated in a mining disaster or two. What? Some 150 died in that last mine collapse. Wasn't that their mine? Paint them black, dirty, fifthly sons-of-bitches that don't give a damn about people. Only profits. Profits. Profits. Greenbacks made at the expense of poor working men that die of black lung at fifty. Coal mines that kill."

Jack said, "I can work with that."

"Jack, I wouldn't tell this to many that have been out of law school a couple of years, but you're ready. This is going to be a big stage. But you're ready. And when it starts, you stand before the court, and you look that prick Juice and the judge in the eye and you say it loud and clear . . ."

"Jack Walker for the Defense."

CHAPTER XLI

Sabby The Cabby

Sabatino Santore was driving his taxi twelve to fourteen hours a day. The family would need the money if he was to be sent to prison.

This night he was near a train station in Colliers, West Virginia, outside of Wheeling to the north and toward Pittsburgh. This was the place where an illegal prizefight was to take place that evening. The train would bring customers to this small town, in from north and south, making it ideal for a prizefight. The police were to be elsewhere. Sabby could make a month's pay from the three men he drove here and their return. If they won a bet, the pay would be even better.

Sabby was parked outside the venue waiting the return of his passengers. He saw a man approaching. He had on a long coat with a turned-up collar and a large fedora pulled down hard to his eyes. Sabby watched him approach, thinking he would just walk by. Instead he approached the taxi and motioned for Sabby to roll down the window. Sabby did and he was looking at hard, dark eyes.

The man said, "Sabatino Santore, is that you?"

"Si, are you Italian? Do I know you?"

"No you don't, and I am Greek."

The man pulled a Smith & Wesson Model 10 .38 Special from his pocket and shot Sabatino Santore three times—twice in the center section of his chest and once in his head, killing him instantly.

He dropped the gun as a car pulled up. The man got in the car, and it sped off toward Wheeling.

The Sunday after the arrest, the Wheeling Intelligencer featured an article on the heist in the Sunday magazine section. It was written by one Alan A. Warwick. It read:

Theft of Nickel from Wheeling Steel. Where was it going?

Mystery Unanswered

"Mack Lyons has worked in security-related jobs at Wheeling Steel for close to eighteen years. Before that he served in the Army, mustered out as a Master Sergeant from the military police.

Now Mr. Lyons seems to be the man of the hour at Wheeling Steel in Benwood.

It started simple enough. Lyons found several hundred bags missing from storage in the warehouse where coal and nickel were housed along with other metals used in the process of making steel and nails. This was an oddity that sent Lyons looking for the why . . . why did they go missing?

He soon found out. A substantial amount of nickel was missing. It is alleged that over twenty thousand pounds of pure nickel nickel had been stolen. Lyons starting snooping and found himself in the middle of what looked like a script written by Agatha Christie, full of surprising plot twists at every turn.

He immediately suspected a new hire at the warehouse, Larry Wells from Vinton County, Ohio, who was the nightwatchman. He put a watch on the rotund watchman. What they saw every night for five nights was a nightwatchman sleeping in a storage bin that Wells had turned into a hidden bedroom.

Things changed on the sixth night of the watch that was watching the watchman. On that night Wells let several men into the facility. They had a large Kelly-Springfield truck with them. They proceeded to load a ton of nickel into the truck and left, all with Wells's alleged assistance.

Lyons concluded they would be back. He notified the law authorities, but no one at Wheeling Steel. Lyons feared a leak within the mill.

Lyons told this reporter, "I wasn't totally sure they would be back, and I didn't know who the inside man was, other than this Wells character, so I was cautious. Me and Sheriff Cletus Boyer over in Moundsville set the trap. As soon as the truck and four men showed up, I called him and he got his people there within the hour. The four men had the nickel metal in the truck and were leaving when the sheriff apprehended the gang."

The other members of gang of five: Lamar McKenna, Bobby T. Wells, Curly Morizzo, and Sabatino Santore, were all arrested, along with the nightwatchman, Larry Wells. Lamar McKenna is well-known to law enforcement officials with a long rap sheet in Marshall County. Bobby T. Wells and Larry Wells also have substantial criminal records, mostly in Ohio. Curly Morizzo, is a well known race car driver at off tracks in and around the Wheeling area. He is suspected of being a bootleg driver as well. Sabatino Santore is an unknown party, but is believed to be a recent immigrant from Italy.

Until recently, Curly was a barber at Willy Jack's barbershop in McMechen. The barbershop is considered a front for illicit activities such as gambling and running numbers. Willy Jack Walker, the owner of the barbershop, had no comment. He is the father of Jack Walker, the defense lawyer for the five and a well known football player from Union High School and Ohio State University. Walker is an associate of Spencer Sprat, the so called 'The Hillbilly Hotshot'. It appears that Sprat is involved in other cases and will not be an active member of the defense team. The senior Walker, Willy Jack, is married to Loretta McKenna, the twin sister of the oft convicted Lamar McKenna.

Mr. McKenna's father, Pappy McKenna, was convicted for bootlegging and served two years at the Atlanta Federal Prison. Lamar McKenna achieved notoriety as a young man for burning down a hen house of a neighbor in Devil's Run Hollow. A prize rooster named Marty achieved fame for his fierce defense of the hen house, which took his life.

What is not clear is where the nickel going? Who was buying it, and for what purpose? We may need Ms. Christie to put Hercule Poirot on the case to solve this twisted mystery. Be assured, however, this reporter will bulldog this story to find out what a criminal five, now popularly called the Nickelodeon Five, would do with tons of nickel pallets."

Jack tossed aside the paper with disgust. Just as it has always been: lawmen and the press dragging his good parents, and now him, with guilt by association to Lamar. He thought, '... not this time. This time we have a courtroom to expose the truth. And this time we have me.'

Three days later, the Wheeling Intelligencer ran this story:

Nickelodeon Five Member Killed in Taxi Robbery

"Recently arrested member of the Nickelodeon Five, Sabatino Santore, infamous for the mysterious Wheeling Steel nickel metal heist, was found shot and killed last night, an apparent victim of a robbery turned bad. Sabatino Santore, thirty-four, was found shot dead in his taxi cab about two o'clock this morning in Clarion.

Detective Sargent Winslow Fischer said that the murder will be fully investigated, but at this time it did not appear to be related to the theft of the nickel pallets from Wheeling Steel.

He is survived by . . . ."

CHAPTER XLII

AN IMPARTIAL JURY FROM A CROSS-SECTION OF THE COMMUNITY SIXTH AMENDMENT, CONSTITUTION OF THE UNITED STATES

The trial began with the court room packed with reporters, spectators and thirty-five potential jurors seated in the crowded visitor section of the courtroom. What they were calling the Nickelodeon Five trial, had slowly moved from a local burglary story to regional, and now, at the beginning of the trial, The New York Times sent a reporter.

Jack was seated at the defense table with the defendants and his associate, Richard Kennedy, a recent graduate of Harvard Law.

Juice and his team made a dramatic entrance. Juice had two associates carrying his bags. He didn't walk in; he pranced, he preened. He walked as though he owned the courtroom—his place of complete and utter dominance. It was not an entrance; it was a coronation. . A dark blue suit with gray chalk lines, white starched shirt, and a blue polka-dot tie completed his assemble. His hair slicked back. He looked with disdain at Jack and sat down at the prosecution table.

Judge Pickett entered, sat, got his robe comfortable beneath him, and said, "Welcome to my courtroom. This trial will be conducted under my supervision. That means no one talks unless I give them the go-ahead. Right now, our first order of business is to select a jury. Mr. Juice, Mr. Walker, are you ready to proceed?"

Both lawyers said, "Yes, Your honor."

"Then proceed we will. Now I am going to say a word to the potential jurors about what to expect. We have a bunch of you out there—I believe it is about thirty-five—and twelve of you will be selected for the jury. We will also select an additional two to act as alternates in case any one of the jurors doesn't make it to the end of the trial. The United States Constitution and the Constitution of the great state of West Virginia both guarantee the accused, these gentlemen seated there, a jury trial of their peers. That means good citizens from their community. You need to be patient and listen to the facts as they are presented. You should not have a fixed mind as to guilt or innocence. It is an honor and a privilege to serve on a jury, and I expect you to behave like it. Right now, we are going to call each of you one at a time, and the lawyers seated in front of me, will ask you a few questions. They can select you or not, and they don't have to get a reason why they are doing that. We will continue to do this process until we have our fourteen. If you have any questions, you can ask them when you are interviewed. Will the clerk call for the first juror candidate?"

The bailiff said, "Will William Conklin come to the witness stand."

Judge Pickett said, "Mr. Conklin, do you have any questions before we begin?"

William Conklin was dressed in his everyday work clothes: coveralls, work boots, and checked shirt that looked like it hadn't been cleaned in a week or so.

Conklin said, "Judge, I got a work emergency, and I fear I will be at a major loss if I am gone a big piece of time. How long is this thing gonna last?"

"Well, Mr. Conklin, we don't rightly know how long this trial will last. May I ask what is your major emergency?"

"I got a big order for my product and if I don't get to it . . . I'm gonna lose the whole thing."

"What is this product we are taking about?"

"Well." Conklin paused, "It's corn-based and damn good. Lot of demand right now."

The courtroom erupted in laughter.

The judge brought down the gavel, "Enough of that. Quiet. Mr. Conklin, moving your shine to market most definitely does not qualify."

"Do you have any other questions, sir?"

"I guess not, but that don't seem rightly fair."

"Mr. Juice, your first up?"

Juice said, "Your honor, because of the particular livelihood of Mr. Conklin and that livelihood being in close proximity to the very livelihood of the primary defendant, the prosecution exercises its first peremptory challenge on Mr. Conklin."

Jack jumped up and said, "Your honor, this is a jury of the defendant's peers. If we start dismissing every one that comes to the jury pool in coveralls and country work clothes, we wouldn't have a fair jury, and in fact, it would be in violation of the two constitutions you quoted in your opening remarks."

"Mr. Juice, Mr. Walker makes a point, so I am going to admonish you . . . let's not leave out the country folk, and Mr. Conklin it looks like you got your wish and can go tend your crop. You are dismissed from this trial. Thank you. Next."

A jury was cobbled together by three that afternoon. Juice had used six peremptory challenges, Jack, four. Juice was trying to get as many men as possible: working men, ex-military, and if it was a woman . . . teachers, church women, those that believed in regulation, order, and laws. Jack was looking for sympathetic country folks, miners and their relatives that might not look kindly at Wheeling Steel and perhaps lost loved ones in a mining disaster.

Among the twelve selected jurors were three from Devil's Run Hollow: Betty O'Sullivan, Freeman Adams, and Ellie Mae Campbell.

Both sides were pleased with their selections.

Judge Pickett said, "We have daylight left. We are going to take a fifteen-minute break and get back in here for opening statements."

Reconvened, Judge Pickett said, "Let's make these opening statements about facts, gentlemen. No flights of fancy, keep your objections to yourself—you'll have plenty of time for that later. Mr. Juice, you have the floor."

Juice jumped up and said, "Thank you, Your Honor."

He stepped from behind the prosecutor's table and moved toward the jury box. His face was what Jack noticed most. Grave, but thoughtful.

He said, "We are going to be working here, in this courtroom, for the next several days or more. We have a charge, you and me. Your charge is to decide the guilt or innocence of those four men seated at the defense table. My job is to show you the facts of that guilt. My name is J.J. Juice, and called by most simply Juice, and I will show you that on the night of September 24th of this year, these four men were arrested at the gates of Wheeling Steel as they were leaving the mill with two-thousand pounds of a metal called nickel, which they were stealing."

Jack said, "Objection, Your Honor. Stating conclusion."

"Overruled. Let's let him finish up, Mr. Walker."

Juice continued, "It was after two in the morning. Our evidence will show that these same men had been doing this for weeks and had taken more than twenty-four tons of nickel from the plant. They were arrested at the site, in the act, and it will be your civic responsibility to see that these men are punished for their vile acts. Thank you."

Judge Pickett said, "Mr. Walker."

Jack stood. Paused briefly. Walked to the jury box and looked at each of the jurors.

He said, "Mr. Juice gave you some information about the arrest of these men. What he didn't tell you is the list of charges. Twenty counts from burglary to criminal trespass to everything in between. Their arrest is a fact. But what was kept from you was the nature of what they were doing. This alleged crime has no violence, no intent to harm any one individual. No resistance from these men at the time of arrest. So why so many charges? Does it look and feel like this prosecutor is guilty of overreach? Throw the book at these men, when a simple charge of burglary would be enough. Why do they do that? I'll tell you why. Because they can, and these men are from poor families that can be pushed around by those in authority and even exploited by the press in that gallery right there. Have you ever felt like that? A big company or the government pushing you around, just because they can, and you . . . you can't fight City Hall, can you? Maybe even Wheeling Steel, that big company down the road, has pushed you around. We know what happened in the mining disaster that Wheeling Steel let happen, now don't we?

Juice jumped up, face red, "Your Honor, that is outrageous!"

Judge Pickett said, "I'll take that as an objection, which is sustained. Mr. Walker, enough of that kind of talk, and wrap it up, if you would. And jurors, dismiss from your mind what Mr. Walker said about mining disasters."

Jack said, "Yes, Your Honor, I will get to a final summary."

Turning back to the jury, Jack said, "The defense will show the true nature of the events here and will ask only for fairness and reasoned judgment. I am Jack Walker for the Defense."

Judge Pickett said, "Court will convene until 9:00 tomorrow morning."

JON MARPLE

CHAPTER XLIII

IT REALLY DON'T MATTER THAT MUCH

It was twilight in the hollow. Lamar wanted company for the drive up to see Pappy and Lula, so he invited Peaches to go along. Lula served fried chicken, greens, corn, and mashed potatoes. Desert was apple pie.

Peaches took her last bit of the pie, sipped coffee, and said, "Lula, I ate too much. I have had a gracious plenty, and then some."

Lula said, "Well, bless your heart. I love to cook and serve it up."

"It certainly shows, Lula. Thank you."

Lula rose to start the clean-up, and Pappy said, "Would you ladies please excuse us for a bit? I have a need to discuss a thing or two with Lamar."

Lamar and Pappy went to rocking chairs outside. Pappy poured two fruit jars of Mule Kick, half-way full. It was a beautiful cool, but comfortable evening.

Pappy said, "How is Jack treatin' you?"

"Oh, good. Very good. At first I was upset that Sprat wasn't our man. But, Jack doesn't take any shit from that asshole prosecutor."

"Jack never did nothin' in his life he didn't take serious. Same way with lawyerin', he gonna be good at that too."

"I don't know what the hell the defense is gonna be. We got caught red-handed."

"That's what I wanted to talk about. Your defense. You don't have to worry none about that, Son. Your Pappy got it fixed up."

"Fixed up? What's that mean?"

Pappy didn't immediately respond. He took a sip and looked at an early rising moon, not quite full. He said, "It means you're not gonna be found guilty."

Lamar said, "I'll be damned. You got the jury?"

"Might have. We got three people from the hills. They don't like the law comin' down on us. They sure as hell don't like Wheeling Steel, losing a couple of kinfolk in that last mine explosion. This may be their payback time."

"So you think this might happen?"

"I surely do."

The morning after Lamar talked to Pappy, Jack walked into Juice's Office.

Jack said, "Counselor."

"Hey, you can just call me Juice."

"So what did you have in mind, Juice, with this little sit-down?"

"Jack, you can't possibly win this. It's prima facie. We got the evidence. Hell, we have some photos. Probably should have some moving picture cameras there as well. And, for you, this being your first big case on a big stage . . . you really don't want to get beat up this badly, now do you?"

"I'll take care of myself, thank you. Whatcha got in mind?"

"I want the rest of the story. Where were they selling this stuff? I want the fence and where it went. I can cut the prison time from ten to five for that deal."

"Juice, you know how these boys, all of them, feel about rattin' out somebody."

"Not all of them."

"Go on."

"One of your flock might be going soft."

"You got a name?"

"You want him to get what that cabby got?"

"Of course not."

"Then we better keep the name out of it."

"Not hard to figure, Juice." Jack paused and said, "Make it two years and we may have something to talk about."

"Four."

"Three. I'll talk to my clients."

"Done."

Jack left Juice's office and went to the house on 21st Street. Peaches said, "Oh, Jack, Lamar is real eager to talk to you, and here you are."

Peach took Jack into the kitchen. Seated at the table were Lamar and Larry.

Peaches said, "I know you Mormon's don't drink coffee, but you might today. Cassandra made these incredible cinnamon rolls, and they just go together."

Jack said, "I'll have the coffee, but hold the roll. Lamar, Larry. Listen up, boys. Winning this case would be almost impossible. You have little legal defense. We would have to play on the sympathy of the jury and hope it's a hung jury. Which would probably mean another trial. They want to cut a deal."

Lamar said, still leaning forward, "We don't have to cut a deal. We got people . . ."

Jack held up both hands and said, "Stop, Stop. Stop. Don't say anything. I can't hear this, whatever it is."

"Yeah, but Pappy said . . ."

"Stop, Lamar! You will compromise me."

Larry and Peaches were in stunned silence at the sudden and aggressive response from Jack.

Lamar said, "Okay. You don't wanna know. But tell the jackass we don't want no deal."

"You best get Curly under control, Lamar. And I don't mean in the Sabby sense. Just tell him what you think. And this is what you think: 'We got some people on the jury that might, just might, get us a hung jury.' You got that?"

"How'd you know that?"

"Know what? That we have three hill folks on the jury? Because I put 'em there for just that reason. And for Gawd's sake, Lamar, don't give them any money."

"I'd only do that after the trial."

"Uncle Lamar, do not tell me anything, I mean anything, about any crimes—past, future, or present—that you are planning. If you do, I have to report it or lose my law license and just might get indicted along with you. So don't do that anymore."

Jack turned to Peaches and said, "Where's your phone? I gotta make a call."

The call with Juice was brief.

Jack said, "Juice, no deal. We are going to trial."

"Are you nuts? Did you talk to Sprat about this?"

Jack said, "See you in court."

And hung up.

Across the street from the Marshall County Courthouse was the Snyder Hotel. It faced the street with a "Restaurant" sign in front and a "Hotel" sign above. For $1.25 a night you got a room with running water. For $2.00 you got a room with a bath. The three jurors from the hollow were Betty O'Sullivan, Freeman Adams, and Ellie Campbell. The women had rooms with a bath. Freeman did not.

To be a member of the jury, the woman had to walk into the courthouse and volunteer. No women were served a jury summons to appear. Only men were summoned. Women could serve on a jury, but just were never ask to do so...they had to ask. Women were needed because working men couldn't always get off work. This trial had an unusual amount of women on the jury because it had attracted so much attention.

The judge told the jurors not to talk about the case, even with their fellow jurors.

At dinner, the three from Devil's Run Hollow agreed to get together in Betty's room.

Freeman had to bring an extra chair so they all could sit.

Freeman was a large man with a full beard, long hair, wearing coveralls. He had a still that was not particularly well-run, and he was a poor. Pappy had said once to Lula, "That Freeman is a good worker, but he just don't do things right. He's always in the poorhouse. Truth be known, he should be named 'Poorman' rather than Freeman."

Freeman said, "This jury thing is not bad. I get to go to town and stay in a first-class place and get my meals paid for. If'n I knew it was this good, I would've come sooner."

Betty said, "That pot roast tonight was better than mine."

Ellie said, "I think, Betty, it's cause they weren't serving up possum, raccoon, or squirrel. It makes a difference when got you cow in there."

"You right about that," Freeman said. "So what'd you think about the trial today?"

"I liked the opening remarks," Betty said. "That government attorney . . . what's his name?"

"Juice Juice," Ellie said.

"That boy is full of his-self," said Freeman.

"Yep, and gonna run for governor they say," Betty said. "He's so full of himself, he thinks the sun comes up just to hear him crow."

Ellie said, "Ain't that the truth. Pappy's grandson—now that boy is something else. No strutting around like some minstrel banjo player. No, he looks you in the eye, and I just want to melt. That man could put his shoes under my bed any day of the week. How 'bout you, Betty?"

"Ellie, I do believe we are no longer attractive to young men in their . . . what? mid-twenties?"

"I don't know how you can say that; we could teach those young bucks a few tricks. I got plenty of men eager to give it a go . . . young and old."

Freeman said, "Do you two know, I'm sittin' here? This kind of talk from women is very unsettling."

That stopped the conversation for a moment, and then Freeman said, "How much they payin' you?"

Ellie said, "Freeman, they said don't tell anybody."

"Well, I ain't ashamed. You know I lost a son in that Benwood mine collapse. Anything to hurt that company, I'm in on it. They givin' me a thousand dollars. I've never had that much money at any one time in my life."

Ellie said, "I told 'em, no money. But they insisted. I got my daughter's weddin' comin' up, and I want to give her a good sendoff. They givin' me five hundred dollars."

Betty said, "Parker has us fixed pretty good, and what with the prohibition and all, he's making more money than ever, so I don't need money right now, and I'm just lookin' to protect what we have up in that holler."

Freeman said, "I wonder what they gonna do tomorrow?"

Betty said, "I don't see how it matters that much."

CHAPTER XLIV

THE FBI SEEKS JUSTICE

Lou Corn's secretary said, "You have a call from a guy calls himself Chief William Flynn, from Washington, DC."

Lou's heart skipped a beat. He thought, 'Oh, shit, the director of the FBI'.

He went to his desk and picked up the phone and said, "Lou Corns here."

"Mr. Corns, this is William Flynn, FBI. I'm calling you from Washington, DC, at the direction of President Wilson."

"Yes, sir. I know who you are."

"Mr. Corns, I sent two of my best special agents to see you. I am going to request that you see them tomorrow afternoon at 2:00 pm, at the Erie Federal Courthouse over on State Street. Are you familiar?"

"Yep."

"There will be no need for you to have an attorney present. We just have to get some clarification on some of your shipments. Will you do that? Be there at two and by yourself?"

"I will do that."

"This involves some sensitive matters of national security. We are sending these agents to solve a serious national security problem. You needn't fear anything. Just questions, nothing more."

"OK."

"Room 122. Two o'clock."

"I'll be there."

"Thank you, my boys will see you then."

They hung up. Lou started thinking, 'They know about my sales to the army. Bad news is I could be walking into a trap. But Flynn seemed to indicate that I had no fear of arrest. So, what do they want? They know I made the sale of the nickel. I told the colonel that I bought it in good faith and sold it to them in good faith. So they know, but they're not going to, at least at this time, arrest me as a co-conspirator in receiving known stolen goods. So what do they want? I guess I'll find out tomorrow'.

Lou walked into Room 122 at the courthouse. The two agents were seated at a conference table. They both were in their mid-thirties, spit-shined from head to toe. Sober-looking gentlemen. Serious.

The shorter of the two said, "Mr. Corns, pleased to meet you. My name is Special Agent Bill Thompson, and this is Special Agent Johnny Lee Morris. If you would just take a seat, we can get started."

Lou sat, folding his hands in front of him, and said, "Gentlemen, agents, you do have my curiosity piqued."

"Let's get right to the point then, shall we?" said Agent Thompson. "Johnny Lee, why don't you start."

Johnny Lee moved some papers in front of him closer to get a better look. He said, "Mr. Corns, here is what we know: You sold nickel metal, some twenty-four tons of the nickel to the United States Army. Is that correct?"

"Yes, I did."

"Where did you get those metals?"

"I bought them from deliveries that were made to my scrapyard. It's a fairly large facility, and I have done quite a bit of business with the government before. Never a hitch that I know of."

"And these deliveries were made by whom?"

"Two guys in a truck. Never saw them."

"Lou . . . may I call you Lou?"

"Certainly."

"Lou, let's not play run around here. Telling us is not going to hurt you. We know it's the Wheeling Steel load. And we know that the so-called Nickelodeon Five, now down to four, is being tried in a federal courtroom this very day in Moundsville, West Virginia. So I'll ask again. Who sold you the metals?"

"That would be Lamar McKenna."

"Who is?"

"My wife's brother is married to Loretta McKenna. Loretta and Lamar are twins."

"When you bought the metals, you were aware, were you not, that Lamar had not dealt in metals before, and you knew of his criminal record?"

"I'm beginning to feel like it might be better to have you talk with my lawyer."

"I will assume from that answer that you knew of Lamar's extensive criminal record."

"I didn't know Lamar at all. Never met him, in fact, until he came into my office promising metals that I deal in."

"You knew nothing of your nephew?"

"Well, I heard talk around the supper table."

The agent stopped, poured a glass of water, and said, "Would you like a drink?"

Lou said, "Yes, but it probably should be stronger than what you have in your hand."

Both the agents smiled at that.

Agent Morris said, "Bill, I think that would do it for me. You what the baton?"

Agent Thompson said, "Lou, you have been quite the topic of conversation in DC. Even the president got involved. The president and the director concluded that if the United States government, through the Army, was buying contraband from you, or anyone else, it would be a huge embarrassment for the government and this administration. Huge."

Lou said, "I hadn't thought of it quite that way, but yes, I can see how it might make the government look like monkeys."

Thompson laughed and said, "Yeah, my thought too. So here's the deal. We don't want a word of this to get out. It's a matter of national security and that's it. One of the gang of five, which is now four, gave you up for leniency. So if we disclosed this, you would be looking at ten years in prison. That won't happen if you abide by a few simple rules. You think you can do that?"

"So I wouldn't be charged with anything and that will be permanent?"

"As long as you keep quiet, the FBI would not, could not, charge you. If you start blabbing, the full force of the FBI and the government of the United States of America would come down on you hard."

"Seems like a simple decision to me."

"It is," said agent Thompson.

"Where do I sign?"

On the morning of the third day of the trial, both lawyers made their closing arguments. Juice flamboyantly pointing out facts that would lead to a certain conviction. Jack's appeal made Wheeling Steel a company whose greed deserved no mercy or leniency.

Judge Pickett addressed the jurors and said, "It is a privilege that you have today, because today you are participating in democracy as you never have and perhaps never will, because you are the sole judge of the facts and the credibility of what has been presented, including the witnesses. Please remember that the opening and closing arguments of the lawyers are not evidence. The burden of proof is on the government. That means you vote 'guilty' if you find the evidence and the facts beyond a reasonable doubt to be true. You vote 'not guilty' if you feel that the government has not met that standard of reasonable doubt. You will select a foreperson. One of you to speak for the group and lead the discussion. Do you have any questions?"

Freeman raised his hand.

The judge said, "Go ahead."

"What we doin' about lunch and maybe dinner?"

Spectators raised a hoot and Judge Pickett brought down the gavel and said, "Enough of that. Freeman has a serious question, although Freeman, it doesn't look like you've missed too many meals." More laughter brought the gavel down again.

"Well, Freeman, lunch and dinner will be brought to you in the deliberation room. The bailiff will assist getting you set up. Thank you again."

The judge brought the gavel down once more and the jurors were led away.

In the deliberation room, the bailiff got everyone seated. The bailiff was a tall, heavy-set woman dressed in a tan police uniform. The room was dominated by a large oak table, with oak chairs that had padded seats and wooden slats on the back. There were four water pitchers and cups on a side table. Windows were on one side of the room. There were fourteen writing pads, spaced at each chair, and a pencil for each.

The bailiff said, "My name is Bailiff Strong, and I will be your contact to get anything you need. To contact me, push that button next to the door, and I will respond as fast as I can. When I come back to the door, I will knock three times like this. . ." She hit the table with a knuckled fist three times. "I will not listen to, nor will anyone else, listen to your deliberations. You may not leave the room for any reason, unless you get me and I escort you. If you need to ask the judge or the lawyers a questions, write it down, and I will take it to them. You may ask to see certain pieces of evidence if you need to. Every two hours you will have a water and bathroom break. Any questions?"

Freeman said, "How long this gonna take?"

"Until you reach a verdict. We will stop at five today. Those of you that our local will go home and be back here at eight sharp. Our hotel guests will stay at the Snyder."

The bailiff paused and looked around the room and said, "Okay, the first thing you do is elect a spokesperson. That's what the judge called a foreperson, the technical name for that position. That person will chair this meeting and take the vote. I will leave you to do that. You can take as many votes as you want, and they can be hands raised or secret by voting ballot by paper. Unless you have anything else, I will leave you to your deliberations."

The bailiff paused and then left the room.

No one spoke. The fourteen in the room had been together over four days now. They had found certain cliques. There were the three from the hollow—Betty, Freeman, and Ellie. Four others were retired. Of these, there was a retired fireman, a teacher, a nurse, and a mine worker. Three housewives, all from Moundsville . . . a barber, two carpenters, and a drugstore employee.

The teacher, whose name was Barbara, had taught third grade for twenty-two years. She was a sparse, small woman that Freeman thought looked like a hawk. She said, "Well, this is pretty straightforward. I think we all know each other, so we don't need formal introductions. Let's get on with it. Anyone want to be the foreperson?"

No one raised their hand.

Ruby, the nurse said, "Can I nominate someone?"

Barbara, the teacher said, "Of course. That looks like what we will have to do. Who did you want to nominate, Ruby?"

"I nominate Bob." She nodded to the retired fireman.

"Who else?" said the stern teacher.

Freeman said, "I would like Betty here. She's the one right there doin' the knittin'. By the way, Betty, I been meaning to ask, what is that thing you keep workin' on?"

Betty said, "Well, a knit hat for a grandbaby that is comin' into the world next month."

Freeman says, "So why is it yellow? Shouldn't it be blue or pink or somethin' like that?"

Barbara looked at Freeman as if were a third-grader and said in her teacher voice, "Freeman. Let's stay on point here. So we have Bob and Betty, any others?"

One of the housewives said, "Well, Barbara here, Ms. Gable, is a wonderful teacher. Taught two of my kids. And she taught them good and really kept them in line, so I nominate her."

Barbara said, "Any more?"

Bob, the fireman, said, "I want to second the nomination of Barbara. And Ruby, thank you for my nomination, but I think Barbara will be just fine."

Betty said, "Suits me just fine as well. Freeman, that was sweet of you, but our teacher friend seems more than qualified. Besides, I would like to keep up on my knittin'."

Barbara gave an approving look and said, "Any objections?" There were none.

Barbara took charge as if she had been doing this all her life. She said, "Well, for my money, we don't have to waste a lot more of our time. These boys look like been doing a lot of stealing for a lot of time, and they were caught right there with the contraband. I suggest we take an immediate vote."

Bob said, "Barbara, I don't think we should be voting on how these men look."

"But Bob, they are. Criminals, that is," Barbara said.

The coal miner said, "Aren't they supposed to be innocent until proven guilty?"

One of the housewives said, "That's what we are going to do, say they are guilty."

Barbara said in a harsh voice, "Let's get back to it. Let's take a vote."

"All voting for guilty, raise your hand."

Barbara said, "You two don't vote, so put your hands down. You're alternates. So let's try this again. All for guilty, raise your hands. Looks like eight."

Barbara said, "Those for not guilty, raise your hands."

Four hands went up. The three from the hollow and the coal miner.

Bob said, "How can you not vote for guilty, Freeman? They got caught at the scene."

Freeman said, "Cause that's the way I'm votin', that's why!"

The other three were mute. Betty, with her sweet smile, just kept looking down at her knitting. The coal miner looked stern and angry. Freeman, belligerent.

They argued for three hours. No one budged. Vote after vote. Same result. Finally after the final break of the day, Barbara said, "This is going nowhere. I think they call this a hung jury. Do we all concur that this is a hung jury?"

No one objected.

"Well, let's go tell the judge," Barbara said. "Ring that buzzer and let's get the bailiff in here."

The jurors were seated. Judge Pickett came to the bench. Reporters and spectators rushed back into the court, all expecting to see Judge Pickett throw down the hammer of his gavel and say, "Guilty as charged."

Judge Pickett said, "Madam Foreperson, what is your verdict?"

Barbara handed the written verdict to the bailiff, who in turn handed it to the judge. Judge Pickett adjusted his reading glasses and silently read the verdict.

He turned to the defendants and said, "Gentlemen, please stand."

Judge Pickett said, "The jury is unable to reach a verdict. The vote was eight for guilty and four, not guilty. Madam Foreperson, I would encourage you to deliberate further."

Barbara said, "That would be meaningless. We beat on those four for over three hours. And we got after them hard. They are steadfast."

The judge said, "Alright. Jurors, thank you for your time and effort. Looks like you did your best. You are dismissed."

Turning to the accused, he said, "Gentlemen, you are free to go. Follow the bailiff and she'll get the paperwork done, return your personal items, and you can go."

Curly said, "May I ask a question, Sir?"

"What is it? Yes, go ahead."

"Where's my truck? I gotta get my truck back."

The judge said, "Right now, it's at the impound yard. Mr. Walker will help you get your truck."

Lamar turned to Curly and said, "That ain't your truck. Don't forget that."

Jack was not jubilant. He knew that his first big win was tainted . . . tainted badly, and he had not spoken out.

Juice turned to Jack and shouted, "This is a fucking outrage, Jack. What did you do?"

Jack jumped up and got within inches of Juice's face and said in a white rage, "You better be Goddamn careful what you say, you self-preening prick. You got beat, Juice. Just like Sprat beat you. You say anything to me like that again, and I swear I will find you, and I will give you a beating with my fist that will put you in traction. You got that, Counselor?"

Jack stormed out of the courtroom. Reporters were yelling questions at him. He ignored them all.

Jack lived in a loft in downtown Wheeling. It overlooked the Ohio River. Two blocks down was a shabby bar. Not a place where lawyers or professional people hung out—a drinker's bar, where people knew each other's first names because many would be there every night and half the day. Barflies. Mostly men, but always a few women. They all looked like alcoholics.

Jack sat at the far end of the bar, isolated from everyone, and said to the bartender, "Gimme a bourbon, double." The barman poured the bourbon into a shot glass. Jack picked up the drink and finished it. His first drink of alcohol in his life. He tapped the glass on the bar, and it was filled again. He kept them coming. Three hours later he weaved his way back to his apartment. The first drunk of his life.

CHAPTER XLV

FBI...We're Here To Help

As soon as FBI Special Agents Johnson and Morris got Lou Corn's signature, they boarded a train and headed to Moundsville.

At the same time, FBI Director William Flynn made a phone call to District Attorney J. J. Juice

Flynn said, "Good morning, Juice. Bill Flynn."

Juice said, "Well, this is a pleasant surprise. Hope you have recovered from that night on the town at the convention."

"That was a time, wasn't it? Got me to lay off booze entirely for a time or two."

"Prohibition will get the best of us on occasion. So, what's up, Chief?"

"Juice, I got two of my best special agents on a train coming to see you. They'll get in late; what about you seeing them tomorrow morning. Will that work?"

"Got a staff meeting at nine. Put together the retrial of those buffoons that robbed Wheeling Steel. That'll take a couple of hours. I want those bastards, Chief."

That brought a moment of silence from Flynn. Then he said, "I know how you feel, Juice, particularly after their lawyer threatened you like that."

"How'd you know that?"

"Because I read The New York Times, Juice."

"That's in there?"

"Apparently, word by word."

"Son of a bitch. I could get him disbarred."

"Juice, cancel your planning session. Meet with the agents. They'll give you a briefing on the case."

"The Wheeling Steel case?"

"Yes."

"What's to talk about? I'm filing tomorrow."

"Don't do that. That's a direct order from not only from me, but from the Big Guy himself."

"Wilson is involved in this? I'll be damned."

"Why can't we just handle it now?"

"Because, you are going to talk to the agents tomorrow, that's why. They will bring you up to speed. Talk to you later. Goodbye, Juice."

Juice sat there staring at the phone.

He thought, 'What the hell is this all about'?

At nine the next morning, Special Agents Thompson and Morris walked into Juice's office. Juice said, "Take a seat, boys, I'm the D.A."

The agents introduced themselves and sat down.

Thompson said, "So, you're the next governor?"

"After yesterday's fiasco, I'm not as confident as I once was."

"That's why we are here. To talk about that trial."

"Go on."

Morris said, "You're a good friend of the Director, right? Good Democrat too. Got your appointment by President Wilson."

"All true, but . . . what?" He shrugged his shoulders, extending hands out, palms up.

Thompson said, "What we say here, stays in this room. Got it?"

"Of course. Almost everything I do is confidential."

"Not everything you do is in the interest of national security," Morris said.

"Why don't you just tell me what you came here to tell me."

Thompson said, "Let's do that. First, you will not demand a retrial. Second, you will not appeal. In short, this case is over. And before you get your tit in a ringer, you know these boys will be back in your courtroom within a very short period of time, and you can throw the book at them."

"What the hell. I'll look like a horse's ass doing that."

"This gang has a lot of public sympathy; you might even pick up some votes from doing this very thing."

"There's more," Thompson said. "Don't do anything about Jack Walker's outburst. Let it go. The president wants this entire case, and everything associated with it, to be ancient history, and quite frankly, Juice, you don't want the specter of this trial haunting you right up to election day."

"You gonna tell me what the national security interest is, that reaches all the way down to our little village on the river?"

"We'll get to that, but right now there is one more thing. Do not pursue, in any way, the fence or destination."

Juice brought his hands over his face, rubbed his eyes, and said, "So what in hell's damnation is this all about, boys? They gonna let you tell me?"

Morris said, "Sign this and we can divulge the rest of the story."

Morris handed Juice a two-page document.

Thompson said, "Take your time."

"Thanks for the legal advice, Counselor."

Juice did take his time. Even made some notes.

"Well, this is pretty clear. I keep all the shit you tell me to myself, and if I don't, I will be put into a public stockade and given an undetermined amount of lashes with a horsewhip. Is that about it, boys?"

The agents didn't respond.

Juice took a pen and signed.

Thompson said, "All of the metal was bought by the United States government, specifically the Army. All paid from the US Treasury and signed by the Treasury Secretary."

Juice paused to think.

"Signed by the US Treasurer, McAdoo?"

"Yes."

"The president's son-in-law, that McAdoo "

"I believe so."

Juice sat back in his chair and thought, "Well now, this is beginning to make a little sense."

At the time the agents were meeting with Juice, Jack walked into the law firm office of Spencer Sprat, deep in thought. He hadn't disclosed what he should have, an ethical violation. He was ashamed of his coarse language and threats against Juice. His letter of resignation was in his inner coat pocket.

He stepped through the office door, head bowed, alone with his thoughts. The noise brought him out of melancholy. Everyone, including Spencer, was standing and applauding, shouting. That started a chant of "Jack, Jack, Jack" that when on far too long to suit Jack. There was a big sign stretched across the corner office that said, "Hail to the Victor!" Jack smiled reading the sign. Spence had posted the title to the Michigan Wolverines fight song to honor Jack, the Buckeye.

Spencer stepped into the middle of the floor with orange juice in hand, held it high, and said, "Toast to you, Jackie Boy. You did the impossible. I heard your close brought tears to the eyes of hardened coal miners. I told anybody that would listen to me that this young man had the it factor. That indefinable something that made the good, the great. If I didn't know better, I would say he was a Michigan Man. To Jack Walker."

Shouts of "Hear, hear" and the Jack chant started again. Jack put up his hand and said, "Ya'll, this really is too much, but thank you. Spence, thank you for those kind words. You always did have a way with hyperbole. You ever think about being a lawyer? But, Spence, you just had to the add that insult of me being a Michigan Man. Just had to do it, didn't you, Spence?"

Spence raised his glass again with a big smile, everybody enjoying their exchange.

"And yes, Spence, I picked up on that very, very subtle sign over there. So everybody, you gotta join me in pokin' the boss a little here. So let's run this back the other way. Folks, you know how this works." Then Jack cheered out, "O-H."

A few voices came back with, "I-O."

Jack said in a louder voice, "I didn't hear you! O-H!"

This time everyone roared back, "I-O!"

"Now, that's more like it!"

Spence said, "Well done, Jack. Okay, back to the salt mines. Let's save some sorry asses today."

Spence held out his hand to Jack. They shook and Jack said, "Spence, may I have a word?"

"I was just about to say the same thing. Let's go to your office."

Jack moved toward his small office with no window.

Spence said, "Hey, Counselor, you are moving in the wrong direction. Follow me."

They started moving to the corner office, with the banner above.

Jack said, "Nice touch with the banner, Spence."

"I thought you would like."

They walked into the corner office, and Spence said, "How do you like this?"

Jack saw that his office had been moved here. Even his parents' picture.

Jack said, "Spence, this is too much; you didn't have to do this."

"Since you're in a corner office, it doesn't give you the right to start bossing me around either," he said with a big smile. "Check the letterhead on your desk."

It read:

Sprat and Walker

Attorneys-at-Law

Spencer said, "Full partnership, Jack. I'm ready to cut back. Take only those cases I care for . . . or pay way too much. I told you it would take you five years. I was wrong. Took three."

Jack sat down. Not at the desk chair, which was a beautiful dark green, high-backed leather. But in a wood chair for clients. He said, "Spence, I really appreciate all this, but I have to discuss some irregularities stemming from the trial."

Spence sat in the desk chair.

Jack said, "I think the jurors that voted for acquittal were plants and maybe even paid off."

"Damn, Jack, when did you come to that conclusion? Everyone is aware of that. Were you a party to that?"

"No, of course not, but Lamar started to tell me about the three jurors from Devil's Run, and I stopped him from saying anything."

"Were you aware of any payments?"

"No, but I wouldn't be surprised if they were paid."

"You wouldn't be surprised! Jack, everybody, and I mean everybody, would be surprised if they weren't paid. What the hell do you think you did?"

"I didn't disclose. It was unethical not to do so."

"What were you going to disclose, that you thought, that maybe, just maybe, not sure, but thought that a few people from up in the hollow might protect their own? Believe me, every criminal lawyer in the country looks the other way on occasion. We deal with criminals. They don't play by the rules. But unless you see them paying money for a fix, you ain't got nothing, Mister."

"So you think I'm okay with what I did, or didn't do?"

"Damn right. Don't give it another thought."

"Well, I had an outburst with Juice at the end of the trial. I think he could have me disbarred for what I said."

"Jack, I've said worse. We have all done what you did with Juice, although I gotta admit, Jack, you put your heart into it better than most. But it's just 'heat of the battle' talk. Nothing more. A disbarment over that? We wouldn't have a criminal bar if that was the standard."

"Wait. You know what I said?"

"Didn't you read the paper this morning?"

"No, I slept in."

"Your whole diatribe is on the front page. You had a bunch of reporters standing right there. Everybody local and—you'll love this—The New York Times ran with it. Picture too, of the big moment. Jack, my boy, that diatribe has made you a celebrity. Who likes prosecutors? No one. Not even other prosecutors. Plus your description of that supercilious Juice the Jerk was terrific. We got three or four of the young women in this office that have it clipped and on their desk. You're a good-looking guy, Jack. It's caught the girls' attention, although it has been a matter of discussion that you don't seem to be overly interested in the girls."

Jack laughed and said, "Oh, I got plenty of interest, but the law is a jealous mistress. No time. But, about my resignation letter . . ."

"Give me that damn thing."

Jack handed it over.

Spence tore it to shreds and said, "When you gonna lose the choirboy thing? Oh, and one other thing. Our largest-billing client is giving a big shindig at his house tonight for his granddaughter's twenty-first. Jane will give you the directions. It's an all-day affair, but we don't have to be there until cocktails at five, dinner thereafter. He's got some big band coming in from New York City, I'm told. And Jack, that granddaughter of his, Sofia, is a real knockout."

"Okay. What's his name?"

"Big Gio. You've heard of him, I'm sure, but you need to meet him; you're going to be our main contact man with him. He's your client now."

CHAPTER XLVI

THE RED DRESS AT BIG GIO'S

Big Gio lived on ten acres in an area of Wheeling called Pleasant Valley. The house was set back from the road for a good half mile, the property guarded by a gate and a security guard. Jack pulled up to the guard and gave his name. The guard checked his clipboard and opened the gate.

The front yard was scattered with playthings for children. He could see a petting zoo, with two ponies for the children to ride and farm animals they could pet.

In a large area in front of the house was a gazebo for a band. In front of that, a platform for dancing. Six tents provided shelter, food, and drinks. More than a hundred people mulling around, most of them carrying drinks. Jack thought it spectacular.

A valet took his car, and he looked around for Spence.

He spotted him standing next to a big man. Georgi Gioapoulas . . . Big Gio, mob boss of the West Virginal Panhandle. They were talking and laughing.

Spence spotted Jack and waved him over.

"Jack, Jack, get over here. Jack, this is Georgi Gioapoulas. Big Gio."

Big Gio said, "So this is the young hotshot. And a new partner in the firm to boot."

"Nice to meet you, Mr. Gioap . . ." Jack stumbled over the name ever so slightly.

Big Gio said, "Just call me Gio, everybody does."

Jack smiled and said, "That's a relief."

Gio said, "You owe me a hundred bucks, Jack."

Jack said, "I thought you paid the lawyers and not the other way around?"

Gio laughed and said, "Well, we pay you plenty, don't we Spence? No Jack, here's the thing—I took Ohio State and got five points on the Michigan game. Put a hundred on our local boy to beat Spence's old team. You guys didn't quite have it that day. Still had the Chic Harley hangover."

"Yeah, Chic was tough to replace."

After some meaningless chatter, Jack got a Coke and started looking around the grounds. Near the front of the house a bar was set up. Jack asked the bar man if there was a washroom inside.

"Inside first hall to the left, second door."

The foyer was as big as Jack's apartment with a sweeping double staircase, one on either side off the entrance. Black and white tile on the floors. In the middle of the foyer was a long, glass table with a gorgeous bouquet of fresh pink flowers. Above it all, a large glistening chandelier.

Jack was coming out of the washroom and heard the rustle of silk stockings, above and to his left. Because of the curvature of the staircase, all he could see was a woman's high-heeled red shoes, showing shapely ankles and strong tanned legs, coming down the steps. Now he could see the bottom half of her red dress, slightly above the knee. She moved slowly, unhurried, everything in unison with swaying, full hips. Now he could see her breast moving softly moving within her dress. Now he saw spaghetti straps going up and over her shoulders, tied in a delicate bow at the top. Now he could see a diamond necklace around a slender, perfectly formed neck.

She stopped her descent when she saw him looking at her, but he could still not see her face, which was blocked by the woodwork of the banister. She just stood there. Then she moved into Jack's view. Now he could see full lips, blue-green bright eyes, diamond earrings. Now her long, raven-colored hair, tousled into lush curls.

Her mouth parted in a slight smile.

Sofia Gioapoulas on her twenty-first birthday. A full-bodied woman. Beautiful, but more than that. She was sexy. She radiated it . . . a sexy 'come try to catch me' look about her.

Jack flushed, startled to see she was looking at him. Jack, was lost for words. This was a woman in full blossom.

She said, "My, aren't you the attentive one?"

"You caught my attention."

"Yes, there's a lot of that going around."

"So, you are aware that you don't look like every other woman on the planet."

"Now that is a bit far fetched, isn't it?"

"Not at all. I am not exaggerating, but you are the most beautiful creature I have ever seen."

"You must have lived a very sheltered life. Do you get around that much?"

Jack laughed and said, "Apparently, not enough."

"Do I know you? You look familiar. Tell me your name."

"Jack Walker."

"Jack Walker. Where did I see that . . . oh, in the paper. The foul mouthed lawyer that works with Spencer. You are a handsome devil though, aren't you? That picture in the paper didn't do you justice."

"Believe me, I don't usually talk like that."

"You don't? That's too bad. I read that and I just couldn't stop laughing. That was fabulous, Jack. If you usually don't talk like that, you should do it more often. You scared the shit out of Juice."

"You know Juice?"

"He was the prosecutor in a trial with my grandfather. What a prick."

"I should know this, but what is your name?"

"Sofia."

"Sofia, before you go outside, let me buy you a drink. The bar set up is just outside the door. I'll get the drinks, and maybe in this little house we could find a place to talk for just a few minutes before you make your formal entrance to what would no doubt be an adoring audience."

"Good looks and a silver tongue and with a body that would look good on an Olympian. So are as you always as aggressive as you look in the newspaper."

"Oh, I can be a tiger."

"I bet you can. Get me a Manhattan and come into the study right over there."

Jack went to the bartender and said, "Give me a Manhattan and a Coke . . . no, let's make that a double bourbon." Jack had no idea what a Manhattan was.

Sofia was sitting in the corner of a soft leather sofa, her legs drawn up under her. A right hand was softly caressing her exposed calf—slowly and softly, moving her hand up and down.

Her left hand was playing with the bow on the strap. Her dress was pulled slightly downward and her full breasts were more exposed. She had taken her high-heeled red shoes off.

Jack swallowed hard at the sight.

Sofia took a sip and said, "So the Hotshot is giving you Papa's account?"

"How'd you know that?"

"Big Gio's little granddaughter knows everything. You hear the strangest things around here."

"Do you need some help with that strap?"

Sofia laughed and said, "You're not going to play games, are you, Jackie?"

"No, Sofia, I am not, and if you are game, consider me a predator. I'll be looking for you."

Jack was seated as close to Sofia as he could get. Sofia took more than a sip of her Manhattan . . . paused, and drank the rest. She let the glass fall from her hand to the sofa and it bounced quietly to the rich carpet. Then her body seemed to slowly float toward him as she placed her hand on his face. Jack leaned over in perfect harmony and Sofia kissed him softly, gently on the lips. They lingered in that kiss. Jack's free hand went to her waist and pulled her lush body to his chest as the kiss became more urgent. They separated slowly, not wanting to leave that first kiss.

Sofia said, "Oh, my."

The rest of Big Gio's party was a blur to Jack. When they went outside, Sofia was taken from him by the one hundred and fifty people now in attendance. He lost her in the swirl of the crowd. He couldn't find her, and the crowd was thinning. He decided to leave and returned to his apartment. His only thoughts were of this woman and the impact she had made on him.

Jack's loft apartment seemed empty when he got home. His mind was consumed by the thought of Sofia. 'How am I going to contact her? Should I ask Big G for permission for me to take her on date? I'll have to talk to Spence about that'.

He showered and went to bed.

Less than an hour later, he heard a knock on his door, something he hadn't remembered hearing before. Few people came to his apartment, especially at this time of night.

He threw on a silk robe and went to the door.

It was her. She had a light shawl around her. She had a bottle of champagne in one hand and held it up. She said, "A night cap, Buster?"

Now they were on Jack's sofa with a glass of Dom Perignon, sipping and talking and laughing.

Her glass was half empty. She drank it at once, stood up, and took Jack by the hand.

"Which way to your bedroom?"

She led Jack there. They stood by the bed. She opened Jack's robe and let it drop to the floor. They kissed. This time passionately, lips tight together, tongues exploring each other.

She touched Jack and said, "My, oh my. And I thought your shoulders and chest were big. You are just full of surprises, aren't you? Give me a minute. I'll be right back, Big Boy."

Jack didn't reply.

When she returned she, she walked toward Jack naked. The room was dark except for street lights, which cast a light haze over Sofia as she moved toward the bed. Jack had never seen such beauty. His desire was beyond anything he had ever felt. He literally ached to hold this woman. To love this woman. To love and kiss her tenderly and sweetly. By the bed, she paused and stood, not moving. Jack just lay there looking at her. She was perfection. Her body a rich copper tone. Her breast were perfection. Her lips were parted. Her eyes bright with anticipation.

Jack reached out and grabbed a wrist and pulled her to him.

In bed their bodies pressed together. She said, "Jack, I've got to tell you something. I'm a virgin. I've never done this before."

Jack laughed and said "This may shock you, but so am I."

"Don't lie to me, Jack."

"I'm not."

"Well, we learn together."

"Just let it flow."

Jack knew his life would never be the same.

And it wasn't.

CHAPTER XLVII

MULE KICK, KICKS IN

Jack was at his desk, writing a letter of resignation from his position in the Church. He knew his mother would be devastated. But his youth was gone. He was on a different path now, and he loved it. Loretta would call it the devil's way. Jack was a man now. He thought it so strange that a woman could make a man feel like a real man—a man that could conquer all before him.

Big Gio called and wanted him out to his estate as soon as he could be there. Jack said to Spence, "Gio called. He wants to see me."

"Well, you better go then, pronto."

Gio was in his study, sitting in a chair by the sofa. Jack sat on the sofa where he and Sofia first kissed. It seemed so long ago to Jack.

Gio said, "Jack, you want some coffee? Wake you up a bit."

"You know what, Big G, I think I'll take you up on that. This will surprise you, but this is my second cup of coffee in all my day's upon this fair Earth."

"That Mormon thing Loretta got you into, right?"

"Yeah, that's right. You know my mother?"

"Jack, my family has been doing business with your family for a long, long time. Hell, I remember Henry, your grandfather, from when I was a kid. Man scared me to death. Mean old sumbitch. Carried that hickory cane around, and he wasn't afraid of using it. Now Pappy is likable and easy to work with. He makes his shine. Gives me a great price. A nice little discount, and that damn Mule Kick is the absolute best. Lamar is Lamar. How'd you save his ass, anyway? They had him dead to rights."

"Gio, I don't thing I did much at all. Might have been a little activity in the background."

"Oh, paying off some of the jury. I figured as much. In fact, everybody figured about the same. The important thing is this . . . you got him off and that picture with you in Juice's face made you a star. Everybody will want you as their lawyer now."

"Oh yeah, Spence is all excited—I think we are getting every criminal defendant that comes along. They all want the guy that got up in Juice's face."

They both had a laugh.

"Jack, you know I like doing business with Pappy. That's what I wanted to talk to you about. Just to review a little information that you already know, but to put us both on the same path here, that Yost Act brought prohibition to West Virginia in thirteen. Now we got the whole country dry because of that Constitutional amendment. Shiners got well when West Virginia went dry. They made some good money. Now we are looking at the whole country dry. And I got news for you, Jack, nobody is going to stop drinking. Can't be done. What this represents for my family and yours is the greatest opportunity to make real wealth in the history of this grand land of ours."

"I think Pappy is doing pretty well, right now."

"Yes, he is Jack, but I'm talking about my family and your family not doing pretty well, but creating Rockefeller wealth. Millions. Maybe hundreds of millions."

"Big Gio. You know, I am a criminal defense lawyer. I don't get involved in the family business."

"I know you don't Jack. But you wouldn't be that involved. Just help out with the business side, not the illegal side. Organizational, accounting, legal defense. All legal. Stuff like that."

"So what would we be doing?"

"I got connections, right? I know and pay tribute to most of them. Capone, Luciano. All friends of mine. They need shine. They need booze. They are absolutely desperate to get booze, and they got these speakeasies, and without the booze, they got nothing. We need to get it all organized to ship outta here to Youngstown, Pittsburgh, Newport, KY, Cleveland, and then Chicago, New York, Philly. Pappy and the others need to be working as well and turn out ten times the shine. It needs to be organized. That's what you would do. It's like doing paperwork, legal work, for them."

Jack sipped his coffee. He said, "You know, I really like this stuff."

"The idea?"

"Well, yeah, but I was referring to the coffee."

"So, you on board?"

"Everything else is changing in my life. Maybe it will get my family out of these petty bullshit crimes and with enough money to go legit. Give me a day or two to think how we could put it together. I'll talk to Lamar too. He's got the damnedest truck you ever did see and I'm told it is bootleggin' ready."

"Yeah, I saw a picture of that."

"How about we meet here, same time, in two days. I'll draft some plans."

"Thank you, Jack. Oh, there is one other thing."

"Yes?"

"You break my little girl's heart, and I will, for certain, break both your legs."

"I can't imagine that would ever happen, G."

"Make sure it don't."

Jack was thrilled with the idea. Make a real killing and get the family out of the crime business. He pointing his car south and headed for the house on 21st Street.

Peaches again opened the door. Jack said, "I hope the boys are here."

"You're in luck. Lamar and Larry are in the kitchen."

Jack joined them at the kitchen table, and had Peaches pour him his second cup of coffee of the day. Larry was trying to roll a cigarette. Lamar was drinking orange juice with a slight light color showing through—a little Mule Kick. Peaches was fussing with the coffee and orange juice.

Jack said, "Little family business, Lamar. You want it private? It's not a small matter."

"These two are family now, Jack. Peaches and me are pretending to be a couple So let's get down to it."

Jack explained Big Gio's plan and opportunity.

Lamar said, "So you will get us organized and all that, and we would have Big Gio's protection?"

Jack said, "We would have more than his protection, as partners, as equals."

Lamar stood and got four shot glasses. Filled three with Mule Kick and started to put orange juice in the fourth.

Jack said, "Lamar, I'll have some Kick."

Lamar, Larry, and Peaches stared at Jack. No one made a sound.

Then Lamar said, "Here's to filling up every gawdamn speakeasy in Chicago to New York and everything else up and down the Ohio River."

Larry struggled with a Quirly. Pieces of tobacco were on his hands, face, clothing, table and floor. He said, "I think I'm going to give up tryin' to roll my own." Lamar said, "It's about damn time.

To be continued in Book 2

Moonshine Mafia: The Good Son